The Abused Werewolf
Rescue Group

The Abused Werewolf Rescue Group

Catherine Jinks

Quercus

First published in Great Britain in 2011 by

Quercus
21 Bloomsbury Square
London
WC1A 2NS

A CIP catalogue reference for this book is available
from the British Library

ISBN 978 1 84916 324 8

This book is a work of fiction. Names, characters,
businesses, organizations, places and events are
either the product of the author's imagination
or are used fictitiously. Any resemblance to
actual persons, living or dead, events or
locales is entirely coincidental.

Printe   ves plc.

To Thomas and Matthew Jinks

Chapter One

You've probably heard of me. I'm the guy they found in a dingo pen at Featherdale Wildlife Park.

It was all over the news. If I'd been found in a playground, or on a beach, or by the side of the road, I wouldn't have scored much coverage. Maybe I'd have ended up on page five of some local rag. But the whole dingo angle meant that I got national exposure. Hell, I got *international* exposure. People read about me in all kinds of places, like England and Canada and the United States. I know, because I checked. All I had to do was google 'dingo pen' and – POW! There I was.

Not that anyone mentioned my name, of course. Journalists aren't supposed to identify teenagers. In the *Sydney Morning Herald*, this is all they said:

> *A 13-year-old boy is in a stable condition at Mount Druitt Hospital after being found unconscious in a dingo pen at Featherdale Wildlife Park, in Sydney's west, early this morning. A park spokesman says that a dingo in the same pen sustained minor injuries, which were probably inflicted by another dingo. Police are urging anyone with information about the incident to contact them.*

1

As you can see, it wasn't exactly a double-page spread. And just as well, too, because when I was found, I was in the buff. Naked. Yes, that's right: I'd lost my gear. Don't ask me how – I can't tell you how. All I know is that I'm the luckiest guy alive. Being Dingo Boy was bad enough, but being *naked* Dingo Boy would have been much, much worse. I wouldn't have survived the jokes. Can you imagine the kind of abuse I'd have copped on my first day back at school? It would have been a massacre. That's why I'm so relieved that nobody printed a word about the missing clothes. Or the damaged fence. Or the cuts and bruises. Either the newspapers weren't interested, or the police weren't talking. (Both, probably.) And I never told anyone that I was naked. Not even my best friends. *Especially* not my best friends.

I mean, I'm not a complete idiot.

So there I was, in the dingo pen at Featherdale Wildlife Park, and I don't remember a thing about it. Not one thing. I remember lying in my own bed at around 10.00 PM, fiddling with a pen-torch, and then I remember waking up in hospital. That's all. I swear to God, I wasn't fiddling with a tube of glue, or a bottle of scotch; it was an ordinary pen-torch. Next thing I knew, I was having a CT scan. I was stretched out on a gurney, with my head in a machine.

No wonder I panicked.

'It's all right. You're all right,' people were saying. 'Can you hear me? Toby? Your mum's on her way.'

I think I might have mumbled something about breakfast then, as I tried to pull off my pulse oximeter. I was a bit confused. I was, in fact, semiconscious. That's what Mum told me afterwards; I was semiconscious with a suspected head injury. When you're semiconscious, it's usually because

2

you've damaged your head or your spine. In the ambulance, on your way to hospital, you have to wear an oxygen mask and a neck collar. And once you reach the Emergency Department, they start checking you for things like leaking cerebral fluid. (Ugh.)

I wasn't semiconscious for very long, though. At first I didn't quite know where I was. I couldn't understand why I was lying down, or what all the beeping monitors were for. But the fog in my head soon cleared, and I realised that I was in trouble. Big trouble.

Again.

Just six months before, I'd been in the same Emergency Department with two broken fingers, after my friend Fergus and I had taped rollerskates to a surfboard. (I don't recommend grass-surfing, just in case you're interested; it's impossible to stand up.) So I recognised the swinging doors, and the funny smell, and the bed-curtains. Even a couple of the faces around me were vaguely familiar.

'What happened?' I asked, as I was being wheeled around like a shopping trolley full of beer cans. 'Did I get hurt?'

There was a doctor looming over me. I could see straight up her nose. 'Don't you remember?' she said.

'Nuh.'

'What's the last thing you *can* remember?'

'Um...' I tried to think, but it wasn't easy. Not while I was being poked and prodded by about a dozen different people.

'Do you have a headache?' someone inquired.

'No.'

'Do you feel sick in the stomach?'

'A bit.'

'Can you look over here, please, Toby? It *is* Toby, isn't it?'

3

'Yeah. Course.' At the time, I thought that they knew me from my previous visit. I was wrong, though. They were only calling me Toby because Mum had panicked. She'd walked into my bedroom at 6.00 AM, seen my empty bed, searched the house, realised that I didn't have my phone, and notified the police. I don't suppose they were very concerned at that point. (It wasn't as if I was five years old.) All the same, they'd asked for a name and description.

So when I showed up at Featherdale, without any ID, it didn't really matter. The police were already on the lookout for a very tall, very skinny thirteen-year-old with brown hair, brown eyes and big feet.

One of the nurses told me later that she didn't recognise me when I first came in because there was so much blood and dirt all over my face.

'Can you tell us your full name, Toby?' was the next question pitched at me, from somewhere off to my right.

'Uh – Tobias Richard Vandevelde.'

'And your address?'

I told them that, too. Then I spotted the big, jagged cut on my leg.

'What happened?' I said, with mounting alarm. 'Is Mum all right?'

'Your mum's fine. She's on her way here now. The police called her.'

'The *police*?' This was bad news. This was *terrible* news. 'Why? What have I done?'

'Nothing. As far as we know.'

'Then—'

'You're breathing a bit fast, Toby, so what I'm going to do now is run a blood gas test...'

I couldn't get a straight answer from any of them, but I didn't want to kick up a fuss. Not while they were trying to figure out what was wrong with me. They kept asking if I was in pain, and if I could see properly, and if I knew what year it was, and then at last the crowd around my bed began to disperse. It didn't take me long to realise that people were drifting away because I wasn't going to die. I mean, I'd obviously been downgraded from someone who might spring a leak or pitch a fit at any moment to someone who could be safely left in a holding bay, with a couple of machines and a really young doctor.

'Not all of these cuts are going to heal by themselves,' the really young doctor said cheerfully, as he pulled out his box of catgut (or whatever it was). 'We might give you a local before we stitch you up. Do you know when you had your last tetanus shot?'

Dumb question. Of course I didn't. You'd be better off asking me how many eyelashes I have.

'No.'

'Fair enough.' He didn't seem too surprised. 'Maybe your mum can tell me.'

'Maybe I can tell you what?' said a voice – and all of a sudden, there was my mum. She'd obviously had a bad morning. Though she was dressed in her work clothes, with earrings and fancy shoes and her good handbag, she hadn't put on her make-up or her contact lenses. And without make-up or contact lenses she looks like . . . well, she looks like a nun or something. It's partly because she's so pale and tired and washed-out, and partly because she wears big, chunky, librarian-style glasses.

'I'm Rowena Vandevelde,' she said. 'Is there something you wanted to ask me?'

'Oh. Ah. Yes.' The very young doctor forgot to introduce himself. 'I was wondering when Toby last had a tetanus shot...'

Mum knew the answer to that, of course. She also knew my Medicare number, and the exact date of my last hospital visit, and all the other boring details that I couldn't have remembered in a million years. Because she's a *mother*, right? It's her job to keep track of that stuff.

I kind of tuned out while she was debriefing various people with clipboards. I might even have dozed off for a few minutes, because I was really tired. But I woke up again quick smart when the very young doctor started jabbing needles into me. That was no fun, I can tell you. And it seemed to last forever, even though Mum tried to distract me with her questions.

The first thing she wanted to know was: what happened?

'You tell me,' was all I could say.

'Don't you remember?'

'Nope.'

'Nothing at all?'

I shook my head, then winced. 'Ouch,' I complained. And the very young doctor said, 'Nearly finished.'

'What's the last thing you do remember?' Mum queried. 'Do you remember leaving the house?'

'No.' A sort of chill ran through me. 'Is that what I did?'

'You weren't in bed this morning.' Mum's voice wobbled a bit, but she managed to hold it together. 'They found you at Featherdale.'

'*Featherdale?*'

'In the dingo pen.'

I'd better explain that I live quite close to Featherdale Wildlife

Park, so I've been there a few times. And I've seen the dingo pen.

'Oh, man,' I croaked. It was hard to believe. But one look at Mum's face told me that she wasn't kidding.

'Are you sure you don't know how you got there, Toby?'

'Nup.'

'Do you remember going to bed?'

Casting my mind back, I could recall throwing off my doona because it was so hot. I'd picked up my pen-torch and shone it at the stickers on the ceiling. The fan had been whirling round and round overhead.

Could it have hypnotised me, somehow?

'You weren't very well,' Mum continued. 'That's why you went to bed earlier than usual.'

'Yeah.' It was true. I'd been feeling seedy, though not in any specific way. I hadn't been suffering from a headache or a sore throat or a nagging cough. I'd just felt bad. 'My stomach's still bothering me.'

'Dr Passlow will be here soon,' the very young doctor remarked. 'He's the paediatrician. You can discuss those symptoms with him.' Then he patted my wrist. 'All finished. Well done. You're a real hero.'

As he packed up his catgut and his bits of bloodstained gauze, I tried and tried to recollect what had happened. I'm a light sleeper, so there's no way I could have been dragged out of bed and carried off like a baby. If I'd left the house, I would have done it under my own steam.

But why? And how?

'You must have crawled out the window,' Mum volunteered, as if reading my mind. 'All the geraniums underneath it were trampled.'

7

'Oh,' I said. 'Sorry.' Though I didn't even know what geraniums were, I figured they must have been important. Not to mention fragile. 'I don't remember that.'

'Listen, Toby.' Mum leaned forward. She looked like a total wreck – what with her twitching nerves and puffy, bloodshot eyes – but her voice was still sweet and calm. Even when she's mad at me, she doesn't sound as if she's yelling or nagging. I guess it's because she's a speech therapist.

Maybe she's spent so many years teaching people to talk nicely that she can't stop doing it herself.

'If there's something you don't want to tell me,' she said, 'you can always talk to a professional. A counsellor. I know how easy it is to buy drugs these days—'

'Mum!'

'—and if you were experimenting—'

'I wasn't.'

'—that would certainly explain what happened.'

'I *wasn't*, Mum!'

'Are you sure?' She stared at me long and hard. 'Think about it. Are you *absolutely sure*?'

I couldn't be sure. That was the trouble. I couldn't remember anything, so I couldn't be sure of anything. Except, of course, that I don't usually mess around with drugs. The only cigarette I've ever smoked made me really, really sick; I smoked it at school, during recess, and when the bell went for class I was too cheap to throw it away because it was only half-finished. So I quickly smoked the rest – in about ten seconds flat.

Man, but that was a bad idea. I nearly passed out. I thought I was going to die. (From nicotine poisoning?) Practically the same thing happened at Amin's house, when we discovered an ancient bottle of port in his garage. We tried to drink the whole lot before his dad came home, and I was puking for *hours* afterwards.

That was when I decided there are better ways to have fun – like grass-surfing, for instance. I might have broken a few fingers doing it, but at least I had fun. Sculling port, on the other hand, isn't fun. That stuff tastes like cough syrup. As for smoking cigarettes... well, I'd rather make sticky-bombs any day.

'I couldn't have been stoned.' Upon mulling things over, I was convinced of this. 'I don't *have* any drugs. Not even glue or smelly marking pens.' The thing about drugs is, they're expensive. Fergus has a brother called Liam who smokes a lot of marijuana, and he never lets Fergus sample his stash because it costs so much. It's kept under lock and key, too; there's no way Fergus could have got to it. And since I can't afford an iPhone, I'm certainly not going to be shelling out huge amounts of dosh for a few puffs of hydroponic. 'There were no drugs in my bedroom, swear to God.'

'But could you have gone out to get some, Toby?'

'No!' By this time, I have to admit, I was starting to panic. It's no joke when a whole chunk of your life has suddenly gone missing. 'Why would I have done that?'

Mum sighed. 'Because Fergus asked you to?' she suggested.

I suppose I'd better explain that Mum doesn't like Fergus very much. She doesn't mind my friend Amin, but she thinks Fergus is a bad influence. It's probably no surprise that she wanted to blame Fergus for what had happened.

To be honest, I couldn't help wondering about that myself.

'If you got involved in some prank, Toby, and you're scared to admit it—'

'I don't know.' That was the frightening thing. I really didn't know. 'I can't remember.'

'I won't get mad, I promise. I'd be relieved.'

'Mum, I told you. I *can't remember!*' I didn't want to start crying, so I decided to get mad instead. 'Why don't you believe me? It's not *my* fault I can't remember!'

'Okay. All right.'

'Why wouldn't I tell you? I mean, I'm in enough trouble as it is; how could it possibly get any worse?' I'd hardly finished speaking when I was struck by a horrible thought. 'I didn't kill any dingoes, did I?'

'No,' said Mum. 'But the fence was damaged.'

'What fence?'

'The one at Featherdale.'

'Oh.'

'Which doesn't necessarily mean that you were responsible,' Mum quickly added, just as somebody pushed back the curtains that were drawn around my bed.

I looked up to see a pair of uniformed police officers flashing tight-lipped, professional smiles at me. One was a short blonde woman who smelled of soap. The other was a tall dark man who smelled like fish and chips.

'Hello,' said the man. 'How are you doing? Mind if we have a quick word?'

Chapter Two

I'd better explain why my dad wasn't at the hospital. Basically, he wasn't there because he's dead. I'm not talking about my *biological* father; my biological father could still be alive, for all I know. But my adoptive father, Ian Vandevelde, died when I was two years old.

That's why I don't remember him. That's also why Mum has to work two jobs every so often. See, my dad was a lawyer, who earned a lot of money. It was his salary that paid for the big house where we lived when I was a baby, over on the northern beaches. But when he died, Mum couldn't pay the mortgage – because speech therapists don't earn very much. She had to sell the house, the Volvo and the timeshare unit, just to pay off all our debts.

Now we live in Doonside, without the pool or the sea view or any of the other luxuries that Mum's always talking about. But we're doing okay. I guess we'd be doing even better if it wasn't for my school fees. I keep telling Mum that I'd be just as happy at one of the local schools. (Happier, in fact, since I wouldn't have to spend so long on the train every day.) My mum, however, has very firm views on education. So unless I get expelled, I'll be switching schools over her dead body.

Mind you, I nearly *was* expelled last year. And when it happened, I felt really bad – because no matter how often I told Mum that it was all my fault, she kept on blaming herself. She seemed to think that if my dad had been around, I wouldn't have dropped a foil wrapper into hydrochloric acid during science class.

She feels guilty that she can't provide enough guidance and discipline.

Maybe that's why she sounded so apologetic when she greeted the two police officers who showed up at my bedside. She had this look on her face, as if she was bracing herself for a well-deserved putdown. But the police didn't start laying into her. They didn't get stuck into me, either. They were very polite.

After he'd introduced himself as Tino, and his partner as Michelle (I can't remember their last names), the policeman said, 'So you've had a bit of a rough night, eh, Toby?'

I grunted.

'Dr Passlow tells me you don't appear to have any major problems, which is good,' Tino went on.

I glanced at Mum, who immediately came to my rescue.

'We – we haven't really talked to any doctors yet,' she stammered. 'Is Dr Passlow the paediatrician? We haven't talked to the paediatrician.'

'Oh.' Tino seemed surprised. 'Okay. Well, I'm sure he'll be heading over here in a minute. And before he does, I just want to see if we can clarify a few things.' He turned back to me. 'According to the doctor, you don't remember what happened last night. Is that correct?'

I nodded. Then Tino nodded. But his nod and my nod were very different. There was a resigned quality to his nod.

'I see,' he said with a sigh. 'And do you know where you ended up this morning?'

'Yeah,' I rejoined. 'Mum told me.'

'And you've no idea how you got there? Who might have left you there?'

'No.' Suddenly I realised what he was getting at. 'Hang on – are you saying someone actually did this to me?'

'That's what we're trying to establish. Do you *suspect* someone of doing this to you?'

Talk about a loaded question! I just stared at him, open-mouthed. I couldn't believe he was serious.

That was when Mum spoke up.

'I'm not sure my son should be discussing this right now,' she objected, sounding perfectly serene even though she wasn't. (She had lots of crinkles on her forehead, and her mouth had gone stiff.) 'He's not in a fit state...'

'We aren't trying to pin anything on Toby, Mrs Vandevelde,' Tino assured her. 'Even if he *was* responsible for the damage at Featherdale, there's no way of proving it. And quite frankly, we don't believe he is to blame. We think other people were involved.' He fixed me with a benign but penetrating look. 'Have you been fighting with the kids at school, by any chance?'

'No.'

'What about the ones in your neighbourhood? I know a few of them can be pretty rough. Are they giving you trouble?'

'Course not!' What did he think I was, a geek? A nerd? A natural-born target? 'Why would anybody want to pick on me?'

'Listen.' All at once Michelle took over. Even though she was smaller than Tino, she had a harder face and a gruffer voice. 'You shouldn't be afraid to tell us if some bully's been giving you a hard time,' she said flatly. 'We've got zero tolerance for bullying. If you don't nip it in the bud, it gets worse and worse. Someone might end up getting killed. That's why we take these situations very seriously, and why we'll make sure there won't be any repercussions if you decide you want to give us a few details.'

'But I can't.' It was like talking to a brick wall. 'I told you, I don't know what happened. I can't remember.'

Michelle sniffed. I got the distinct impression that she didn't believe me. Mum must have thought so too, because she leaped to my defence.

'My son was unconscious,' she pointed out. 'The nurse said he might have amnesia. *Post-traumatic* amnesia.'

'Huh?' I didn't like the sound of that. I didn't like the word 'post-traumatic'. 'What do you mean, traumatic?'

'Well—'

'You mean I saw something bad? Like a murder? Is that what you mean?'

Mum blinked. Michelle said, very sharply, '*Did* you see a murder?' And I had to take a deep breath before replying.

'Are you deaf?' I growled. 'For the millionth time, I *don't know.*'

'I'm sure the nurse meant physical trauma, not mental trauma,' Mum interposed hurriedly. 'Like a blow to the head. Being knocked out can cause amnesia. It happens all the time.'

'Mmmph,' said Tino.

'When Toby recovers, his memory might come back to him,' Mum concluded. 'That's why I don't think he should be answering questions right now. He's just not well enough.'

Tino and Michelle exchanged glances. There was a brief

14

pause. Finally Michelle said to my mother, 'Are there any troubles at home?'

Poor Mum. She flushed and gasped. She was speechless.

I was pretty gobsmacked myself.

'We have to ask these questions, Mrs Vandevelde,' Michelle continued. 'Has there been a new man in your life lately?'

'Of course not!' Mum cried, in a strangled voice.

'No ex-husband or ex-boyfriend who might have been giving you grief?'

God knows what Mum would have said to *that*, if Dr Passlow hadn't appeared. I knew it was Dr Passlow because of his name tag; he was a small man in a crumpled suit, who twitched back the bed-curtains with casual authority, behaving as if the police weren't there.

His reddish hair was thinning on top, and there were bags under his eyes. Even from a distance, I could smell the mint on his breath.

'Hello. I'm the paediatrician, Glen Passlow,' he announced. 'How are you feeling, Toby? How's the stomach?'

'Umm...' I thought about it. 'Better.'

'You're looking better,' he informed me, then turned to Mum. 'Are you Mrs Vandevelde? Yes? How are you holding up?'

'Oh. Well...' Mum obviously didn't know what to say. 'I – uh—'

'Sorry I couldn't talk to you earlier,' Dr Passlow interrupted, as if he was pressed for time and couldn't wait around until Mum had managed to think of a response. He talked very quickly, in a bracing tone. And he refused to acknowledge the police, despite the fact that their guns and badges were very hard to ignore. 'I want to tell you how pleased I am with Toby,' he declared. 'We thought he might have a fractured skull or some sort of spinal injury, but there's no evidence of that. No fractures of any kind, no internal bleeding, no invasive wounds...'

'Thank God,' said Mum.

'My one concern is that he was unconscious for so long. With concussion, there's often a delayed recovery period. That's why I want to keep you here until tomorrow, Toby.' All at once Dr Passlow was speaking to me again. 'It's just a precaution. We'll find you a bed in the children's ward, and observe you overnight, and if everything's still okay in the morning, we'll let you go. Does that sound reasonable?'

I love the way adults do that – as if they're genuinely interested in what *you* want. Suppose my answer had been: 'No way! Get stuffed!' Would they have listened?

Would they hell.

'Guess so,' I mumbled.

'But you should come back later in the week for an EEG,' the doctor advised. 'That's a kind of brain scan, and it's nothing to be alarmed about.'

You should have seen Mum's face! 'But—'

'When Toby first arrived, we did an arterial blood gas test. That test showed elevated lactate, which indicates a massive metabolic disturbance. Like a *grand mal* seizure, for example.' Dr Passlow raised his hand, as if to repel a barrage of furious objections. 'I'm not saying that Toby *did* have an epileptic fit. It's just something we have to explore.'

An epileptic fit? I didn't know what that meant. There was a kid at our school who had epilepsy, and she'd always acted just like a normal person. Except that she was an ABBA fan.

'But Toby's never had a fit in his life,' Mum said faintly. 'Not even when he was running a temperature.'

The doctor shrugged. 'Sometimes seizures go completely

unnoticed,' he observed, before launching into a long spiel about different kinds of epileptic fits. I didn't listen to that. I couldn't see how it was relevant.

Because the more I thought about it, the more likely it seemed that Fergus and Amin were to blame for my troubles. Fergus was always playing tricks. He could easily have lured me through the bedroom window with some dumb idea – and when that dumb idea had gone belly-up, he'd probably panicked. *I* certainly would have panicked.

I have to talk to Fergus was the decision I made, as Dr Passlow said his piece about recent advances in the treatment of epilepsy, and Mum chewed on her bottom lip, looking anxious. I wasn't anxious. I was convinced that Fergus (or possibly Amin) would be able to explain everything.

What I needed was a phone.

'So do epileptics sometimes lose the plot when they have a seizure?' Tino asked, once the doctor had finished. 'I mean, do they act in an irrational way, like they've been drugged?'

Dr Passlow didn't appreciate being questioned by the police. This was clear from his raised eyebrows and pursed lips.

'Epilepsy isn't a psychosis,' he said crisply, without even glancing in Tino's direction.

'Yes, but—'

'Some people do experience tension or anxiety before a seizure, just as some people experience temperature changes. I suppose you could describe that as an irrational response, though it's hardly the same as an irrational *act*.' The doctor finally dragged his gaze away from my mother, fixing it on Tino instead. 'You'll excuse me if I don't feel entirely comfortable discussing the details of this case with you, since there's been no proper diagnosis.'

It was such a put-down that it silenced Tino. He cleared his throat, his expression blank.

Michelle, however, was made of sterner stuff.

'But if the kid had a fit,' she said, in her harsh and nasal monotone, 'would he have felt so hot that he had to take off his pyjamas? Would he have been scared enough to run away?'

Dr Passlow sighed. 'As I've already told you, I'm not able to comment at this point,' he retorted.

'Yeah, but I'm asking if it's *possible*—' Michelle began, then broke off when Tino nudged her in the ribs.

She shot him a sullen look, which he disregarded.

'We ought to be going,' he said. 'If there's anything more you want to discuss, just ring me at the station.' He offered Mum his phone number on a card. 'We'll be keen to hear from Toby if his memory improves. And of course we'd appreciate an update on his condition, once the test results are in. Just in case they have any bearing on last night's incident.'

For a moment my mother sat there dumbly, staring at the card in her hand. Then she raised her eyes and gazed at Dr Passlow.

'Do you think his condition *might* be to blame?' she asked. 'Do you think it's why Toby ended up where he did?'

Something about this question must have pained the doctor, because he grimaced as he sucked air through his teeth. You could tell that he was trying to be patient.

'Mrs Vandevelde,' he said, 'Toby doesn't *have* a condition. Not as far as we know. My concerns might prove to be utterly unfounded.'

'Yes, I realise that, but—'

'You shouldn't worry about your son. He's a healthy lad, and those cuts of his are fairly superficial. I'm sure he could do with a few hours' sleep, though.' Dr Passlow suddenly rounded on the two police officers. 'Which he's not going to get if he's constantly disturbed.'

I've never much fancied being a doctor, but you have to admit there's an upside. Who else could have talked to the police like that and got away with it? Michelle was certainly cheesed off; her mouth tightened as she shifted her weight from foot to foot. Her partner swallowed, his expression becoming a little strained.

'Okay. Well, I don't think there's anything else,' he remarked. 'We might leave you to it and check in later. Good luck on the scan. I'm glad things turned out better than we all expected.'

I think he meant what he said. He was a nice guy. And I don't blame him for thinking that I was a liar. After all, my own mother had jumped to the same conclusion.

As for me, I guess you could say that I also jumped to conclusions. I was *so sure* that Fergus must have engineered some sort of joke or trick or scheme; something involving drugs, perhaps, or dingoes, or nudity, or all of the above. Something that I couldn't remember, owing to the lingering effects of whatever substance I'd been sampling.

Because there seemed to be no other explanation. I didn't have an enemy in the world, so why would anyone have wanted to kidnap me and dump me in that dingo pen? More to the point, *how* could anyone have done such a thing? Even if some twisted creep had decided to sneak into my room and slap a chloroformed rag over my nose while I was sleeping, surely there would have been a few moments of consciousness? Surely I would have had a faint, confused memory of the struggle?

As my mind veered away from this extremely unpleasant scenario, I quickly decided that I was being over-dramatic. *No*,

I thought, *that's all spy-thriller stuff. That doesn't happen in real life.* In real life, crazy friends like Fergus dreamed up ideas that sounded hilarious when you first heard them, like the time we took all the firewood out of a firewood cage at Nurragingy Reserve, before hanging a sign on the cage that said FREE CHILD RESTRAINT FACILITY. Of course it all went wrong when Fergus decided to stick a few bits of playground equipment inside the cage; there's a fenced yard full of old plastic spring animals at Nurragingy, and when we tried to rescue one of those, we nearly got caught.

But that's the kind of idea I'm talking about – the kind where you can really screw up. It seemed to me that the whole dingo-pen affair was a typical Fergus Duffy extravaganza.

And I thought to myself, *Fergus, you are dead meat on a doner kebab, my friend.*

Chapter Three

I stayed in the children's ward overnight. It wasn't much fun, because the food was lousy, the sheets smelled weird, and you had to pay for the TV (even though it was just ordinary free-to-air, not cable). I was sharing my room with a four-year-old kid who kept yak-yak-yakking about every tiny thing that popped into his head. You know the way some kids will give you a running commentary on stuff that most people take for granted? Like how water comes out of taps, or how cars have four wheels? Well, the kid I'm talking about was that kind of kid. And when he wasn't babbling, he was coughing like a bull walrus. I swear to God, it was hard to believe the kind of monster coughs that kept coming out of his bony little chest.

Apparently he had pneumonia. That's what his mother told my mother, anyway. I felt sorry for his mother, who had to sit at his bedside all day long wearing mental earplugs while he exercised his mouth. She didn't even go home to sleep in the evening; instead, she bunked down next to her son, on a kind of narrow sofa-bed that squeaked every time she turned over.

Luckily, Mum didn't do anything like that. She packed up and left when the lights went out, promising to come back first thing in the morning. But by that time, of course, it was too late to call Fergus. All day I'd been waiting and waiting for

Mum to leave, so I could pick up the bedside phone and dial his mobile number. I'd been asking her if she wanted to go out and buy some food, or move the car, or check her email. Not once, however, had she disappeared for more than three minutes at a stretch – not even when she went to the toilet. The bathroom wasn't very far away, you see; I was sharing it with the Pneumonia Kid, and from where I was lying you could hear people flush even when they'd closed the bathroom door.

So there was no way I could have used my phone without alerting Mum. That's why I had to put off calling Fergus until bedtime, when I discovered that I couldn't get through. I'm not sure why. Maybe you had to pay for outside calls. Maybe Fergus was out of range. Whatever the reason, I'd left it too long.

Fergus was unreachable.

After that, I was kept awake for most of the night by all the squeaking and coughing. I knew that there was no point calling Fergus too early, because he always sleeps late during the holidays – and because he turns off his phone when he goes to bed. So I didn't even *try* to make contact before breakfast. But by nine o'clock I was starting to panic; I had a nasty suspicion that Mum might be along any second, lugging the clothes and shoes and toiletry bag she'd promised to bring. She'd already told me that she was taking another day off work. I figured she was bound to show up as soon as she could, and I was worried that she might interrupt me while I was giving Fergus an earful.

That's why I decided not to use my bedside phone. That's why I wandered around the ward – holding my stupid hospital gown together at the back – until I found an empty office with a telephone in it. I should tell you, by the way, that I was feeling fine. Wandering around the ward didn't trouble me in the *least*. Though still a bit sore, I wasn't dizzy or limping. And I began to think that there was nothing much wrong with me.

I'd felt ten times worse after my nicotine overdose, which I'd managed to survive without a trip to the hospital.

Needless to say, I shut the office door before dialling Fergus's number. My call went straight through. Fergus answered on the second ring, sounding cautious; he wouldn't have recognised my caller ID, I suppose.

'*Yeah?*' he said.

'You bastard.'

'*Toby?*'

'This had better be good.' I was already in a rage. 'What the hell happened?'

'*Huh?*'

'I don't remember what happened, Fergus.'

'*What happened when?*'

'Don't gimme that.'

There was a long and loaded pause. Then Fergus said, '*Are you stoned or what?*'

'Get stuffed!'

'*You're not making any sense, okay? Just tell me what the problem is.*'

'Oh, right. Like you don't know.'

'*I don't know.*'

'Bull.'

'*I do not!*'

I took a deep breath. 'This isn't funny, okay? Whatever you gave me, it messed with my head. I can't remember a thing.

23

So you'd better tell me exactly what happened, or I'll bloody kill you.' When Fergus didn't respond, I added shrilly, 'You dumped me in it, you dickhead! I've had the cops on my back and everything! The hospital wants to do all these tests, thanks to you!'

'What?'

'Just tell me how I got into that dingo pen! If you tell me what we did, I won't mention your name. I'll say I don't remember.'

There was a sudden gasp at the other end of the line.

'Don't tell me it was you in that dingo pen?' he squeaked. 'Man, you were all over the news!'

If this was supposed to impress or distract me, it didn't work. All it did was make me even madder.

'Oh yeah?' I growled. 'Well, guess what? You'll be all over the news, if you don't 'fess up!'

'Whaddaya mean?' Fergus protested. 'Don't blame me, I wasn't there!'

'You were too.'

'Was not. I haven't been near your house since Saturday.' During the silence that followed, I could almost hear Fergus turning things over in his head. 'Maybe it was Amin. Have you asked him?'

'No,' I had to admit. 'But Amin can't get out at night. You know that.' Fergus can come and go as he pleases, because his mother is usually at her boyfriend's house. Amin, on the other hand, is one of eight kids. He can hardly turn around without bumping into somebody. 'Are you sure this isn't down to you, Fergus?'

'I swear to God.' He was pretty convincing. 'Why would I lie?'

24

'Because you killed someone?'

'*What?*'

'By accident,' I hastily amended. 'I mean, you might lie if you killed someone by accident.'

'*Well, I didn't!*' he cried. '*Jeez, Toby!*'

'It was just an example.'

'*You're a really great friend, you know that? First you ask me if I left you in a dingo pen, then you ask me if I killed someone!*'

'*By accident.*'

Fergus sniffed.

'What about your brother?' I went on, feeling more and more confused. 'Could he have done it?'

'*Who – Liam?*'

'Yeah. He's got drugs.'

'*Liam gave you drugs?*'

'I dunno. I can't remember.'

'*Toby, Liam never gives anyone drugs. He always charges for them.*' Fergus abruptly changed the subject. '*On the news it said you were in hospital.*'

'Yeah. I still am.'

'*Really? How come?*'

'I dunno. Because I was knocked out? There's nothing much wrong with me.' If I sounded a little absentminded, it was because the *slap-slap-slap* of approaching feet had caught my attention. 'Ah – listen, Fergus, I've gotta go.'

'*Hang on—*'

'I'll call you later, dude.'

I hung up just as the footsteps passed me by. It was a lucky break, and I took full advantage of it. Carefully opening the door a crack, I checked the adjoining passageway. No one was looking in my direction. There were people around, but they had their backs turned or their eyes fixed elsewhere. They were too busy and preoccupied to be worrying about a barefoot kid in a blue smock.

So I slipped out of the office and began to walk, briskly but calmly, back to my room.

It worried me that Mum might have shown up while I was away. I couldn't think of an excuse that would explain my absence. In the end, however, I didn't need a cover story, because Mum wasn't waiting beside the bed when I returned. Nobody was. Even Pneumonia Boy had disappeared. The room was deserted.

All the same, I realised that someone had been there. Envelopes aren't like birds or bees; they don't just land on pillows without human intervention. The envelope sitting on *my* pillow had 'Toby Vandevelde' scrawled across it – so my phantom visitor must have known who I was.

Mystified, I picked up the envelope. It smelled faintly of antiseptic. There was a letter inside, addressed to the Vandevelde family and signed by a priest called Father Ramon Alvarez. I was pretty sure I didn't know him. My mother isn't religious, so we don't mix with priests. Or nuns.

To the Vandevelde family, forgive me for intruding at this time. Having read about Toby's plight in the newspaper, I am concerned that you might not be fully informed about what probably occurred. There is a very good chance that Toby suffers from a rare condition that isn't widely known or commonly treated, especially in the western world. I have a friend with the same condition, and he would be more than willing to discuss it with Toby. Before you take any further steps, would you consider calling me? We could arrange a

meeting – for Toby's sake, as well as for your own. If I'm
correct (and I think I am), it's important that you understand
what you'll soon have to deal with.

In the top right-hand corner of the page there was a picture
of what was probably Father Ramon's house – St Agatha's
presbytery – with its phone and fax numbers listed underneath.
When I saw that he lived in Sydney's inner west, I realised that
Fergus had been right. I *must* have been all over the news.

'Toby? What are you doing?' a puzzled voice said. With a
start, I looked up.

Mum was standing on the threshold.

'Oh. Hi,' I muttered. There must have been something weird
about my expression, because she asked, 'Are you all right?'

'Yeah. Course.'

'I brought your clothes and your toothbrush,' she announced,
dumping her bags on the floor. 'And your Nintendo, naturally.
What's that, a get-well card?'

'Uh – no.' I held out the letter. 'I think it's for you.'

'For me?'

I had a feeling that she wasn't going to like that letter. As a
matter of fact, I didn't really know how I felt about it myself.

All this talk about my so-called 'condition' was freaking me
out. I didn't have a condition. I didn't *want* a condition.

'What on earth . . . ?' Mum's eyes widened as they travelled
down the page, finally coming to rest on Father Ramon's
signature. She blinked, then raised her head. 'Where did this
come from?'

I gave a shrug. 'It was on my pillow. Someone left it.'

'Who?'

'I dunno.'

'But you must have seen. Weren't you here?'

Ouch. I tried not to wince.

'I had to go to the toilet,' was my lame excuse. Talk about feeble! But Mum seemed to buy it. She frowned, her gaze dropping to the letter again.

'This really isn't appropriate,' she said. 'I don't care if he *is* a priest, he shouldn't be writing letters like this. And how does he know who you are? Who could have told him your name?'

I didn't bother answering, because I couldn't. Instead I snatched up a bag full of clothes and retreated into the bathroom, where Pneumonia Boy had left his Thomas-the-Tank-Engine toothbrush. At that point I was beginning to wonder if there might be something wrong with me after all. My heart was racing. My skin was clammy. Surely it had to mean that I was sick?

It's only now, when I look back, that I realise how scared I must have been. If Fergus wasn't to blame for what had happened, then my life had suddenly become *way* more ominous. I mean, it's not easy to accept that you have a 'condition'. Not when you're thirteen years old. The whole idea is just too much to cope with.

That's probably why I let myself get distracted. As I pulled on my baggy old jeans (trying not to snag them on any gauze dressings), I was suddenly struck by a terrible thought.

Had Mum been poking around in my stuff?

My heart sank at the possibility. Where had she found my Nintendo, for instance? It might have been sitting on my desk or in my schoolbag, but what if it had become tangled up with a whole lot of other things – things that I didn't want her to see?

Like that length of PVC pipe? Or that wiring diagram? Or that bottle of vinegar? Could I tell her I needed the vinegar to clean my windows?

Nup. Not a hope. I knew she'd never believe it.

I was still trying to remember what I'd done with the padlock shim that I'd made out of a soft-drink can (using instructions from the Internet) when I opened the bathroom door again. To my surprise, I found that Mum had been joined by Dr Passlow. He was parked by the bed, looking creased and puffy. The priest's letter was in his hand.

'Hello, there,' he said, glancing in my direction. 'I see you're ready to go.' Before I could reply, he added, 'How's the stomach?'

'Okay.' It wasn't a lie. Though I was pouring sweat and my heart was racing, I didn't feel nauseous.

'You've been eating all right,' he remarked, jerking his chin at the breakfast tray still sitting on my bedside cabinet.

'Yeah.' I could have made some joke about the food (which was bad enough to make *anyone* feel sick) but I didn't.

Dr Passlow nodded.

'I'm pretty pleased with your progress,' he said. 'We might just run a few more checks, and if everything's in order, you can be discharged.'

'Great.'

'What we need to do first, though, is set up an appointment at the neurological outpatients' clinic for an EEG,' he continued. 'Then I'll want to discuss the results with you both, and perhaps give you a referral, depending on the indications.'

'But what about this?' Mum demanded. She tapped the letter he was holding. 'What does this mean?'

'I have no idea.'

'Is Father Alvarez some kind of hospital chaplain? Does he actually work here?'

'I'm not sure,' Dr Passlow confessed. 'I'll have to follow it up.'

'If he is, I don't think he should be writing things like this and leaving them on children's beds.' Poor Mum was in a state. I can always tell, though it isn't easy; most people think she's just a little concerned when she rambles on in her soft, breathy voice. They don't realise that Mum's agitated ramblings are the exact equivalent of another person's screaming hysterical attack. 'It's not appropriate,' she complained. 'My son shouldn't have to read this sort of stuff. His medical advice should come from you, not from a hospital chaplain...'

She went on and on, but no one was listening. I'd tuned out, the way I often do. So had Dr Passlow. Watching him, I realised that he was actually giving the letter his serious consideration. Something in it had sparked his interest.

When he finally looked up again, he caught my eye.

'Ahem,' he said, clearing his throat. Mum immediately shut up. She and I both waited, staring at him.

I don't know what we expected. The answer to all our problems, perhaps? If so, we didn't get it. Dr Passlow wasn't about to spill any beans.

'I'll make some inquiries,' he promised. 'As you say, it's all rather troubling. Do you mind if I copy this? For my own records?'

'You can keep it.' Mum folded her arms. 'I don't want anything to do with it.'

'That's probably wise.'

'I'm just grateful we're leaving. What if this priest actually tries to *visit* Toby?' After hesitating a moment, she suddenly changed tack. 'Do you know what rare condition he's referring to?' she asked, sounding a bit shamefaced. 'I mean, do you think it's worth pursuing, or... ?'

She trailed off weakly. Dr Passlow was tucking the letter safely back into its envelope, his eyes downcast. Without lifting his gaze he said, 'It's impossible to know what this so-called "condition" might be, without more details.'

'Oh.'

'But what we have to do first is rule out all the obvious problems. Fretting about exotic diseases isn't going to help anyone.' He glanced up, smiling professionally. 'For all we know, this blackout of Toby's might never be repeated. I don't want you panicking because ignorant people are poking their noses into your business. Father Alvarez might be a hospital chaplain, but he's going way beyond his remit. And I'll make sure it doesn't happen again.'

I remember feeling relieved. I remember thinking, *That's one scary thing I don't have to worry about anymore.*

God, I was stupid.

Chapter Four

It was just as I'd feared. While I was in hospital, Mum had 'cleaned up' my bedroom, uncovering all kinds of sinister and suspicious objects. Her search for my Nintendo had become a contraband shakedown.

For some reason, the soda-can padlock shim hadn't rung any of her alarm bells. Neither had the really, *really* gross computer game lent to me by Fergus. But Mum isn't a complete fool. She knows a bit about chemical reactions. That's why my length of pipe, my bottle of vinegar and my little plastic bag full of baking soda were all lined up accusingly on the desk when I opened my bedroom door.

'That bicarbonate of soda gave me a real fright,' she admitted, before I could say anything. She was standing right behind me. 'I thought it was cocaine for a minute.'

'Yeah. I figured you would.' This was a total lie, of course, but I was trying to brazen things out. 'That's why I put it there. It was meant to be a joke.'

'Toby, I know *perfectly well* what happens when you mix vinegar and baking soda. Don't you remember that volcano we made when you were six?'

'No.'

'I suppose I should be grateful. When it comes to science

experiments, you could be growing your own marijuana, or distilling your own alcohol.' She sighed into my ear. 'So there's absolutely *nothing* you want to tell me about Monday night? Before we start all these medical tests?'

'No!' I snapped. (Why didn't she believe me?) As I marched forward to reclaim my room, she followed me in, fiddling and fidgeting. I'm used to that by now. I'm used to the way she can't pass my open door without darting across the threshold to pick up a sock, or shut the wardrobe, or adjust my curtains. She has to fix things the way some people have to smoke cigarettes.

This time, however, there wasn't much left to fix. She'd already cleared out all the dirty laundry and half-eaten sandwiches, so she had to be satisfied with smoothing down the curled edges of my Fred Astaire poster. Yes, that's right. I have a poster of Fred Astaire. So what? He was a good dancer – though I prefer Gregory Hines. I'd like to see *you* doing what Fred Astaire used to do. I've tried it myself and it's impossible. Especially when you have to practise on a shag-pile carpet in a cluttered bedroom.

Maybe my moves would be better if I had access to a converted warehouse, with a whole wall of mirrors and a shiny wooden floor. But where am I going to find a converted warehouse? Unless I start taking proper lessons, of course, and the trouble with that is . . . well, you know what the trouble with that is. I mean, come on. Lessons? Surrounded by hundreds of little girls in tap shoes? No *thanks*. I'm not Billy Elliot, for God's sake. I'd rather be Dingo Boy than Twinkle Toes.

Besides, it's just a hobby. I *enjoy* it. I don't want to ruin it with a bunch of lessons. Maybe if there was some kind of B-boy workshop at the local community centre, I'd consider joining that – though it would depend on who else was there.

If the place was full of wannabe gangstas, with their fingers stuck out and their baseball caps turned back to front, then I wouldn't want to go. Deadheads like that are worse than little girls in tap shoes.

I guess I just prefer working things out on my own.

'Do you think Fergus might be involved?' said Mum, as I foraged in my schoolbag. 'I realise you can't remember what happened, but do you think it's likely?'

'Fergus had nothing to do with it,' I retorted.

'How do you know? If you can't remember—'

'I already asked him.' At last I found my phone. 'I rang him up and he didn't know what I was talking about.'

Mum absorbed this for a moment. Then she said, 'Are you sure he was telling the truth?'

I was draped across the bed at that point, scrolling through my messages as if everything was back to normal. I didn't want to discuss my mysterious blackout. I wanted to forget that it had ever happened. The whole subject was like a dark shadow, lurking just outside; I felt that if I even glanced its way, it would pour through my window and engulf me.

But I had to answer Mum's question. Otherwise she would have assumed that I didn't believe what Fergus had said.

'Oh yes,' I mumbled, lifting my gaze. 'Fergus was telling the truth, all right.'

I have to admit, there was a slight wobble in my voice. Mum must have heard that – or perhaps she saw a hint of panic in my expression – because she gave me a long, grave, sympathetic look before leaning down to press my shoulder.

'It'll be all right,' she assured me. 'You heard what the doctor said. Even if you *do* have epilepsy, it's an easy condition to manage these days. You can live a perfectly normal life.'

There it was again; that word. 'Condition'. God, how I hated it.

'Anyway, we don't want to get ahead of ourselves,' Mum continued. 'There's no use worrying before we have to.'

At that very instant, the kitchen phone rang. Mum immediately rushed off, crying, 'I hope that's not the hospital!' So I never did get a chance to say, '*You* think I've got it, though, don't you?'

Because she did. I could tell. She was already bracing herself for the bad news – and I couldn't really blame her. When you think about it, what's easier to cope with: drugs, epilepsy, kidnapping, or some weird rare disease?

I can understand why she picked epilepsy.

In the end, it wasn't the hospital calling. It was Fergus. He'd been trying to reach me all day; most of the text messages on my phone were his, and most of them were about the dingo pen. Fergus had lots of very dumb and far-fetched theories about my dingo-pen escapade, involving things like bikies and aliens and magnetic fields. That's why I didn't want to talk to him. I was having a hard enough time coming to terms with the whole epilepsy scenario. Discussing Satan worshippers or multiple personalities was way beyond my scope.

So I was pleased when Mum told Fergus that I couldn't speak to him. I was too tired, she said. Naturally, Fergus tried to call me on my mobile, but I turned it off. For the rest of the afternoon I played a really fast computer game, which called for lightning response times and didn't give me enough headspace to think about anything else.

Meanwhile, the calls kept coming. There were calls from Mum's friends, asking how I was. There was a call from the hospital to say that I could have an outpatient's appointment the next morning, because someone else had cancelled. There was even a call from a journalist – or at least, that was what Mum thought. When she answered the phone, a voice said, 'Mrs Vandevelde?' And after Mum confirmed that she *was* Mrs Vandevelde, the voice asked, 'Are you Toby's mother?'

Mum's immediate response was, 'No comment.' She told me later that hanging up was a kind of reflex. It was only after she'd done it that she began to wish she hadn't. 'What if it was someone who saw you the other night?' she fretted. 'What if they were ringing to tell me what happened to you?'

I wondered about that myself. 'Was it a kid?' I inquired.

'No. I don't think so.'

'Was it a man or a woman?'

'A man.'

'Oh well.' I shrugged. She was interrupting my computer game. 'If they saw something weird, and they want to report it, they'll probably ring the police.' In an effort to change the subject, I added, 'What's for dinner, Mum?'

Dinner was my favourite: Chinese takeaway. Afterwards I stayed up as long as I could, putting off the moment when I would finally have to climb under the sheets and stare at the revolving fan above my bed. When Mum caught me locking my bedroom window, she offered to bunk down beside me on an inflatable mattress. 'Or you could sleep on the mattress yourself, in my room,' she said.

I turned her down. I didn't want her to know how scared I was. I didn't want to face up to it myself; in fact I was so determined not to look like a wimp that I refused to leave my bedroom door open, even a crack. When she suggested a nightlight, I scoffed at the idea. And when she started talking about homemade alarm systems – things like wind chimes, squeaky toys or crunchy gravel arranged in front of every access point – I poured scorn on the whole concept.

'Are you crazy?' I said. 'Do you *want* this place to look like the Miscallefs'? Because I don't.'

I should probably explain that the Miscallefs, unlike most of the families on our street, live knee-deep in crap. There are always bikes, blades, shoes, car parts, dog bowls, fluffy toys and old barbecue grills scattered around their front yard. Now, don't get me wrong; I know that my own room is a real mess. And I also know that when you have a lot of kids, it's hard to keep things clean. But every time I pass that house in someone else's company, it always gets the same reaction. Mum's friends always say something like, 'What are the unemployment figures in this area?' And *my* friends say something like, 'There's a kid who lives around here, and he's got four different fathers, and they're all fighting over which one's his real dad.'

It's not fair, because the Miscallefs are okay. I like them. They're friendly. But that whole junkyard look is the kiss of death in this part of town. You should hear Mr Grisdale talk about the Miscallefs! Grisdale is a grumpy old bastard who lives three doors down from us. He yells at every kid who even pauses outside his front gate, so it's not as if anybody pays much attention when he calls the Miscallefs 'trash' and 'scum' and 'bludgers'. The thing is, though, he isn't the only one. I've heard Mrs Savvides badmouthing the Miscallefs, too. And Mrs Savvides is a nice person; she feeds the birds and sends us a card at Christmas. But she's really mean about the Miscallefs. She says they live like pigs, let their kids run wild, and stink up the whole street because they're always forgetting to put out their rubbish for collection. 'People like that,' she says, 'shouldn't be *allowed* to have kids.'

I swear to God, I must have heard this a million times – and not just from Mrs Savvides. The guy on the corner, the retired couple across the street, and the new people at the end of the block have all said the same thing. There's only one poor soul who cops it even worse than the Miscallefs, and that's the alcoholic living behind us. I don't know her name. I've never actually seen her, since she hardly ever goes out. But *her* house is messy, too. So even though she's as quiet as a mouse, the whole neighbourhood is constantly moaning about her. *Just because she doesn't tidy up.*

Is it any wonder that I didn't want to leave squeaky toys scattered around? If you do something like that where I live, your neighbours will start telling each other that you're growing marijuana in the garage.

Maybe Mum realised this, because she soon shut up about the homemade security system. She didn't leave any lights on, either. But she did shut all the windows, even though it was a really warm night. Maybe that's why she didn't sleep very well. In fact it was lucky that I had a clinic appointment the next day, otherwise poor Mum might have had to go to work feeling totally trashed.

However, I'm getting ahead of myself. First I should tell you about my night, which was much better than I'd anticipated. I was scared that I'd lie awake for hours, jumping at every noise, and that when I finally *did* fall asleep I would be tormented by horrible nightmares. The funny thing is, though, that I was fine. Having dropped off the instant my head hit the pillow, I plunged into a dreamless stupor, hardly stirring until Mum shook me into consciousness at around 9.00 AM.

Then I climbed out of bed, ate breakfast, cleaned my teeth, and went to the neurological outpatient's clinic.

38

I'll spare you the details of my visit. Let's just say I spent a long time sitting on a hard chair in a lemon-scented waiting room, playing with my Nintendo and trying not to look at some of the other patients, who were... well, in a bad way, quite frankly. You don't want to know what some poor people have to live with. *I* didn't want to know, that's for sure. So I kept my head down until the doctors decided that they were ready to stick electrodes all over it.

Actually, the EEG was pretty cool. I was hooked up to a computer and given things to look at, so that the doctors could map my brain's electrical activity. It was like being a lab rat or a science-fiction hero. (*'You think you can outsmart us, Consumer Unit 2792, but we are able to see what you are thinking...'*) Fergus would have loved it. So would Amin. I guess I would have loved it too, if I hadn't been so worried about the results. No matter how hard I tried, I couldn't forget that all this whiz-bang technology was being used to search for a nasty, lurking, terrible thing – like sniffer dogs tracking down a corpse. I was so worried, in fact, that I kept expecting someone to notice. I was sure that my worry would show up on the brain scans.

But nobody said a single word about my EEG. Not then, anyway. I was supposed to wait for the results, which Dr Passlow would explain to me during my next appointment with him. So after all that fuss, I emerged from the clinic still not knowing if I had epilepsy or not.

It was a real bummer. I was so pissed off that I spent the whole trip home in a sulk, with my arms folded and a scowl on my face. And my mood didn't exactly improve when I spotted Fergus sitting on our front steps. Fergus was the *last* person I wanted to see just then. Mum couldn't have been too happy, either; she didn't have much food in the fridge, and Fergus eats like a swarm of locusts.

'Oh, God,' she said with a sigh, as she pulled into the driveway, 'I don't have a thing for lunch. Why on earth does he always turn up at mealtimes?'

Because his brothers eat everything at his house, I thought. But I didn't say it. Instead I climbed out of the car and slammed the door shut behind me.

Before I could even open my mouth, Fergus jumped up.

'Man, where have you *been*?' he cried. 'What's happened to your phone? Did you lose it or something?'

He had nicked one of Liam's T-shirts, which was much too big for him. Not that I'm saying big is bad. I always wear baggy clothes myself, because when you're as skinny as I am, you have to bulk up with extra layers. Fergus, however, is a lot shorter than me. And though he seems to like dressing in his brothers' T-shirts, with the hems hanging down past his knees and the shoulders flopping around his elbows, I think oversized gear makes him look like a performing dog.

Of course, this wouldn't worry Fergus. He honestly couldn't care less about his hand-me-downs, or his chipped front tooth, or his lousy haircuts. He doesn't even mind that he's short. Some people might, but not Fergus.

I wish I was like that.

'Maybe you left your phone in the dingo pen,' he gabbled, without waiting for a reply. 'Maybe we should go back and see if it's there!'

'Don't be stupid,' I snapped. And Mum said, very calmly, 'We've just been at the hospital, Fergus. There are some parts of the hospital where you're not supposed to leave your phone on.'

Fergus grunted. He dodged Mum as she moved past him to unlock the front door, never once meeting her gaze. She's used to that, though. He hardly ever catches her eye or answers her questions. I don't know if he's afraid or embarrassed or what.

'I suppose you're staying for lunch, are you, Fergus?' Mum queried. As usual, he squirmed and glanced at me for input, as if he didn't understand English.

I couldn't help feeling impatient.

'Well?' I demanded. 'Are you staying or not? Make up your mind.'

'Yeah, sure,' he said, happy to be addressing me instead of Mum. 'I'll stay.'

'Because if you come in,' I warned, 'we're not talking about Monday night. No way.'

'But—'

'Forget it. Don't even go there. It's none of your business.'

Fergus blinked. He stared at me for a moment, drop-jawed and goggle-eyed, before shuffling into the house.

'Jeez,' he moaned. 'What's got up *your* bum?'

'You have,' I told him.

'Why?'

'I dunno.' It occurred to me suddenly that I was being unfair. 'I just don't want to talk about any of this.'

'So you don't want to know what happened?'

'Of course I do!'

'Well, how are you going to find out if you don't talk to people?'

He had a point. He was also extremely unsquashable. The thing about Fergus is, whatever he wants to do, he does it.

Without a second thought. That's why he gets into so much trouble at school.

'I was thinking, if someone's to blame for what happened, we can pay 'em back,' he suggested, following me into my bedroom. 'We can work out what they did, and then do the same to them.'

'Don't be such an idiot.' I could hear Mum banging kitchen drawers in her search for something edible. 'This isn't funny. This isn't a joke. It's *really serious*.'

'I know! That's what I'm saying! Whoever's responsible should be made to suffer!'

'Just drop it.' I scanned my possessions, eager to distract him. 'Do you wanna play that computer game you got off Liam, or what?'

Fergus seemed taken aback. He eyed me in a perplexed sort of way, then pulled a face and scratched his chin.

'Did some pervert get hold of you?' he asked quietly.

'*No!*' I was stung. 'Jesus!'

'Well, why are you acting so weird?'

'Because you're really bugging me, that's why!'

'Were you with a girl?'

'Of course not! Why the hell would I take a girl to a dingo pen?'

Fergus shrugged. 'Some people are really strange when it comes to sex,' he announced.

I laughed: a short, sharp honk.

'Like you'd even know,' I said witheringly.

'Was it a boy?' he inquired, as if struck by a sudden thought. 'Are you gay?'

'Don't be stupid.'

'Was it a dare?'

42

'Just *leave me alone*, will you?'

'Why? What's the big deal?' He wouldn't stop pestering me – and at last I blew my top.

'The big deal is that I might be epileptic! Okay?' I barked. 'Are you satisfied? Huh? Will you shut up, now?'

Of course not. Dumb question.

'What do you mean?' He was frowning. 'How can you be epileptic?'

'I dunno, Fergus! Go figure!'

'But—'

'I might have had a seizure on Monday night. I might have lost it. And now I can't remember what happened.'

I braced as Fergus caught his breath.

'But that's *fantastic*!' he exclaimed.

I gawped at him. 'What?'

'Don't you see?' He grabbed a handful of my T-shirt. 'You've got a free pass, you lucky bastard!'

I still didn't get it, though. He had to spell it out.

'You can do anything you want,' he said, 'and you'll never get in trouble. Because you can always blame the epilepsy. Man, you've got it *made*.'

He was right. The truth slowly dawned on me as I gazed at his widening grin. I now had the perfect excuse. For everything. There was no end to what I could get away with, providing I didn't push my luck.

'You know what?' I said slowly. 'Yesterday the doctor was talking about these things called absence seizures, where you just sit there and stare into space.' Lowering my voice so that Mum couldn't hear, I hissed, 'What if I pretended to have one of those during an exam?'

'You wouldn't have to answer any questions!'

'I know!'

'You could do it in class!'

'Exactly!'

'You could say you didn't do your homework because you had a seizure . . .'

That's what I like about Fergus: he's a real silver-lining kind of guy. We soon worked out a whole bunch of tricks that we could play, thanks to my dreaded 'condition'. He put an entirely new spin on something that I'd been viewing as a total disaster. Thanks to Fergus, I was no longer scared to talk about what had happened. On the contrary, we discussed it at length. We laughed. We made plans. We tried to imitate the various kinds of epileptic seizures. Looking back, I guess it sounds pretty gross, but we did have a lot of fun. And by the time Fergus went home, I wasn't worried anymore. I was in a terrific mood. The world seemed to be full of exciting possibilities.

It didn't last, though. When Father Ramon Alvarez turned up, everything went pear-shaped.

Chapter Five

The doorbell rang after dinner. It was about seven o'clock, and the light was only just beginning to fade. Mum and I were in the kitchen, cleaning up.

'I bet that's the Mormons,' Mum said with a sigh. 'I saw a couple in Blacktown the other day.'

'What if they're looking for donations?' I asked, as I headed out of the room.

'Tell them we donate online,' Mum called after me. I was still in a pretty good mood, thanks to Fergus. In fact I was in *such* a good mood that I practised my dance moves all the way to the front door – which I yanked open without checking through the peephole.

Imagine my surprise when I found myself staring at a Catholic priest.

I knew he was a priest because I'd recently watched *The Exorcist*. There are Catholic priests in that movie, and they all wear black robes and clerical collars like the guy who was standing on our welcome mat. I figured that he must be collecting for charity, so I was about to tell him that we always donate online when he murmured, 'Are you Toby Vandevelde?'

My heart seemed to do a backflip.

'I'm Father Ramon Alvarez,' he continued, before gesturing at the man just behind him. 'This is my friend Reuben Schneider. We were wondering if we could have a word with your mum?'

I raised my voice. '*Mum!*'

'It's very important or we wouldn't have come here like this. We don't want to annoy or frighten you.' The priest certainly didn't *look* frightening, with his soft brown eyes and worried expression. He had one of those creased, pouchy, unthreatening faces, topped by a dense thatch of silver-grey hair. He smelled faintly of flowers.

Reuben Schneider, on the other hand, had trouble written all over him. It wasn't just his age (early twenties, by the look of it), or the fact that he was dressed in clothes that must have been borrowed from someone else (like his grey tweed jacket, for instance, which was too tight across the shoulders). No; what freaked me out was the way he stood with every muscle tensed, as if he wanted to lunge forward. There were other disturbing things about him too: the jagged scars on his neck and hands; his split lip and bandaged fingers; the fact that he'd smoothed back all his thick, wild, curly brown hair to make his appearance less alarming.

It didn't work, though. I was alarmed.

'*Mum!*' I yelled again, retreating a step or two.

'We're really sorry to bother you at such a late hour,' the priest murmured. He was already gazing over my shoulder at Mum, who was hurrying down the hallway towards us.

'It's that priest,' I said, turning to address her. 'The one from the hospital.'

'Oh, I'm not from the hospital—' Father Ramon began. Mum, however, wouldn't let him finish.

'What are you doing here?' she shrilled. 'How did you find us?'

'Mrs Vandevelde.' The priest spread his hands, as if to show her that he was unarmed. 'Forgive me for intruding. I realise how irregular this must seem. But I didn't know what else to do.'

'*How did you find us?*' she repeated.

After a moment's hesitation, the priest replied, 'To be honest, you're the only Vandevelde in the phone book who lives anywhere near Featherdale Wildlife Park.' He spoke so quietly and humbly that I almost felt sorry for him. 'And when I called to ask about your son, you said 'no comment'. Which made me think that you'd been dealing with the media at some point—'

'That was *you*?' Mum interrupted. '*You* made that call?'

'Yes. I had to.'

'And you wrote that letter? The one about Toby?'

'I'm afraid so.'

'Well, you shouldn't have!' Mum exclaimed. She kept trying to push me back into the house, but I wouldn't let her. I had a firm grip on the doorknob. 'You shouldn't be leaving notes on teenagers' beds! If there's something you want to say about my son's health, you should go through the official channels!'

'What official channels?' Reuben asked. He'd been watching me intently, his green eyes raking me up and down like a pair of laser beams. All at once they swivelled towards my mother. 'You want us to go to the *police*?'

Mum didn't answer him. She was still talking to Father Ramon.

'If you're a hospital chaplain,' she said, 'you should have spoken to Dr Passlow.'

Reuben gave a snort. The priest winced.

'I'm not a hospital chaplain,' he confessed. 'I'm just a wellwisher. A concerned party. I'm genuinely worried about your son, Mrs Vandevelde.'

'And so am I,' Reuben cut in. 'Because I think he's got the same thing as me. I'm *sure* he's got the same thing as me.'

But Mum wasn't interested in Reuben. She was still trying to absorb what the priest had said.

'You're not from the hospital at *all*?' she demanded.

'No.' By now Father Ramon's hands were folded meekly in front of him. 'I have a friend who works there as a volunteer, and she found out Toby's name.'

'Then you can leave right now,' said Mum, her soft voice trembling with anger. 'Get out of here or I'll call the police.'

'Please, Mrs Vandevelde—'

'I'm not listening. How dare you? You're just stickybeaks! I'm not interested in what you have to say!'

'You will be,' Reuben warned. He wasn't looking at Mum, though. His hard stare had shifted back to me – and something about it was deeply disconcerting. 'There are things you have to be told. For your own safety.'

'Is that a *threat*?' Mum cried.

'No, no.' Father Ramon unlocked his hands, flapping them about in a beseeching gesture. 'We have information, that's all.'

'Well, I don't want to hear it!'

Suddenly I glimpsed a small, bright object whizzing towards me. I caught it without thinking; my muscles moved automatically to intercept it.

It was a bunch of keys that Reuben had thrown.

'*That's* one of my symptoms,' he pointed out. 'Quick reflexes. Like you.'

There was a brief, stunned silence. Then Reuben added, 'Does your hair grow really fast? Do you need a lot of haircuts?'

I don't know if I can describe the peculiar, sinking sensation that I felt when he said this. Because the thing is, my hair does grow fast. Mum's always complaining about it. If I don't have a haircut every two weeks, I look like a hippie.

'*My* hair grows fast,' Reuben continued. 'I mean, you'd never believe I shaved this morning, would you?' His fingers scraped across his scrubby jaw.

I was so shaken, I couldn't even nod. It was Mum who spoke.

'Get out!' she snapped. Reuben promptly rounded on her, all bared teeth and flashing eyes.

'Your son needs to hear this!' he barked.

'Nonsense.' She wasn't even listening. She was in too much of a state. 'I'll count to three, and if you haven't left by then, I'm calling the police.'

'Mrs Vandevelde—'

'One.'

'You'll regret it!' said Reuben.

'Two...'

'Mum.' I grabbed her arm. 'He's right.'

Talk about a bombshell. Even Reuben blinked. Poor Mum was so shocked that she just stood there with her mouth open, staring at me.

'Don't you think we should at least listen?' I mumbled. 'It might be important.'

'It *is* important.' Reuben was butting in again. 'It's genetic. Hormonal. How many brothers do you have?'

This time it was my turn to blink. 'What?'

'You've got six brothers, right? Six older brothers?'

I glanced at Mum, totally confounded. And she stepped up to the plate for me, declaring in a frigid tone, 'My son is adopted, if that's any of your business.'

Father Ramon clicked his tongue. 'Ah,' he said with a nod.

Reuben grimaced. 'So you don't even know how many brothers you have?' he asked.

'No.' I was aware that there must have been a few, because my junkie biological mother had been such a useless parent that her kids had been taken away from her. But I'd never bothered to learn all the details. Why go looking for trouble? 'I don't care about my brothers. *Or* my sisters.'

'Well, you should.' The way Reuben talked, he and I could have been alone on a desert island. He didn't seem to notice that Mum was about to blow her top. 'If you're number seven, then that pretty much clinches it,' he briskly decided. '*I'm* number seven. And I've also got a Portuguese background.'

'Uh – Reuben?' the priest interposed. Unlike his friend, he was stealing anxious looks at my mother's flushed cheeks and compressed lips. 'Perhaps we should hold off until we have more privacy. This is hardly the appropriate spot.'

He jerked his chin at the scene behind him: the dusky sky, the glowing windows, the nearby houses. A few Miscallefs were playing football down the other end of the road. Mr Savvides was walking his dog.

'Could we please step inside, Mrs Vandevelde?' Father Ramon pleaded. 'Just for ten minutes? So I can explain?'

Mum didn't know what to do. She dithered on the doorstep, unable to make up her mind. Perhaps she was afraid that the

50

whole thing was a scam – that Reuben was going to rob her or something.

But I was keen to hear more about these so-called 'symptoms'. How could quick reflexes possibly be a 'symptom'? And who could have told Reuben about my hair?

'All right. You can come in,' I announced, tossing the keys back at him. His hand shot out abruptly, catching them without the slightest effort. He didn't even *look* at the bloody things. 'Just don't expect me to believe you, that's all,' I added, stepping aside like a good host.

Reuben gave me the hairy eyeball as he passed. Father Ramon smiled gently. They both proceeded into the living room, stopping when they reached our sectional sofa.

Bringing up the rear, Mum whisked a pair of dirty socks off the carpet.

The priest didn't sit down. I think he was waiting for an invitation. Reuben also remained standing, though not out of politeness; he just couldn't keep still. His restless gaze flitted from our TV to our sideboard to our rocking chair. He paced like a caged animal, stopping here and there to finger a souvenir or study a family photograph.

When he picked up one of her Japanese dolls, Mum said sharply, 'Please don't touch that!'

Reuben immediately put it down again, flushing. I suddenly realised that he was younger than I'd thought.

'I fidget a lot,' he had to admit, before turning to me. 'Do you fidget a lot?'

'Uh...'

'I'm not sure if that's a symptom,' he allowed. 'But a good sense of smell *definitely* is. I bet you have a good sense of smell.'

He was bang on. I couldn't believe it. My sense of smell is so damn good, it's annoying. Everywhere I go, I'm assailed by the stench of mouldy drains, or burnt food, or dog shit, or really rank body odour. Other people hardly notice the stink, but to me it's like being gas-bombed. I hate it. I hate being able to tell if someone's eaten garlic within the past forty-eight hours.

'Yes,' I said hoarsely, as I lowered myself into the rocking chair. 'I can smell anything.'

'Me too. I can smell your conditioner from here. Coconut, right?' Reuben gave a satisfied grunt when I nodded. 'Thought so.'

I wanted to ask him how he knew all this. I tried to. For some reason, however, I couldn't force the words through my constricted throat.

I think Mum saw how freaked I was, because she broke in harshly, glaring at Reuben. 'Will you sit *down*, please? You're making me nervous.'

Reuben sat down. So did Father Ramon. But Mum didn't; she stood over them with her arms folded, looking quite fierce even though she was wearing fluffy slippers and a very old pink cardigan.

'Well?' she asked.

The two men exchanged glances. Then the priest took a deep breath. 'Are you aware if Toby is of Spanish or Portuguese descent?' he murmured.

There it was again. The Portuguese angle.

'What's that got to do with anything?' Mum wanted to know.

'I told you. It's genetic.' Reuben couldn't seem to restrain himself. He seized control of the conversation, sitting on the edge of the sofa, his knees jiggling with suppressed impatience.

'My mother had Portuguese blood, and I was her seventh son. This thing only happens to boys who are the seventh sons of women with Spanish or Portuguese backgrounds. So you tend to find it in South America.'

'And the Philippines,' Father Ramon interjected.

'Yeah. That's right. And Goa.'

'What are you talking about?' Mum was already lost. 'What do you find in the Philippines? You're not making sense.'

'I'm sorry,' said the priest. And he really did sound sorry. 'It's confusing, I know. What we're referring to is a very rare condition that begins to affect certain boys at puberty. That's not to say they don't share a number of characteristics from birth—'

'Like the hair and the reflexes,' Reuben piped up.

'Exactly. But acute symptoms only appear from the age of fourteen or so.' Before Mum could even open her mouth, Father Ramon proceeded to describe these 'acute symptoms' in a careful and hesitant sort of way. 'It's basically a transformation,' he murmured. 'Once a month, for a single night, there's a huge metabolic change that causes . . . um . . .' He cleared his throat. 'I suppose you could call them behavioural problems.'

'*Behavioural* problems?' Mum echoed, all at sea. By this time Reuben was shifting about like someone sitting on a hotplate.

'I turn into a wild animal,' he said roughly. 'No one can stop it.' He wiped his hand across his mouth as he stared at the floor. A muscle in his cheek was twitching. 'It's dangerous,' he finally concluded. 'If you don't take precautions, things can get . . .' He trailed off.

After a moment's silence, Father Ramon finished the sentence for him. 'Things can get out of control. People can get hurt.'

The priest placed his palms together, leaning forward, brow furrowed. 'That's why we had to warn you. If Toby is affected, then his condition will have to be managed properly. Otherwise he might attack someone.'

Attack someone? I couldn't believe my ears.

Neither could Mum.

'Don't be ridiculous,' she scoffed. 'Toby wouldn't hurt a fly.'

'Not in his normal state. Of course he wouldn't.' The priest smiled at me. 'But when he's symptomatic, he's not himself.'

'He's a wild animal,' Reuben elaborated. 'We all are. I told you. We can't help it.'

By this stage I was as tense as a cornered chihuahua, all quivering limbs and popping eyes. Though Mum made a gallant attempt to reassure me, it didn't do much good. Her voice was about an octave higher than usual.

'This is nonsense,' she said. 'You're not psychotic, Toby. Remember what Dr Passlow said? Psychosis and epilepsy are completely unrelated.'

'Epilepsy?' Reuben was flummoxed. 'Who said anything about epilepsy?'

Father Ramon sighed. When he rubbed his face, the loose pouches of skin were pulled about like folds of fabric. He looked exhausted. 'This isn't just a psychological problem, Mrs Vandevelde,' he pointed out. 'You can't treat it with therapy or anti-psychotic drugs.'

'I've tried. It didn't work,' said Reuben, butting in again.

'This is *physical*. It's very much a physical phenomenon.'

All at once Reuben sprang to his feet – so unexpectedly that my mother stumbled backwards. But he wasn't trying to pounce on her. He was pulling a digital camera out of his pocket.

'We took some photos,' he revealed, pushing various buttons on the device. 'They're not of me. No one's ever managed to get any shots of me, because I smash everything when I'm on a rampage.' He thrust the camera in my direction. 'You can see the scratches I've left, though. And the tooth marks. That's a concrete wall. *Reinforced* concrete. It's the wall of a bank vault, it's not some plasterboard thing.'

Obediently, I studied the camera's display screen. On it I could vaguely identify a pattern of shapes – some lighter, some darker – although I couldn't really see what these shapes were. The picture wasn't clear enough.

'That bank vault is one of our precautions,' Father Ramon ventured. 'Every full moon, Reuben has to be restrained for a night. It's what Toby will have to do. We'll have to find him a secure facility—'

'*Restrained?*' Mum interrupted, latching onto that word the way a tick latches onto a dog. Apparently she hadn't noticed the two words that had caught *my* attention.

Full moon?

'I lock myself up,' Reuben assured her. 'I have to. It's voluntary.'

'You want Toby to be *locked up?*'

'It's only one night a month,' he said, as if this made all the difference. Mum, however, wasn't persuaded.

'Why on earth would I even *consider* doing something like that?' was her very reasonable question. To which Father Ramon replied, 'For your own safety.'

'Otherwise Toby will rip your head off and eat it,' Reuben insisted. 'You're lucky he didn't do it on Monday night.'

Mum regarded him for a moment with a mixture of scorn and disbelief. At last she said, 'You're mad.'

Reuben flushed again. His brows snapped together.

'Rip my head off and eat it?' Mum pulled a face. 'You've been watching too many horror movies.'

'Mrs Vandevelde—'

'And if someone's been locking you up in a bank vault, Mr Schneider, you should go to the police,' she finished. 'There's no excuse for doing that to a person.'

'But I'm *not* a person!' Reuben snarled. 'Not on those nights!'

Mum shook her head in disgust. 'Don't be ridiculous.'

'I'm an animal! I told you! I *turn into an animal!*'

'You're behaving like an animal now – which doesn't mean you are one,' she scolded. I don't know what else she might have said, given the chance; it seemed to me that she was only just warming up. Before she could really get stuck into Reuben, though, I finally found my voice again.

'If you turn into an animal when it's a full moon,' I croaked, 'doesn't that make you a werewolf?'

I was being sarcastic. At least, I *think* I was being sarcastic. Maybe I was hoping for an outraged response, which would have laid my niggling fears to rest once and for all.

If so, I was disappointed. Because Reuben swung his head around, looked me straight in the eye, and said with a kind of shamefaced defiance, 'That's right. I'm a werewolf. Just like you.'

Chapter Six

As soon as werewolves were mentioned, everything changed. Mum hit the roof. I mean, *werewolves*? Puh-*lease*.

'Get outta here,' I said with disgust. 'You guys are so full of it.'

'Toby, go and call the police,' Mum ordered. 'The number's on the fridge. Tell them two intruders are on our property and are refusing to leave!'

It didn't take me long to find the number of our local police station. But by the time I'd started punching digits into our kitchen phone, Father Ramon and his friend were already on their way out. I heard footsteps. The front door slammed. Then Mum appeared at my elbow.

'It's okay,' she announced. 'They're gone.'

I hung up, hugely relieved.

'Oh, man.' My heart was still racing. 'They nearly had me fooled, for a second.'

'He gave me his card! Can you believe it?' Mum tossed a little white rectangle of cardboard into the bin. 'I bet it's not even his real name. And I bet the other one's not even a real priest!'

'Do you reckon it was a joke?' I asked. But Mum didn't answer. She was following her own train of thought.

'I got their numberplate,' was all she said.

'Werewolves,' I muttered. 'Did they really think we'd fall for a dumb stunt like that?'

It's funny how one word can hit you like a train. Reuben had been making good progress until he'd mentioned werewolves. That was when I'd stopped listening. That was when all his arguments about quick reflexes and fast-growing hair had been blown to atoms.

Werewolve? I thought, as I climbed into bed that night. *What kind of losers would believe in werewolves?*

I can't tell you what a relief it was to know that Father Ramon was either lying or deluded. It meant that I didn't have to worry about a 'rare disease' anymore. The only thing I had to worry about was epilepsy – and that wasn't the end of the world. Especially if it gave me a foolproof excuse for just about everything.

So I went to sleep feeling pretty calm, all things considered, and woke up the next morning eager to tell Fergus my weirdo-invasion story. Amin and Fergus always have lots of weirdo-invasion stories (*'Eeep! Eeep! Eeep! Weirdo Invasion!'*), because Amin's enormous extended family is full of drama queens and psycho in-laws, and because Fergus's brother has friends who get very drunk. But at last I had a story as good as anyone's.

That's why I was happy to be spending the day at Amin's place. That's also why I secretly fished Reuben's card out of the bin. I wanted proof, see. I didn't want anyone thinking I'd made the whole thing up.

By ten to eight I was in the car, pumped and ready to roll. I wasn't fretting about my blackout anymore – not after two full nights of undisturbed sleep. You could almost say that the whole amnesia episode had slipped my mind. (Ha ha.) Mum was the same. Rather than dwelling on gloomy things like *grand mal* seizures, she preferred to bitch about unprincipled priests who preyed on the fears of vulnerable families. 'They were obviously trying to sell something,' she said of our two recent visitors, as she navigated the sunbaked streets of Doonside. 'They must have had some treatment they wanted to flog. No one would go to that much trouble if there wasn't money involved.'

'Maybe they build underground bunkers,' I hazarded. 'Remember they wanted to lock me up?'

'It's a disgrace. I'm going to tell Dr Passlow. He should be warned.'

She went on and on until at last we pulled into Amin's driveway. Amin lives quite near us, in a two-storey brick house so huge that it doesn't have much of a garden. There's a patch of grass out the front, and a patio with grape vines down the back, but the rest is all house. It has to be, because Amin has eight brothers and sisters, plus a live-in grandmother. With a family that big, you need at least five bedrooms (plus three bathrooms, an industrial-sized laundry, and a two-car garage).

It's no wonder Mrs Kairouz doesn't work. Running that house must be a full-time job. But she doesn't seem to mind – or to care how many extra children are running around. In fact, I used to spend most of my school holidays with Amin. And even though I'm old enough to look after myself now, I still end up at his house once in a while. Especially if I'm sick.

Not that I was sick that particular Thursday morning. But Mum had come to the conclusion that I was still 'convalescing', so she had appealed to Mrs Kairouz for help. That's why I found myself standing on Amin's doorstep, ringing his doorbell as

Mum waited in the car. That's also why she wouldn't leave until Amin had ushered me over his threshold. She was probably worried that if I had to stand in the sun for too long, I might keel over.

But the sight of Amin reassured her. She beeped her farewell before reversing back into the street.

'Fergus is here,' was the first thing Amin said to me, once we were both inside. 'Just as well, or I wouldn't even know what happened. Why didn't you answer my messages?'

'Because I figured that Fergus would tell you everything. He usually does.' I decided not to comment on Amin's geeky Pokemon T-shirt. Like Fergus, Amin tends to wear hand-me-downs; the clothes in the Kairouz family keep getting recycled until they practically fall apart, so I recognised Amin's T-shirt, which had once belonged to his brother Rayan. It didn't fit very well because Amin's a lot fatter than Rayan used to be. That's one reason why Amin cops a lot of abuse from bullies at bus stops, though it's not the only reason. There's something about Amin that brings out the worst in brainless kids. Maybe it's his high voice or his dimples. Maybe it's his doggy brown eyes.

'Is your mum babysitting or what?' I asked, as a tornado of little kids burst into the hallway, nearly drowning my voice. (There seemed to be more of them than usual.) 'I don't remember that bald one from last time.'

Amin grimaced.

'My cousins are here,' he replied. 'We should go upstairs before we get trampled.'

So we went upstairs together, retreating from the chaos on the ground floor. Luckily, Amin's older brothers weren't home; this meant that he had full custody of a bedroom that he normally has to share. In fact the entire top floor was pretty quiet, for a change. We didn't even have to fight our way past gaggles of teenage girls.

'Fergus said you had an epileptic fit,' Amin remarked, following me into his room. 'But I still don't understand how you ended up in that dingo pen.'

'Neither do I.' Having spotted Fergus on Amin's bed, I launched straight into my weirdo-invasion story. 'You're not going to believe who came to *my* house last night. Fergus? Are you listening? You're not going to believe this.'

'Hang on.' Fergus was hunched over Amin's Nintendo. 'Wait – just wait—'

'Who was it?' said Amin. 'Not the guy from the wildlife park?'

'No. Better than that.'

'Who?'

'A Catholic priest,' I replied. Then, when I saw that Fergus wasn't even listening, I added, 'Oh – *and* a werewolf. Don't let's forget the werewolf.'

Amin gasped. Fergus raised his head. 'What's that supposed to mean?' he said.

'I told you. A priest came to visit, and he brought a werewolf with him.' I was enjoying the impact I'd made. 'Not that this guy *looked* like a werewolf. He looked just like a regular guy. But he said he was a werewolf.'

'Are you joking?' Fergus asked suspiciously.

'Nuh.'

'Someone came to your house and told you he was a *werewolf*?'

'That's right.' I nodded. 'He also told me that *I'm* a werewolf. So you'd better watch out, Fergus. Don't mess with the werewolf, bud.'

I'd been saving the best for last, and it was fantastic. Fergus almost dropped his Nintendo. Amin gave a squeak. Then Fergus recovered enough to drawl, 'Yeah, right.'

'It's true.'

Fergus snorted.

'He left me his card.' I pulled it out of my pocket. 'See? That's him. Reuben Schneider. And the priest was called Father Ramon Alvarez.'

As I'd expected, the card was proof enough. Even Fergus wavered. To study it, he had to put down his Nintendo.

Amin gazed at me, round-eyed.

'Why would anyone think you're a werewolf?' he wanted to know.

So I told him. I told the entire story, in such detail that it must have taken me at least ten minutes. By the end of it, we were all huddled together on Amin's bed, bouncing with excitement.

'Oh, man,' Fergus kept saying. 'Oh, man. Oh, *man*.'

'But the strange thing is, he was right.' I saw Amin's jaw drop. 'Not about being a werewolf, dummy!' I snapped. 'About my hair. And my nose. And my reflexes.'

'You do have really quick reflexes,' Amin gravely confirmed.

'I know. It's weird, isn't it?'

'Maybe you *are* a werewolf,' Fergus joked.

'Ha ha.'

'God, I'd love to be a werewolf,' said Amin. His tone was wistful. 'Can you imagine how cool that would be? No one would ever mess with you in a million years.'

'Yeah, but I'm *not* one. Okay?'

'I know. I'm just saying.'

62

'You should call him.' Fergus looked up from the card in his hand. 'Why don't you?'

'Huh?'

'Why don't you give this werewolf a call? I wanna hear what else he says.'

I recoiled. 'Oh no.'

'Go on.'

'No.'

'It'll be fun!' Fergus insisted. 'It'll be great!'

I shook my head.

'He won't mind,' Fergus pointed out. 'He *asked* you to call him, remember?'

'So what?'

'Toby, this isn't just your average nut, okay? He's a once-in-a-lifetime loony. We can't miss a chance like this.' Fergus appealed to Amin. 'Don't *you* wanna know what's going on?'

Amin nodded. 'Yes.'

'Come on, Tobe. I dare you. Come *on* – it's not like there's anything else to do around here.'

As I said before, whatever Fergus wants, he gets. He's unsquashable. In the end he made me feel like such a killjoy that I couldn't argue, because I couldn't admit to being scared – not even to myself. And *certainly* not to Fergus.

Fergus wasn't scared. He almost never is.

'Your mum won't find out,' he assured me. 'She wouldn't listen to this werewolf guy – you said so yourself. She doesn't want anything to do with him.'

'I'm not worried about my *mum*.' What did he think I was, a two-year-old? 'I just don't know what to tell him, that's all.'

'Tell him you want proof,' Fergus suggested. 'Tell him you want a photo.'

63

'He doesn't have any photos, remember? Because he always tears the camera apart.'

'Yeah, right.' Fergus sniffed. 'A likely story.'

'Tell him you want a sample,' Amin butted in. 'Like a tooth or a hair. Or werewolf poo.'

'Tell him you want to do a school project.'

'Ask him if he's got a website.'

'Hey – no – you should ask him if he'll come and give a talk to your biology class!'

By this time the two of them were writhing with amusement. Fergus was snickering and Amin was giggling and even I could see the funny side of it all – though my own smile was a little lopsided.

'He's not a complete psycho, Fergus,' I growled. 'He's gunna know it's the summer holidays.'

'Yeah, yeah. I was only joking.' Fergus lapsed into thought. 'Okay, how about this?' he said at last. 'You ring him and you ask for proof. *Physical* proof. And we'll see what he comes up with.'

'A claw would be good,' Amin elaborated.

'Or a paw print.'

'Or a DNA test on werewolf spit . . .'

They wouldn't let up. I finally had to key in that number, or there would have been hell to pay. They would never have let me forget it.

Reuben Schneider answered on the second ring.

'*Hello?*'

'Oh – ah . . .' I grimaced at Fergus, because he was breathing down my neck. 'Is this Reuben?'

'*Speaking.*'

'This is Toby. Vandevelde. From last night.'

There was a brief pause. Fergus gave me a thumbs-up, flashing his teeth and waggling his eyebrows.

'*Oh yeah?*' Reuben sounded cautious. '*Okay.*'

'Can I talk to you?'

'*Sure.*'

'About werewolves?'

'*Any time.*' He waited. I waited. At last he said, '*What do you want to know?*'

'Um...well...' I covered the mouthpiece, so flustered that I couldn't think straight. 'What do we want to know?' I mouthed at Fergus.

He rolled his eyes impatiently.

'We want proof!' he whispered.

'Oh, yeah.' I cleared my throat, then addressed the phone again. 'You have to show me proof. How can I believe you, otherwise? I need proof.'

Reuben grunted.

'*Right,*' he said thoughtfully. '*Yeah. I don't blame you.*' After a moment's hesitation, he added, '*Is your mum there?*'

'No.' I was pushing Fergus away, as Amin mimed at me. 'She's at work.'

'*Uh-huh.*'

'Have you got any evidence? Like...um...paw prints? Or a tooth or something? I know you said you didn't have photos—'

'*Listen.*' Reuben raised his voice over a metallic screech in the background. I couldn't tell if it was machinery or car-brakes or even a bird of some sort. '*I've been wondering why no one saw you the other night. You musta been wondering about that yourself, eh?*'

'Yeah. I guess.' Actually, I hadn't. I'd just figured

that the whole of Doonside must have been in bed asleep.

'*I've been looking at my street directory,*' Reuben continued, '*and I think I know where you musta gone. I think you went to that big reserve near your house. The one with the lake in it.*'

'Nurragingy?'

'*That's the one.*' Reuben's tone warmed up a little. '*If you were running around in there, you wouldn't have been in people's gardens, killing pet guinea pigs. Whatever you did wouldn't have been very obvious.*'

'How do you mean, killing pet guinea pigs?' I repeated, so Fergus could hear. He nudged Amin, who smothered a gurgle of delight. 'Why would I want to do that?'

'*Because they're edible,*' Reuben rejoined. Then he changed the subject – or seemed to. '*Did you feel sick when you woke up that morning? After your blackout?*'

I felt a sudden chill. 'Why?' I asked.

'*You did, didn't you?*'

'Maybe.'

'*That's because you ate something rank. Like a rat or a dead pigeon.*' Though he couldn't have seen me wince, Reuben must have sensed my discomfort. '*We've all done that,*' he said. '*It's no big deal. Pigeons are nothing; it's people we've gotta worry about.*'

At this point Fergus couldn't contain himself any longer. He had been avidly studying my face, and my expression was driving him wild. 'What is it?' he hissed. 'Tell me!'

But I shushed him instead, because Reuben was still talking.

'*You were lucky, mate. If that reserve hadn't been there, you woulda been chewing up aviaries and attacking drunks. I'm surprised you didn't mangle a few mailboxes.*' His flat voice became suddenly brisk, as if he was running out of time. *'The proof you want will be in that park. I'll bet money on it. Just go there and have a poke around – you'll see.'*

'See what?' I demanded. 'What should I look for?'

'Damage.'

'Huh?'

'DAMAGE. You know. When things get busted.'

'Things are always getting busted around here. There's nothing much else to do.' I wasn't impressed. Vandalism? What kind of proof was *that*? 'I know lots of people who like pulling up bushes. It doesn't make them werewolves.'

'Check the garbage bins. You'll have gone for the garbage bins.'

'Yeah, but *everyone* goes for the garbage bins. That's not proof.' By this time, I have to admit, I was growing angry. How stupid did he think I was? Did he really expect me to believe such blatant lies? 'This is all crap. What are you really after? What's this all about?'

'Toby, I just wanna help.'

Suddenly Fergus grabbed my arm and whispered, 'Tell him you've gotta meet him!' When I shook my head, he began to nod frantically. 'Yes! Yes! We'll do it in the park!'

'Sorry.' Reuben must have heard something. *'I didn't catch that.'*

'It's nothing,' I replied, glaring at Fergus – who wouldn't take 'no' for an answer. He put his lips to my free ear.

'We'll play a trick,' he buzzed. 'We'll fool him with fake paw prints. It'll be a total set-up.'

'Toby? Are you there?'

'Get him to meet you and I'll film it,' Fergus instructed, under his breath. 'With my mobile.'

'Hello? Toby?'

67

'Hang on,' I told Reuben, before covering the mouthpiece again. 'What's wrong with you?' I squeaked. 'This guy's a head case, remember? If he finds out I'm having him on, he might go for me!'

Fergus, however, flapped my objections aside as if they were mosquitoes. 'You'll be fine. I told you, I'll film it. Me and Amin can hide in the bushes, so if anything happens, it'll be three against one.'

I hesitated. It was a tempting plan. Tricking the guy who had tried to trick me would be an enjoyable case of poetic justice.

'Maybe you'd better come and show me all this stuff yourself,' I said into the phone. 'Why don't we meet at the reserve and go from there?' A pause. 'Hello?' No answer. *'Hello?'*

'Jeez, mate.' When Reuben finally spoke, he did it very, very reluctantly. *'I dunno about that.'*

'Why not?'

'Well, I'm not sure if Father Ramon is available.'

'So come by yourself.'

'I can't. Your mum wouldn't like it.'

'She won't even know.'

'Exactly,' Reuben muttered. *'It would look bad. Meeting you in a park? I could get arrested. People might think I was there for . . . uh . . . well—'*

'The wrong reasons?' All at once I could see what he was getting at. The thought hadn't even crossed my mind. 'Like you're a pervert or something?'

'Which I'm not,' he growled, then added, *'You're not trying to get me arrested, by any chance?'*

'No!'

'Because if you are, you'll rue the day.'

68

Though his matter-of-fact tone was chilling, all it did was make me mad. Really mad.

I often get mad when I'm frightened.

'So you're threatening me now?' I retorted. 'Nice move.'

'*Toby, what the hell do you want?*'

'What do *you* want?'

'*I'll tell you what I want. I want to make sure that no one gets killed.*' He was fast losing patience. I could tell. '*You're dangerous. Do you realise that? You're a threat to society.*'

'Oh, yeah. Right.' Man, but I was pissed off. 'So you're *scared* to meet me, is that it?'

'*I'm not scared.*'

'That's funny. You sound scared.'

'*Jesus,*' he spat. '*You think I can't take care of myself?*'

'Well, if you're that tough, what's the problem?'

'*I'm not scared to meet you. I'm scared of what will happen if I don't meet you. I'm scared you'll end up killing someone.*'

'Then what are you waiting for? Come and convince me.' By this time, I have to admit, I was already half convinced. Something about our heated exchange had opened a door in my head, and I desperately wanted to shut it again. I was anxious to see his so-called proof, so that I could dismiss it as complete rubbish. 'Put your money where your mouth is, why don't you?'

'*I would, if I could be sure you were on the level.*'

'Me?' I couldn't believe my ears. 'That's pretty rich, coming from a guy who says he's a werewolf!'

'*I'm not trying to pull a fast one—*'

'Prove it.'

'*Fine.*' All of a sudden he capitulated, sounding weary. '*Where should I meet you? At the park?*'

It took me a moment to switch tracks. His about-face had come as a complete surprise.

'Uh – yeah,' I agreed, glancing at Fergus. 'At the park. Around two o'clock?'

Fergus nodded. There was a big grin on his face.

'*Okay. Two o'clock this afternoon,*' said Reuben.

'On the steps by the lake. In front of the conference centre,' I suggested. It was the most obvious place I could think of. 'Have you been there before?'

'*No.*'

'Well, you can't miss it. Just follow the signs.'

'*I'll be there.*'

Click. Reuben hung up before I could, like someone slamming a door in my ear. Fergus scowled at me.

'Where are we gunna hide, if you meet this bloke near Deathwater Pier?' he demanded. 'You should have told him Ambush Alley, or the Culling Fields!'

'But we don't have to hide,' Amin broke in. 'We can pretend to be buying stuff at the kiosk.'

'That's true,' Fergus had to concede. 'Yeah, you're right. That wouldn't look suspicious.'

'And you could follow me from there.' My hands were shaking, but not my voice. I was proud of that. 'We could put some tracks in the swamp. Right near the boardwalk, where he'll see them.'

'*Man*, this'll be great!' Fergus yelped. His eyes were bright with joyful malice. 'We are *so* gunna get this guy! This guy is *toast on a spit!*'

'I hope so,' was all I could say.

Though I didn't want to admit it, I was already beginning to regret the whole crazy idea.

Chapter Seven

I know what you must be thinking. You're thinking, 'Ambush Alley? The Culling Fields? What kind of a place *is* Nurragingy Reserve?' You're wondering if it's a park or a war zone.

But those names aren't for real. My friends and I just made them up. Ambush Alley is really Parkland's Track. The Culling Fields are actually the Barbecue Grounds. Even Deathwater is only a small lake with ducks on it. We call it Deathwater because we've spent so many years playing games at Nurragingy that some of our old fantasy names have stuck. In the Barbecue Grounds, for instance, we used to pretend that the play equipment was going to entrap us – that the climbing frames were cages, designed to lure us in before they snapped shut, and that the slippery-slides had quicksand at the bottom. Where other people saw an innocent stretch of lawn, we saw an arena. Where other people ate their picnic lunches, we fought world-shaking battles with bits of borrowed firewood.

So don't be misled; there's nothing especially dangerous about Nurragingy. Not unless you pull the kind of stunts that Fergus and Amin and I used to pull – like the time we planted a stink bomb in the Wedding Garden, for example. (*That* nearly got us killed.) And there was the famous grass-surfing stunt, of course, not to mention our firewood treehouse, which nearly

71

collapsed on top of my head. Both of those stunts were pretty dangerous, though not because they were against the rules. We've always been careful not to break the rules. Mind you, there are so many rules at Nurragingy that it's kind of hard to figure out what you're actually *allowed* to do; you're certainly not allowed to swim, litter, skateboard, fly kites, ride horses, play hockey, climb on the water feature, or let your dog off the leash. On the other hand, there are no signs anywhere forbidding you to grass-surf, or build treehouses, or piss in the lake. That's always been our defence, in fact: 'Where are the signs that say we can't?' Usually it's a good enough argument to keep us out of major trouble, especially since nothing we do is ever *really* bad. I mean, none of it's as bad as vandalising the toilet blocks or carving graffiti into the trees at the top of the waterfall. You should see those trees; they're like notice boards, except that they never have anything interesting to say. It's all just names and dates and four-letter words.

Personally, if I was going to take that kind of risk, I'd be doing it for something worthwhile – like a riddle or a poem. If those trees were covered in treasure-hunt clues, I could see the point. But I guess it's like Fergus says: deadheads have no class.

And there are always lots of deadheads at Nurragingy.

Not that the deadheads make it dangerous. They don't. Even Mum doesn't mind Nurragingy, despite the fact that I've broken several bones there. According to Mum, hanging out in the park is a whole lot safer than hanging out on the street, or at the mall. And Mrs Kairouz is always delighted to see us go. 'Yes! Good idea! Get some fresh air!' she'll say. 'You need to run around!'

She said it again on Thursday afternoon, when Amin asked if we could wander down to the reserve for a little while.

This was after the three of us had spent most of the morning shut up in his room making a werewolf paw out of modelling clay. The result was pretty good, I thought, even though it was pink and shiny. (We'd had to borrow the modelling clay from Amin's little sister, so we'd ended up with a paw full of sparkly bits, like glitter-glue.) We'd then run a few tests, leaving some paw-shaped impressions in various substances around the house: cocoa, washing powder, margarine. Only when we were satisfied that the paw really worked did we feel ready to head for the park.

'Yes! Good idea!' Mrs Kairouz said, as usual. 'It's a nice day – go and run around!'

So we did. We took our phones, some money, Amin's sister's digital camera, and the pretty pink paw wrapped up in a plastic shopping bag. On our way to Nurragingy, we discussed certain technical challenges, like sound recording. Fergus didn't think that the camera would be able to pick up Reuben's voice from a distance. He was wondering if I could use my phone as well.

'I don't see how,' was my opinion. 'There's no way Reuben's gunna let me take pictures of him – why should he?'

'It's not the pictures I'm worried about. It's the audio,' said Fergus. 'We've gotta have audio.'

'Maybe Toby could take shots of the paw prints,' Amin suggested. '*That* would look normal.'

'You're right.' Fergus favoured Amin with an approving nod. 'It's what most people would do. They'd whip out their phones and start filming.' As we trudged along the side of the road, he turned to address me again. 'You should ask questions while you're at it. Get him to talk about werewolves. Then we'll have a soundtrack of him lying.'

'I guess so.' Though the prospect didn't exactly thrill me, I could offer no alternative plan. 'But how will I make sure he finds the paw prints?'

'By putting 'em everywhere,' Fergus replied. 'The more there are, the easier it'll be.'

There was no arguing with logic like that. It made perfect sense. When we reached the park, however, we soon realised how difficult it would be to stamp any paw prints into the dry, sunbaked earth. Nurragingy isn't too lush in the middle of summer. Where the ground isn't covered with mulch or tarmac or yellow grass, it's often as hard and unyielding as concrete. We tried (and failed) in various spots: near the blacksmith's shed, around the Memorial Garden, under the windmill. There wasn't even a sandpit where we could leave our werewolf tracks.

Finally we were forced into some of the boggier areas – like Lorikeet Marsh, for instance. Lorikeet Marsh was tricky. There's a boardwalk built across it, and you're not supposed to step off that boardwalk. (We used to pretend that if we *did* fall off, we'd be swallowed up by a tar-pit, or a lava-flow, or a swamp full of acid.) But now we didn't have a choice. One of us had to leave the boardwalk and break the rules.

That's why Fergus volunteered to plant werewolf tracks in the mud. He's good at breaking rules – and he also doesn't weigh a lot. By the time he'd finished, there were only a few shallow, indistinct human footprints scattered around. You could hardly see them. They weren't nearly as noticeable as the paw prints, which were deep and regular, though probably not quite far enough apart.

'We should have spread them out more,' I lamented, as I stood with Amin, gazing down at Fergus's handiwork. 'Those feet are really big, but the stride's really small. Like the werewolf's got tiny legs.'

'Maybe it's got a limp,' Amin replied. 'Or maybe it's stalking its prey. You know...stopping and listening. Stopping and listening.'

'You *guys*.' It was Fergus. He hadn't retraced his steps across the swamp, in case he left more footprints. Instead he had come back the long way, through the bush that ringed Lorikeet Marsh. Amin and I had been so deep in conversation, neither of us had heard the pad of approaching feet along the boardwalk. 'I thought you were supposed to be keeping watch?'

'It doesn't matter, now you're finished,' Amin rejoined. 'No one can prove that *we* did this.'

'They can if they see our paw.' Fergus gestured at the plastic-wrapped parcel under his arm. 'Let's get outta here quick, before somebody else shows up. I wanna check the lake. See if there's any mud around there.'

'Fergus, don't you think these tracks are too close together?' I interrupted. 'It looks like the werewolf has really short legs. And a werewolf wouldn't have really short legs.'

'Dude.' Fergus cut me off. His tone was one of strained patience. 'Of course he's not gunna *buy* it. We're not trying to convince this guy Reuben that werewolves exist. We're trying to get him on film, lying to you.'

'Oh. Yeah.' Of course. Somehow I'd become too focused on the details.

'Come on,' said Fergus. 'Let's not stand around pointing like a bunch of bozos. We're running out of time.'

He led the way back to Deathwater, where we found a bit of mud along the lake shore. While Fergus busied himself at the water's edge, in a grove of date palms, Amin and I created a diversion by running around and screaming like lunatics.

It was a good move, because it did more than simply attract people's attention. It also frightened them away.

By the time Fergus had finished, Amin was puffing like a steam engine. Even I was a little out of breath.

'What now?' Amin panted, as the three of us went into huddle. 'Should we try somewhere else?'

'I don't think so.' My watch said 1:48. 'Reuben might be early. We should split up.'

'Do you think we've got enough paw prints?' asked Fergus, who was all muddy around the knees. 'Maybe I should do some more. He might not see them, otherwise.'

'He'll see them,' I promised. 'Don't worry. I'll make sure he sees them.'

Nervously I glanced towards the function centre.' You guys shouldn't stay with me,' I said. 'You should hang around here for a few minutes before you hit the kiosk, okay?'

'Yeah, yeah.' Fergus gave me a push. 'Go on, then. If you wanna go, go.'

So I went. I headed straight for the flight of steps that lay between the lake and the function centre. Once there, I sat down to wait, wishing that I'd brought my sunglasses. The reserve wasn't too crowded. It never is, on a weekday – not even around the lake. From my vantage point, I could easily keep track of everyone who wandered across my field of vision. I saw two joggers, a dog-walker, and a woman on a bike. I saw a mum with a stroller, and a couple smooching in the shade. But I didn't see Reuben until he was practically on top of me.

He must have parked behind the function centre and come around the side. I smelled him before I saw him; the scent of his deodorant made me turn with a start. Then I scrambled to my feet, because he looked so damned scary.

'Hello,' he said. 'I know I'm late, but it was a helluva drive. I had to come all the way from Burwood.'

This time he hadn't even tried to spruce himself up. The grey tweed jacket was gone, as was the musky hair gel. He wore a T-shirt that revealed tattoos on both arms, plus knee-length shorts that showed off the scars on his legs. I could see my face reflected in his mirror-lens sunglasses. His lip was still split and his fingers were still bandaged. And despite the fact that his tan and his cheekbones and his curly brown hair made him look like a rock star, I suddenly realised what a bad idea it would be to mess with the guy.

In the full light of day, on neutral ground, without the priest beside him, he seemed much more hard-edged than he had in our living room. I couldn't believe that Fergus had talked me into his dumb paw-print idea. I couldn't believe that I'd even *considered* screwing with a bloke like Reuben Schneider. His fuse was as short as he was; I could sense that, somehow. And I figured he had a brain in his head, as well.

Oh, man, I thought, inwardly quaking. *This is a big mistake*.

'I like this park. It's nice,' he observed, slowly scanning the view. 'I never even knew it was here.' The waterbirds seemed to catch his eye for a moment. Then he abruptly got down to business, jerking his chin at the structure behind him. 'Didja see the bins out back?' he asked.

'Huh?'

'There are wheelie bins out the back of this restaurant. Didja see 'em?'

'It's not a restaurant,' I feebly corrected, 'it's a function centre.'

'Well, whatever it is, it's got bins,' he said. 'And I wanna show you what's happened to 'em.'

God, but he was a fast mover. The words had barely left his mouth before he was out of sight; I had to run to catch up as he ducked around the side of the building, which was locked and empty of people. He was retracing his steps, heading back towards the rear entrance.

I wondered what Fergus was going to do. If he and Amin had been hanging around the centre's kiosk, they might have caught a glimpse of Reuben.

Would they be having second thoughts at the sight of all those scars and tattoos?

'There,' said Reuben, pointing. 'See that bite mark? I reckon you did that.'

Dazed, I peered at the two wheelie bins near the kitchen door. One had had its lid ripped off; the plastic hinges were squashed or frayed, as if savaged by a very powerful set of pliers. The other one was full of jagged puncture-marks, its rim scored by deep cuts and tears. Both bins were cracked, dented and completely unusable.

'Jeez,' I croaked. 'What happened to *them*?'

'You did.' Reuben nudged me closer. 'Look at that. And that. Your tooth went through there.'

'It didn't.'

'It did.'

'It's a bullet hole!'

'Gimme a break.' Reuben couldn't conceal his scorn, though he tried to. 'Have you ever *seen* a bullet hole? This isn't a bullet hole.' Before I could protest, he forestalled me. 'If you can bite through bone, you can bite through plastic. And you *can* bite through bone, mate. We both can.'

But I was shaking my head. I was backing away.

'No,' I said. All at once I felt cold, even though the sun was beating down. Something about those bins had hit me like a hammer. 'Nuh. Uh-uh. I don't believe you.'

'Toby—'

'You did this.' It was the only explanation – and it freaked me out. 'You got here early and you did this yourself. With tools and stuff.'

'Don't be ridiculous.'

'You tore up these bins after I phoned you!'

Reuben's eyebrows climbed his forehead.

'In broad daylight?' he exclaimed. 'Next to a car park? Are you crazy?'

'*You're* the one who's crazy.' I turned on my heel, catching sight of Fergus as I did so. He was up ahead, peering around the side of the kiosk, camera in hand. But he vanished before I could do more than blink.

'Toby. Wait.' Reuben grabbed my arm. 'You said you *wanted* proof.'

'That isn't proof. That's just sick,' I quavered, pulling free. Then I stumbled blindly away from him, my mouth dry, my heart pounding. I must have been in a state of shock, because I'd forgotten all about the plan I'd made with Fergus and Amin. I just wanted to escape.

'Well, why don't we go look somewhere else?' Reuben called after me. Though he raised his voice, he didn't move. 'Why don't you think of a spot, and we'll see what's there?'

'No.'

'I didn't smash up these bins, Toby!'

When I swerved around the corner of the kiosk, I found myself face to face with Fergus, who scowled like a gargoyle. '*You're not finished!*' he hissed, flapping his free hand. Behind him, Amin was shrinking back against the wall. There was no one else in sight.

Mutely, I shook my head.

'*He's trying to snow you!*' Fergus breathed. '*Keep going and he'll lie about the paw prints!*'

'I know you're scared!' Reuben continued, from somewhere behind me. 'I felt the same way, at first, because it's a scary thing. It's hard to cope with, right?' In the pause that followed, Fergus fixed me with a reproachful look, urging me silently to proceed. 'Toby?' Reuben implored. He was still out of sight. 'I'm not trying to scare you, here—'

'I'm not *scared*!' Given a choice, I would have run all the way home, like a five-year-old. But I didn't have a choice. Not in front of witnesses. I *had* to stand my ground. 'Don't keep saying that!'

'Sorry,' said Reuben. He was definitely coming after me; I could hear him drawing closer. And as I turned to confront him, Fergus and Amin began to retreat. They probably wanted to scoot around the corner, to the front of the building. But they were much too slow off the mark. Reuben emerged from behind the kiosk before they could hide themselves.

When he saw them, he froze. We all froze. There was a long, long silence – which Reuben was the first to break.

'So,' he said, 'I guess you're Toby's friends, huh?'

Chapter Eight

It was a blood-chilling moment. I didn't know what to say.

Luckily Fergus did. He turned to Reuben.

'Is that what you were told?' asked Fergus, with barely concealed contempt. 'That I'm a *friend* of his?'

He was giving me my cue, and I took it.

'We go to the same school,' I announced in a flat, grudging voice. I couldn't pretend that Fergus and I were strangers; the whole atmosphere was too loaded for that. My face was too tense. My body language was all wrong.

Instead I had to convince Reuben that I wasn't thrilled to see Fergus. And Fergus, of course, had to follow my lead.

'Who's this, then? Your big brother?' Fergus scornfully inquired, jerking his chin at Reuben. I have to admit, it was a master stroke. In just six short words, Fergus not only demonstrated complete ignorance of my family life; he also managed to suggest, very subtly, that I was the sort of loser who couldn't go anywhere without a bodyguard.

'No,' was my sullen response. 'He's just a friend.'

'Oh yeah?' Fergus drawled. 'Well, it's good when you've got at least *one* friend, eh?' By this he meant to convey his firm belief that I couldn't possibly have much of a social life. 'I guess you wanna buy something at the kiosk?' he continued. 'Like maybe a lollipop? Lollipops are great when you're feeling scared.'

I didn't even have to fake my wince. As for Reuben, he narrowed his eyes. But he didn't say anything.

'Is that what *you* do when you're scared? Suck on a lollipop?' was the only comeback I could think of. It was pretty lame. I used it as my exit line, though, because I was desperate to leave before someone screwed up. Amin, for instance, was sweating bullets. I've never *seen* anyone look so guilty. And Fergus isn't always reliable in these situations. His lies can easily spiral out of control.

That's why I headed for the lake, hoping that Reuben would come after me. I wasn't trying to lure him towards the werewolf tracks. I just wanted to draw him away from Fergus.

'See you at school!' Fergus cried, as I bolted. Amin was smart enough to keep his mouth shut. I prayed that they would both have the sense to hang back; if they followed me too soon, Reuben would probably spot them. And if he did, I knew, there would be hell to pay.

I figured that things might get pretty hairy, once Reuben became suspicious.

So I loped off, trying to put as much distance as possible between myself and Fergus – without, at the same time, giving the impression that I was in a hurry. I didn't really set a course. I had no destination in mind. I just put one foot in front of the other.

'Hey! Wait! Hang on!' It was Reuben, right on my tail. He wasn't even out of breath. 'Toby, listen. This is important.'

But I didn't stop. I couldn't. I had to keep moving.

'There's something I've gotta tell you,' he growled into my ear. It was impossible to shake him off. He kept pace with me, so he didn't have to raise his voice. 'When I was your age, I was locked in an underground tank. I spent five years in that tank, and I don't want the same thing to happen to you. Okay?'

That made me stop. I stared at him, speechless, as he scanned our immediate surroundings. We were on the outskirts of the Memorial Gardens, where some kids were playing under the pergola. But they were very young kids, and they were screaming like mandrakes. It was pretty obvious that they weren't going to be interested in anything that Reuben said.

'I was raised in the country,' he went on, 'and one morning, when I was your age, I woke up in a field. Couldn't remember how I got there. But I had a brother who liked to party, and I'd been drinking with him the night before, so I figured it had something to do with that. I didn't connect it with all the dead sheep around town. I thought wild dogs were responsible. Which was what most people thought.'

He paused, as if expecting me to comment. Once again, though, I was lost for words. What do you say in these situations? *No wonder you're so screwed up, if you were locked in a tank for five years?* It suddenly occurred to me that Reuben might be genuinely mad – that he might be suffering from some kind of post-traumatic thing.

You can imagine how happy I felt when *that* thought popped into my head.

'There were only two people who guessed the truth,' he said (after realising that I had nothing to contribute), 'and they weren't locals. They were two guys who knew what to look for. The McKinnons. They'd watch out for reports of wild dog attacks, and whenever they heard of an attack that happened on the night of a full moon, they'd investigate. They'd come to town asking questions about families with seven sons, and kids with behavioural problems.'

This time, when Reuben stopped, it wasn't because he was waiting for input. It was because his voice had failed him. He had to clear his throat and lick his lips before proceeding.

'The McKinnons kidnapped me,' he finally declared, his tone so harsh that it sounded like a concrete slab being dragged down a gravel road. 'Then they locked me up. And every full moon they'd let me out to fight another werewolf. In a pit, with people watching. Those bastards would lay bets, like they do at dogfights.' Something in my blank expression must have warned him that I wasn't buying this, because he thrust his face into mine, pushing aside his tangled curls to display a scar like a trench above his left ear. 'How do you think I got all these scars?' he demanded roughly. 'These are *bite marks*. These are *claw marks*. I killed six people, and they went down fighting. Do you think that's easy to live with?'

'No,' I mumbled, shrinking back. He was really, *really* freaking me out.

'In the end I escaped,' he concluded, 'and those guys – the kidnappers – they got what they deserved. But you can make big money out of blood sports, so there'll always be people somewhere in the world going after that money. I know there's a guy in America who never got caught. Name of Forrest Darwell. He's probably still staging fights and buying kids from the Philippines. In fact he once came over here to buy *me*, only it didn't pan out.' Reuben's eyes became blazing green slits. 'One day,' he said slowly, spitting out every word, 'I'm gunna track down that bastard. When I've got enough money saved, I'll head to America and introduce myself. Then I'll teach him a few lessons about fighting for his life.'

Oh, man, I thought, swallowing hard. I don't know if I can convey to you how goddamn *scary* Reuben was, at that moment.

You got the distinct impression that he could barely keep a lid on the red-hot fury that was seething behind his clenched fists and bared teeth.

All the same, I had to ask the obvious question.

'Why don't you just tell the police?' I said. 'If you know where this Darwell bloke actually is—'

Reuben cut me off.

'No,' he snapped. 'That's the whole point. We can't go around *telling* everyone, it's too risky. Once the news gets out, people totally lose it. They treat you like an animal. They lock you in a tank or pull your teeth out.'

'Pull your *teeth* out?'

'It's what happened to a guy I know. Someone like us. He had a bad time when he was a kid, even before the McKinnons got hold of him. His grandfather said he was a threat to society and pulled some of his teeth out. Kept him chained and muzzled. It was way off in the boondocks, so no one ever noticed – except the McKinnons, of course.' Distracted by painful memories, Reuben hadn't been paying much attention to the outside world. But all at once he emerged from this reverie; he grabbed my arm and pulled me close. 'If you wanna end up living like Danny Ruiz,' he added, 'out in the desert with a buncha dogs, then you should keep shooting your mouth off.'

'*Me?*' I was aghast. (How did he know?) 'I haven't said a word to anyone!'

He didn't reply. He didn't have to. His expression was enough.

'It's true!' I protested. But he just shook his head.

'You've cooked up some scheme with those friends of yours,' he flatly declared. 'You think I couldn't work that out? I'm not a complete idiot.'

'What friends?' My motto has always been: if you've told a lie, then stick with it. Because sometimes, if you stick with it long enough, it might actually start to sound like the truth. 'What are you talking about?'

'You told me to come here so your mate with the freckles could have a squiz at the crazy guy,' said Reuben. 'You just wanna laugh. You don't really want me to find you any proof.'

'I do!'

'Yeah, right.'

'I swear! I'm really interested! I am!'

Reuben sighed. He put his hands on his hips, letting his gaze drift towards the pergola as if he couldn't bear to look at me anymore.

'You know what? If I could, I'd tell you to stuff it,' he said at last. 'But I can't. I can't just sit back and let you kill someone.'

He was watching the little kids as they scurried around not far from us; I guess they must have struck him as natural werewolf bait. As for me, I glanced nervously in the other direction, hoping that I wouldn't catch sight of Fergus.

To my relief, there was no one skulking behind any nearby hedges.

'So you want proof?' Reuben suddenly asked. 'Is that what you really came here for?'

'Yeah.' I nodded madly, like one of those bobble-headed toys. *Humour him*, I thought. *Don't annoy him.* 'Yes. That's what I came here for.'

'Okay. Well…choose your spot.' He waved at the scenery. 'Tell me where you wanna go, and we'll see if you left any traces there on Monday.'

By this time, let me tell you, I had things all worked out. Reuben was a bad-news guy. I had to get away from him. But I couldn't just run; he'd come after me for sure. He knew where I lived. He had a weird, compulsive agenda of some kind. What I had to do was *scare* him away, so he'd never return.

The problem was that I couldn't exactly threaten him with severe bodily harm. Though taller than Reuben, I didn't have the muscle. He would have wiped the floor with me. So my best bet was blackmail. If I could record him claiming that the fake paw prints were real, it would give me a bit of leverage. I could say to him, 'Back off or I'll use this. I'll stick it on the Net. I'll show it to the police.'

It was my only weapon. In the heat of the moment, I could think of no alternative.

'O-okay,' I stammered. 'Let's try the lake.'

'The lake?'

I shrugged. 'It's where everyone else always goes.'

He studied me for a few seconds, then gave a nod. 'Fair enough,' he said. 'I reckon you're right. I reckon those ducks would have got you interested when you were on the rampage.' As he spun around, I stealthily fingered my phone, unlocking the keypad without even glancing at it. 'You might even have stopped at the lake for a drink,' Reuben continued, up ahead. 'Since it was a hot night on Monday.'

I grunted, then followed him to the lake. While most of the lakeside is lawn right down to the water, in two or three places someone has lined the shore with reeds and bushes and big, jagged rocks. Around the waterfall it's like that; it's also like that near the little white bridge. And in both locations, you get a lot of birds as well as a lot of mud.

So I guess it wasn't surprising that Reuben headed straight for the very grove where Fergus had left his paw prints.

'We'll try in here,' Reuben suggested. He was still on the path, which had begun to wind between two thick walls of foliage. But he soon stopped to look for an opening among the dense, spiky clumps of palm trees and ornamental grass that blocked his route to the lakeside.

'Can you smell that?' he asked suddenly.

I stared at him in confusion. 'What?'

'Can you smell that?' he repeated, sniffing the air. 'I can.'

Cautiously I followed his example. Sniff, sniff. Australian native plants have a distinctive scent, very spicy and antiseptic; it was dominating the Nurragingy smellscape, as usual. I could also smell jasmine, exhaust fumes and hot chips. But there was something else as well – something faint and rank that caught at the back of my throat.

'Dog poo,' I concluded.

Reuben clicked his tongue impatiently, shifting from foot to foot. 'Not that. I'm not talking about that.'

'Cigarette smoke?'

'Come here.' He beckoned to me with one hand while parting branches with the other. 'Have a whiff of that. Can't you smell it?'

For some reason (don't ask me why) I wanted to show him that my nose was just as good as his, if not better. So I willingly thrust my head into a murky thicket that stank of squashed dates and stagnant water and . . . possum?

'Is it a dead possum?'

He stared at me, bug-eyed. *'Possum?'* he squawked. 'What the hell kind of man-eating possums do you have around here, anyway?'

'Fox?' I guessed. 'Or...I dunno...tomcat?'

'It's you, Toby.' Reuben stepped off the path into the undergrowth. 'Either that or someone else in this neighbourhood has the same condition.'

It was my turn to gape at him.

'What are you *talking* about?' I exclaimed. 'Are you off your nut? I don't smell like that!'

'You did on Monday night,' he retorted. 'This smells just like my bank vault does, after I've been knocking around in it for a few hours.' All at once he bent over, his hands on his knees. 'Mmph,' he said, peering at the ground. 'That's interesting.'

I was certain he'd spotted our paw prints, so I ploughed into the bush after him. The musky smell was much stronger beneath the canopy of palm fronds.

'Look,' he said, pointing. My heart sank. Even in the dim light, it was obvious that he hadn't found any paw prints. Instead he'd stumbled on a scattering of feathers. 'See that?' he queried. 'See the way they're all stuck together in clumps? Dried blood makes 'em do that.'

'So?'

'So something's been eating the ducks.' He began to forge ahead, down a shallow slope towards the lake. Branches caught at his loose, tangled hair. They scraped across his bare arms and legs.

Then he stopped, so abruptly that I almost ran into him from behind. I'd been distracted because I'd walked straight through a spider's web and was still trying to peel it off my eyelashes.

'Ugh...yuck...' I muttered, before realising that I was right at the water's edge. Over Reuben's shoulder, I could see the fountain, the flags, and the function centre.

I could also see Fergus's paw prints. Reuben was gazing down at them.

'Nice try,' he said.

'What?'

He folded his arms and pulled a face. But he didn't say anything else. He just turned and headed out of the undergrowth, a red flush slowly staining his olive cheeks.

Damn, I thought. *Damn, damn, damn.*

'What is it?' I called after him. 'Hey! Did you see these? What do you think they could be?'

'You should know,' he growled, crashing over dead leaves and dry sticks. 'You put 'em there.'

God, was that ever a sucker punch! I was floored. My stomach seemed to drop through the soles of my feet. I would have jumped in the lake and swum for it, if my phone hadn't been in my pocket.

But as Reuben kept retreating, my panic began to subside. I realised that he wasn't searching for a blunt instrument. He really was marching away, before he totally lost his temper. Those prints had been the last straw.

He was pissed off with me, big-time.

For a split second I felt relieved. Then it occurred to me that pissed off doesn't mean scared off. What was to stop him getting madder and madder and coming after me at a later date? Nothing. I had no defence. Unless I calmed him down – unless I lied my head off – he would turn into a ticking time bomb.

'Hey!' I yelped. 'Wait!'

When he didn't even pause, I tried to close the gap between us.

'Hey! Hang on! Ouch!' A branch had slapped me in the face. 'What's the problem? What did I do?'

Still no answer. By this time he had reached the path; I saw him silhouetted against the glare for an instant as he hesitated, glancing from side to side. Then he disappeared, swerving off to the right at a rapid trot. I figured he was making for the car park near the function centre.

But if that was his ultimate goal, he had to deal with a few obstacles along the way. When I staggered out of the undergrowth, scattering leaves and twigs, I saw him rooted to the spot not half a dozen metres from where I stood. He was staring at a mangy-looking shrub, behind which two hunched figures were clearly visible.

'Oh, man...' The words popped out before I could swallow them. They weren't very loud, though; I don't think Reuben heard me. He was too busy intimidating my friends.

Amin was certainly intimidated. I could tell by the set of his shoulders. Fergus, however, rose to the challenge. He must have made a snap decision to brazen it out, because he emerged from the undergrowth with a lot of noise and movement, as if to demonstrate that he wasn't hiding from anyone. He wore a huge grin, and was fiddling with his fly.

'Hey!' he said. 'It's you! Are you stalking us, by any chance?'

Reuben's jaw-muscles twitched.

'I was *busting*,' Fergus added breezily, by way of explanation. 'There aren't enough toilets in this park, eh?'

I don't know if he was expecting an answer, but he certainly didn't get one. Reuben fixed his gaze on Amin, who had followed Fergus onto the path.

'Oh!' Amin coloured. 'It wasn't like – I mean, I wasn't watching him pee, or anything.'

'God, no!' Fergus yipped, momentarily aghast. His

grin vanished. 'Amin was just looking for his...um, you know...'

'My football!' Amin exclaimed. 'I kicked my football into the bushes.'

Fergus rolled his eyes. I couldn't blame him. For one thing, neither he nor Amin had been carrying a ball back at the kiosk. And for another, Amin doesn't look like someone who plays football. Though certainly *shaped* like a ball, he's the sort of kid who always ends up at the bottom of every pile-up. I used to play on the same soccer team as Amin – as central midfielder, because of my fancy dancer's footwork – and I never even saw him touch the ball. *Ever.* He just couldn't get anywhere near it.

Reuben must have realised this, because he wasn't fooled for a second. As he leaned forward to prod Amin in the chest with a one grimy finger, his expression was a mixture of rage and disgust.

'Let me tell you something, Mr Smartarse,' he hissed. 'Next full moon, chances are that *you'll* be Toby's first meal. And you won't be laughing then, mate.'

Amin swallowed. It was Fergus who opened his mouth to reply. But before he could think of a suitably cutting rejoinder, Reuben had gone. *Phht!* Just like that.

It was enough to make you believe in teleportation.

Chapter Nine

The next morning I had an appointment with Dr Passlow.

Mum came with me. I guess she wanted to be there in case the doctor announced that I was an epileptic. By this time, I'm sure, she'd convinced herself that I was – though of course she wouldn't admit to it. 'There's no point worrying until we have the results back,' she kept saying. But she was doing Internet searches on subjects like anti-convulsive medication; I know this because I found some of her notes on Thursday night. She was preparing herself for the worst, I think.

So it must have been a big shock when Dr Passlow declared, 'There's no evidence of seizure activity in Toby's brain. No lesions. Nothing untoward. The scans were perfectly clean.'

Mum blinked. Even I was startled. A clean brain? That didn't sound like me.

'You mean he *isn't* epileptic?' she asked.

'Well...' The doctor preferred not to pass judgement. 'Let's just say the indications aren't there on the scans. Which aren't conclusive. What this means is that we still don't have a firm diagnosis.'

'So he *could* have epilepsy. Is that it?' said Mum.

Dr Passlow leaned back in his chair. It was a posh kind of chair, with a high back and leather upholstery, but the rest of his consulting room wasn't very posh at all. The carpet was stained, the walls were covered with scribbles and fingermarks, and the whole place stank of old baby spew. There was a plastic crate full of toys in one corner, right underneath a photo of a happy toddler who'd had all his immunisation shots.

I couldn't help feeling that I was in the wrong place.

'Let me put it this way,' Dr Passlow continued. 'At the hospital there's a registrar who remembers having a couple of absence seizures in the classroom when he was at high school. He didn't mention them to anyone, and it never happened again.' When Mum didn't react, the doctor placed his hand on top of my file. 'At this stage, we shouldn't be using words like 'epilepsy'. We should be thinking in terms of individual seizures, and taking each episode as it comes. A watching brief, in other words.'

'That's all?' Mum didn't sound impressed – at least, not to my ears. But I know her pretty well. She's so soft-spoken that Dr Passlow might have been fooled into thinking she was only a little bit confused. 'Isn't there something else we should be doing?'

'If he has another episode? Absolutely.'

Mum stiffened. 'But he can't afford to have another episode!' she protested. 'He was lucky to survive the first one!'

'Mrs Vandevelde—'

'If it wasn't an epileptic fit, then what was it? What happened to him?'

'I don't know.' Dr Passlow spread his hands, eyebrows raised. You've got to give the guy his due; a lot of doctors wouldn't have admitted that they were stumped. They would have thrown up a screen of gobbledygook to hide behind. 'We'll see how things pan out,' he proposed. 'I doubt it was an allergic reaction, but that might be worth looking into if any other symptoms manifest themselves. Alternatively, I do know of a study being done in the US on possible links between specific erratic behaviours and certain chemical responses in adolescent males—'

'Are you talking about drugs?' she demanded, much to my annoyance.

'Jeez, Mum.' It was hard to keep calm. 'I *didn't take any drugs*, all right?'

'I don't mean drugs,' the doctor assured us quickly, intervening before any arguments broke out. 'I'm referring to chemical changes in the body. Elevated lactate, for instance. I was doing sabbatical work in Chicago recently, specialising in Child and Adolescent Mental Health, and a colleague there was interested in two cases similar to Toby's, whereby a possibly physical condition had presented as a psychiatric one.'

Mum caught her breath. I nearly had a heart attack.

'*Mental health?*' I squawked faintly. If there's a word you don't want to hear sitting right in front of 'health', it's 'mental'.

Dr Passlow must have realised this, because he looked me straight in the eye and said, 'Toby, I don't think you have a psychological problem. That isn't what I'm saying.'

Whew! I was *so* relieved. As long as I wasn't going mad, nothing else mattered much. He could have told me that I had rabies and it would have been welcome news in comparison.

'My point is that if you continue to experience blackouts, there are more unusual avenues that we can explore. I just don't believe it would be particularly helpful to do so yet, because I wouldn't be surprised if this whole event was a one-off.' Turning back to my mother, Dr Passlow adopted a soothing tone – though his gaze did flick towards the clock on the wall.

'Toby is a normal thirteen-year-old boy who's had one aberrant metabolic reading,' he observed. 'I'd be very reluctant to panic or take extreme measures at this time. It's contraindicated.'

The way he spoke, you could tell that he was keen to wind up our session. (His waiting room had been pretty full.) Mum, however, didn't respond immediately. She sat for a moment, pondering, as the doctor closed my file.

'So – so Toby doesn't have a brain tumour?' she said at last.

'No.'

'And he wasn't drugged?'

'Ah. Well. That I can't tell you.' There was something slightly detached about the way Dr Passlow answered her, as if he didn't want to become involved in the whole teenage-drug-and-alcohol-abuse debate. 'Drug screening isn't an automatic procedure in casualty, plus there was no legal requirement that it be done,' he revealed. 'Besides which, a drug like rohypnol is very hard to detect. It leaves minimal amounts of residue.'

What could you say to that? Nothing. It was a dead end – and poor Mum had run out of steam. She looked so defeated that Dr Passlow must have felt safe enough to ask if she had any more questions. I doubt that he was expecting any.

He certainly seemed surprised when I put up my hand.

'What happened to the kids in Illinois?' I said, because I was genuinely interested. 'Did they lose their memories too?'

The doctor raised his eyebrows. 'They did, yes,' he replied. 'They had elevated lactate and short-term amnesia.' For some reason he suddenly became more animated, leaning across the desk towards me. 'As a medical practitioner, when you see an unclassified group of symptoms presenting itself over and over again, you tend to look for what we call a "case series" before jumping to conclusions,' he explained. 'I thought I might have identified a similar case in Australia, last year, but... well, I wasn't able to follow through on that one. I'm not sure if it was an isolated incident or whether there was a pattern of repeated episodes.'

'Why not?' asked Mum, before I could say anything. The doctor immediately shifted his attention to her.

'It was a Community Services case,' he explained. 'The boy was being badly treated at home as a result of this symptom cluster – apparently the parents had very primitive religious beliefs.' Dr Passlow pulled the kind of face you normally pull when you bite into a rotten apple. 'He was removed and placed into residential care, but he ran away and no one's seen him since. I only wish I'd had a chance to monitor his progress, because everything was pointing towards a clinical profile similar to the ones in Illinois.'

He'd been rattling on with mounting enthusiasm, but something about my mother's pursed lips suddenly pulled him up short.

'Not that this has anything to do with you,' he told me. 'I wouldn't even *begin* to make assumptions about your case right now.'

'But if something else happens...' Mum began, before trailing off.

'If something else happens, I might put a call through to my colleague in Chicago. With your permission,' the doctor agreed, finishing Mum's sentence for her. He then rose, thrusting out his hand for her to shake. 'In the meantime, you should get on with your lives and not worry too much. This clean scan is *good* news. It's the sort of thing I *like* to see.'

And that was the end of my appointment. What a flop. Once

again, Mum and I came away from a medical consultation with no clear answers; we *still* didn't know what had happened on Monday night. I was so disappointed that I couldn't eat all of my lunch afterwards. I guess I'd been counting on a diagnosis so that I didn't have to worry about Reuben's dire warnings anymore.

As for Mum, she was already talking about a second opinion. 'I don't like that man,' she complained, over coffee and lasagna. 'He's too ambitious. Doctors like him are only interested in making a name for themselves. They don't care about their patients; all they care about is getting research funds and publishing articles in the *Lancet*.' She peered at me across the red plastic tablecloth. 'Do *you* want to get involved in some obscure American clinical study?'

'No.'

'No. I'm not surprised.' After chewing her way through a mouthful of pasta, she added, 'I'll get another referral. I'll find someone who doesn't go on and on about case files. You can't trust a doctor who calls people "cases".' She patted my hand. 'Don't worry. We'll figure something out, I promise.'

Once we'd finished eating, Mum paid the bill. Then she dropped me at Amin's house on her way back to work. I can't say I was all that keen to visit Amin; we'd had a bit of a disagreement the previous afternoon, because neither he nor Fergus had been able to stop talking about Reuben (even though I'd asked them very nicely if they could please just give it a rest for five minutes). After insisting that I repeat every single thing that Reuben had told me, they'd launched into an endless discussion about how we should deal with him in the future – completely ignoring the fact that I wanted to change the subject.

In the heat of the moment Fergus had accused me of being a scaredy-cat *and* a bossy-boots, not to mention a spoilsport.

Though we'd calmed down over a shared bowl of popcorn and a DVD of *X-Men*, I still wasn't looking forward to spending Friday afternoon squabbling with Fergus – who was bound to be at Amin's place, since he had nowhere else to go. But when I considered the alternatives, I realised that they were even bleaker. I could watch TV by myself, or play computer games by myself, or practise dance steps by myself. And I knew that if I did any of these things, I'd be moping and fretting the whole time.

So I agreed to visit Amin – and it was the right thing to do. Because when I finally reached the Kairouz house, I discovered that he and Fergus had already lost interest in the whole topic of werewolves. Reuben was old news by then; much more intriguing was the microwave oven that Fergus had found sitting by the road in a heap of junk that someone had put out for collection. Fergus hadn't expected that the microwave would actually *work*. He'd lugged it all the way to Amin's house because he'd wanted to dismantle it, in case the problem was just a loose wire. According to Fergus, if the magnetron and the capacitor and the HV diode were still functional, we could maybe follow the instructions he'd discovered on a website and create ball lightning.

It turned out, however, that the microwave did work. It had probably been thrown away because the clock was faulty, though there might have been other problems as well: a leaky seal, perhaps, or a broken glass plate. But we didn't need fancy things like clocks or glass plates – not to run an experiment. All we needed was an electrical socket and a bunch of interesting things to zap.

We found the perfect socket in Amin's garage, well away from 'the swarm' (as Amin likes to call his family). Here we watched the effects of microwaves on various things: a bar of soap; coins in a pyrex dish; a light bulb resting in a third of a cup of water. Fergus wanted to follow another Internet recommendation – namely, petrol in a metal dog bowl – but Amin and I were reluctant. For one thing, Amin didn't have a big enough yard or a long enough extension cord. For another, I've always drawn the line at messing around with petrol. You can really screw up with petrol; I know this for a fact. 'Once bitten, twice shy' is what I always say.

We were still arguing when my mobile phone rang.

'Hello?' Since I was fully expecting Mum to reply, I nearly dropped the phone when a voice said, *'Toby? It's Father Ramon.'*

The shock must have shown in my face, because Fergus mouthed, 'Who is it?'

'I'm calling you because I felt you probably wouldn't want to talk to Reuben,' the priest went on. *'I don't think he handled things very well yesterday; I'm afraid he tends to lose his temper. It's something he has a problem with . . .'* As I remained speechless, he added, *'Hello? Are you there?'*

'How – how did you get my number?' I managed to croak.

'From Reuben,' the priest replied. *'You called him, remember? You left your number on his phone.'*

'Who is it?' hissed Fergus. I shook my head, turning my back on him. I had to concentrate.

'What do you want?' I demanded, addressing the priest. 'Why don't you leave me alone?'

'Because we can't,' Father Ramon said apologetically. *'Not*

until you realise what a threat you'll be if you don't make proper arrangements for the next full moon. You have to think of it like a public health issue. Every month, for one night, you'll be suffering from something that's as dangerous as a communicable disease. What you have to do is take precautions—'

'That's all crap,' I interposed, my voice shaking. 'You're lying. Or loony. I don't want to talk to you.'

'I know you don't. But this needn't be so very frightening. It's just one night a month, and if you take the proper precautions, it won't affect anything else in your life.'

'Look – I'm not a werewolf. Okay? Werewolves don't exist. End of story.' I saw Fergus raise his eyebrows at Amin, as the voice on the other end of the line said, 'Please won't you give us one more chance? Reuben thinks you should come and look at the bank vault where he spends every full moon. He wants you to see the marks on the walls. He says you might recognise the smell.' Before I could tell him where he could stuff his bank vault, he quickly offered, 'You can talk to some of his other friends too. They know what he's like when he's ... um ...' There was a pause. 'When he's not himself. Two of them have actually seen him like that. They can give you an eyewitness description.'

You might be wondering why I didn't just hang up. Well, I'll tell you why. It was that little hesitation. That fleeting pause. When I heard that, something seemed to go *clang* inside me, like an anvil hitting the bottom of an elevator shaft.

Because he was trying to be kind. I was sure of it. Rather than say, 'They know what he's like when he's acting like a rabid dog and gnawing at doorjambs,' he had delicately skirted the whole subject of Reuben's more feral moments.

And why do that if you're lying through your teeth? Why even bother?

'*You'll like these people,*' Father Ramon insisted, talking very quickly, as if he feared that I might hang up at any moment. '*They're nice people. There's an elderly lady called Bridget, and a young girl about your age called Nina, and a doctor called Sanford. They've all been helping Reuben. Like a support group.*'

I couldn't believe my ears. A werewolf support group? 'Gimme a break.'

'*They could be your friends too, if that's what you want,*' said the priest.

I snorted. 'Thanks very much, but I've already got friends.'

'*Ah. Yes. I was going to ask about your friends.*' Father Ramon went on to suggest that, since I'd apparently been discussing Reuben with at least two other boys, I might like to bring them with me when I inspected the bank vault. '*A little knowledge can be a dangerous thing,*' the priest pointed out. '*We thought that your friends might be less likely to gossip about Reuben if we were to convince them that he's telling the truth. Once they understand his predicament, they'll realise that publicity of any kind is something we need to avoid at all costs.*' He stopped for a moment, as if expecting a reply; when at last he proceeded, his tone had softened. '*And you'll feel much safer if they do come along. Isn't that so?*'

It was all moving a bit too fast for me. I could hardly catch my breath. An excursion? To meet a werewolf support group? With Amin and Fergus along for the ride?

'I dunno...I mean...this is crazy,' I stammered. 'You're out of your minds. Really. I'm not a werewolf.'

'*You just want to believe that—*'

'I *do* believe that!'

'*—because you're scared. And you don't have to be. I realise it's*' come as a shock, but in the long run this is a much better outcome than most of the other alternatives.' It's hard to convey how reassuring the priest sounded. He had such a sympathetic, matter-of-fact quality to his voice. 'You mentioned epilepsy,' he continued. 'As a rule, you need to take medication for epilepsy. But there are no drugs involved in your condition. You don't have treat it, you only have to adjust to it. And it's not a big adjustment to make. The only major change is the one affecting your self-image.'

By this time Fergus was practically jumping up and down, trying to communicate something with a lot of hand gestures and exaggerated facial contortions. Amin was waving a piece of paper at me; on it, he'd written, WHERE IS WEREWOLF FIGHTING PIT?

I felt like strangling both of them.

'You can bring your mother too,' Father Ramon was saying. 'Though I doubt she'd be amenable.'

'She wouldn't have a bar of it,' I retorted.

'No. Of course not.'

'She'd stop me from coming.' Even as the words left my mouth, I had an idea. And I realised that I would have to do it – I would have to visit the bank vault. Because if I did, I would be able to find out whether Father Ramon and his pals were lying or not.

'Would you be there? At this place?' I asked.

'Oh – well – yes. Certainly. If that's what you'd prefer.'

'How far would I have to go?' I clicked my fingers at Amin, then mimed a pen. He handed me his scrap of paper before looking around for something to write with. 'Is it near a train station, or what?'

Father Ramon recited the address, which was in Strathfield. I'd never been to Strathfield, though I knew it had to be at least half an hour away by train. When I made inquiries about the timetable, however, the priest demurred.

'*We'll pay for a cab*,' he promised, as I scribbled away. '*I wouldn't want you catching a train at night.*'

'At night?'

'*Uh – yes.*' He went on to say that there was a slight problem. I would have to inspect the bank vault at night because Sanford – who owned it – was at work during the day. '*Of course I realise how much this will complicate matters. On the whole, I'd prefer it if we could somehow get your mother on board—*'

'No.' By that time I had everything worked out. I knew that if Mum were told, she would stop me from going. And if I couldn't go, I wouldn't be able to execute my plan. And if I couldn't do *that*, then I would remain in a terrible state of anxiety and indecision until the next full moon, when Reuben would probably try to kidnap me. 'No,' I declared. 'It's no good getting Mum involved. She'll just put her foot down.'

'*But if you return home very late—*'

'Don't worry. I'll take care of it.' All I needed was a good cover story. 'So what time should we be there?'

'*What time?*'

'In Strathfield?' Sensing a lack of comprehension, I wondered if I'd misunderstood him.'You want us there tonight, don't you?'

He gasped. '*Oh!*'

'Is that a problem?'

'*No, I – I don't think so.*' During the lull that followed, I could just make out a faint murmur in the background – and I realised that he was consulting somebody. Reuben, perhaps? '*Yes, that should be fine,*' the priest finally confirmed. '*If you get here about ten, it would give me enough time to make arrangements.*'

Though ten was a little later than I'd expected, I agreed to it anyway. 'Ten. Right. Gotcha,' I said.

'*Make sure you take a cab. I'll pay for it when you get to Sanford's house.*'

'Okay.'

'*It shouldn't take too long. We'll have you back home by eleven thirty.*'

'Whatever.' I was keen to get off the phone, since I had my own arrangements to make. 'But this'd better be good,' I warned. 'And you'd better not be trying to set me up. Because I have a friend who's a drug dealer, and if anything happens to me, he'll come after you.'

Fergus immediately scowled. He knew that I was talking about Liam.

'*Oh dear.*' The priest clicked his tongue. '*I really don't think you should be mixing with drug dealers, Toby . . .*'

'Yeah, yeah. Just keep it in mind, okay?' Before he could start lecturing me on the evils of addictive substances, I pulled the rug out from under him. 'See you tonight, then. Ten o'clock. Bye.'

Click. As soon as I cut the connection, Fergus weighed in.

'Liam's not a drug dealer!' he protested. 'You made him sound like a bikie or something!'

'I know. Sorry. It was just a bluff.'

'What's all this about Strathfield, anyway?' said Amin. 'What's happening at ten o'clock?'

'That's what I've gotta tell you.' Extending both arms, I put one hand on Fergus's shoulder and one on Amin's. Then I drew them towards me. 'Listen up,' I murmured. 'Because I've had this brilliant idea, but I'm gunna need your help . . .'

Chapter Ten

You don't even want to know how much the cab fare was that night. I mean, from Mount Druitt mall to Strathfield? Forget about it.

But I'm getting ahead of myself. First, let me just explain that I went to the mall because of my cover story. Mum had been told that I was going to a movie there, with Amin and Fergus. Upon hearing that our preferred session started at 9.15 PM, she'd simply asked me if there was an earlier one.

'No,' I replied. 'Except for the one this morning, but we missed that.'

'Okay – well – I'll pick you up afterwards,' she said. 'All of you. I don't want anyone making their own way home at . . . what is it? Eleven?'

'Eleven thirty.'

'Then I'll pick you up outside the cinema. If it finishes early, you can give me a call.'

In other words: permission granted. I had cleared the first hurdle. My next problem was a technical one; how was I going to turn my mobile phone into a bug? Though I knew it was possible – having dipped into a lot of Internet discussions on the subject – I'd never experimented with the technique myself.

And I certainly didn't own any hands-free headphones, which were a basic requirement for electronic eavesdropping.

So Amin was forced to borrow his father's headphones. Then we ran a few tests. By planting my reprogrammed mobile in various bedrooms around the Kairouz house, I was able to listen to Amin's sisters arguing about wardrobe space, Amin's grandmother singing something in Lebanese, and Amin's brother playing computer games.

On the whole, I was satisfied with these results. And so were my friends.

'But how are you going to get your phone back?' This was Amin's one concern. 'Your mum will kill you if you lose your phone, Toby.'

'I won't lose it. I'll call up Reuben tomorrow and say I left it behind. By accident.'

'But what if they turn out to be lying sleazebags? What if they're such crooks that they won't give it back?'

'Then I'll tell Mum, and she'll call the police. Don't worry, okay? This is going to work. I *know* this is going to work.'

All the same, I wasn't as confident as I sounded. In fact I hardly ate any dinner that night – and when Mum drove me to the mall, I spent the whole trip praying to God that she wouldn't suddenly decide to go to the movies herself. Luckily, she didn't even get out of the car; I think she wanted to rush back home so she could watch the beginning of *Law & Order*. You can imagine how relieved I was when I saw her waving goodbye.

It was also a relief to see Amin and Fergus. They both showed up at the cinema on time, though Amin confessed that he'd had a bit of a close call. His older brother had been toying with the idea of coming with us, and had changed his mind only at the last minute. 'We would have been stuffed,' said Amin, who was still sweating. 'Unless we'd bribed him.'

'Not me,' Fergus rejoined. 'I'm broke.' He fixed me with a stern look. 'By the way, are you *sure* we don't have to pay for this cab? What happens if we reach the bank vault and nobody's there?'

'If that happens, then we really are stuffed,' I admitted. 'We'll have to take the cab back to my place, and Mum will have to pay for it.'

'Which means she'll kill you,' Fergus warned.

'Yeah. But I don't think the priest will stand me up. You should have heard him. He was *desperate* for me to go. He was *begging*.'

'Which is pretty strange in itself, don't you think? Makes you wonder.' Before I could respond, Fergus gently kicked his backpack, which was sitting on the cinema's well-worn carpet. 'I bought some Exit Mould, just in case. And an icepick.'

'Exit Mould?' Amin was mystified. 'What's that for?'

'For spraying in their eyes!' Fergus spat. 'We were supposed to come prepared, remember?'

'I know.' Amin was immediately on the defensive. 'I didn't forget.'

'Me neither,' I said, though finding a weapon in my house had been next to impossible. Mum would have spotted a missing kitchen knife in three seconds flat, because all our knives are kept in a wooden block on the kitchen benchtop. What's more, she doesn't like leaving dangerous chemicals around. 'I brought a screwdriver,' was my feeble contribution, which sounded even more feeble when Amin suddenly announced, 'I brought my dad's nail gun.'

Fergus and I stared at him, awe-struck.

'Wow,' said Fergus.

'Gee, Amin, that's really...' I tried to think of a word. '...really major.'

'Can I carry it?' Fergus pleaded.

'Nope,' said Amin.

'Why not?'

'Because Dad doesn't like people touching it.'

'*You* touched it.'

'Yeah, but I didn't shoot it.'

'I won't shoot it...'

They were still arguing as they followed me outside. Since it was a Friday night in summer, there were quite a few cabs around. I'd barely reached the footpath before a taxi pulled up in front of me and disgorged a jabbering mob of girls, one of whom looked vaguely familiar.

She lifted her hand when she caught my eye. But then Fergus pulled a dumb, drooling face, at which point she decided that I wasn't worth knowing after all.

'That's Jasmine what's-her-name,' said Amin. 'From sixth class. I remember her.'

'Taxi!' I shouted. 'Hey!'

'Isn't she the one with the pet frog?' asked Fergus.

But I didn't reply; I was already in the cab, talking to the driver. I don't usually catch cabs – not without Mum, anyway – so it felt weird telling the driver where I wanted to go. It felt especially weird because I was practically penniless; I didn't have enough cash on me to pay for a ride to Strathfield.

Maybe the driver sensed this, because he glanced up into the rear-view mirror and said, 'That's a pretty long trip. You boys got the money for that?'

'My uncle will pay when we get there,' I promised, before adding, 'He's a priest.'

Maybe 'priest' was the magic word – or maybe the driver couldn't bring himself to blow off such an enormous fare. Whatever the reason, he sighed, shrugged, and waited for Amin and Fergus to climb into the back seat.

Then we pulled away from the kerb.

My heart was pounding like a hip-hop song by this time. Even Fergus seemed subdued. We didn't say much as we headed onto the motorway, where the traffic was pretty heavy; I guess the driver's presence put a dampener on things. He had the radio on, so we all listened in silence to some pathetic top-forty program until we reached Parramatta Road. Then came a painfully slow crawl through one set of traffic lights after another, while the countdown gave way to the news, and then to somebody talking about mental health.

I kept looking at the meter. It was giving me vertigo.

'My cousin used to work there,' said Amin, pointing at a used-car yard.

Fergus wasn't interested. He leaned towards me. 'Did you ever read about that guy who was executed with a nail gun?' he whispered into my ear. 'The police found something like thirty nails in his skull. Gross, eh?'

I grunted, but my heart sank. Sometimes you suddenly *know* that you've made a mistake. Sitting in that unfamiliar cab, smelling the driver's deodorant and watching all the coloured lights flash past, I felt as if I'd been cut adrift in a totally strange world. Not a computer-generated world – a real one. Full of real people and real consequences.

What the hell did I think I was doing? Was I out of my *mind*?

'I bet you forgot to bring nails,' Fergus said to Amin, just as the car began to slow.

'What's that number again?' the driver queried. 'Are you sure this is the place you want?'

We'd reached a small clump of shops on a modest intersection. There was a newsagency, a hairdresser's, a pub, a drycleaner's and a place selling office equipment. There were also several buildings that were hard to identify. One might have been a doctor's surgery, or perhaps a dental clinic; it was hard to tell in the dark. Another was either a post office or a police station. And there was a two-storey structure that obviously wasn't a house, though it didn't look much like a business, either. For one thing, it didn't have any signs affixed to its blank, imposing facade.

The driver halted in front of it.

'Number sixty-eight,' he announced.

Fergus, Amin and I peered out the window.

'That looks like an old bank to me,' said Amin.

'Yeah.' I swallowed. 'You wait here.'

'I can come too,' Fergus offered.

'No. Both of you wait here.'

I scrambled out of the car, then approached an imposing set of double doors flanked by two stone pillars. To my surprise, the doorbell was just an ordinary plastic button; I was expecting some kind of elaborate, wrought-iron thing. Overhead a light was burning.

One of the doors swung open before I could even announce my arrival.

'Ah!' said Father Ramon. He was standing on the threshold, wearing his cassock. 'You're early. Excellent. Did you bring your two friends?'

111

My mouth was so dry that I couldn't talk. So I jerked my chin at the cab.

Father Ramon responded by slapping his brow.

'Oh!' he exclaimed. 'That's right. There's a fare to pay. Let me take care of that...'

As he hurried past, I saw someone else hovering behind him, just inside the front door. It wasn't Reuben; it was a little old lady with white hair and a walking stick. Her blue eyes looked enormous, enlarged by the coke-bottle lenses of her steel-rimmed spectacles.

'Hello,' she croaked. 'I'm Bridget.'

As my eyes adjusted to the dimness, I saw a small group of people standing in an enormous room. Above them, two glowing balls of frosted glass hung from a cavernous ceiling. Glass screens were attached to a distant row of counter tops. The floor was made of polished stone. Every window had been sealed behind a set of massive, reinforced security shutters.

It was an old bank, all right – and it was being used as an art studio. It smelled strongly of turpentine. An easel had been set up. There were canvases stacked against the walls.

'Hi, Toby,' said Reuben, who was lurking in one corner near a half-finished still life. He was wearing greasy blue overalls. Beside him were two other people: a pale girl in a long floral dress, with dark hair and matchstick arms, and an old woman with steel-wool hair, who was smoking a cigarette.

Thinking back, I could recall that Father Ramon had mentioned a girl – someone called Nina. I figured this had to be the same girl. But the old woman didn't ring any bells. I didn't like the look of her. I didn't like her hacking cough, or the way she kept blowing smoke around.

I liked the look of Nina, though. She had the most Gothic

face I'd ever seen, all blanched skin and dark smudges. But she wasn't dressed like a Goth, so I could tell that she was *naturally* gloomy and mysterious. She wasn't putting it on, like all those other girls who strut around in black lipstick and purple velvet and fishnet stockings. She wasn't trying too hard.

Maybe it was Nina who suddenly cheered me up. Or maybe I was reassured by a whole range of things: Nina's pink sandals, and Bridget's walking stick, and the person who introduced himself to me as Dr Sanford Plackett – who had to be the world's straightest guy. He was a thin, pasty-faced, middle-aged man wearing a three-piece suit and a boring moustache, like an old-fashioned bank manager. It was impossible to be scared of him. Or of Nina. Or of Bridget.

I thought, *These people aren't going to hurt me. No way. They're just a bunch of losers*.

So I took a deep breath and went inside.

'Where's your gang?' Reuben asked. 'Didn't you bring them?' He was trying to be jovial, I think, but I wasn't amused. Not one little bit.

'They're just coming,' I rejoined. 'And they're *not* my gang. I don't have a gang.' Even as I gestured towards the front entrance, Fergus and Amin stumbled into the room behind me. Amin looked scared and harmless. Fergus, on the other hand, was wearing camouflage pants and Blundstone boots.

'This is Amin Kairouz, and this is Fergus Duffy,' I said, by way of introduction. The words were barely out of my mouth before it occurred to me: should I have used aliases?

'Hello, Amin. Hello, Fergus.' Dr Plackett gave a nod. 'Welcome to my home. I'm Dr Sanford Plackett, and this is Nina Harrison, and Estelle Harrison.' He pointed at the pale girl, then the old smoker. 'And this is Bridget Doherty, and you know Reuben Schneider, of course.'

Fergus grinned when he spotted Reuben. Amin winced. Then they both shuffled aside to admit Father Ramon, who closed the big double doors behind him.

With the doors shut, everything seemed a lot more shadowy and mysterious.

'Thanks for coming,' said Reuben. In response to a reproving glance from the doctor, he reluctantly added, 'Sorry I lost my temper yesterday.'

I shrugged. Father Ramon offered me a nervous little smile.

'Shall we have a cup of tea?' he suggested. 'There's a proper living room out the back, where we can sit and talk.'

'It's the old manager's residence,' Dr Plackett broke in. 'I don't really use this area very much. It's too hard to heat in winter. I spend most of my time out the back. And in the rooms upstairs.'

'I baked some scones,' Bridget quavered.

Hearing this, I couldn't help sneaking a look at Fergus. Tea and scones? What the hell were these people *up* to?

Fergus obviously thought they were dithering about. 'We wanna see the vault,' he declared. And Amin echoed, 'Yeah. We wanna see the vault.'

'But we'll have some scones afterwards,' I said hastily, because I suspected that Reuben and his friends wouldn't be discussing me in the old bank vault once I'd left. They would probably talk in a comfortable place, where they could sit down with a nice cup of tea. For that reason, I decided to leave my mobile phone in the living room, under a sofa cushion or behind a pot plant.

'All right.' Dr Plackett turned to the priest, who nodded. 'We'll do the bank vault first. Not you, though, Bridget. Those stairs would be too much for your hips.'

'I'll go and set the table,' Bridget volunteered. 'Do you have any paper doilies, Sanford?'

'Of course not. Why on earth would I have paper doilies?'

'Never mind.' Bridget began to stump away. 'Napkins are just as good...'

It was interesting to see how everyone reacted to this exchange. Reuben heaved an impatient sigh. Estelle snorted. Amin screwed up his face in sheer bewilderment; I don't think he even knew what doilies were.

Nina caught my eye and smiled without showing her teeth.

'Are you really thirteen?' she asked.

'Yeah,' I said. 'Are you?'

She shook her head. 'You're tall for your age,' she observed, 'but you *are* a lot like Reuben.'

'No, I'm not.'

'Yes, you are,' she insisted. 'You're all fizzy and glowing.'

Fizzy and *glowing*? Fergus gave a honk of laughter. Reuben said sourly, 'Come on. Shake a leg. We haven't got all night.'

Various people began to move, heading for a door behind the old teller's counter. Watching them, I wondered if I was making a big mistake. Should I really be going into an underground vault with a crowd of total strangers?

Amin must have been thinking the same thing. 'Maybe I should stay up here,' he squeaked. I saw that his forehead was damp.

Reuben spun around to glare at him.

115

'What's the matter with you?' asked Reuben. 'I thought you *wanted* to see the vault?'

'He's scared,' said Estelle. She removed the cigarette from her mouth before addressing Amin. 'Isn't that right, love? You don't feel safe.'

'Oh, for—' Reuben stopped himself just in time. He took a deep, steadying breath as Father Ramon protested, 'We're not going to hurt you, boys. We're trying to *help*.'

Amin didn't seem convinced. But then Fergus spoke up.

'Amin, that cab driver saw us, remember? And Toby's girlfriend used the same cab before we got into it. So if something happens, the coppers will know where to look. Okay?'

Man, I hate it when Fergus does that. 'She's not my *girlfriend*, Fergus! I don't even *know* her!'

'Yeah, yeah.' Fergus waved me aside as he made for the next room. 'Anyway, my brother's a drug dealer. He chops off people's feet. He'll go *mental* if anything happens to us.' Upon reaching the exit, he stopped to gaze back at a ring of astonished, deeply disturbed expressions. He seemed surprised that no one was coming after him. 'So is it down these stairs through here, or what?'

'Er...yes,' Dr Plackett agreed. He was the first to set off in pursuit of Fergus. Reuben was next in line. Then Amin darted forward.

I finally found myself clattering down the stairs at the rear of the group, beside Nina Harrison. She was very small; the top of her head barely reached my shoulder.

She smelled vaguely of dust, like old potpourri.

'So where do you go to school?' was the only question I could think of to ask her. It wasn't much, but it was a start.

'I don't go to school.' After a moment's pause, she explained, 'I get taught at home.'

'Oh.'

'Mum does it.' She cocked her thumb at Estelle, who was shuffling along behind us in a pair of rundown moccasins.

I blinked. Estelle was her *mum*?

'She calls me Mum because I raised her,' Estelle interjected, then broke into a fit of coughing. Nina added quickly, 'She's my grandmother, really. Mum's dead. So's my dad.'

'Oh yeah?' That was a coincidence. 'My dad's dead too.' I might have said more if we hadn't reached the bottom of the stairs just then. All at once I realised that I was standing in front of an honest-to-goodness bank vault, like the ones you see in the movies. Behind a big, iron-barred gate lay a grey steel door that had to be at least half a metre thick; although it was very old-fashioned, with no digital locks or fancy laser alarms attached to it, this door was still impressive. I especially liked the giant bolts and tumblers.

'Oh, man,' Fergus exclaimed. 'That is *so cool.*'

Even Amin had perked up. Reuben, however, wasn't interested in him – or in Fergus. Reuben was watching *my* face.

'Now, this is where Reuben comes every full moon,' Dr Plackett remarked. He pulled the vault door open until its inner surface was revealed. 'See that? And that?' he continued, indicating damage on the painted metal. 'They're marks left by Reuben. You can see where he's been scratching at it, trying to get out. And this is where he chipped a tooth on the hinge. And if you come and look at this little patch, there's a smear of blood here with some hairs embedded in it. We didn't clean those off because we wanted you to examine them, Toby.' To my amazement, the doctor suddenly produced a heavy, silver-rimmed magnifying glass from somewhere beneath his jacket, like a magician pulling a scarf out of someone's ear. 'You can even take those hairs with you, if you want,' he said, thrusting the glass into my hand. 'Give them to any laboratory and you'll find that no one can identify the species. It's a unique DNA signature. I can provide you with a sterile specimen bag, of course...'

Every eye was fixed on me. Everyone was waiting to see what I would do. Father Ramon smiled his encouragement.

Fergus said, 'It's okay, Toby.' And he crooked his trigger finger, his gaze flicking towards Amin's back. *If anything goes wrong*, he was trying to say (without actually speaking), *I'll whip out the nail gun*.

'For God's sake...' I muttered, wishing that I was a million miles away. But I couldn't leave. I had to step forward and inspect the smear of blood. I had to appear cooperative if I wanted to be invited into the living room afterwards.

Besides, Nina was watching. And I didn't want to look like a snivelling kid in front of *her*.

'It's just here by the door,' Dr Plackett instructed. As I drew near him, I caught a whiff of his cologne, which was very strong. When I stuck my head into the bank vault, however, his piney scent was blasted away by a stench like a tidal wave. That stench – I kid you not – hit me with the force of a ten-tonne truck. I reeled back. I couldn't breathe. It did something weird to my muscles, which all contracted at once. It made my head spin, and my heart race, and the blood burn red-hot under my skin. It gripped my stomach like a fist.

'Toby?' said Father Ramon. 'Are you all right?'

I had to get out. I was frantic. Something was after me – I had to get out before it tore me to pieces!

Choking and gasping, I hurtled back upstairs.

Chapter Eleven

Next thing I knew, I was surrounded by sticky paintings of flowers and apples and teapots. They were crowding in on me. But I couldn't escape because someone was holding me back.

'Let go!' I cried, struggling and kicking.

'Calm down,' said Reuben. 'It's all right.' His arms were clamped firmly across my chest like steel bars. And when I tried to buck him off, he drove the front of his knee into the back of mine.

'Ow!' My left leg crumpled.

'Toby, listen. No one's going to hurt you.' This was probably Father Ramon's voice, though I couldn't be sure. I wasn't really paying attention. As I threw myself backwards, Reuben staggered a little. For a moment I thought he was going to collapse under my weight.

'Jesus!' He managed to brace himself against the impact. '*Calm down*, or I *will* bloody hurt you!'

'No, you won't.' Dr Plackett was talking from somewhere in my immediate vicinity. He lowered his voice to add, 'This is a post-traumatic response. Something to do with those specialised olfactory organs—'

'For God's sake,' Estelle interrupted. I recognised her smoker's rasp. 'Shut up and give the kid a valium or something, can't you?'

'Toby? Toby!' All at once I felt a cold little hand on my cheek. It was Nina's hand. The shock of that icy touch snapped me out of my panic; I stopped fighting to stare at her.

'Relax,' she said. 'You're okay. What's wrong?'

'It was the smell,' Reuben growled into my ear. 'It was the smell, wasn't it? Eh?' He shifted his grip. 'There's nothing in that vault, mate. Just the smell.'

'Why is your hand so cold?' I mumbled. I was addressing Nina, who shrugged as she retreated a step.

'I don't know. I'm just a cold person,' she replied.

'But it's the middle of summer...' I was dazed and confused. My legs were shaking. I'd dropped the magnifying glass. When I looked around, I saw that I was in the big front room, near the tellers' counter. 'How did I get up here?' I demanded, with mounting alarm. 'Who brought me?'

'You need something hot. With sugar in it,' Dr Plackett decreed. 'Come and sit down in the living room.'

'Did I have another blackout?' Suddenly I spotted Fergus and Amin. They were standing together some distance away, looking utterly clueless. 'Hey! You guys! Was I drugged?'

They shook their heads slowly. Even Fergus seemed to be at a loss. For once he didn't crack any smart-arse jokes or make any hair-raising suggestions. He just stood there like a little kid.

'Come on, mate.' Having released me (at long last), Reuben put his arm around my shoulders. 'You'll be fine. I know it's tough at first, but you'll get over it.'

'What happened?' I still couldn't work it out. Then I saw that we were retracing our steps. 'Oh no,' I squawked, digging my heels in. 'No way. I'm not going back down there.'

'You won't have to,' Father Ramon assured me. 'We're not going downstairs. Sanford's living room is on the other side of the stairwell.'

'But that thing...' I couldn't finish. When I shuddered, Reuben frowned.

'What thing?' he asked.

'In the – in the vault...'

'There's nothing in the vault,' said Dr Plackett. He turned to my friends. 'Tell him. Did *you* see anything?'

Once more, Amin and Fergus shook their heads.

'You're just scared of *yourself,* Toby. That's all,' Reuben theorised. 'Come and sit down and we'll talk about it.' As he nudged me back into the stairwell, he and Dr Plackett began to argue about whose job it had been to buy lemonade. Nina kept patting my arm while Father Ramon hurried ahead into the living room. Nina's grandmother was bringing up the rear; she had rescued my backpack, which Fergus and Amin had forgotten to pick up.

'Here,' she said, shoving it at Fergus. '*You* take this. I've got arthritis.'

The living-room walls were covered in paintings. That was the first thing I noticed when I crossed the threshold: all those splodgy flowers hanging from the picture rails. Then I saw that the paintings matched the carpet, which was printed with an old-fashioned floral pattern. Even the cushions had flowers on them. Everywhere you looked there were flowers.

'Is this really where you live?' I asked Dr Plackett, who didn't seem like a flowery kind of guy. I would have expected to see nautical maps and tartan rugs in his house. Then I spotted a sepia photograph of a puffy-haired woman wearing a huge hat covered in flowers, and suddenly it all made sense. Of course. This wasn't *his* taste; it was hers. 'I guess that's your mother, hey?'

'Uh...y-e-e-es.' For some reason, the doctor didn't seem one-hundred-per-cent sure. He waved at an antique sofa with a dip in its back and a curled animal claw at the end of each leg. 'Sit down,' he ordered. 'Have a scone.'

So I sat down. To be honest, I was glad to; my knees were still trembling, and I wanted to get away from Reuben. I didn't realise that he was going to sit down right next to me.

Then Bridget suddenly spoke, making me jump. I hadn't seen her because she was practically engulfed by the flowery, overstuffed wingback chair in which she was huddled.

'What would you like on your scone, dear?' she queried, in her cracked little voice. 'Jam and cream, or just butter?'

'Um...' I had to clear my throat. 'Actually I'm – uh – not very hungry.'

'Tea?'

'No, thanks.'

Around me the room was filling up. Nina had found an ottoman. Dr Plackett was perched on a piano stool. Fergus and Amin were both wedged into a kind of miniature pew with a carved back and a padded seat. Only the priest remained standing.

'When does your mother expect you back?' he asked. When I told him 11:30 PM, he checked his watch. 'Not much time,' he observed. 'We'd better get a move on.'

But no one seemed to know how. We exchanged uncertain looks until finally Nina said, 'Maybe Toby has some questions he'd like answered.'

Yet again, all eyes swivelled towards me. The attention left me tongue-tied; I had so many questions that I couldn't decide where to begin. I wanted to say, 'How do you know each other? Why are you doing this? Where do you live? What are you *really* here for?' The trouble was, all these words became tangled up on their way out. They stuck in my larynx.

After a long pause, Dr Plackett finally declared, 'I think we should treat this like an ordinary meeting. Reuben, why don't you tell us your life story?'

Reuben scowled. 'You already know my life story,' he replied.

'Toby doesn't.'

'Yes, he does. I told him about being locked up. I told him why it's important that he doesn't shoot his mouth off.' Reuben glared at Fergus. 'I told him we need to keep a low profile, if we don't want to cop a lot of abuse.'

'That's right,' said Father Ramon. Then he turned to me. '"Werewolf" is a very emotive word. It has bad connotations. But it's a word that's bound to be used if the general public finds out about your condition, Toby. At which point you'll become a target for hatred and prejudice and violence.'

'Like I did,' Reuben broke in. 'And poor old Danny Ruiz. Remember I told you about Danny? He's the one who lives in the desert.'

There was a muted murmur; clearly I wasn't the only one who had been told about Danny Ruiz. Nina shook her head sadly. Father Ramon sighed.

'Danny's really messed up,' Reuben continued. 'He can't cope with other people. He's not a big threat now, but if anyone ever came after him with a camera...'

He trailed off. There was more solemn head-shaking. At last Dr Plackett said, 'That unfortunate man is *damaged*. He needs help. If only he'd get some therapy, he'd be a lot better off.'

'Sanford, he'd eat you for breakfast,' Reuben rejoined. Then he flushed as Estelle chuckled. 'I mean – not literally, but ... you know.'

'Metaphorically speaking,' said the priest.

'Yeah.'

'I do think we should keep trying, though,' Bridget quavered. 'We can't just abandon him because he's so hard to help, poor thing.'

Reuben shifted impatiently. 'Yeah, but you haven't *met* him, Bridge. None of you have. You dunno what he's like – the guy's a full-on menace. He totally freaked me out.' Catching my eye, Reuben was quick to offer reassurance. 'I'm not saying he's crazy because of his condition. It's the way he was treated. *Anyone* would start to lose it after being treated like an animal for twenty-odd years.'

'It's post-traumatic,' was Dr Plackett's diagnosis.

'Yeah. I guess,' Reuben agreed, his gaze still boring into me. 'See, Danny never learned how to trust people. No one ever helped him. I was rescued, but Danny wasn't. He escaped from that underground tank all by himself, and then he went bush. I only found him because ... well ...'

He hesitated, furiously rubbing his jaw. It was the priest who finished his sentence for him.

'Because Danny's kidnappers had a change of heart,' said Father Ramon. When Nina raised her eyebrows, he added, 'In a manner of speaking.'

'A change of heart. Yeah, right,' Reuben said drily. 'I guess you could call it that.'

'I think we *should* call it that,' said Dr Plackett. 'Since we're all friends now.'

Only Bridget, however, backed him up. Though she began to nod and smile in an encouraging way, no one else seemed very enthusiastic. Estelle sniffed. Reuben glowered. Even the priest looked doubtful.

'Speak for yourself!' Nina snapped. 'Personally, I don't care if I never see the McKinnons ever again!'

'Hear, hear,' said Reuben – much to Bridget's distress. Her forehead puckered and her smile began to fade.

Father Ramon eyed Reuben reproachfully. 'The McKinnons are doing their best, Reuben, and they've been very helpful.'

'Hah!'

'If it weren't for the McKinnons, we wouldn't have found Danny,' the priest insisted. He flicked me an inquiring glance. 'Has Toby heard about the McKinnons?'

'Oh yeah. He's heard about the McKinnons, all right.' Reuben answered before I could. 'I told him how they locked me in an underground tank and made me fight in a pit—'

'Not anymore, though,' Dr Plackett said firmly. 'Credit where credit's due.'

'That's right,' Father Ramon concurred. 'They want to repair the damage they've done.' Ignoring Reuben's sneer, he began to elaborate, still watching me closely. 'When the McKinnons were making their money off blood sports, they had a friend who used to alert them to various dog attacks around the state. This friend was a dogger, so he was always the first to hear about wild dog activity.' My blank expression made him falter for an instant. 'Do you know what a dogger is?' he asked.

I shook my head.

126

'Doggers hunt wild dogs,' Reuben volunteered. 'They trap 'em and shoot 'em.'

'And this particular dogger used to collect a small fee every time he gave the McKinnons a good tip.' Father Ramon went on to recount how the McKinnons had never informed their dogger friend that they were no longer in the business of kidnapping people. So the dogger was still conveying news of the latest sheep losses, which the McKinnons, in turn, were relaying to Reuben. 'They told us about some attacks near Dubbo last year, and Reuben went out there to investigate,' the priest finished. 'Which is how he located poor Danny.'

'See, he wasn't properly organised,' Reuben explained. 'Danny, I mean. He'd been taking precautions, but they weren't good enough. You can't just chain yourself up every full moon – it doesn't work. After a few months of really rough treatment, something's always gunna give. Like a link or a bolt or something.'

'Which is what happened to Danny,' said Nina.

'Which is what happened to Danny,' Reuben confirmed. 'He kept yanking at that chain until he pulled it out. Then he ended up killing his own dogs, poor bugger.' There was a regretful clicking of tongues all around the room. 'I told him, *you need a secure facility*. So we fixed up an old mine shaft—'

'I don't think Toby's too interested in the details, love,' Estelle suddenly remarked. She was grinding her cigarette stub into a brass ashtray. 'Not right now, at least.'

'Good lord, no.' Dr Plackett was peering at the clock on the mantelpiece. 'We're running out of time.'

'The point we're trying to make, Toby, is that you're not the first person we've approached. And you probably won't be the last,' Father Ramon declared. He spoke in a slightly formal manner, as if he were delivering a sermon. 'Because although you have an extremely rare condition, you're not alone.'

'Not by a long shot,' said the doctor. 'We're here to help.'

'Any support you might need, whether practical or emotional – all you have to do is ask,' Father Ramon continued. 'Every one of us in this room has a special burden to carry, and we know that a shared burden is always much lighter. "Woe to him that is alone when he falleth, for he hath not another to help him up."'

'Amen,' Bridget muttered.

The priest ploughed on. 'We're here because we believe that we have a responsibility both to you, as a fellow human being in trouble, and to society as a whole. And we each have something special to contribute, whether it be advice or comfort—'

'—or a wine cellar.' Reuben weighed in. Seeing Nina grimace, he went on the defensive. 'What? Aren't we gunna talk about the wine cellar?'

Estelle flapped her hand at him. 'For God's sake, take it easy, will you?' she croaked, between coughs. 'The poor kid's still reeling.'

'Yeah, but there isn't much *time*.' Reuben was becoming restless. He didn't just turn his head to look at me; his whole body spun around. 'We've got a friend who's got a wine cellar,' he explained. 'It needs a bit of work, but we think it would be a really good option for you. And it's not too far away – it's in Haberfield.' He paused, then began to twitch and fidget when I didn't respond. 'We can't *both* go in the bank vault, mate, we'd rip each other apart!'

Still I couldn't say anything. I sat there dumbly, my mind a blank, only vaguely aware of Reuben's impatience, and Nina's sympathetic regard, and the plate of scones hovering under my nose.

'Are you sure you won't have one?' Bridget offered, in a gesture of helpless goodwill.

'No, thanks.' My voice was barely audible. Amin was chewing on his thumbnail, round-eyed.

'Listen, Toby.' Dr Plackett leaned forward in a brisk, no-nonsense fashion, his bony hands clasped between his knees. 'We'll show you the wine cellar before you make any final decisions – don't worry about that. You'd be involved in the whole renovation process.'

'Oh sure,' said Reuben. 'And we'd be doing most of the work ourselves, so it wouldn't cost you much.'

'It wouldn't cost you *anything*,' the doctor corrected, still talking to me. 'Maybe when you're older, with a good job and a solid asset base, you can make your own contribution. The way Reuben has.'

'And of course you're free to consult your mother,' Father Ramon advised. The rumble of protest that greeted this announcement made him add, 'As long as you're able to convince her that we have your best interests at heart.'

'And hers, too,' Estelle pointed out. 'God knows, *I* wouldn't want to be sharing a bathroom with Toby, next time he has a bad spell.'

'No, no. Of course not.' Dr Plackett took over again. 'But if you don't think your mother can be persuaded, Toby, we'll have to arrange some kind of cover story. Maybe your friends can help.' Focusing his gimlet eye on Amin and Fergus, he addressed them with barely concealed distaste. 'I daresay you all take part in the occasional overnight camping trip, or some such thing...?'

Amin gawked. Fergus said, '*Camping trip?*' as if he'd never heard anything so ridiculous in his whole life.

'You must have sleepovers,' Nina suggested. Then she appealed to me. 'Don't you have sleepovers?'

I didn't want to be rude. I really wanted to answer her. But it was a huge effort. 'I've stayed at Amin's house a couple of times,' was all that I could manage, even after a lot of throat-clearing and lip-moistening.

It seemed to satisfy the doctor, though.

'There you are, then. We can sort something out,' he said. 'The important thing is that the police don't get involved. We simply can't afford to alert them.'

'Because of me,' Reuben confessed.

'Not *just* because of you—'

'Because I've killed people. Lots of people. I could go to gaol for that.'

'But you weren't in your right mind,' Estelle cut in, with the fretful air of someone who's argued the same point a million times before. 'All you'd have to do is plead insanity—'

'—and get put in a hospital for the criminally insane! No *thanks*,' barked Reuben. Dr Plackett, however, wasn't about to be diverted. He kept soldiering on, doggedly making his case.

'We can't risk any kind of public exposure,' he informed me. 'If the police find out, the media will find out. Which would be disastrous.'

'Why?' Fergus demanded. He had regained some of his in-your-face confidence; as everyone stared at him, he stared right back, defiantly. 'I don't get it. Werewolves are cool. People love werewolves.'

Reuben bared his teeth. 'You don't know what you're talking about,' he snapped.

'Yes, I do. It doesn't make sense. Why shouldn't Toby be famous? Why shouldn't he earn lots of money from going on TV?' Before Reuben could say anything else, Fergus began to harangue me, his excitement increasing with every new scenario. 'I bet you'd be famous all over the *world!*' he exclaimed. 'I bet they'd fly you to America and everything! They might even make a movie about you!'

'That's right,' said Nina flatly. 'Toby would be famous. Wherever he decided to go, people would know who he was. All the scientists who'd want to treat him like a lab rat, and all the crazies who'd want to get rid of an unnatural freak, and all the evil billionaires who'd pay big money to have a stuffed werewolf – all those people would know who Toby was.'

Snubbed, Fergus began to deflate beneath her sombre regard. Then Father Ramon spoke up.

'It's one thing to enjoy werewolves when they're part of a paranormal fantasy world,' he said. 'It's another thing when that fantasy becomes reality.'

'I mean, we can't pretend we're harmless, right?' Though still flushed, Reuben was keeping his anger in check. 'It's not like we're fairies or unicorns. We've had *a hundred years* of bad press – that's not going to disappear in a hurry.'

'It's like vampires,' Estelle proposed. For some reason, this comment didn't seem to go down very well; a slight tension was noticeable in the atmosphere as she went on. 'If vampires were real, someone out there would want to kill every one of 'em. Just because they have a bad reputation.'

'But vampires are *dangerous*,' Fergus objected. After a

131

heartbeat's pause, he mumbled, 'I mean, they would be if they were real.'

'Yes. That's certainly what people would think,' said the doctor, with tight-lipped disapproval. 'And they'd think the same thing about you, Toby. Your life as you know it would completely disappear. You'd become a stereotype. A target. You'd be "the werewolf" to everyone, and that's all you'd ever be.'

'Plus you'd never get health insurance,' Estelle remarked. She had shuffled over to the coffee table, where she was pouring herself a cup of tea. 'In fact you might have trouble finding any kind of insurance cover at all,' she conjectured. 'Try telling your average insurance salesman that you wouldn't be ripping up your soft furnishings every month. Do you think he'd believe you? I don't hold out much hope.'

A glum and weary silence settled over the room. Even Fergus had run out of things to say; his arms were folded and he looked sulky. Beside him, Amin was staring at the floor. Nina must have been feeling sick, because her eyes were closed. Estelle was peering at her with obvious concern.

Everyone else was studying me.

'You've been very quiet, Toby,' Father Ramon said at last. 'Is there anything you're particularly worried about? Anything you'd like to ask us?'

'Yeah,' I replied. 'There is.' Then I stood up, shaking off Reuben's steely grasp. 'Can I go home now? Please?' I said. 'All I wanna do is go home.'

Chapter Twelve

Luckily, I didn't have to wait long for a cab – no more than ten minutes. And during that time, no one said much. Estelle called the taxi service that *she* always used, because apparently she lived in Surry Hills, which wasn't that far away. Bridget offered to pack up a few scones so I could take them with me. (I rejected her offer.) Father Ramon gave me his phone number and enough money for the fare back home. Nina vanished; I think she went to the bathroom. Dr Plackett gave Fergus a short lecture about having some consideration for a friend in need. 'Imagine how bad you're going to feel,' said the doctor, 'if Toby ends up dead because you couldn't keep your mouth shut.'

It was Reuben who came outside with me when the cab finally appeared. He'd been trying to arrange a visit to his friend's wine cellar, and was fast losing patience because I wouldn't commit to any kind of schedule. 'Just gimme a rough idea,' he pleaded, following me down the front steps. 'We've gotta do it soon, y'know – we can't just piss about. It's only three weeks until the next full moon.'

'I'll think about it.' All I wanted to do was escape. 'I'll text you.'

'Yeah, but when?' he pestered. Then he seized my arm again.

'Listen – you can't just ignore this, right? It's not gunna go away. It's like being pregnant.' Hearing Fergus snicker, he rounded on both my friends, scowling furiously. 'As for you two, you'd better watch your step, because you're treading on thin ice, okay? You're *really* getting up my nose. And you don't wanna do that. You do *not* want someone like me on your tail.'

Amin flinched. 'I didn't say anything!' he protested, without eliciting the slightest response. Reuben simply turned back to me.

'You can call any time,' he said. 'If you wanna talk, just dial my number. Don't go blabbing to anyone else.' The taxi driver honked his horn impatiently. 'Did Father Ramon give you enough cash?'

'Yes.' It was in my pocket.

'Good. Off you go, then.' He clapped me on the shoulder as I pulled open the taxi's rear passenger door. 'And don't sweat it, okay? You'll be fine.'

I was already climbing into the back seat of the car, so I figured that I didn't have to say anything. Fergus shoved his way in after me, with Amin bringing up the rear. It was Fergus who told the driver that we wanted to go to Mount Druitt. I just stared straight ahead until Reuben slammed the door shut, because I didn't want to catch his eye.

I only glanced back when we started to pull away from the kerb. Reuben was standing in the glow of a streetlight, hands on hips, watching us go with a frown on his face. It was good to see how quickly his figure receded.

'Quick!' said Fergus. He whipped out his mobile and began scrolling down the screen for my number. 'Let's hear what they're saying!'

'It's no use,' I mumbled. Fergus, however, ignored me. Amin was the one who reacted, his eyes widening with dismay.

'Whaddaya mean?' he said.

'It's no use,' I repeated. 'Fergus? There's no point calling my phone. I didn't leave it back there.'

At last my warning sank in. Fergus looked up.

'You might as well not bother,' I continued. 'All you're gunna hear is us, because my phone is right here in my pocket.'

He was speechless. His mouth flapped, but no sound emerged. Then Amin said, 'Did you forget to do it?'

He was talking to me, so I shook my head.

'Are you crazy?' Fergus had found his voice again, though it was high and hoarse. 'That's the whole reason we went there! To plant a bug!'

Amin flicked a nervous look at the driver, who was behaving like one of the three wise monkeys. ('Hear no evil', to be precise.) I swallowed.

'We went there to find out if Reuben was lying,' I said.

'Exactly!' Fergus still didn't get it. 'Which means we're stuffed! This was all a waste of time!'

I turned to stare out the window. Amin, who was way ahead of Fergus, tried to explain why we hadn't been wasting our time at all.

'We didn't need to leave the phone there,' he told Fergus. 'Toby's made up his mind.'

'Huh?'

'Well...' There was a pause. I don't know if Amin was pulling faces or not, because I was still staring out the window. 'Did *you* think Reuben was lying?' he finally asked.

'Of course he was lying!' Fergus yelped. Then the penny dropped. 'Oh, man,' he cried. 'You *believed* all that?'

'Didn't you?' said Amin. 'I mean, it was weird. I thought they might try to jump us, or sell us something, but it was really...' He trailed off.

'Really ordinary,' Fergus supplied.

'Yeah. Kind of respectable.'

'Except for...' Fergus jerked his chin in my direction. 'That thing downstairs. Toby's freak-out.'

'Yeah.'

'Which was spooky,' Fergus agreed. He fixed me with a speculative look. 'What was all *that* about, anyway? Is that what convinced you?'

I nodded.

'Why?'

But I couldn't tell him. I couldn't even begin to describe how I felt. And after a while, he gave up waiting.

'Wow,' he murmured. 'Man. So it's the real deal, huh? That's pretty cool.'

'Yeah,' said Amin.

'That's really amazing. I mean – wow. *Wow*. Toby, of all people!' He was warming to the subject. 'It's gunna be awesome! We're gunna have the *best* time! I wish *I* was a—'

'Fergus!' I snapped, before he could finish. Then I cocked my thumb at the driver.

'Oh. Yeah. Right.' Fergus winced. 'Sorry.'

'I don't wanna talk about it, okay?'

'Okay.'

'And I don't want *you* talking about it.'

'Sure, dude. Gotcha.' Fergus lowered his voice until he was whispering. 'It's great, though, don't you think? It's *way* better than being epileptic!'

I was too stunned to answer him, so I turned back to the

window. And I stayed like that, watching the streetlights slip past, until we reached our destination. I didn't have to fend off any more questions from Fergus, though he probably would have liked to ask some. Perhaps he didn't know how to – not without saying 'werewolf' in front of a totally strange cab driver. Or perhaps he sensed that I didn't want to talk. Whatever the reason, he kept his mouth shut all the way to Mount Druitt. And for that I was very grateful.

We were dropped in front of the cinema, which was shutting for the night. Only half a dozen people were still hanging around. I was the last out of the car because I had to pay our fare; by the time I'd pocketed my change and slammed the door behind me, Mum was already breathing down my neck. I straightened up and there she was: *bang!* So close I could hardly get her into focus.

'This had better be good,' she said, through her teeth.

'Oh. Hi, Mum.' The cab was moving off – and so was Fergus, who was trying to fade away into the night. I checked my watch. 'You're early.'

'Would you like to tell me where you've been?' she requested, before suddenly raising her voice. 'Fergus! Where are *you* going?'

He froze like a spotlit rabbit.

'You can't walk home from here. I'll give you a lift,' Mum offered.

Fergus looked around frantically, as if searching for an escape route.

'Come on, please.' She beckoned to him. 'The car's just over here.'

There was no point resisting; Fergus gave up without a fight, trudging towards Mum's car like someone heading for the guillotine. Amin did the same. As for me, I was feeling so winded – so numb and baffled – that I didn't panic at all. I just climbed into the front seat and waited for the next question.

It didn't come until we were on the road, driving towards Amin's house.

'So. Are you going to answer me?' she asked. 'Where have you been for the last three hours? Because I know you weren't at the movies.'

Fergus was a lost cause; he wasn't going to say anything. And Amin's face was a complete blank. I could see it in the rear-view mirror.

'I was visiting my girlfriend,' was the brilliant excuse that popped into my brain.

Let me tell you, it was a total *winner*. Mum got such a shock, she nearly ran us off the road.

'Your *what*?' she squeaked.

'My girlfriend. Nina Harrison.' I wasn't going to tell her the truth. Not before I'd had time to absorb it myself. And I knew that a girlfriend was the perfect cover story. Mum would be so distracted, she'd never even think about Reuben. 'I've got a girlfriend, okay? Are you happy now?'

She wasn't happy, but she was certainly dumbstruck. I could practically hear the cogs turning in her head as she absorbed my big news. Fergus and Amin were also silent, though Amin flashed me an admiring glance. Once again, I caught a glimpse of his expression in the rear-view mirror.

'Why didn't you mention this before?' Mum finally asked, in sceptical tones. It was a good question. Why hadn't I?

'Dunno,' I mumbled. 'Do I have to tell you everything?'

Another pause. We were nearly at Amin's place. Mum was frowning.

138

'So you *all* decided to visit Nina?' she said at last. '*All* of you?'

'Yeah,' croaked Amin. Fergus grunted.

'Why?'

She doesn't believe me, I thought. And suddenly I felt quite cross. Why *shouldn't* I have a girlfriend? Other people did. Okay – maybe I *was* a bit skinny. Maybe I *did* have to wear extra layers, so I wouldn't look like a handful of chopsticks tied up with string. That still didn't mean I was a complete loser. Some girls seemed to like me. Nina had said that I was fizzy and glowing.

'We went to Nina's house so we could play on her Wii,' Amin piped up. I have to admit, I was impressed. Of course! Why else would a whole bunch of boys want to visit a girl?

If Mum hadn't been watching me, I would have given Amin a thumbs-up sign.

'She's got four remotes,' I elaborated. 'And this enormous widescreen television.'

'In a home theatre.' Amin was on a roll now. 'With surround sound and everything.'

I was half expecting Fergus to join in, but he didn't. By this time we were on Amin's street. As the car rolled to a standstill at the foot of his driveway, Mum turned to Amin and said, 'So Nina's house was better than the movies?'

'Oh yeah,' he replied. With his bedroom window in plain sight, he was already a lot chirpier. I noticed that he was clutching the doorhandle. 'When we spotted Nina, we decided to go straight back to her house.'

'Instead of buying a movie ticket?'

'Yeah.'

'Which is how you paid for the cab?'

139

'Uh-huh.'

'You should have given me a call,' said Mum. 'I could have picked you up and saved you the fare.' As Amin squirmed, she added, 'Where does Nina live, anyway?'

Poor old Amin. He froze up, then; he was stymied. Fortunately, however, I'd been expecting Mum to ask this question, so I had an answer already prepared.

'Surry Hills,' I announced. I didn't even know where it was. I just remembered that Estelle had talked about it.

'*Surry Hills?*' Mum was astonished. 'But that's *miles* away!'

Was it? My heart sank.

'No wonder you needed all your ticket money for the cab!' she went on. Meanwhile, Amin was making his escape. He slammed the car door behind him.

'Bye!' he gabbled through Mum's window. 'Bye, Toby! Bye, Fergus! See you, Mrs Vandevelde!'

He shot up the driveway, beating a hasty retreat. Mum didn't bother to check that he made it inside. She just hauled at the steering wheel and put her foot on the accelerator.

'How on earth did you ever meet a girl from Surry Hills?' she demanded. 'Through school?'

I was about to say 'yes' when it occurred to me that school was too complicated.

'She was at the park,' I said.

'What park?'

'Nurragingy.'

Mum seemed to accept this. At least, she didn't comment on it. No one made another sound until we reached Fergus's place, which was all lit up, as if for a party. There were so many cars in his driveway – and on the nature strip in front of his house – that Mum had to park across the road.

'What's going on?' Mum queried. 'Is it someone's birthday?'

'Nah.' At last Fergus managed to crank out a few words. 'It's just my brother.'

He'd barely finished speaking before the crash of breaking glass reached our ears, faint but unmistakeable. It seemed to come from somewhere beyond the Duffys' front fence. I could hear thudding music as well.

'Are you going to be all right, Fergus?' Mum sounded genuinely worried.

'Yeah. Course,' he said. He was already standing on the footpath; suddenly the door banged shut and he was gone. I saw him threading his way between all the utes and customised street-racing cars, which were parked bumper to bumper.

Mum and I sat watching him for a moment. Then she asked, 'You weren't in *there* tonight, were you?'

'Huh?' It took me a moment to process this question. When I did, I wasn't pleased. 'No! God. Why would I want to go in there?'

'I don't know. For the booze, perhaps?'

I rolled my eyes.

'Just tell me the truth, Toby.'

'I *told* you the truth! Jeez!'

'You were really visiting your girlfriend?'

'*Yes!*'

'Was there booze at *her* house? Were you drinking together?'

By now I was seriously annoyed. It's funny; even though I was lying, I was also furious that she wouldn't believe me.

That's why I folded my arms and sulked.

'Is this something to do with what happened on Monday

141

night?' she pressed. Upon receiving no answer, she kept needling and needling. 'Toby? Look at me. Were you with Nina on Monday? Have you been trying to protect her? Has she been giving you drugs?'

'Don't be stupid!' I was almost alarmed. 'She doesn't do drugs!'

'Then why won't you talk about her?'

'Because I don't *want* to!' God, I was mad, suddenly. I was also scared, and tired, and really confused. 'Why do we always have to *talk* about everything?' I raged. 'Just because you're a speech therapist, you think talking is the best thing in the whole world! Well, it's not! Okay? I don't wanna talk! I want you to *leave me alone*, for once!'

The instant I stopped shouting, I realised that Mum wasn't the only one listening to me. Some guy in the Duffys' front yard had turned to stare in my direction.

Mum must have realised this too, because she immediately pulled out from the kerb.

'All right, then,' she said crisply, as we headed home, 'why don't you call her right now?'

'Huh?'

'If you don't want to talk to *me*, that's fine. But you must want to talk to Nina.'

I didn't, of course. So I said, 'Why should I?'

'Because I need confirmation.' Mum wasn't beating around the bush. She wasn't trying to wheedle and coax. She'd decided to lay her cards on the table. 'I need to know what you were doing tonight.'

'Because you don't trust me!'

'Because you were found unconscious in a dingo pen on Monday morning, Toby! *That's* why!' She pounded on the steering wheel. 'I want to know what's going on! I'm your mother, I'm not just some dumb old idiot who has to be kept in the dark!'

'Oh, don't gimme that...'

'How *can* I believe you when you tell me one thing and do something else?'

'Fine.' I yanked out my phone and started to search for Reuben's number. By that time, I just wanted to prove her wrong. I wanted to *prove* that I had a girlfriend called Nina – even though I didn't. I wanted to demonstrate how mean and nosy and unfair my mother was.

'*Hello?*'

To my surprise, it wasn't Reuben who answered my call. The voice at the other end of the line was a girl's voice.

I'd been hoping that Reuben might still be at Dr Plackett's house, discussing me with his support group. If he'd gone home, I was in trouble.

'Who's that?' I asked, praying that it wasn't Reuben's girlfriend.

'*It's Nina. Who's that?*'

'It's Toby.'

'*Toby?*' She seemed even more surprised than I was. '*What's wrong?*'

'Oh – uh – nothing...'

'*Do you want to talk to Reuben? Only he's driving, you see. He's giving me a lift.*'

'No, no. It's okay. I wanted to talk to you.' I cleared my throat, glancing across at Mum. She was squinting into a trail of approaching headlights. 'My mother's here right now,' I continued, 'and she doesn't believe you're my girlfriend.'

After a loaded pause, Nina murmured, '*I see...*'

'She doesn't believe I was with you tonight. In Surry Hills. So I thought maybe you could put her straight on that.'

'*Um . . .*' Another pause. '*Okay.*'

'I told her we were just playing with your Wii, but she – ow!' Mum had snatched the phone from my hand. 'What's *your* problem?' I protested.

She didn't answer me. Instead she swerved into the nearest gutter and stomped on the brake.

'Hello?' she barked, addressing my phone. 'Who's that?' The reply took longer than I'd anticipated; I can't imagine what Nina was telling her. 'Well, Nina,' Mum finally said, 'I'm Toby's mother, and I'd really like to know how you two spent this evening. Now that I'm actually aware of your existence.' During the interval that followed, she raised her eyebrows and nodded. 'Uh-huh. Uh-huh. And where did this happen?' She pursed her lips as I cringed. 'Oh really? Because Amin said you had a home theatre. With surround sound.'

'Amin's always making things up,' I began, but she raised her hand and glared.

'Shhh!' she hissed. 'I'm having a conversation!'

'Mum—'

'No, no. It's just Toby. What was that?' Turning away, she covered one ear. 'Mm-hmm. I see. Well, that's very interesting. I'm afraid we don't have anything like that at our house, but maybe next time you could come over here. So I could meet you.'

'*Mum!*'

'Can I ask how old you are, Nina? Uh-huh. And would you mind telling me how you and Toby met?'

I was stuffed. I knew it. As she listened to whatever rubbish

144

Nina was spouting, I hid my face by pressing my forehead against the window.

'Oh – all right. If your grandmother wants you, then I guess you'd better go,' Mum said sweetly. 'Nice to talk to you. Yes, I will. Goodbye, Nina. Sorry to bother you at this late hour.'

Beep. She broke the connection. Then she tossed the phone into my lap, flicked on her indicator, and pulled out into the traffic.

'As of tomorrow, you're grounded,' she said.

Chapter Thirteen

I had terrible dreams that night. After lying awake for hours, I finally dropped off at around three in the morning. But I didn't sleep well; I remember sitting bolt upright at half past four, gasping and sweating because I thought I'd been trapped in the dark with something that was closing in – something that I couldn't see, though I could smell its rank odour and hear its rough, heavy breathing. And the worst thing is, I kept having the same nightmare over and over again. I must have had it at least six times.

I didn't drag myself out of bed until ten o'clock. By then, of course, my mother had already left for work, despite the fact that she doesn't usually work on Saturdays. We'd discussed this the night before. Thanks to the way my problems had messed up her schedule, she'd agreed to take a weekend shift for another speech therapist.

'But that doesn't mean you're not grounded,' she'd warned me. 'I'll know if you leave this house, because I'll be speaking to Mrs Savvides before I go. I'll ask her to keep an eye on you.'

'Yeah, yeah.'

'We're not going to talk about this now, Toby. It's much too late. And I don't expect we'll have a lot of time tomorrow morning, either. But I'll be home in the afternoon, and that's when I'll want an explanation.'

Ouch.

'Incidentally, I don't want to hear that Nina or Amin or Fergus have been visiting. Is that clear? I want you to have some time alone, so you can think about what's been going on.'

Most kids would probably have told her where she could shove it. Either that or they would have ignored her. Most kids wouldn't have shuffled off to bed without a word of protest, the way I did.

I guess the sad truth is that I *wanted* some time alone. I *wanted* to think about what had happened. But even after several hours of thinking, followed by a broken night's sleep, I still hadn't fully absorbed the terrible possibility that I might actually be a werewolf. A *werewolf*. I kept stumbling over that word; it made no sense to me. How could I be a werewolf? Werewolves didn't exist. I could grapple with genetic conditions all right. I could face the fact that Reuben and I seemed to share certain characteristics. I could even accept that the human body might react to the phases of the moon (like with menstruation, for instance). But every time I started to put everything together in my head, I'd hit that word again. *Werewolf*. And the whole, carefully built argument would come tumbling down.

I could hardly eat breakfast. My stomach seemed to be screwed up into a tight little knot. What was I going to tell Mum? I couldn't just launch into a no-holds-barred account of my meeting with Reuben's friends. If I did, she'd blow her top. And then she would complain to the police. And then all hell would break loose.

I didn't want that to happen. It would be a disaster. Even if Reuben was deluded about everything, it would still be a disaster. The papers would have a field day. 'Dingo Boy' would become 'Werewolf Boy', and the kids at school would eat me alive.

I was still moping about when the phone rang at ten thirty. Needless to say, I didn't answer it. I let our machine pick up the call. Upon hearing Fergus's voice, however, I began to feel worried. And as soon as he announced that he wanted to meet up 'and discuss some werewolf ideas', I hurled myself at the receiver.

'We can't meet up,' I warned him, without even saying 'hello'. 'I'm grounded.'

'*Toby?*' he said. '*Is that you?*'

'I can't talk. I can't go anywhere. I'm grounded.'

'*Then I'll come over there.*'

'No! Fergus!' I didn't want him anywhere *near* my house. 'Mrs Savvides is spying on me! I'm not meant to be seeing anyone!'

'*So? I'll just get in through the back.*'

'No!'

'*It'll be fine. Mrs Savvides is the one across the road, isn't she?*'

'Yeah, but—'

'*She won't be able to see me from her place. Not if I come over your back fence.*'

'But someone might think you're trying to rob us!'

Fergus actually laughed. '*Are you kidding?*' he scoffed. '*The only person who's got a chance of spotting me is that shut-in who lives behind you, and she's always so drunk she must be used to seeing things in her garden. Like fairies and aliens.*'

'Fergus, I don't want you to come here. Okay? Are you listening? I don't want to get in trouble.'

'*You won't. Swear to God.*'

'Fergus—'

'*See you in a minute!*'

And that was that. He hung up on me. I called him back, of course, but his mobile was either turned off or out of range. As for his home number, I didn't even consider dialling it; if you use that line, you often end up talking to Liam. So I tried Amin's phone, which was engaged. No luck there.

By this time I was getting angry. Why the hell couldn't Fergus ever just *take a hint*? I didn't want to see him! Was that so hard to understand? I moved to the kitchen window – which faces the back garden – and tried to work out if any of our neighbours would be able to spot him coming over the fence. Probably not, I decided. The neighbours to our right were always at work on Saturday mornings, while the neighbours to our left were completely concealed by the enormous hedge they'd planted. As for the woman who lived behind us, her blinds were perpetually drawn...

Suddenly I had an idea. It was one of those brilliant flashes that you get sometimes when you need a bit of distraction from your troubles. I went to the pantry cupboard, where I collected some vital ingredients: flour, honey, jelly crystals, maple-flavoured syrup. Then I added a few more items to the pile because they appealed to me: a can of whipped cream, a jar of hand lotion, a bottle of rose-scented hair conditioner. Working quickly, I combined all this stuff in a mixing bowl. My next stop was the recycling bin, where I discovered an empty plastic ice-cream container with a flip-top lid. This ice cream container was a lucky find; it was way better than a water balloon, though I had to stick it over the laundry door with thumb-tacks while it was still empty. After that, I tied a long piece of string through the lid – *before* inserting my glutinous formula. (There was a little bit of leakage, but it wasn't too bad, because the stuff was more like scrambled egg than liquid soap.) As a final step, I fastened the other end of my string to the doorhandle.

Once that was done, I had nothing to do but sit back and wait.

I have to admit, I was feeling pretty pleased with myself. A booby-trap, for me, was the perfect antidote to anxiety and depression; I was so busy imagining Fergus in a rage that I almost forgot the whole werewolf business, which was thrust to the back of my mind as I placed a chair opposite the doorway leading from the kitchen to the laundry. From that chair, I had a perfect ringside seat. I sat there spraying dollops of whipped cream into my mouth, poised for action, until I heard footsteps on the patio outside.

There were two sets of footsteps – and two voices as well. Fergus had brought Amin along.

The doorhandle turned.

'Hello?' said Amin. It was such a shame. Fergus had been my target, but Amin was in the wrong place at the wrong time (as usual). When he pushed open the door, my sticky-bomb descended like a giant clump of bird poo. *Splat!* I've never seen anything so perfect.

There was a moment's stunned silence, followed by gales of laughter. Fergus, who was just behind Amin, had seen everything.

I sprang to my feet as Amin stood gasping, his head streaked with gunk.

'Oh, oh, oh – that is so *good!*' Fergus doubled over, heaving and snorting. It was the ideal moment. I lunged forward, armed

150

with my can of whipped cream, and let him have it straight between the eyes.

Dodging me, Amin slipped in a pool of goo.

'Aargh!' cried Fergus. He took a blind swipe at the can, but I was too quick for him. I sprayed more cream – *ssst!* – and would have beaten a hasty retreat if it hadn't been for Amin. He was down on the floor, wallowing around in my evil formula. Every time he tried to stand up, his feet would slide out from under him.

I'd forgotten he was there until I sidestepped Fergus. That was when I fell over Amin's outstretched leg.

It was a fatal mistake. Fergus might be small, but he knows how to take advantage of a tactical error. He reached for my can. I held on tight. I fought him off. He scooped up a handful of goo and rubbed it into my mouth. Then he bolted for the kitchen, shedding gobs of whipped cream.

I won't give you a blow-by-blow account of the next five minutes. Everything happened so quickly that the sequence of events is hard to remember. Let's just say that bottles of ketchup and mustard were squirted, cans of soft drink were shaken up, and an egg was thrown. The egg soon put an end to things, because eggs are like nuclear warheads. They're on a whole different level from honey or whipped cream; even Fergus understands that. As soon as the egg hit the window, all three of us calmed down.

'*You* threw the egg,' I told Fergus, panting. 'You can clean it up.'

'You started it.' He was scraping mustard off his hair. 'Why should we clean up if you started it?'

'Because I told you not to come here and you did anyway. Which means it's your fault.'

Fergus disagreed, but offered to lend a hand 'out of friendship'. Amin was already looking for a mop. Luckily, we'd confined ourselves to the kitchen and laundry, so cleaning up wasn't as hard as it could have been. The floors are all tiled in those rooms, and the windows are hung with venetian blinds. Even the tablecloth is made of plastic. With a bucket, a mop and a couple of sponges, we managed to wipe up most of the mess. After rearranging some shelves, and replacing the old tea-towels with fresh ones, I was pretty sure that Mum wouldn't figure out what had happened.

Not unless she saw our clothes.

'We're gunna have to change,' I said. 'You can borrow some of my stuff, and we'll wash all these dirty things before Mum gets back.'

'Why don't you let *her* wash 'em?' Fergus wanted to know. And I shot him a withering glance.

'Because she'll freak,' I rejoined, as I began to search through the laundry cupboard. That was when I found the chlorine bleach – much to Fergus's delight. He pounced on it with a squawk of excitement.

'Hey, great!' he said. 'And we've got whipped cream too!'

'So?'

'So we can make a *bomb*!' Seeing my crinkled forehead, he continued impatiently, 'There's a nitrous oxide bulb inside that whipped cream! It's the perfect combo!'

'You reckon?'

'I've tried it before.'

'Yeah, but—'

'Let's go to the park. We can explode it there.' He looked around. 'Where's Amin?'

'In the shower.'

152

'Aw, jeez,' he complained. Then he stomped off towards the bathroom, yelling at the top of his voice. 'Amin! Hurry up! We're going to Nurragingy!'

At first I wasn't too keen, because I'd been told to stay put. Mrs Savvides was keeping an eye on me. And what if Mum decided to come back early, just to make sure that I was still under house arrest?

Gradually, however, Fergus got me all worked up about finding a suitable bomb-casing; he wanted a cigar tube, but finally settled for the length of copper pipe that I'd hidden away. Then I had to look for matches, because our gas gun wasn't good enough. (We needed sulphur, he said, not an open flame.) And when I told him that he should take the fire extinguisher, he laughed scornfully.

'Don't be stupid!' he exclaimed. 'I'm not dragging a fire extinguisher over the back fence!'

'But it's really dry, Fergus. It's the middle of summer. You don't wanna start a fire.'

'I won't.'

'How do you know?'

'The bomb won't be big enough.'

'That's what you always say.'

'I can't take a bloody *fire extinguisher* into Nurragingy!' he growled. 'I'll get arrested!'

'You can put it in a bag,' I pointed out. 'It's not that big.'

'You can put it in *your* bag,' he corrected. 'Because *I'm* not carrying it. No way.'

'Amin can carry it,' I said. Amin, however, shook his head.

'I'm carrying the clothes,' he reminded me. By this time we'd agreed that we wouldn't try to do a load of washing after

153

all, because we didn't know very much about stain removal. Instead, Amin had offered to smuggle the garments into his own house.

According to Amin, his mother dealt with so much dirty laundry that she wouldn't even notice a few extra pieces of it.

'But I *can't* take the fire extinguisher! I'm not even going!' I don't know how many times I'd already said this. 'I'm grounded, remember? I can't go.'

'Course you can.' Fergus dismissed my scruples with a careless wave. 'Just go through the back yard. No one'll see you.'

'What if Mum calls?'

'Leave the phone off the hook.'

'What if Mrs Savvides drops by?'

'Say you didn't hear the doorbell. Put on some really loud music before we leave.' Fergus rolled his eyes in despair. '*God*, you're such a wuss!' he complained. 'So what if your mum finds out? It's not like she's gunna beat the crap out of you, is it?'

With arguments like these, he managed to chip away at me until I finally gave in. I suppose the truth is that I really *wanted* to go, and didn't need all that much persuading. (What would *you* rather do: sit around worrying, or explode things?) My only real concern was climbing the back fence; I felt that Fergus and Amin would be pushing their luck if they did it again, though I couldn't think of an alternative route. Not with Mrs Savvides watching the front of the house.

In the end, however, escaping wasn't all that difficult. After turning on Mum's CD player, I took the phone off the hook and slipped out quietly – taking care not to bang any doors. Then, upon reaching the fence, I gave Fergus a leg-up before passing him my bag, which contained the fire extinguisher. Next I helped Amin over the splintery wooden palings, because he's smaller than me, and not very agile. I was the last one into my neighbour's garden, where the grass was so high that we didn't have to worry about being seen. As soon as we dropped to our hands and knees, the grass concealed us. We simply crawled through it like a pack of dogs. The whole thing was a cinch.

There was only one nasty moment; it was when we'd reached the front gate and had to stand up again. I knew that any people who might be passing would probably wonder why three teenagers had suddenly popped into view like a row of jack-in-the-boxes, so I climbed to my feet in a casual sort of way, making a conscious attempt not to look rushed or furtive. I even brushed myself off, as if I didn't have a care in the world. And while I was doing that, I suddenly saw a car creeping towards us.

It was moving very slowly. For one awful moment, I thought that the driver was going to stop and ask us what on earth we were doing. But he didn't, thank God. He just rolled on past.

I figured that he must have been searching for somebody's house.

'Did you see that?' said Amin. 'He was staring at us. So was the guy next to him.'

'I'm not surprised,' Fergus growled, eyeing poor Amin – who was bursting out of my very baggiest T-shirt, and whose shorts were drenched with tomato sauce. 'You look like a traffic accident.'

'And *you* look like you got shrunk in the wash,' Amin retorted. It was true. My shorts were as long as knickerbockers on Fergus. 'Maybe you should have worn your own clothes,' Amin continued. 'You couldn't have looked any worse than you do now. So what if there was honey in your pants? You got most of it out, didn't you?'

Fergus just glared at him. I began to head for Nurragingy, weighed down by a bag full of fire extinguisher. Amin and Fergus followed me, bickering and sniping; it didn't take us long to reach the park, though we had to skirt around the lake and pass through the picnic grounds before we arrived at our final destination. It was a small clearing surrounded by thick bush. There were no seats or paths or bits of play equipment anywhere nearby, so we decided that we wouldn't be bothered there. We'd certainly never been bothered there before.

As soon as we stopped, Fergus took charge. He insisted that the bomb was his, because he was the only one who knew how to assemble it. And when I pointed out that *I* had supplied all the components, he went on and on about his expertise being the most important component of all. At last, however, we got down to business, after tossing a coin to see who would put in the last ingredient.

I won.

Fergus was pretty cross, but he needn't have been. I never did get a chance to set off that bomb. We'd only just begun to seal up one end of the pipe when a crunching noise disturbed us – and we looked around to see a little kid stumble into the clearing. He was about five years old, with blond hair and very red cheeks.

Much to our dismay, he marched straight towards us, clutching some kind of fancy toy robot.

'Whatcha doing?' he squeaked.

Amin and I exchanged despairing glances.

'Nothing!' Fergus barked. 'Piss off!'

The little kid froze. He stuck out his bottom lip.

'Go on,' I said. 'Go back to your mum.'

I guess I was too gentle, because he immediately perked up.

'Can *I* play?' he asked.

'No!' snapped Fergus. 'Get lost!'

'We're not playing a game,' Amin added. He spoke calmly yet firmly, with the confidence of someone used to dealing with very small brothers. 'We're doing something you wouldn't like. You're too young.'

'Why?'

'Because it's dangerous,' I said, like a fool. Amin scowled at me. The little kid's whole face lit up.

'Please?' he begged.

'Go away!' Fergus warned.

'Is it a rocket?'

'No!'

'*I* can make a rocket!'

'Just ignore him,' Amin murmured. 'He'll get bored.'

So we tried to ignore the little kid, but it wasn't easy. He kept shuffling around with his thumb in his mouth, peering at this and poking at that. 'I made a truck,' he'd say; or 'Can I have some sticky tape too?' He wouldn't leave Mum's scissors alone – probably because they were so big and sharp. Every time we put them down, he'd pick them up.

At last Fergus couldn't take it anymore. He was on the point of dismantling our aerosol can, but when he tried to retrieve the scissors, our unwelcome guest wouldn't let them go. So Fergus spun around and gave him a face full of whipped cream.

That did the trick, let me tell you. With a piercing scream, the little kid dropped Mum's scissors and ran. He was in such a panic that he actually bumped into a tree on his way out of the

157

clearing. (It was quite funny to watch, as a matter of fact.)

'God, Fergus,' I said. 'You're such a bastard.'

'I know.' He sounded quite pleased with himself.

'*I'll* have to try that some time,' Amin commented. 'Yussy's such a pain in the arse these days, and he won't fall for my spider routine anymore.'

'You just gotta show 'em who's boss,' said Fergus. Having opened our aerosol canister, he was fishing around for the nitrous oxide bulb. 'I don't blame the children, mind you,' he went on, speaking so pompously that I had to laugh. 'It's the parents' fault. They just don't use enough discipline, nowadays.'

'*Hey! Hey you!*' An enormous voice rang out, harsh and deep and menacing. It made us all jump. In perfect unison, we turned our heads to see a big, bald man striding across the grass towards us.

He was holding hands with a familiar little kid, who was crying his eyes out.

'*Who the hell do you think you are?*' the man boomed. '*And what the hell did you do to my son?*'

Chapter Fourteen

Fergus and I locked gazes for an instant.

'Oh, man...' he muttered.

'*What are you up to? Huh?*' the enraged father cried. He was built like a cannonball, and smelled faintly of barbecued lamb. He was also closing in fast, dragging his son behind him. '*Think you can get away with stuff like this, do ya?*'

'We gave him some whipped cream!' was the only answer that I could think of. It didn't impress Baldie, though. He bared his teeth.

'In the *face!*' he spluttered. By this time Amin was shuffling backwards; I could see him out of the corner of my eye.

But I couldn't see Fergus. He'd ducked down below my field of vision.

'Whassa matter – you scared?' Baldie snarled. He was almost on top of us, and I didn't know what to do. Run? Plead? Argue?

'It was a *joke!*' I protested, as his gaze dropped. Suddenly he froze. His expression changed. He threw up one hand in a futile gesture as – *SSHHHZZ!* – a white cloud enveloped him.

Fergus had unleashed the fire-retardant foam.

'*Run!*' he yelled.

I ran. What else could I do? Thanks to Fergus, I had no

choice. But I didn't follow Amin. I wasn't that stupid. There's no safety in numbers when you have an enraged parent after you. The best thing is to just split up and hope. And run. Boy, did I run!

I bolted straight into the bush. I knew I'd have the advantage in there because I'm skinny enough to slip through narrow spaces. I also have quick reflexes; I can dodge any tree trunks that might be coming straight for me. And I have long legs too, so I can leap over spiky undergrowth. Poor Amin doesn't have long legs *or* quick reflexes, but he's very good at hiding. That's what I figured he would do: hide until the coast was clear.

Not me, though. I couldn't afford to hang about. I had to get home before Mum did. So I crashed through bushes and vaulted across fallen logs. I ducked and dodged and swerved. I darted from one piece of cover to the next – from a shrub to a toilet block to a parked car. After a while I began to slow down, because it didn't look as if I was being followed. What's more, I was attracting a lot of attention; I figured that a brisk walk would be less noticeable than a mad dash for the nearest exit.

Checking my watch, I saw that it was lunchtime – and it occurred to me that Mum might have decided to call home. What would happen if she kept getting the engaged signal? She would probably try my mobile number, I decided. The question was, should I answer it? Maybe not. *Maybe I should turn it off*, I thought, before realising that I couldn't. Not while I was waiting for Fergus to ring me. I certainly couldn't call *him*. The wail of a fire-alarm ringtone was the last thing he'd need if he was crouched behind a rubbish bin somewhere.

By now I had reached the main road, and was waiting nervously for the lights to change. I kept glancing over my

160

shoulder, half expecting a big, bald dad to come bursting out of the park. But I'd well and truly shaken him off; no one followed me across the road except a little old lady with a walking stick. All the same, I didn't feel entirely secure until I'd plunged into a comforting tangle of suburban streets, where I was shielded from the park gates by houses and hedges and carports.

It wasn't until I was halfway home that I remembered our fire extinguisher.

The thought of it hit me like a punch. I froze in mid-stride, my jaw dropping. The fire extinguisher! Goddammit! Mum would *kill* me if I lost the fire extinguisher! Standing irresolute on the sunbaked footpath, I wondered if I should retrace my steps. It was possible that Fergus might have discarded the extinguisher. He might have tossed it aside before running away, so its weight wouldn't slow him down. In that case, however, would Baldie have let it lie? Or would he have picked it up as evidence? Could it be in police custody *at this very moment*?

No, I concluded. If the police had been summoned, they would still be on their way to the scene. Only a few minutes had elapsed since my encounter with Baldie; that was why I couldn't call Fergus. There was no guarantee that Fergus had managed to get out of the park. For all I knew, he could still be crawling around in a shrubbery, with Baldie breathing down his neck.

For the time being, at least, there was nothing I could do. I just had to walk on, hoping like hell that Baldie wouldn't press charges. Would a faceful of chemical foam constitute an assault? Surely a squirt of whipped cream wouldn't be taken seriously? As I hurried along, I told myself that everything would be okay providing Fergus and Amin didn't get caught. My bag was still at the scene, but it didn't have my name on it. Neither did the extinguisher. I was still in possession of my phone and my keys and my wallet. As long as Amin and Fergus were free and clear, and hadn't dropped anything during their escape, we would be perfectly fine.

By reasoning like this, I was able to keep calm. The trouble was that it took a lot of effort. I was so busy reassuring myself that I nearly made the serious error of walking straight down my own street. Only at the very last minute did I recall Mrs Savvides and her promise to my mother. Mr Grisdale's roof was already in plain sight when I realised that I was supposed to be climbing over our back fence.

'Bugger,' I growled, stopping short. I had to think for a moment. What would be the best plan? Should I retreat to the nearest intersection and take the long way round? Or should I risk advancing a few metres, before turning into the lane that linked my street with the next?

After weighing my options, I decided that Mrs Savvides would be very unlikely to spot me from such a distance. So I took a deep breath and moved forward, keeping my head down and my shoulders hunched. No one passed me as I crossed the street. The lane, when I reached it, was deserted. It was a narrow strip of gravel pinched between two high paling fences. Some of the palings were overgrown with ivy and honeysuckle, while some of them were covered in graffiti. Passing traffic had pushed bits of debris against them like a tidemark; I could see bottles and bones and empty chip packets and an old shopping trolley that had lost its wheels.

I was skirting around this trolley when a car suddenly appeared at the other end of the lane. It was a big, sleek sedan that looked pretty wide from where I was standing. As it rolled towards me, I flattened myself against the nearest stretch of fence.

But instead of passing by, the car braked when it drew level with me. One tinted window slowly descended, revealing two men in suits. The driver had a grey walrus moustache and the sort of dour, bloodhound face that's all sagging jowls and drooping eyelids. The other man was clean-shaven, with a wide, square jaw and a scar on his upper lip. His curly black hair was neatly trimmed.

I couldn't tell how old he was, because of the suit. He was a whole lot younger than his partner, though.

'Are you Toby Vandevelde?' he asked.

I gaped at him. My heart seemed to do a backflip.

'Wh-what?' I stammered at last.

'*Are you Toby Vandevelde?*' When I didn't answer, the younger guy waved a plastic wallet at me. I caught a glimpse of the word 'police'. 'I'm Detective Constable Santos, and this is Detective Sergeant Green,' he said. 'Now – are you Toby Vandevelde or not?'

For about half a second I toyed with the idea of giving him a false name. Then I decided against it. He already seemed to have made up his mind that I was Toby. Besides, I had a vague idea that giving the police a false name was something you could get arrested for.

'Yeah, that's me. So what?' Though I spoke with as much attitude as I could muster, I was reeling inside, stunned that the police could have caught up with me already. Had Amin spilled the beans? Had he told them where I lived? Had he given them a description?

'You've had a complaint of trespass made against you, Toby,' Detective Constable Santos announced. He had a reedy, drawling voice and a glint in his eye; there was something about him that made me wonder if he was the kind of cop Fergus is always complaining about – the kind that likes to hassle the Duffys for no reason at all.

'Trespass?' I was confused. Wasn't Nurragingy a public park?

'By the owner of Featherdale,' the detective constable explained. That's when I finally understood.

This wasn't about the fire extinguisher. This was about the dingo pen.

'We need to take you down to the station and call your mum,' the younger detective continued. 'I guess she's at work, is she?'

'Uh . . . yeah,' I said.

'There's a procedure we gotta follow. But don't worry – we can't do any interviews unless your mum's present.' For some reason, Detective Constable Santos was doing all the talking. 'Just hop in the back, okay? This won't take long.'

I was in such a state of shock that it took me a while to absorb his instructions. 'You're – you're *arresting* me?' I croaked at last.

'Yeah, but that doesn't mean we'll be laying charges. Personally, I think this is a big waste of time.' If the detective constable hoped to encourage me with his assurance, it didn't work. I just gaped at him in horror. 'Come on,' he said impatiently. 'We're busy people, y'know – we've got *real* fugitives to track down.'

Numbly I scrambled into the back of the car, which smelled of pizza and cigarette smoke. I was still trying to get things straight in my head, so I barely noticed as we emerged from the laneway.

Arrested? It couldn't be true.

'Put on your seatbelt,' Detective Constable Santos reminded me. Then he added, 'You look like you've had a rough day, so far.'

At first I didn't know what he was talking about. Then I glanced down at myself and saw what a mess I was in, all covered in dirt and scratches.

'I was...uh...I was just playing soccer,' I said. 'In the park.'

'Soccer player, are ya?'

'Yeah.'

'Who were you with?'

'Friends.'

'What friends?'

I swallowed. 'Why do you wanna know?' I asked. And the detective constable shrugged.

'Why don't you wanna tell me?' he retorted. 'I was just making conversation.'

'Well – they've gone home now, anyway.' I quickly changed the subject. 'Which police station are we going to?'

'Blacktown.'

'Oh.' I felt sick.

'Do you know your mum's work number?' the detective constable went on. 'It's probably in our case file somewhere, but—'

'Of course I know it!'

'We won't call her yet. It's better to use a landline when you break bad news.' He peered at me over the back of his seat. 'If you'd both been at home, it would have been easier.'

Suddenly a glimmer of light pierced the fog in my head. 'Is that where you were going?' I quavered. 'To my house?'

'Nup. We were on our way *back* from your house. And since we've got a description...' He didn't bother to finish. He didn't need to. I remembered how Mum had reported me missing on Monday night; her description was probably still on file, somewhere.

'It's no big deal,' Detective Constable Santos was saying. 'Your mum'll get a lawyer, and he'll sort things out.'

'But that other policeman – back at the hospital – he said it would all be okay!' My heart was thudding so loudly that I could hardly hear myself speak. 'He said no one could prove I did anything!'

'Yeah, well. I think he's right.'

'And it wasn't my fault! Something happened to me! The doctor thinks I had an epileptic fit!'

'Oh yeah?' Clearly, this was news to the detective constable. 'What doctor is that?'

'Didn't anyone tell you?' I demanded, clenching my fists. He immediately turned to his partner and asked, 'Have *you* seen any medical reports?'

The other detective shook his head.

By this time we were in Blacktown, heading towards the mall and railway station. But we didn't take the route I'd expected. Instead, Detective Sergeant Green swung his car down a backstreet that ran behind a whole row of shops. All I could see were skips and delivery bays and garage doors.

'Hang on,' I said. 'Where are we going? This isn't the way to the police station, is it?'

'It's the scenic route,' Detective Constable Santos drawled. 'We just gotta stop off at the Local Area Command.'

'Huh?'

'The Local Area Command. It's where my boss hangs out.' He flashed me a kind of lazy smirk. 'We can't leave you here, so we've gotta take you inside. But we won't be more'n ten minutes, don't worry.'

'I thought we were going to Blacktown police station?'

'We are. When we're finished here.'

At that instant, Detective Sergeant Green spun the wheel. We bounced over a metal grille into a small, fenced-off area that was paved with cracked concrete. Someone had divided this space into half a dozen parking spots, using white painted lines; the space itself was sitting out the back of a low blue building that appeared to be empty, though it had once been occupied by a DVD rental outlet. On either side loomed the blank, windowless walls of two ugly brown office blocks, each about five or six storeys high.

'It's in there,' said the detective constable, gesturing at the larger, browner office block. Then he fixed his little dark eyes on my face. 'And the thing is, Toby, we're gunna have to cuff ya. Before you get outta the car.'

'*What?*'

'Sorry, mate. It's just that we're not on police property.' Seeing me blanch, he adopted a wheedling tone. 'I mean, having this yard free is great, because the LAC parking is rubbish. There's never enough room. But it means we gotta go down the side there, into a public lane, and that means handcuffs. Isn't that right, Link?'

His partner gave a grunt.

'There's a fire door round the corner – we won't be using the front steps,' Detective Constable Santos continued. 'No one'll see you, I promise.'

'In that case, why do I have to put on handcuffs?' It seemed like a reasonable enough question to me. The detective constable, however, didn't think so.

'Regulations,' he said flatly.

'But—'

'Sooner we get 'em on, sooner we'll get 'em off.' He heaved himself out of the car and yanked open my door. 'Just turn around and put your hands behind you. Thumbs together.'

'Listen—'

'Don't piss me about, Toby, I've been up since five.' He sounded crabby rather than threatening, but I did what I was told. I couldn't help it. Resistance would have required a certain amount of willpower – and all my energy was being channelled towards not bursting into tears.

That's why I tried to concentrate on something other than the cold touch of metal around my wrists. That's why I found myself staring between the front seats, directly at the dashboard. It looked like a perfectly normal dashboard.

And I suddenly thought, *Shouldn't there be some kind of police radio?*

'Okay,' said the detective constable, as his cuffs went *click-click*. Then he grabbed one of my arms. 'Where is it?' he inquired. But he wasn't talking to me. His partner swivelled around, reaching up over the headrest to hand him something.

It was a loaded syringe.

Even now, I don't like to think about what happened next. A moment like that is your very worst nightmare; nothing seems quite so bad to me anymore, because I lived through that moment. It's hard to describe the panic. My heart leaped into my throat. My hair stood on end. For half a second, I forgot how to breathe.

Then I threw myself towards the other door, kicking and yelling.

'*Shuddup!*' At last the older guy spoke. '*Don't move!*' He pointed a gun at me, shoving it between the two front seats.

Do you know what it's like to stare down the barrel of a gun? This particular gun wasn't very big, but it was scary as hell. It looked like a Nazi's gun, all sleek and black and businesslike. An automatic. My brain registered that it wasn't a revolver – don't ask me why. I couldn't have cared less what kind of gun it was.

'Ow!' A jab in my arm made me jerk like a hooked fish. Distracted by the gun, I'd forgotten about Detective Constable Santos.

'There,' he said. 'All finished.'

'*What are you doing?*' As I kicked him in the ribs, he held on grimly. Then I felt the gun barrel against my scalp.

'Don't move,' warned the other one. 'If you move, you'll get hurt.' He had a flat, gravelly voice with an American accent.

'You're not police!' I shrieked. 'What do you want? Lemme go!'

'Shh.'

'*Lemme go!*'

The younger one threw himself on top of me like a wrestler, knocking the air out of my lungs. He planted an elbow in the small of my back. Then he wriggled around, before somehow slamming the door shut behind him.

'For Chrissake, Gary . . .' said the other one.

'I'm doing my best, okay?'

'Someone's gonna hear.'

'He's a bloody *werewolf*, Lincoln! It's not that easy!'

A werewolf?

I stopped struggling. I couldn't believe it. 'Who *are* you?' I wheezed, gasping under Gary's weight. 'How did you know about me?'

'Jesus, can't you shuddim up?' the American growled. 'You're supposed to be the goddamn muscle in this operation.'

'Just drive, then! If you're so worried!'

The American snorted. 'Sure, I guess that's one way to screw the whole deal,' he said, with lumbering sarcasm. 'Hit the lunchtime traffic before he's gone under. Why not just wind down the windows while we're at it?'

'Did Reuben send you?' I clutched at this possibility the way a drowning man might clutch at a lifebelt. If Reuben was involved, then it all made sense. It wasn't so frightening. It was something I could talk my way out of... 'Tell him there's no need to do this!' I squawked. 'You don't *need* to worry about me! I believed him, I swear! I was gunna take precautions!'

But Gary didn't seem interested. He was still talking to his partner. 'I thought you said this wouldn't take long?' he complained.

'It won't,' Lincoln retorted.

'Are you listening? Are you Reuben's friends?' By now I was almost hysterical. I kept thinking, *Reuben wants to lock me up! He's scared I'll kill someone!* 'I won't tell the police, I promise! He convinced me last night! I was gunna ask him what to do!'

Suddenly Gary pushed my head down, so that my face was half buried in the grey upholstery.

'You wanna know what to do?' he spat. 'You should shut your mouth, that's what! Or I'll shut it for ya!'

'Nnn-mmmm-nnn...' When I tried to speak, the words were muffled by layers of foam and viscose. Even *I* couldn't understand what I was saying.

I couldn't breathe, either.

'Don't smother him,' the American said sharply.

'Do you want him quiet, or not?'

'I want him quiet. I don't want him dead.'

You can imagine how relieved I was to hear *that*. And I was even more relieved when Gary shifted his grip, allowing me to raise my head and gulp down some air.

But the extra oxygen didn't seem to help a lot. I still felt dizzy and nauseous.

'This isn't fair,' I mumbled.

'Shuddup! Jeez!' Gary slapped me on the ear. 'Are you deaf? Don't you understand English? *Shut your mouth!*'

I shut my eyes instead. I had to. They wouldn't stay open. 'It's not for weeks, yet,' I whimpered. 'Tell Reuben I was gunna call...'

'Who's Reuben?' said Gary.

'Don't ask me,' the American replied. 'Ask him.'

'Who's Reuben?' Gary repeated, giving me a shake. Despite the chill that ran down my spine, I couldn't answer. I couldn't do anything. I was so sleepy...

'Wait a minute.' The last thing I heard was Lincoln's measured rumble. 'I know that name. There was a Reuben for sale here not long ago. Mr Darwell flew in to do the deal – nearly got himself arrested.' After a brief pause, the American added, 'Looks like we mighta scored us another prospect. Two for the price of one! I like that.'

I didn't. But before I could say so – before I could even think it all through – darkness descended.

I passed out with a question half formed on my tongue.

Chapter Fifteen

I felt *so* bad when I woke up. My head was aching. My bladder was bursting. My stomach was heaving. And when I tried to open my eyes, the eyelids seemed to be stuck together. I had to peel them apart.

'Aaugh...' I groaned, wondering how I was going to move. If I didn't move, I would almost certainly wet myself. But if I tried to get up, something awful was bound to happen. My brain would explode, or I'd regurgitate my own guts.

What on earth was wrong with me?

For a while I didn't even have the strength to think about it. I just lay very still, wincing at every throb of pain. At last, however, sheer discomfort drove me to act. I *had* to piss. Nothing else mattered quite as much – not even the fact that I was all on my own, in a completely strange place.

When I climbed to my feet, I thought I was going to pass out. I had to prop myself against a wall, clutching my head and swallowing my nausea. The wall was made of concrete, rough and grey and cold. The floor was made of concrete, too. I had to shade my eyes from the glare of an overhead light as I squinted around, searching for a bathroom door – or at the very least, an empty bucket.

I certainly didn't expect to see a stainless-steel toilet sharing the room with me. In such a vast, empty space it looked a bit odd, not to mention grimly practical. Even as I staggered towards it, I wondered if I was in gaol. Because you don't normally see beds and toilets sitting next to each other unless you're in a prison cell or a furniture warehouse. And I was pretty damn sure this wasn't a furniture warehouse.

Using the toilet helped me a bit. Once I'd taken a piss, the relief was so enormous that I was able to raise my head and study my surroundings. But what I saw made me feel sick all over again. I was in a windowless, circular dungeon. Apart from the toilet, this dungeon contained only a heater suspended high above me, a manacle chained to the floor, and a metal-frame bed with a mattress on it. One exit was blocked by a door made of painted steel, like a prison door. There was also a very tall barred gate, beyond which lay a long, dark, winding passage.

I could tell that this was a subterranean passage – and not just because its walls were as rough and dusty as the walls of a mine shaft. The whole place smelled of damp soil. Somehow I could feel the earth's weight bearing down on my head. And I also remembered what Reuben had said to me at Nurragingy: *When I was your age, I was locked in an underground tank.*

The more I thought about it, the more certain I became. The room in which I stood was round, and made entirely of concrete. It had no windows. A power cable had been taped across the ceiling in a slapdash kind of way, suggesting that no one had wired the place up when it was first built. As for the door, it was well and truly locked. There wasn't even a handle to turn. And after stumbling over to the gate, I discovered that *it* wouldn't budge either. No matter how hard I shook it.

I was locked in an underground tank. Just like Reuben.

If I hadn't been so unwell, I probably would have had a

nervous breakdown at that point. But the thing about pain is: it's very hard to ignore. Other worries tend to fade into the background when you've got a headache as toxic as mine was. I knew that something very, very bad had happened. I knew that I could probably expect a lot worse. Yet none of this seemed to matter much, compared to the sudden flare of pain that I experienced every time I turned my head or bent over.

I was also distracted by a raging thirst, which was so intense that I caught myself wondering if I could drink out of the toilet. Let me tell you, it's pretty alarming when you find yourself thinking something like *that*; I immediately made a huge effort to snap out of my daze, looking around for an alternative water source.

Then I spotted a plastic water bottle beside the bed. It was like a sign from God. I pounced on the bottle and drained it, without even stopping to make sure that I was squirting water into my mouth instead of urine or methylated spirits. Luckily, that bottle *was* full of water. And after drinking my fill, I felt less seedy. My sore throat went away. My stomach settled a bit. I was able to focus my attention on the fact that I'd been knocked out. With a drug. By two guys who hadn't been policemen after all.

So who were they really?

As my dull gaze drifted towards the underground passage, a bell tolled somewhere in the dim recesses of my brain. I remembered the name 'Darwell'. Reuben had mentioned someone called Darwell, as had the two fake policemen. Did this mean that they were all part of the same plot?

I struggled to concentrate on my last, dim recollection of the kidnappers. They'd been asking me who Reuben was. They'd referred to a 'Mr Darwell'. *There was a Reuben for sale here not long ago*, the American had said. *Mr Darwell flew in to do the deal.* But how did Mr Darwell fit into Reuben Schneider's story? No matter how hard I tried, I couldn't dredge up the exact details. There had been some kind of illegal racket. Reuben had been forced to fight other werewolves – or so he claimed. And he had spoken of Mr Darwell in this context, along with someone else...

Suddenly I recalled another name: 'McKinnon'. Reuben's story was that the McKinnons had locked him up for five years. Had the McKinnons locked *me* up as well? Had I been kidnapped by the McKinnons?

It was all too confusing. I couldn't think straight. And besides, I had a more urgent job to do. Before anything else, I had to get out.

I felt in my pocket, but my phone was gone – along with my keys, my watch and my wallet. *Bastards*, I thought, through a sickening spasm of pain. *Bloody stinking bastards.* My shoes were also missing; I couldn't see them anywhere. I was still wearing my socks, though, and the rest of my wardrobe as well. No one had tried to strip me of all my layers.

I was just making sure that my T-shirts were all present and accounted for when I had a flash of inspiration. And if you're wondering why I was dressed in more than one T-shirt... well, the truth is, I get embarrassed. I've told you that I'm skinny and that I wear baggy clothes. What I haven't told you is that my arms are as puny as pipe-cleaners and that my chest is all narrow and knobbly. My hips stick out like a skeleton's pelvis. My knees bulge like two beads on strings. I look as if I've been stretched on a rack, and I'm not happy about it.

That's why I bulk up with extra T-shirts. That's why I wear trackpants under my jeans, even in summer. It might get hot, but at least I don't have people asking me how much I eat. Because I eat plenty, in case you're interested. There's nothing wrong with *my* appetite.

Mum says that I haven't grown into my height yet. She says I'll fill out when I get older. And while I certainly hope that's true, I suppose it's just as well that I was so underweight when the two fake policemen kidnapped me. If I hadn't been swaddled in layers of fabric, they might have realised how thin I was. They might have worked out that I was spindly enough to squeeze through the bars of their cage.

They might have chained me to the floor instead of leaving me on the bed, unfettered.

Even from a distance, I could tell that I had a good chance of escaping. Though the bars were thick, they were also widely spaced; I figured that if I could just push my head between them, the rest would be a cinch. My only concern was what this might do to my ears. I was very concerned about my ears. They stick out a bit, and I didn't want them torn or crushed. My headache was bad enough without the added burden of mangled ear cartilage.

I wasn't worried about hidden cameras. To be honest, the thought of electronic surveillance never crossed my mind. It should have, of course. Checking for cameras should have been my first priority. But I wasn't reasoning too well just then. In fact I didn't even stop to consider what might happen once I was out of my cell. Right at that moment, I couldn't see past step number one.

First I stripped down to my underpants. Then I pushed every other piece of clothing through the gate into the tunnel. At least I was thinking clearly enough to realise that I would need to put them back on again.

Then I forced myself through the bars, nearly ripping my head off in the process. It was an agonising experience, like being stuck in a vice. For one really bad moment, I thought I was going to be trapped there. My skull seemed to be wedged into the narrow space as tightly as a nut in a nutcracker.

But I managed to pull free at last, leaving some blood and hair behind me. As expected, my ears had taken the worst beating; they felt bruised and flattened. My headache hadn't improved, either. Every time I bent down to pick up a T-shirt or a sock, the pain was so bad that I had to close my eyes. Getting dressed was awful. Just keeping my *balance* was a strain.

In the end, though, I found myself fully clothed, upright and more or less in one piece. The tunnel stretched out before me, disappearing into blackness. A disturbing smell wafted out of the shadows; I couldn't identify its source, or why it seemed so alarming, but it raised the hairs on the back of my neck. All the same, I had to move forward. What else could I do? Turning back was out of the question.

So I advanced reluctantly, pressing against the wall as my vision adjusted to the fading light. Wires running along the roof of the tunnel were attached to a fuse box near the gate, but I wasn't tempted to throw any switches. I didn't want to draw attention to myself. Wearing socks, I was able to tread almost noiselessly over the rocky, uneven surface of the floor. Though I was pouring sweat – though my legs were shaking and my head was throbbing – I was able to ignore these symptoms, because fear does such a great job of concentrating your mind. I didn't even hiss when I stubbed my toe. My only concern was getting out unnoticed. I was living from heartbeat to heartbeat.

Then I hit a fork in the tunnel. Another tunnel joined mine, after running on an almost parallel course. I was faced with an unwelcome choice: should I keep going in the same direction or not? I didn't like the idea of doubling back down the parallel tunnel. On the other hand, there seemed to be very little light up ahead at the end of my tunnel – and I noticed that the converging tunnel led back towards a faint, golden glow.

After a moment's thought, I opted for the darkness. At least in the darkness I couldn't be seen. And I was much more afraid of being spotted by a fake policeman than I was of falling down a crevasse.

This has to lead somewhere, I decided, before continuing on my way.

Luckily, the tunnel didn't wind around too many corners. It did swerve a bit, but not enough to block out every trace of light from the cell behind me. So I didn't break my nose on the first obstacle that I encountered; I was able to see just well enough to pull up short before I ran straight into a metal hatch, which was bolted shut from the inside. For a few seconds I groped around, fingering the bolt and the hinges and the wire that ran from the latch through a hole in the ceiling. Then, very slowly and carefully, I drew the bolt, lifted the latch, and pushed the hatch open.

Needless to say, I didn't want to announce my arrival. Instead of giving the hatch a huge, careless shove, I nudged it open just a crack, wincing at the squeak it made. Though I couldn't hear any voices, I *could* smell fresh air. My heart leaped as I realised that I was peering through the hatchway at a large space drenched in moonlight.

I was out. I'd escaped from the underground tank.

You can imagine how relieved I was – at least for a moment. The night air immediately whisked away that rank, raw odour that had frightened me so much. A peppery bushland scent seemed to flood through my veins like a reviving drug. My headache vanished. My mood lifted. I pushed open the hatch a little further, admiring the emptiness of the roofless space beyond it. There was no one around! I had stumbled upon a large, rectangular pit under a starry sky. The pit was fully tiled and very deep. *It's an old pool,* I thought, noting a drainage outlet in the floor. High above, the pool's rim was edged with razor wire. I couldn't see any steps.

And at that very instant, my hopes began to fade.

How could I possibly scale those sheer, slippery walls without the aid of some steps? No ladders or ropes were lying around at the bottom of the pool. Its pale tiles reflected so much moonlight that I could see at a glance every piece of rubbish that had collected near the drain: a stick, a beer can, a crumpled plastic wrapper. The shadows weren't dense enough to conceal anything as big as another hatch. There were no iron rungs hammered into the tiles.

Gazing up at the pool's edge, I felt like a spider in a bath. Unless someone reached down to help me – unless a friendly face appeared overhead – I would *never* get out.

That's why I went back inside. You might think I was brave, but I wasn't. I didn't have a choice; I had to find a ladder or another exit. And I had to do it quickly, before my kidnappers realised what was going on. I had to escape while the coast was clear.

Maybe these guys are all asleep, I pondered, having no idea what time it was. My watch had been stolen, so I couldn't tell how long I'd been unconscious. If it was still before midnight, I might not have to rush. If it was nearly dawn, however, every second would count. I sensed that I might be out in the bush (it certainly smelled that way) and country people, I knew, often woke up early.

I didn't want to retrace my steps. When I drew back into the tunnel, closing the hatch behind me, it was like climbing back into my own grave. I hated having to shut out all that wonderful light and air. Even though I'd decided that an open hatch might raise the alarm, I had to force myself to do the sensible thing. You probably won't believe this, but my headache returned as soon as the latch clicked into place. I had to swallow again and again, to stop myself from throwing up. Every nerve in my body was screaming *NO!*

But I had to ignore what my nerves were telling me. I had to set off towards the fork in the tunnel, teeth clenched and eyes peeled, hoping that I would stumble across a ladder, or a rope, or a cable – something, at any rate, that I could use in a daring escape attempt. When I reached the second tunnel, I nearly chickened out; advancing into unexplored territory took a lot more courage than I had, by that time. What if I was heading straight into the arms of the fake policemen? What if there were dogs or guns or instruments of torture at the end of the tunnel? For a minute or so I couldn't even move. I just stood there sweating, with my heart in my mouth. It was so unfair. I didn't deserve any of this. How come it had happened to *me*?

Finally, a voice in my head snarled, *Get going, ya wuss* – and I obeyed. Step by cautious step, I picked my way down the curving tunnel, which grew brighter and brighter. A soft radiance began to seep across the walls. Somewhere up ahead, I knew, an electric light must be burning. The question was: had it been left on in an empty space, or was someone actually using it?

I was so intent on what lay in store for me that I forgot to look down. I stopped paying attention to my own feet. And that was a fatal mistake, because I didn't see the metal drum until I bumped into it. *Crash!* The noise was like an explosion; it seemed to ricochet off the walls. As I fell, the drum rolled away from me, making a hollow *boom-boom-boom*. I banged my knee and scraped my right hand.

A distant voice said, 'Hello? Who's there?'

I froze. I think my heart might have stopped beating. I certainly held my breath.

'Hello?' The voice was young and high-pitched. It didn't belong to either of the fake policemen. 'Is that you, Gary?'

Gary. I knew that name. Gary and Lincoln – my two kidnappers.

Very slowly and quietly, I pushed myself upright again. One of my knee-joints clicked.

'Who is it?' the voice entreated. 'Say something!'

I couldn't hear footsteps. Was no one going to come after me? I took a step backwards, wincing at the soft *crunch* it made as loose pebbles slid from under my heel.

'Please! Help me! I'm trapped here!' The voice cracked on a shrill note. Something rattled. 'You gotta get me out! You gotta call the police! Don't go! Wait! Help!'

This time, when I froze, it was because of shock – not fear. Help? Someone wanted *help*?

'I've been kidnapped!' the voice cried, sounding more and more desperate. 'Are you there? Can you hear me? Who is that?' *Rattle, rattle.* 'Don't be scared! I'm all alone! There's no one else!'

Oh my God, I thought. *It's another kid! Just like me!*

181

If I hadn't clutched at the wall, I might have lost my balance.

'Oh, *please* help me, *please!*' the voice moaned. It was horrible to listen to. I wanted to cover my ears. 'Don't go...don't leave me...I gotta get out...'

What could I do? What choice did I have? If you'd heard that despair – that hopeless misery – you wouldn't have walked away either. You would have done exactly what I did; you would have taken a deep breath, licked your dry lips, and moved forward.

One step, two steps, three steps...after eight long strides, I found myself staring at a barred gate identical to the one I'd just squeezed through. Beyond it lay a concrete cell bathed in harsh electric light. This cell contained some standard-looking items, like the metal-frame bedstead and stainless-steel toilet, together with a scattering of more unfamiliar objects: an apple core, some sheets, a dirty plastic plate, a couple of dog-eared comic books. But I didn't really notice these minor details at first. Because they couldn't compete with the sight of a long-haired boy, about my age, who was clinging to the bars as if he needed their support.

Though shorter than me, he was wider, with a nuggetty frame and a big head (which might have looked bigger than it really was, owing to all the fuzzy blonde hair sprouting out of it in tightly coiled ringlets). He had huge pale eyes, a slightly flattened nose and almost invisible eyelashes; his clothes were grubby and his colour was bad.

Normally, I don't know what Mum means when she says that someone's colour is bad. I'll take one look and think, *What's wrong with that colour? It's not bright blue or orange.* This time, however, even *I* could see that something was wrong. The face behind the bars had a kind of pasty, greenish cast to it. There were purple rings around the kid's eyes and a yellowish bruise near his mouth, which fell open as I approached him.

For a second or two we just stood there, gaping at each other.

Then he burst into tears.

Chapter Sixteen

'Help me!' he sobbed. 'Get me outta here, *please!*'

'Yeah, all right...' What else could I say? He was bawling like a baby. 'Can't you squeeze through the bars, then?'

'No! Of course not!' The gate rattled furiously. 'D'you think I haven't tried?'

'Okay, okay. Calm down.' I made a 'shushing' motion, because I was afraid that someone might hear him. Then I scanned the sides of the gate, looking for a latch or release button.

'It's padlocked,' he informed me, pointing. 'Up there...'

'Oh.' That was bad news. I could see the padlock and chain high above my head. The padlock was enormous. 'Bummer.'

'You can stand on the drum!' he said shrilly. 'That's how *they* always do it!'

'Who?'

'Huh?'

'Who are you talking about?' I demanded. 'Who did this?'

He stared at me as if I were insane.

'Gary and Lincoln!' he cried. 'Who else?'

'So they got you too?'

'Of course they did!' *Rattle, rattle* went the gate. 'And they'll come down if you don't hurry up!'

'Down from where? Where are we?' I asked. But he wasn't about to answer any more questions.

'Just *break the lock*!' he screeched, as if it were the easiest thing in the world. I glanced at the padlock doubtfully. 'How am I supposed to do that? I'd need a big rock or something...'

'So find one! Quick!'

He was ordering me around – and I have to admit, I didn't like it. That's why I said, in a sulky sort of way, 'There's no point. We can't get out through the tunnel – it leads straight into the bottom of an old pool.'

'I know that! D'you think I don't know that?' His voice broke as he pressed against the bars. 'I've been out there! I've seen it!'

I frowned. 'Then—'

'We can use the drum!' he explained. 'You can stand on the drum and I can stand on you—'

'—and you might reach the top,' I finished, nodding in agreement. Then something else occurred to me. 'We can tie your sheets together and make a rope,' I suggested. 'So you can pull me up after you.'

'I'll do that. Sure I will,' he said tearfully. 'If you can just get the gate open...'

We both raised our eyes to the padlock again. It looked awfully solid.

'I don't think I could lift the drum that high,' was my doleful conclusion.

'No, no! Don't hit it with the drum!' he pleaded, his teeth chattering with fear. 'It would make too much noise! They'd hear you!'

'Would they?' My gaze followed his, towards the iron door in his cell. 'Are they close by?' I whispered.

'Maybe.'

'In the next room?'

'Upstairs.'

'Do they live upstairs, then?'

'How should *I* know?' he yelped. 'It's not like they let me use their toilet!'

'Okay, okay...'

'Just *get me out of here!*'

'Shh! Okay!' Unnerved by his mounting hysteria, I was tempted to beat a retreat. But since my only escape route led into the bottom of a swimming pool...

Suddenly I had a flash of inspiration.

'Hang on – wait – I've got an idea,' I said, turning.

'No! Don't go!'

'Shh. I'll be back.'

'*Don't leave me here!*'

'I'm not! Okay? I'm just getting something.'

He didn't believe me, though. I could hear him begging piteously as I raced back down the tunnel; it was pretty obvious that he was in a bad way. Any minute now, I felt sure, he would flip his lid and start screaming like a maniac. So I didn't linger when I finally reached the pool. Without a moment's hesitation I burst through the hatch, stumbled over to the drainage outlet, and snatched up the aluminium beer can that someone had left there. I didn't even pause to check for unexpected noises or movements.

Then I returned to my fuzzy-haired friend, who had fallen to his knees in despair.

'It's okay,' I assured him. 'Look – see? I had to get this.'

He was sobbing too hard to ask why. But his expression, as he stared at the beer can, told me exactly what he was thinking.

He was thinking, *What the hell use is a beer can?*

'I'm gunna make a shim. I've done it before.' Not only that, I had successfully used my beer-can shim to pick a lock. 'You can tear this stuff with your bare hands, if you fold it properly first.'

'How – how—'

'Just gimme a minute, all right?'

I can't pretend it was easy, making that shim. Ripping up aluminium requires a lot of patience; unless you concentrate hard, you end up with crooked rips (not to mention cut fingers). With so much whimpering going on, I found it hard to focus.

'So what's your name?' I said at last, when the impatient atmosphere got too much for me. I wanted to distract the guy from his fretting and fuming. 'Mine's Toby Vandevelde.'

'I'm Sergio. Pereira.'

'How long have you been here, Sergio?'

'I dunno. How should *I* know? They took my watch. I got no calendar...' He sounded peevish, but at least he wasn't jigging up and down. 'I guess you're a werewolf too, huh?' he said, wringing the tears from his eyes.

I grunted, not quite sure how to respond. The jury was still out on my status as a werewolf...

'It's a family curse,' Sergio continued. 'That's what the priest told us. My parents thought I had a demon in me, but when they called the priest, he couldn't get rid of it. He said it was genetic. Seventh son. You know?'

'Mmmm...'

'They didn't believe him. They didn't believe that *they* had

187

bad blood, so they tried to beat the devil out of me. They locked me in a pizza oven.'

'A *pizza oven*?'

'Wood-fired. You know. Very thick.'

'But—'

'When the police found out, they put me in a foster home. Is that what happened to you?'

'Nuh.' I was nearly finished. 'I live with my mum.'

'Does she lock you up?'

'No.'

'And you haven't killed her?'

'Of course not!' He was beginning to freak me out. I didn't want to listen to any more of his weird family history. 'Okay – so this is done now. I just have to haul the drum over here . . .'

'*I* killed someone. It wasn't my fault. Gary and Lincoln – they *made* me do it.'

'Uh-huh.' Boy, I was squirming. 'Hang on a tick.'

'They wanted me to!' he groaned. 'I woke up and he was dead! I couldn't help it!'

'Sure – fine – but d'you think we could talk about this later, please?' The drum was even heavier than I'd expected. I found myself panting as I dragged it towards the gate. Meanwhile, Sergio just went on and on and on, as if he *couldn't* shut his trap.

'They said they were police,' he gabbled. 'That's why I went with them. They knew my name. They knew where I was living. I thought, "They must be police." But they weren't . . .'

I climbed up onto the drum, trying to ignore his high-pitched chatter. By stretching my arms above my head, I could reach the padlock without too much trouble. I soon realised, however, that actually *picking* the damn lock wasn't going to be a piece of cake. Not from that position.

'I don't know how they found out where I was,' Sergio was saying. 'Someone must have told them about me. Like my dad. Or my brother. Maybe my dad was scared that I'd come and get him one night. Maybe he wanted someone else to lock me up.'

Fiddle, fiddle. Flick, flick. I was sweating bullets, and my arms were beginning to shake. *Come on*, I thought, *you bastard lock!*

'Except that Dad didn't know my address,' Sergio added. 'The social worker wouldn't tell him. That was her story, anyway. Maybe she was lying. Maybe *she* was the one who told Gary.'

'Goddammit!' That lock just wouldn't cooperate. So I took a couple of long, deep breaths before trying again.

Flick-flick. Flick-flick-flick.

'It could have been her,' croaked Sergio, oblivious to my struggles. He was staring off into space. 'She knew where I was. But so did the lawyer. And Dr Olsen. And Dr Passlow. And Mrs Tennant—'

'Dr Passlow?' I interrupted, cutting him off. 'You *know* Dr Passlow?'

Sergio goggled up at me. 'Huh?'

'Dr *Glen* Passlow? From Mount Druitt hospital?'

Sergio shook his head. 'I've never been to Mount Druitt,' he mumbled. 'I come from Orange. They took me to Orange Base Hospital . . .'

But he was missing the point. 'Paediatrician?' I pressed. 'Balding? Ginger hair? Ring a bell?'

He nodded slowly. 'I guess,' he faltered. 'Except that he was in Orange.'

'When?'

'Huh?'

'When were you in hospital?'

'Well...' He thought for a minute. 'I was in hospital after the pizza oven. Before I went to foster care. And I was in foster care for three months.'

'There you are, then. He could have moved hospitals.' I suddenly realised that I wasn't doing what I was supposed to be doing, so I fixed my attention on the padlock again. *Flick, flick. Flick-flick-flick.* 'If you ask me,' I said, conscious that my face was growing hot with the effort of keeping my arms raised, 'Dr Passlow must have something to do with this. Unless it was the priest. What was your priest's name? Was he called Ramon Alvarez?'

'No.'

'Did he ever *mention* anyone called Ramon Alvarez?'

'I don't think so.' Sergio sounded completely dazed.

'What about Reuben Schneider? Have you heard of him?'

'No.'

'Sanford Plackett? Nina Harrison? Bridget Doherty?'

'Why are you asking me this?' Sergio whined. 'I don't know any of those people. Why should I?'

'Just wondered.' At that moment something went *click* – and the padlock released its clenched jaw. I can't tell you how unbelievably good it felt when that happened. I was so surprised, I nearly fell off my drum.

'Oh!' I exclaimed. 'Oh my God!'

'What?'

'I've done it!' The chain clinked as I pulled it through the bars. 'Look! Oh my God!'

'Shh! Not so loud!'

'Yeah. Right. Sorry,' I muttered, climbing down to the dusty floor. It occurred to me that the chain would make a very good weapon. 'We should keep this,' I proposed, swinging it like a lasso. 'I bet you could really hurt someone with it.'

But Sergio wasn't listening. He had pushed the gate open, and was squeezing through the gap he'd made for himself. Without even stopping to say 'thank you', he bolted past me down the tunnel.

'Hey! Wait!' I called after him. 'What about the drum?'

'Shh!' He hit the brakes and whirled around. 'Stop *shouting*!'

'I'm not shouting. I'm asking nicely.' Lowering my voice to a hiss, I fixed him with a stony glare. 'You wanna help me with this drum, or what?'

To give him his due, he came straight back. Though he didn't say anything that I actually wanted to hear (like 'sorry' or 'thanks' or even 'I owe you'), he picked up one end of the drum and began to retrace his steps – facing backwards.

'Hang on,' I said, from the other end of the drum. I'd slung the chain around my neck like a scarf. 'We should do this sideways.'

'It's okay. I'm fine.'

'You'll fall.'

'No, I won't.'

'You will if you can't see where you're going,' I insisted. 'It's *dark* down there.'

'Just hurry, will you?' He was frantic. 'Stop farting about!'

With a shrug I gave in – and we shuffled off into the shadows. Sure enough, Sergio soon came a cropper; because he was moving too fast and couldn't see where he was going, he caught his heel in a shallow dip that caused him to sit down abruptly, dropping his end of the drum.

It made a hollow *bong* as it hit the ground.

'See? I told you.' Impatiently I readjusted the thing until it was sitting at a sensible angle, with each end facing a wall. 'If we do it like this, we can both keep our eyes peeled, and it'll be much quicker...' I trailed off when I realised that he was crying again. 'What's wrong?' I said. 'Did you hurt yourself?'

'I'll never get out,' he sobbed. 'I'll never get out.'

'Course you will. We're nearly there.'

'I'm gunna die in this hole...'

'Sergio!' I spoke sharply because he was dragging me down. His terror was infectious. 'Snap out of it! Stop being such a wuss!'

'You dunno what's it like,' he moaned, then yelped as I gave him a hard little kick on the shin. 'Ouch! What are you doing?'

'I'm getting you out of here, okay? Stand up!'

'All right, all right. You don't have to yell at me...'

I did, though. I had to yell at him at least twice – once when he thought he'd heard a noise (and nearly lost the plot), and another time when his legs suddenly buckled, for no apparent reason, so that he slid to his knees with a squeak of dismay.

'I can't breathe!' he croaked. 'I can't – I can't—'

'You're fine,' I said crossly.

'I feel sick!'

'It's just a panic attack,' I hazarded. 'It's nothing.'

'It is! I can't see!'

'Of course you can't see. It's pitch black in this tunnel.' He didn't move, though, and I lost my temper. 'Get up! Right now! Or I'll leave you here!'

192

'No! Don't leave me!'

'I will if you don't move!' Needless to say, this was an empty threat. Without Sergio's help, I had no way of climbing out of the pool. But he was too distraught to remember this all-important fact – and I certainly wasn't about to remind him of it. 'You don't hear *me* complain, and my head is splitting!' I concluded. 'So why don't you just suck it up and gimme a break?'

When at last we arrived at the hatch, I was fully prepared to punch Sergio in the nose if he gave me any more trouble. I realise now that I was being unfair. The poor guy was half crazy, thanks to what he'd been through; it wasn't his fault that he kept sniffing and whining and being a total nuisance. Luckily the fresh air did wonders for him. As soon as I pushed the hatch open, his mood changed. He became a different person, enthusiastically spouting helpful suggestions while we manoeuvred our drum through the narrow opening.

'We forgot the sheets!' he lamented. 'Should I go back for them?'

'No.' I couldn't believe he was even offering. 'We can use the chain instead. It might be long enough.'

'I wish we had a torch,' he whispered, scanning the rim of the pool. Above us, the moon was still glowing in an inky sky. 'I wish we had shoes.'

'Yeah. Well – I wish we had a lot of things.'

'Do you know where we are?'

'Nup.'

'It doesn't smell like a town, does it?'

I flashed him a look, thinking: *So you really are like me.* For the first time, I felt as if we were on exactly the same wavelength. 'You can smell that, huh?' I inquired.

'Yeah. Can't you?'

'Oh sure.'

'What about trying a corner? That corner over there might work, don't you think?'

I agreed. The corner of the pool was a good place to start. By wedging myself into the angle where two walls met, I would have more support while Sergio was balancing on my shoulders. That was Sergio's theory, anyway – and it made a lot of sense. So we positioned our steel drum in one corner; then I gave Sergio my chain and climbed onto the drum, before Sergio tried to climb onto me.

Boy, he was heavy. I hadn't been expecting such a dead weight. When I squatted down so that he could sit on my shoulders, I wasn't able to rise again. Even with my forearms pressed against the enfolding walls, I didn't have what it took to launch him skywards. My knees weren't strong enough.

'Okay, wait,' he said. 'I'll get off so you can stand up. Then I'll start again.'

'How do you mean?' I wasn't reassured. 'What are you going to do?'

'I'm going to pretend you're a ladder,' he rejoined. And that's exactly what he did. While I stood with my shoulders hunched, my chin tucked into my chest and my face pushed into the corner, Sergio hoisted himself onto my back. Using my hipbones as footholds, he wriggled up until his knees were clamped on either side of my neck.

I was surprised at how nimble he was, until I remembered how nimble *I* was. Perhaps he had quick-growing hair as well.

'This is great!' he breathed. 'I can almost touch the edge!'

'Ow! Ouch!' It felt as if my collarbones were about to snap. 'Be careful...'

194

'I'm gunna stand up now. Okay?'

'Hang on—'

'I won't tread on your ears, I promise,' he assured me.

The next bit was dire. I couldn't help squealing. He placed one foot on my left shoulder and shoved down hard, before lurching upright with a mighty grunt. I nearly toppled.

'Look out!' I squawked.

'Got it! I got it!'

'*Yeowch!*'

'Gimme a push, quick!'

I did my best. Bracing myself against the wall, I reached up to grip his ankles. Then I gave a huge shove, nearly dislocating half a dozen joints in the process.

'*Gnnn!*' Flailing around desperately, he caught me a glancing blow on the head with his foot. '*Aah-aah—*'

'Yeowch!'

Suddenly the weight was off my shoulders. I could breathe again. My arms and neck were aching.

I peered up and saw the black silhouette of a leg against a paler, star-studded canopy.

'Sergio?'

'Ooof!' The leg vanished.

'Are you okay?'

'Ow!' A pause. 'Bloody hell!' he continued, his voice sounding faint and muffled. 'There's razor wire!'

'Oh. Yeah.' I'd forgotten to warn him.

'It's okay. It's not high. I'm stepping over it.'

I heard a scuffling noise, followed by a few more grunts. I waited. And waited.

'Sergio?' When he didn't speak, I began to feel scared. '*Sergio?*'

'Aw, jeez...' he said at last. His tone wasn't encouraging. 'Aw, jeez.'

'What?'

'This is bad. It looks bad.'

'*What?*'

'I think it's the desert. It looks like the desert. I can't really...it's so dark.'

'Aren't there any houses?'

'No. Yes. There's one, I think.'

'Where? Is it close?'

But Sergio didn't seem to hear. Once again, he was losing his cool.

'This fence is bad,' he quavered. 'It's got barbed wire on top. We'll *never* get over *that*.'

I frowned. 'Didn't you say you could step over it?' I asked, kneading my sore muscles.

'That's the razor wire. That's different. Oh!' He caught his breath. 'Oh, man!'

'What?'

'Oh wow!'

'For God's sake!' I was ready to throttle him. 'Will you tell me what's going on?'

'I think it's...hang on...just let me...'

I tried to be patient. As he squeaked and cursed and scurried about overhead, I clenched my fists and closed my eyes. *You can do this*, I told myself. *You're halfway there. You're gunna make it.*

Then a metallic *clank* reached my ears – and my eyelids snapped open.

'Hey! Hey, Toby!' Sergio spluttered. I glanced up to see his fuzzy hair glinting in the moonlight. 'Guess what I found?'

196

He was so excited that I jumped to conclusions.

'A phone!' I exclaimed.

'No.'

'A bus stop?'

'It's a ladder!' he shrilled. 'And there's a gate in the fence! With a padlock!'

'Oh...'

'All you have to do is pick the lock!' He was practically hyperventilating. 'Just one lock and we'll be out! Free! We can make a run for it!' At this point he broke off with a gasp, left momentarily speechless as something dreadful occurred to him. 'You still have that shim, don't you?' he finally found the strength to ask. 'Toby? Did you keep it? *Did you keep the shim?*'

Chapter Seventeen

Well, of course I'd kept the shim. It was in my pocket. I told Sergio this before instructing him, fiercely, to pass me the damn ladder.

'Just push it down here, will you?' I urged. 'I wanna get the hell out!'

'It's heavy.'

'So what?'

'Be careful. I might drop it.'

But he didn't. With a lot of scraping and swearing, he lowered it into the pool until I was able to grab the bottom rung – which seemed to be made of aluminium. The whole ladder clanged and rattled as I guided it into position; aluminium's much noisier than wood when it bounces off a tiled wall.

'Shh!' Sergio hissed, getting more and more anxious. 'Keep it down, or they'll hear!'

'I'm trying. Okay? I'm not doing it on purpose.'

'They could be in that house. They might not be asleep...'

Though the ladder was certainly long enough, it didn't feel very stable. Even with Sergio holding the shafts up top, the whole thing creaked and shook with every rung that I climbed. At last, however, I reached the edge of the pool, where Sergio was squatting on a narrow strip of concrete between a razor-sharp tripwire and a four-metre drop back into the pool.

'Jesus.' That tripwire was the first thing I saw from the topmost rung. Moonlight glinted off jagged shards of steel shaped like deadly bow-ties. The wire itself was about twenty centimetres off the ground; it had been threaded through a kind of picket fence made from widely spaced, raggedly cut lengths of metal pipe. 'What the hell is that for?' I wheezed.

'It's for keeping *us* in,' Sergio softly rejoined.

'But we can step over it!'

'Only when we're like this.' He grabbed my wrist, pulling me up. 'If it was a full moon and we managed to jump out, we'd probably run straight into that wire.'

I felt a sudden chill, though the night was pretty warm. And I was grateful when Sergio changed the subject. Gesturing into the darkness, he said, 'The padlock's over there.' At which point I realised that we were penned in by a high fence made of steel mesh and barbed wire.

It was so close, I could reach out and touch it.

'Jesus,' I said again, appalled at the size of the thing. 'They're really serious, eh?'

'That's what the people stand behind.'

'Huh?'

'The people who come to watch.' Sergio's low-pitched voice became unsteady. 'I was down in the pool and I saw them, once. Before sunset. While I could still...'

He choked up, thank God, because I didn't want to hear. No way.

'This is gunna be tricky,' I announced, as I carefully stepped over the tripwire. It was hard to see. Everything was hard to see. Beyond the mesh fence lay a dim, uneven, grey-washed landscape that seemed to roll on forever. It was covered in mysterious black tufts. The only bright spot was a distant square of golden light – possibly a lamp in a window – which was embedded in a dense, shadowy, squared-off shape and surmounted by a sheet of something that had a faint gleam to it.

'There's the house,' I murmured, unnecessarily. I was surprised at how far away it was. Why build your pool so far from your back door? 'I thought it would be closer than that.'

'It's still too close for comfort,' was Sergio's jittery response. 'We gotta get out. Sooner the better.'

'Yeah, but that's what I'm trying to tell you. It won't be easy. I've never picked a lock in the dark before.' Taking care to avoid the razor wire that lurked at my heels, I groped along the fence until I reached the gate that Sergio had mentioned. As promised, it was padlocked shut. 'You know what you should do?' I said quietly, fingering the lock. (It was smaller than the last one.) 'You should go get your mattress. Just in case.'

'What?'

'See, I'm not sure if this'll work. And even if it does, I'm not sure how long it will take.' I began to fish in my pocket for the shim. 'But we could easily climb this fence if we had something to put over the barbed wire on top. Like a mattress, for instance.'

Sergio swallowed. I could actually hear him do it.

And I sympathised.

'I know you don't wanna go back. Who does? It's just that we need a plan B,' I went on. 'And now that we've got the ladder, it won't be too hard – not with a foam mattress, anyway. Those things are really light.' As he hesitated, I was struck by a sudden misgiving. 'Is your mattress down there a foam one?' I asked. 'Because mine was.'

After a moment's silence, he mumbled, 'Yes.'

'Good. Okay. I figured it would be.' My gaze wandered away from the padlock towards our barely visible escape route: an endless stretch of scrubby terrain that smelled as dry as wood ash. 'You should bring back your bottle of water, so we won't die of thirst out there,' I added. 'It looks like we're miles from the nearest town.' When Sergio didn't reply, I turned my head – and saw, to my astonishment, that his shadowy form had retreated to the edge of the pool. 'Will you be okay?' I said. 'Do you want me to hold that ladder?'

'No.' The top rung creaked under his weight. 'I'll be fine.'

He didn't sound fine, but I let him go. To be honest, I wasn't too hopeful about the lock in my hand; it felt a bit rusty (though I couldn't be sure, because the light wasn't good enough for a close look), and I didn't think rusty tumblers would be a cinch to pick. It seemed to me that climbing the fence would be much easier and quicker than standing around for half an hour, flick-flick-flicking away with my shim.

So I tackled the lock in a half-hearted kind of way, casting worried glances at the house while I listened for any telltale noises down in the pool. I heard the pad of Sergio's footsteps. I heard the hatch creak open as he crawled back into the tunnel. After that, there was dead silence for quite some time, except for a breeze rustling through leaf litter and the tap-tap-tap of the shim that I was jiggling.

Left alone, I was suddenly conscious of the vast, mysterious space in which I stood. *We could be anywhere*, I thought. *We could be in the Simpson Desert*. I felt sure that I was still in Australia, because the stars looked familiar and the air smelled of native plants. Until the sun rose, however, I wouldn't even know my compass points. So how would I find a way out? Where was the nearest road? What if we walked off into the wilderness and died of thirst in the baking summer heat?

I could feel a nasty surge of panic bubbling up inside my chest, like rapidly boiling water. Then all of a sudden – *click!* The lock fell open. I couldn't believe it. Were my ears playing tricks on me? Cautiously I felt around, tugging at the lock, sliding back the bolt, pushing at the gate. When the hinges squealed, I knew that I wasn't mistaken.

I'd done it. I was free.

The trouble was, I now faced another problem. What should I do about Sergio? It crossed my mind (very briefly) that I could make a dash for it and leave him to fend for himself. But I dismissed this thought almost at once. It wasn't only mean, it was impractical. Why run off and leave Sergio with the water? More to the point, why run off and leave him with the mattress? Because we were going to need the mattress. I realised that as soon as I took a step through the gate and felt something hard and sharp prick at my bare heel.

'Hey! Sergio!' I rasped, trying to call his name without making too much noise. I'd been hoping that he might be on his way back, but he wasn't. No one replied. So I pocketed the shim and retraced my steps until I was standing in front of the hatchway again, shoulders hunched, peering into a long dark hole.

'Hey! Sergio!' I repeated, even more softly. Still nothing. To say I was nervous is an understatement. The *last* thing I wanted to do was to climb into that tunnel again. As I tried to stoke up my courage, however, I became aware of a scraping, shuffling sound. And I held my breath to listen.

It wasn't the sort of commotion made by two people fighting.

Straining my ears, I decided that someone was dragging something down the tunnel towards me. Was it Sergio dragging the mattress? Or was it an armed gaoler dragging Sergio? In case the news was bad, I stationed myself to one side of the gaping hatch, with my back pressed against the tiles.

I had picked up the chain, which Sergio had discarded at the pool's edge; with a length of swinging metal in my hand I felt more secure, though the pounding of my heart was so loud that it deafened me to the noises in the tunnel. I couldn't hear much – and I couldn't see much, either. Only when a hushed voice said 'Toby?' did I realise that I was safe.

'Sergio?' I croaked.

There was an extended pause. Then Sergio whispered, 'Where are you?'

'Here.' I swung around to face the hatchway, beyond which I could just make out some vague, glimmering, pale patches that moved as I spoke. 'Here I am.'

'Why?' Sergio asked breathlessly, out of the darkness. 'What's wrong?'

'Nothing. I've picked the lock.'

'Oh, *man*.' For some reason, he seemed cross rather than overjoyed. 'You mean I didn't have to do this after all?'

'Don't worry. We need this mattress,' I assured him. 'We won't be getting far without it.' And as I helped him to bundle the mattress into the pool, I quietly explained how we could put together some makeshift shoes out of foam rubber and ticking. 'I just hope my shim is sharp enough,' I added, gingerly pressing my thumb against the jagged piece of metal.

It was certainly sharp enough to poke a hole through the ticking, which Sergio then tore into strips with his bare hands. But by the time he'd finished, I was still sawing away grimly at the foam – which was very hard to cut and almost impossible to tear. When at last I managed to detach a large, uneven chunk from the main body of the mattress, we decided to abandon the shim and slice our foam fragment into smaller pieces using razor wire. At least, *I* decided to use razor wire. Sergio wanted to abandon the whole project, until I pointed out that there might be snakes out in the desert.

I guess he must have been scared of snakes, because he suddenly became very keen on my idea. Instead of grumbling about the delay, he began to help me carve up our piece of foam. Within minutes we each had two thick chunks of the stuff, which we bound to our feet with several layers of ticking. The result was ... well, let's just say it wasn't ideal.

'They're not exactly Nikes,' I muttered, 'but they'll have to do.'

I suppose they were better than nothing, though after about ten minutes spent hobbling over rough ground, I was beginning to wonder how much more we could take. Have you ever gone on a cross-country walk wearing bits of mattress tied to your feet? Take my advice: don't. It's very, *very* uncomfortable. In fact it was so uncomfortable that it distracted me from the looming horror of our situation. There we were, stumbling through the darkness in the middle of nowhere, with no shoes, no map, no compass, only half a bottle of water, and not the slightest notion of how to reach the nearest settlement. The one thing we *did* know was that we should steer well clear of the house near the pool. We both agreed that our first goal should be to put as much distance as possible between ourselves and the light in the window.

Then, after about fifteen minutes, it suddenly occurred to me: what if the house was on a road?

'There must be some way to reach that place by car,' I said with a cough. When Sergio didn't reply, I pressed him more urgently. 'If we walk around the house in a big, wide circle, we might find a track. It'd be better than wandering off like this.'

Sergio, however, didn't agree.

'No,' he said.

'But—'

'Keep your voice down.'

'Okay.' I adjusted my volume. 'But people die in the outback, Sergio. Especially in summer.'

'We should keep off the roads,' was Sergio's stubborn response. 'Otherwise they'll see us.'

'Not necessarily.' I knew that he was referring to Gary and Lincoln. 'Not if we're careful—'

'It's the first place they'll look!' he interrupted. 'They'll jump in their car and hit the road! It's where they'll *expect* to find us!'

He had a point. 'Yeah, but we'll hear 'em coming a mile off, won't we?' I said. 'And we can take cover before they're anywhere near us.'

'Take cover? Behind what?' He waved an arm. 'There aren't any trees! There's nothing!'

'There are bushes. And ditches.'

'You're crazy!'

I stopped in my tracks. 'Listen,' I begged, trying to reason with him, 'there are things we can do. We can roll around in the dust to camouflage ourselves. We can stay off the road, as long we keep it in sight.' I could understand why he was terrified of running into Gary again, but when he kept on walking, I grabbed his arm. 'Someone else might come along!' I argued.

'We might be able to hitchhike! Wouldn't that be better than dying of heatstroke on a salt pan somewhere?'

'Let go.'

'Will you listen to me?'

'No.'

'Don't be such a wuss!' I said – and instantly regretted it. He batted me off with a shove, his teeth snapping.

'*Get off!*'

'Sorry . . .' I fell back, thoroughly intimidated.

'Don't *touch* me!'

'I won't. Okay? It's all right.' The words had barely left my mouth when I heard a faint buzz, which made us both fall silent and listen hard. Within seconds, the buzz had grown louder. It became more of a whine.

If I hadn't been so shaken up, I probably would have recognised it sooner.

'That's a car,' I squeaked. Sergio's head began to snap back and forth wildly.

'Where – where . . . ?' he stammered.

'I dunno.'

I couldn't see any headlights. The engine's low growl was very misleading; I'd think at first that it was coming from one direction, before changing my mind, then changing it again.

'It's heading for the house!' Sergio yelped, ducking down onto his haunches.

I followed suit. 'You reckon?'

'Maybe they were out. Maybe that's why they didn't hear us.'

'Unless it isn't them in that car,' I said. And after a minute or two of intense concentration, I added, 'That isn't the same car.'

'What?'

'That's not the car they were driving in Sydney.' I focused on the throaty roar as it grew louder and louder. 'I don't even think it is a car. I think it's some sort of truck.'

As I straightened my knees and raised my head, Sergio pulled me back down again with a jerk – but not before I'd glimpsed the approaching vehicle. It was closer than I'd expected. In fact, as I cowered behind a low, prickly shrub, I heard the crunch of gravel and the squeal of brakes.

Oh my God, I thought. *It's stopped.*

There was no mistaking the rattle-and-throb of an idling engine. I held my breath. Sergio clutched my arm. We both waited, paralysed.

Then the engine died. A door slammed. I recognised the grinding squeal of a tailgate being lowered. But it was the snuffling that really scared me – that and the clicking of toenails on metal. I could smell dogs.

'They saw you,' Sergio breathed into my ear.

'Shh!'

He began to grope about for a rock. I didn't know what to do. Use my chain? Make a run for it? So far, I could only hear one set of footsteps.

'Hey. Toby. Is that you?' somebody said.

My heart skipped a beat.

'I can smell you, okay?' The voice was a rough-edged drawl, too low to be Gary's and too Australian to be Lincoln's. 'Reuben sent me. I'm Danny Ruiz.'

Danny Ruiz? *That* rang a bell. Reuben and Sanford had both mentioned Danny Ruiz. Danny was the one from the desert. The damaged one.

The menace.

207

'You gunna come out? Or will I send me dogs in after ya?' he growled. Then there was a ratcheting noise that I recognised instantly as a rifle-bolt being drawn – don't ask me how. (Television, maybe? I'd never laid eyes on a *real* rifle.) 'Whyn't you say something?' he demanded. 'Hey! Is that Toby or not?'

Beside me, Sergio suddenly moved. He exploded into the air like shrapnel from a landmine. '*Yaagh!*' he screamed, hurling something heavy. It hit solid metal with a ringing *clang!* A dog yipped. Danny swore. Sergio bolted.

Even now, I'm not sure exactly what happened. It was dark and I was confused. Somebody whistled. There seemed to be dogs everywhere. As I sprang to my feet, four of them bounded past me, two on each side. Then a dark shape loomed up and shoved a long, metal tube under my nose.

I froze as I realised that the tube was the barrel of a gun, gleaming dully in the moonlight.

'You *are* just a kid,' said Danny, from the other end of the gun. 'I thought so.' Raising his voice, he added, 'Move a muscle and they'll go for ya! I swear to God!'

That was when I became conscious of the low rumble behind me. It made the hairs rise on the back of my neck. Glancing around, I saw that Sergio had been surrounded by snarling dogs – four tense silhouettes with raised hackles and glinting teeth.

I lifted both hands, dropping my chain.

'So which one's Toby?' Danny asked. I had to clear my throat before answering.

'M-me,' I stuttered.

'And who's that?' The gun jerked slightly, indicating Sergio.

'That's – um – that's...' My mind was a blank. I couldn't think. I was shaking and sweating, and I felt nauseous.

Maybe Danny sensed this, because all at once he lowered his gun.

'Listen,' he said, 'I'm on your side. I came to get yiz out. I never figured you woulda done it on your own.' He gave a harsh chuckle, which sounded like two pieces of sandpaper rubbing together. I couldn't see much of his face in the shadows, but his outline was tall and lanky, and his wispy hair seemed to be worn quite long. 'How in the hell didja pull it off?' he asked. Then, in a chatty tone, he added, 'I went for the jugular, meself. Got shot a few times, but I kept on going. Bulled me way out.'

Sergio gasped. He'd been standing like a statue, with one knee up and one arm bent, staring at the dogs. But now he turned his head to look at Danny. 'You mean – you mean you were locked down there? In a tank? Like us?' he quavered.

Danny gave a snort.

'Too bloody right I was! Didn't you work that out already?' He shouldered his rifle, as if to demonstrate that we were all allies. 'I'm a werewolf. Just like you,' he said. 'And I'm here to make those bastards suffer.'

Chapter Eighteen

Wait a second.' My voice was hoarse and my hands were still up. 'How – how did you know I was here?'

'I just told you, didn't I?' Danny growled. 'Reuben Schneider called me.'

'Yeah, but how did *he* know?' *Unless,* I thought, *he was in on this deal.* 'Who would have told him?'

Danny shrugged. He didn't seem interested. 'Reuben called me – I dunno – round four hours ago?' he replied. 'Said some blokes were back at Wolgaroo, running fights again. Said they'd probably snatched a frienda his, called Toby.' Peering at Sergio, he added, 'Didn't mention this guy. What's your name?'

'S-Sergio.'

Danny grunted. Then he clicked his tongue at the dogs, calling them to heel. They immediately abandoned their posts, slinking back towards their master.

Sergio heaved a long, quivering sigh as he adopted a more comfortable position, with both feet planted firmly on the ground.

'You can drop your hands,' Danny informed me. 'I'm not gunna shoot ya.' The next instant, however, he unslung his rifle in a threatening kind of way – not exactly aiming it, but making sure that everyone knew it was there. 'Where'dja think *you're* going?' he barked at Sergio, who was heading for Danny's vehicle.

Sergio halted. 'I thought – aren't you taking us away?' he shrilled.

'Not yet,' said Danny. 'Not until I deal with the bastards who brought yiz here.' Then he turned back to me, still cradling his gun. 'So how did yiz both get out, exactly? Gimme a blow-by-blow.'

I licked my lips and lowered my hands. Though I didn't trust him, there was no way on earth I could avoid giving him some kind of explanation. Not while he was armed with a bolt-action rifle. 'I squeezed through the bars,' was what I finally told him, keeping one eye firmly on the dogs.

'Y'mean the bars in the gate?' he queried. 'The gate to the tunnel?'

'That's right.' He obviously knew his stuff; I could tell that he was familiar with the underground tanks. But I didn't find this reassuring.

On the contrary.

'And then what?' he asked.

'Then I picked the lock on Sergio's gate.'

'Oh yeah?' Danny sounded surprised. 'How'd you manage that?'

'With a shim,' I mumbled. 'That I made out of a beer can.'

Though I can't be absolutely sure, I think Danny might have cracked a smile at this. But all he said was, 'And then what?'

'Then we took a big steel drum, and I stood on that, and Sergio stood on me. So he could climb out of the pool.' As I went on to describe the ladder, and the tripwire, and the padlock, the barrel of Danny's gun slowly sagged towards the

211

ground. He seemed to be concentrating fiercely. At last, when I'd finished, he said, 'How many are there? D'you know?'

I was stumped. 'What do you mean?'

'I mean, who's in the house? How many people?' When I didn't answer, Danny swung around to address Sergio. 'What about you? Do *you* know?'

'We don't even know if anyone's there at all,' Sergio rejoined sullenly. 'We thought your truck might be them, coming back.'

'Okay.' Danny pondered for a moment. 'So how many *have* you seen? Since you got here?'

'Two. No – three.' When Sergio corrected himself, I stared at him in astonishment. There were three kidnappers? He'd never mentioned that. 'I only saw one of 'em once,' he admitted. 'Not long ago. Maybe yesterday or the day before . . . it's hard to tell the time, down there . . .' He trailed off, his head drooping.

'Mmmph.' Danny nodded. Then he swivelled around to study the small square of light in the distance. 'How many cars are parked outside?' he asked.

Sergio and I stared at each other. We waited. Neither of us, however, could provide that information. 'We didn't notice,' I said at last.

'Okay. So how many guns've they got?' was Danny's next inquiry. I was startled when Sergio spoke up.

'One each,' he said, after a short bout of mental arithmetic. Then he amended this total. 'No. Hang on. The third guy was carrying Lincoln's gun. I remember that.'

'Which is?'

'A shotgun. Ten-gauge.' Sergio seemed to be warming to the subject. 'The other one's a handgun. A Glock. Gary told me.'

'Gary *told* you?' I echoed. And Sergio stiffened before muttering, 'Yeah. When he stuck it in my face and said he'd blow me away with it. *That's* when he told me.' After a long, drawn-out silence, he added, through clenched teeth, 'I wanna do the same to him. And then I wanna pull the trigger.'

My jaw dropped. I caught my breath. But Danny was completely unfazed.

'Yeah. I hear ya,' he remarked carelessly. 'But we gotta catch 'em first.' Having shouldered his rifle again, he checked the illuminated dial on his watch. 'It's half past two,' he went on. 'They might not check on yiz both until breakfast, if we're lucky. Which'll give us a bit of time to get in there. Set up an ambush.'

He's crazy, I decided. Reuben's warning popped into my head: *Danny's really messed up . . . he's a full-on menace . . .*

What's more, he still hadn't satisfied my curiosity. Okay; so he'd heard about me from Reuben. But how had Reuben found out where I was, if he didn't know Gary or Lincoln? What if this was all some elaborate plot, to get Sergio and me back in our cages without shooting us?

'Nuh-uh,' I announced. 'Not me. I'm not going back in there. I wanna go home.'

Danny regarded me for a moment. I heard him sniff. 'Don't worry,' he said, in faintly scornful accents. 'You'll be safe with old Danny around.'

But he was missing the point.

'So what?' I countered. 'Who cares? I just wanna go home.' Anticipating a sharp response, I quickly went on the offensive. 'Aren't you here to take us home? Isn't that why Reuben sent you?' I demanded.

213

'What – home to Sydney?' Danny gave a snort. 'No bloody way. Reuben can do that.'

'Huh?'

'Reuben can do that,' Danny repeated. 'He's driving up from Sydney now. Should be about...I dunno...four hours? Five?'

'*Five hours?*' Sergio butted in. 'Where *are* we?'

'Outside of Cobar. Near Broken Hill.' If Danny expected some kind of reaction, he was doomed to disappointment. I'd never heard of Cobar. *Or* Broken Hill. Neither had Sergio, by the look of it. He scratched his head.

'So we're in the outback?' he wanted to know.

'Miles from anywhere,' Danny confirmed. 'That's why I can't leave. Not yet. Or they'll scoot off before I can bag 'em.'

He seemed to realise that I was the one who needed persuading, because all at once he yanked me towards him. Up close, despite the poor light, I could just make out that he was missing some teeth, and that a scar was dragging down the corner of his left eye.

There were other scars, too. All over his face.

'See, if those bastards are in there, and they find out you're gone, they won't hang around. They'll fly the coop. Just like that.' He snapped his fingers. 'And we'll lose 'em for good, because it's not like they'll leave a forwarding address.' When I still didn't comment, he scowled at me. 'You want that to happen?' he chided. 'You want 'em to kidnap some other poor kid?'

I recoiled from his bad breath, which smelled of sour milk and fried onions.

214

'They won't get away with it,' I insisted. 'The police will track them down.'

'The *police*?' spluttered Danny. And Sergio exclaimed, 'They *are* police, you moron!'

'No, they're not,' I said.

'Yes, they are!'

'Sergio, they were just pretending. So they could get us into their car.'

'How do *you* know?'

I didn't, of course. I just had a hunch. Danny hawked and spat.

'Forget the police,' he declared. 'I got no dealings with the police. Not *ever*.'

Oh great, I thought. And aloud I said, 'There's no way the police won't get involved. My mum would have called 'em already. She'll be frantic.' The thought of how Mum must be feeling brought tears to my eyes. I was so homesick, all of a sudden, that I wanted to curl up and bawl like a baby. That's probably why I got mad instead. 'I need to phone Mum right now!' I snapped. '*I need to tell her I'm safe!*'

'Fine. You do that,' said Danny. Then he jerked his thumb at the house. 'But you'll have to use their phone, since I don't have a mobile.'

He obviously felt that he had said something funny, because he cracked a grin so wide that I could actually see it in the dimness. As for me, I wasn't amused. Not only that – I wasn't convinced.

'You don't have a *mobile phone*?' I asked, in disbelief. 'You drive around in the outback and you don't have a mobile with you?'

Danny shrugged. 'No coverage,' he replied, before abruptly

changing tack. 'See, all I'm gunna do is, I'm gunna make sure those bastards stay put until Reuben arrives,' he explained. 'Then we can take it from there. Okay? Figure out what the hell we should do. Sounds good to me.'

I was about to object when he suddenly turned on his heel and headed for the back of his ute. Though I couldn't see exactly what he was doing, all the clinks and clunks and rattles told me that he was searching through a metal locker or toolbox.

The dogs appeared to be even more confused than I was. They certainly stared after him in a lost kind of way. But they cheered up when he called to them.

'Come by!' he yipped, then muttered 'Gotcha!' as he stuffed something long and thin under his arm. *Clang* went the lid of a toolbox.

'Don't satellite phones work out here?' I asked, in the belief that Danny and I were still having a conversation. But he didn't answer. He simply walked on by, moving towards the house – and for a moment I didn't understand. What was he doing? Where was he going?

The dogs surged after him, silently obedient. That was when I realised: he didn't intend to hang around any longer. He was off to do some damage instead.

A pair of boltcutters was dangling from his right hand.

'Wait!' I cried. 'What about us?'

'I'm going with *him*,' Sergio decided. And he began to follow Danny.

'But what about the ute?' I said feebly. 'Aren't you gunna drive?'

'Oh sure.' Danny's sarcastic retort floated back to me over his shoulder, like a whiff of stale air. 'I'll drive right up to the front door with me headlights on, just to give 'em some warning.' He uttered a honk of laughter. 'Maybe I'll ask 'em if they wanna be chained to the floor, as well.'

I stood watching as he marched away, his rifle on his back and his raincoat flapping open. Moonlight glinted off the top of his balding scalp. His big heavy boots thudded and crunched over the parched ground, while his dogs padded along beside them. Sergio, I thought, looked a bit like one of the dogs; he was scurrying behind Danny with his head down.

I suppose I could pretend that I followed them both because I wanted to call Mum, or because I was keen to stop anything really bad from happening. But it wouldn't be true. The fact is, I couldn't bear the thought of being stuck out in the middle of nowhere all on my own. As Danny's dark silhouette receded further and further into the shadowy distance, I became more and more uneasy. Don't ask me why. It wasn't as if the guy was going to protect me, since he was obviously trouble on steroids. Maybe I had a pack mentality, back then. Maybe I was programmed to follow the alpha dog.

Not anymore, though. Boy, have I learned my lesson. These days, believe me, I would stay with the truck. You know that old saying, 'safety in numbers'? Well, it's not always true. Sometimes the more people there are, the more dangerous it gets.

Anyway, I followed Danny and Sergio back to the pool, even though I was almost screaming with anxiety and frustration. Danny didn't say anything about my change of heart. He was too busy formulating a plan of attack.

'What we *don't* want is a shootout,' he declared. 'But we'll get one if we storm the front door, or try to crawl through a window. We're outgunned, so we gotta be careful. We gotta take 'em by surprise and sneak in through the tanks.' When

I pointed out that the house couldn't be reached from the tanks, because both interconnecting doors were still locked, Danny waved my protest aside. 'We'll fix that,' he promised. 'Don't worry.'

Then he insisted that each of us carry one dog down the ladder into the pool, while his fourth dog remained up top, on guard. It was a stupid idea. All of the dogs were big and mean and heavy – American Staffordshire terriers, for the most part – and they didn't want to be picked up. They certainly didn't want to be picked up by *me*. In the end, I dismantled my homemade shoes and tied the strips of mattress ticking through the holes in Danny's coat, transforming it into a kind of sling that we used to lower the dogs down, one by one. Danny and Sergio did the lowering, while I supported the dogs from underneath.

Afterwards, when Danny descended the ladder to join his dogs, he told me to retrieve Sergio's mutilated mattress. 'That has to go back where it came from,' he insisted, 'or things won't look normal.' He went on to emphasise that, unless everything looked absolutely normal, the ambush wouldn't work.

So that's how I ended up in charge of Sergio's mattress. I had to lug it through the tunnel, manoeuvre it into his cell, and heave it back onto his iron bedstead. Sergio was supposed to help me, but he was shaking too hard to be of much use; the smell of the tanks made him hyperventilate. The only thing he *could* do was crawl into bed and pull the covers over him, so that the mangled bit of mattress wasn't visible.

'Just lie there and pretend to be asleep,' Danny instructed, very quietly. 'I'll be back in a tick.' He himself was carrying the steel drum, which he'd shouldered back at the pool; his free hand was still wrapped around the boltcutters. In the penetrating light from the overhead bulb, he looked scarier than ever. His nose was so crooked, it was probably broken. His jagged teeth were brown, where they weren't completely gone. His eyes were the same lifeless grey as his straggly hair, which barely concealed all the dents and scars on his scalp. As for the rest of his scars, they were savage. I've already mentioned the scar that was dragging down one eyelid. There was another bisecting his chin, and a hole in his left cheek. It was also pretty obvious that something had been chewing on his Adam's apple, because a huge chunk of his neck was missing.

I guess I can't blame Sergio for getting the shakes. I nearly freaked out myself, when I first saw Danny in the fully illuminated flesh. *No wonder he lives on his own*, I thought, as he shoved the boltcutters into my hands.

'Hold these,' he barked.

'Where are you going?' Sergio squeaked from the bed. 'Don't leave me!'

'Calm down. Psycho's gunna stay,' said Danny, though not with the air of someone trying to offer comfort. It was more of a command. Then he told one of his dogs to lie under the bed, disregarding Sergio's protests. My orders were to shut Sergio's gate behind me and make sure the padlock looked as if it was closed up tight.

Next thing I knew, Danny was dragging me towards the cell I'd already abandoned.

'What we need to do,' he remarked, 'is lull those bastards into a false sense of security. We need 'em to come in before they know what the score is. They can't get suspicious.' He let me go upon reaching my cell, which looked completely undisturbed. The light was still on. The gate was still locked.

The water bottle hadn't been moved. 'This hasn't bloody changed,' he announced, as if reading my mind. 'I don't think they've even washed the sheets since I was here last.'

I stood and waited while he positioned his drum beneath the padlock, mutely handing him the boltcutters when he asked for them. I couldn't quite see why he wanted me there. After he'd climbed up onto the drum – without assistance – it didn't take him long to snip through the lock. And it wasn't as if his dogs needed watching; the two that had followed us sat rigidly by my side, panting a little, their gazes riveted to Danny's every move. He didn't even hand me the boltcutters when he jumped down again; instead he took them into my cell and hid them under the bed.

Only when he asked me to restore the drum to its proper place did I finally make a genuine contribution. 'I want it exactly where yiz left it,' he warned. 'Everything's gotta look the same. That's why I shut the gate back there. Understand?'

I understood, all right. I wasn't stupid. I also understood why he made the two dogs – Tagger and Mutt – crawl into my bed, under the covers. From a distance, their combined bulk was very misleading. 'When our friend comes down to give yiz a bite to eat, all he'll see is a lump,' Danny said. 'With any luck, he'll think it's you. I'll hide behind the door and surprise him. And if it's a standoff for some reason, the dogs'll go for this throat.'

It seemed like a workable (thought slightly bloodcurdling) plan, thanks to the cell's layout. But I could see a possible complication. 'What if he checks on Sergio before he comes in here?' I asked.

'He won't.' Danny sounded absolutely confident. 'Sergio's not the one with a Rohypnol hangover.' As I absorbed this chilling comment (*Rohypnol? Is that what they used on me?*), Danny went on to say, 'And if I'm wrong, it's no big deal. Psycho's hiding under the bed in there, so no one'll see *him*. Chances are this guy'll just dump Sergio's breakfast before coming straight over here.'

'What if they *both* come down, though? Gary and Lincoln? What if one comes in here and the other goes in there?'

Danny shrugged. 'I can handle two,' he promised. 'With three dogs, it won't be too hard. Not as long as you get the guns off 'em quick enough.'

'*Me?*'

'That's what you're here for, mate.' Danny fixed me with a hard, cold, speculative look. 'When the first one drops his weapon, I want yiz on it like a dog on a rat. Before the next one arrives.'

'But I've never even *fired* a gun!'

'It's easy. I'll show ya.'

'But—'

'Feel that. Feel the weight. Not too heavy, is it? You can handle that, no problem.'

I can't count how many times I've been warned about guns. My mother once showed me a picture of a patient who'd tried to shoot himself in the mouth. 'That,' she cautioned, 'is the kind of damage a firearm can inflict. Guns aren't fun, Toby. They're *made to kill people.*' I think she was worried that Fergus might acquire a gun from someone (his brother, perhaps) and do something hair-raising with it. And I can understand why she was so scared, because if Fergus ever *did* get hold of a gun, there'd be hell to pay. No question.

But the thing is, he's never even laid eyes on a gun. Maybe guns are more common in the countryside, and maybe there are drug dealers around Sydney who keep guns squirreled away under their beds. In my neighbourhood, though, I've never met a kid who's ever handled a real, live gun. (And believe me, if they'd done it, they would have boasted about it.)

That's why it took my breath away when Danny suddenly dumped his rifle into my arms. It was solid and smooth, and still warm from Danny's touch. It had a wooden stock. And it was loaded. With *bullets*.

When I raised it to aim at the wall, I was almost tempted to pull the trigger.

'See?' Danny said. 'You got the hang of it already. You're a natural. Just make sure the safety's off, and you're all set.' Watching me adjust my grip on the thing, he declared, 'You'll be as safe as houses behind a cocked .22, as long as you know how to use it. And that goes for any other gun you might pick up.'

As an afterthought, Danny suggested that if I *did* pick up Lincoln's shotgun, I should probably swap it for the rifle. Because a shotgun, he said, needed careful handling.

'Anyway, whatever they bring down, just make sure you get ahold of it quick smart,' he finished, relieving me of his weapon. Without it, I felt strangely exposed. That might be why I joined him so promptly when he took up his position near the door.

'Do you think Sergio's gunna be okay?' I asked, keeping my voice down. Danny glanced at his watch and said, 'He'll be fine. Psycho's in there too.'

By this he probably meant that Sergio was being guarded. 'Yeah, but... what if he freaks out?' I pressed.

'Psycho never freaks out.'

'No, I mean Sergio. What if Sergio freaks out?'

'Not while Psycho's there,' he said quietly, as if Psycho was a trained counsellor. It really got up my nose. How could a dog be the answer to everything? Unless he was supposed to *scare* Sergio into a tranquil frame of mind.

'But what if it's *Psycho* who freaks him out?' I whispered, at which point Danny turned his pale, empty gaze on me.

'You wanna shut the hell up?' he rasped. 'Because those bastards could be down here any minute. And if they hear you talking, they're gunna wonder who you're talking to. And you know what'll happen then?'

I could only assume that he was asking a rhetorical question. But I answered it anyway. 'We won't take them by surprise?' I hazarded.

Danny shook his head. 'What'll happen then is, you won't live long enough to die in the pit,' he growled. 'Since I'll bloody well kill ya meself.'

And that was where the conversation ended.

Chapter Nineteen

We waited for nearly four hours.

At first I was frightened. Then the edge wore off my fear, until I was merely anxious. After that I became impatient, then bored, then insanely restless. It was like being stuck on a station platform, only worse. At least when your train is delayed you can read a newspaper, or make a call on your mobile. Sometimes you can even buy a snack from the nearest vending machine.

Down in the tanks, however, there were no phones, no newspapers, and no vending machines. There was a toilet, but no booth. When Mutt took a piss, he did it in a corner. When *I* took a piss (just once), I had to do it in front of Danny. Not that he paid any attention, thank God; he seemed to have slipped into a kind of trance, leaning against the wall with his eyes half shut. Occasionally he'd mutter under his breath. Occasionally he'd scratch himself, or shift his weight, or adjust his grip on the gun. But apart from that, he was like a hibernating bear. The only time he said a word was when Sergio appeared, at about five o'clock. Poor Sergio had fallen asleep for an hour or two – and upon waking up, had immediately panicked. 'I thought you must have left!' he whimpered, through the bars of the gate. 'I thought you'd gone off and left me here!' With his puffy eyes, heaving chest and trembling hands, he cut a pretty pathetic figure. Even *I* felt sorry for him. And I wasn't looking too good myself, right then.

Danny, however, was unmoved. 'Get back to bed,' he snarled, 'or I'll sic the bloody dogs on ya!' I don't think he was serious. For one thing, a dog attack would have made too much noise. But his tone was so menacing that Sergio scampered off without a word of protest.

About half an hour later, I heard a sharp *bang*.

Danny stiffened beside me. His knees cracked as he straightened up, pushing away from the wall. I followed his example. It felt as if I'd stopped breathing. The dogs squirmed slightly, but froze at the nearly inaudible hiss that Danny made by pushing air through his teeth.

Footsteps sounded on a wooden staircase outside the cell door. I could tell that it was a staircase because the feet were descending – and I could tell that the staircase was made of wood because of the way the treads squeaked. *Thump-squeak-thump-squeak.* There was a jingle that had to be keys, and a muttered curse from someone with an American accent.

Lincoln.

To say that I was terrified is an understatement. I was so tense that I was vibrating. Sweat poured off me, but my mouth was bone dry. Blood pounded into my head. *You can do it,* I kept telling myself. *You can do it you can do it you can do it.*

There was a funny little *snap*, which must have been the door's spy-hole cover flicking open (or shut). Then, unmistakably, came the squeal and clank of a bolt being pulled.

'I've got a gun here, kid, so don't try anything,' Lincoln announced. I nearly jumped out of my skin, but Danny didn't move. He was already in position, every muscle fully engaged.

I cut a quick glance at his clenched jaw and staring eyes, before the door suddenly swung towards us.

Lincoln was carrying a shotgun. That was the first thing I noticed, because its barrel entered the room ahead of him. He wasn't far behind, though; I saw the outline of his shoulder, a slice of cheekbone and the back of his ear. It was just a momentary glimpse before Danny's hulking form blocked my view.

'*Freeze!*' he rapped out.

God, but his voice was scary! It didn't sound human. Or maybe I'm mixing it up with the dogs' snarls, since everything happened so fast. The barrel of Danny's gun had only just made contact with Lincoln's shoulder blades when the dogs jumped up like a two-headed jack-in-the-box, all yellow fangs and mad, glaring eyes. As Lincoln recoiled, I lunged for his weapon.

'*Drop it!*' Danny snapped – even though he didn't need to. Shocked by the dogs, Lincoln had slackened his grip; I was able to whisk his shotgun away quite easily.

'Hands behind your head,' Danny growled, prodding Lincoln with the rifle. 'Kneel down. That's the way. Toby? Don't point that thing at me.'

'What? Oh. Sorry...'

'I want you to unload it,' Danny continued. Before I could open my mouth to protest, he added, 'The safety's already on. You just gotta press that little release button near the trigger guard. See that?'

'Yeah.'

'Now slide back the action bar until the first round pops outta the chamber...'

Though my hands were slippery with sweat, I managed to

remove three shells from both the chamber and magazine tube of Lincoln's shotgun. Meanwhile, Lincoln himself remained silent and motionless. He didn't even turn his head.

I had a nasty feeling that he was biding his time.

'Okay,' said Danny, pocketing the shells – which were so huge they looked like coin-rolls wrapped in brown paper. 'See those keys?'

I saw them all right. They were hanging from a clip on Lincoln's belt, which was holding up a pair of neatly ironed trousers. He was still dressed like a policeman, in a white shirt, striped tie and shiny shoes. His haircut was immaculate and he smelled strongly of aftershave. Only his drooping jowls looked untidy.

'I want you to get those keys and unlock the other door,' Danny instructed, talking to me without taking his eyes off Lincoln. 'Then come straight back here with your mate. Don't be too noisy, all right? And don't forget that shotgun. If anything happens, you can pretend it's still loaded.'

If anything happens. It took me a while to figure out what he meant by this. At first I was too busy unhooking the keys from Lincoln's belt – a manoeuvre that seemed risky enough, since Lincoln could easily have grabbed me in a headlock if I'd leaned in too close. But once I had the keys, I realised that step number two was even more dangerous. Beyond the cell door, I could see a brick-lined stairwell containing several other doors and the flight of wooden stairs. There was no way of telling what might lie in wait behind those doors, or at the top of those stairs.

Basically, Danny was asking me to walk into a possible ambush with nothing but an unloaded gun as protection.

I guess I wouldn't have done it if I hadn't been so scared of him. By that time, I knew, Danny was on a knife edge. I could smell it, somehow. I could hear it in his voice as he pressed the barrel of his gun into Lincoln's back, pushing Lincoln further and further towards the ground.

'Who else is up there?' Danny rumbled. Then, when he received no answer, he gave Lincoln a kick. *'Who else is up there, you scumbag?'*

Lincoln gasped. I got out. I didn't want to see Danny beat up an unarmed man, no matter how big a scumbag that man might be.

So I charged into the stairwell and made straight for the nearest door.

'Sergio?' I muttered. 'Where are you?'

'Toby?'

He must have been standing right there, behind the door I'd chosen; when I flicked open the spy-hole, his bloodshot eyes nearly gave me a heart attack.

'Hang on,' I croaked, tucking the shotgun under my arm. 'Let me just find the key . . .'

'Hurry! Quick!'

The bolt on his cell door was padlocked – and there were an awful lot of padlock keys hanging from Lincoln's key ring. I had to try at least three before I found the right one. Meanwhile, Sergio was whimpering, Psycho was snuffling, and floorboards were creaking rhythmically overhead.

'D'you hear that?' asked Sergio, in a strangled whisper. 'Someone's upstairs!'

'I know.'

'You've gotta hurry!'

'I know, I know.'

Luckily my fourth key turned in the lock, or I think he would

228

have tried to crawl through the spy-hole. As it was, he nearly knocked me over when he burst out of his cell and made a grab for Lincoln's shotgun.

'Gimme that!' he said with a gasp.

'No—'

'*Let go!*'

'It's not even loaded!' I hissed. But he'd already yanked the thing off me. As he headed towards my cell, Psycho and I were right behind him. The instant we crossed the threshold, however, Sergio broke away. He suddenly darted forward, waving the shotgun like a club.

If it hadn't been for my quick reflexes, I don't know *what* would have happened to Lincoln. He was lying on his stomach at the far end of the room, with both hands clasped behind his head and one leg manacled to the floor. So there was nothing he could have done to defend himself if Sergio had started pounding a gun-butt into his ribs.

I guess you could say that I was Lincoln's guardian angel. When Sergio swung the shotgun, I caught it before it could hit anything. And I hung off it grimly, even though Sergio aimed a few kicks at my ankles.

'Let go!' he exclaimed, tugging and twisting. Don't ask me why I held on. It wasn't as if Lincoln would have done the same for me. Maybe it's just that I had a bad feeling. Only later did it cross my mind that if Sergio had ended up leaving bits of Lincoln's brain all over the wall, I would have become an accessory to murder.

'Shh!' said Danny. 'Shut up!' He was so angry, he even trained his rifle in our direction. But it was too late.

From somewhere off in the distance, high above us, a muffled voice cried, '*Link? What's up?*'

Everyone froze. Even Sergio stopped moving. For a split second there was absolute silence.

Then Danny broke the spell.

'Say one single word, and my dogs'll rip your throat out,' he spat. I thought that he was talking to me, until I realised that he was actually addressing Lincoln – who by now was being guarded by Tagger and Mutt. They were stationed on either side of Lincoln's head, so close that he must have been able to smell them.

'Get behind that door,' Danny told me. 'Don't come out unless I call ya.'

He ducked into the stairwell, with Psycho at his heels, as I cut a glance at Sergio. But I needn't have worried. Sergio had snapped out of his blind rage. He was shaking all over, so frightened that he could barely keep a grip on the shotgun.

Before he had a chance to drop the thing, I plucked it from his hand. Then I hustled him into the shadow cast by the open door.

From there, of course, I couldn't see anything much – except for Lincoln's motionless shape, which was flanked by Mutt and Tagger.

Mutt was drooling onto the floor.

'Oh God,' breathed Sergio. 'Oh God oh God oh God…'

'Shh.' I was trying to work out what I should do if Danny got shot. Run for the pool? Use the dogs? Set up an ambush?

'Lincoln?' It was Gary. 'What are you doing?'

I heard him hurrying downstairs – *thumpa-thumpa-thumpa.* Then all hell broke loose. There was a shriek and a yelp, followed by a quick cascade of crashes and cracks and thuds and grunts.

But no gunshots. Definitely no gunshots.

'Toby!' Danny roared. 'Get in here!'

And I went. Just like that. Without a second thought.

In the next room, I found a scene that stopped me in my tracks. Gary was sprawled at the bottom of the stairs in a tangle of bent limbs and blood-spotted clothing. Danny was near him, stooping to retrieve a pistol from the floor. Psycho was sniffing around Gary's outstretched hand, which was moving feebly.

'Bloody idiot just came rushing down,' said Danny, with obvious satisfaction. 'All I had to do was stick me gun between the treads and – *whoomp!* He tripped over it. Wasn't watching his feet, goddamn fool.'

'Is he . . . ?' I couldn't say it. But I didn't need to. Danny knew what I was talking about.

'He's fine,' Danny muttered. By now Sergio was right behind me, wielding Danny's boltcutters. There was such a nasty look in his eye that I moved instinctively to block his path, just in case he tried to stomp on Gary's head. Luckily, Danny stepped forward with the pistol.

'Here,' he said, thrusting it into Sergio's free hand. 'Hold this.'

Sergio was speechless. He gazed down at the little black gun, his expression a mixture of awe and delight.

I was speechless too, but not with delight.

'Gimme that.' Danny grabbed the shotgun, passing me his rifle instead. Then he fished around in his pocket for the shotgun shells. 'You can chain this guy to the floor,' he rasped. 'In Sergio's room. The keys'll be on that key ring.'

'But—'

He didn't let me finish. 'I'm gunna check the house,' he announced quietly, his gaze fixed on a patchwork of green cupboards and yellow ceiling that was visible at the top of the stairs. When he stepped over Gary, it was as if he were stepping over a discarded sweatshirt. 'Don't do anything stupid.'

'But, Danny—' I began.

'*Shhh!*'

I was worried about Sergio. I was *very* worried about Sergio. So I did the only thing I could; I whirled around to confront him before he even had a chance to aim his gun. 'If you shoot either of them,' I warned, 'then you're no better than they are.'

Sergio scowled. From close up, he looked pretty scary.

His pistol looked even scarier.

'You'll go to gaol,' I added, under my breath. 'You wanna get locked up for another ten years?'

That sure worked. It had some impact, at least – I could see it in his eyes. All of a sudden he was thinking like a human being instead of a werewolf.

'You owe me, Sergio. I got you out. You owe me big,' I continued. Then I adjusted my grip on the rifle. It wasn't a threat, exactly; it was just a reminder that I was also armed. 'Is that how you wanna pay me back?' I finished. 'By making me an accessory? Gee, thanks.'

Psycho had followed Danny up the stairs. I could hear the dog's toenails clicking away overhead, as the floor creaked under his master's weight.

Then Gary moaned. He was rolling his head around.

'Quick!' I whispered. 'We have to get him chained up before he comes to!'

'Yeah, but—'

'Come *on*, Sergio!'

Urgent action was all it took. By keeping Sergio busy, I stopped him from wreaking his revenge. He was so shocked and disoriented that he couldn't focus on more than one thing at a time.

'You take his feet,' I softly suggested, slinging the rifle over my shoulder. Sergio blinked. He glanced down at his pistol as I seized Gary under the armpits.

'Is the safety catch on?' I said, in a further attempt to distract and confuse. 'You'd better put it on before you stick that thing in your pants.'

'I – I dunno,' Sergio mumbled. 'Where's the safety catch?'

'Don't ask me.'

Gary moaned again. His eyelids fluttered.

'We probably shouldn't be moving him,' I remarked. Being so close to Gary made my skin crawl. 'He might have broken his back.'

'God, yes! Wouldn't *that* be good?' Sergio exclaimed, just a bit too loudly. Then he laid down the pistol and boltcutters, picking up Gary's ankles instead.

Grunting and heaving, I shuffled backwards through the door to Sergio's cell. For a small guy, Gary weighed an awful lot; I was gasping for breath by the time I reached the manacle and chain. As for Gary, he was groping around vaguely with one hand. When I let him slide to the floor, he said 'Ow!' and opened his bleary eyes.

'Quick! Put that thing on him!' I was fumbling with my rifle. Sergio let go of one leg, which landed on the concrete with a lifeless kind of *thump*. He then manacled Gary's other leg, locking it into a thick band of steel.

'What the hell . . . ?' Gary slurred. He gave me such a fright, I nearly dropped my gun.

'Shut up!' I yelped, waving it at him. 'Don't move!'

'Wha . . . ?'

'I'll get the other gun,' Sergio offered, before retreating into the stairwell. I backed right away from Gary, so that he couldn't make a grab for me. I still hadn't figured out where the safety catch was.

'For Chrissake!' Gary croaked. He'd obviously just realised what had happened. 'Jesus...'

'Shut up!'

'Oh Jesus.' He rattled his chain. The big red lump on his forehead was already turning purple. 'I don't believe it. I don't bloody believe it...'

'You'd *better* believe it!' Sergio spluttered. Framed in the doorway, pointing a black automatic, he frightened the life out of me. (God knows how Gary must have felt.)

'Turn over! Onto your stomach!' I told Gary, hoping that he would have the sense to obey. I wanted Sergio to think that ordering Gary around would be a lot more fun than shooting him.

But Gary didn't seem to hear.

'Oh no,' he quavered. Staring down the barrel of Sergio's gun, he began to shake uncontrollably, as white as salt beneath his dark stubble. 'Please... please don't...'

It was awful. Really awful. He thought that he was going to die.

'Not so funny now, is it?' Sergio barked, slowly advancing. 'Not such a big joke now, eh?'

'Sergio! Hey!' *Goddammit*, I thought, because he wasn't listening to me. 'Be cool, all right? Sergio!'

'Let's see *you* eat dirt on your knees!'

'Sergio!'

Click-click. He pulled the trigger. Twice. But nothing happened.

234

I nearly fainted.

'The safety's on, thickhead,' Danny drawled. He had appeared behind Sergio and was standing on the threshold, cradling his shotgun. 'Here. Give it to me.'

In a dazed sort of fashion, Sergio passed him the pistol. I felt like vomiting. Gary was making the most dreadful noises; he had his head down and his hands up.

Danny slipped the pistol into his pocket.

'I didn't tell you to shoot the bastard, did I?' he growled. 'Can't yiz understand plain English?' Upon receiving no answer from Sergio, he rounded on Gary. 'Shut the hell up, or I'll shoot you meself!' he snapped. Then he clicked his tongue at Psycho, who had slipped into the room like a cold breeze.

Obediently, the dog padded over to where Gary was cowering.

'Okay – see this dog? This dog is werewolf-trained,' Danny continued. He was still talking to Gary. 'If you move, he'll rip your throat out. If you say *one word*, he'll rip your throat out. Got that?'

Gary nodded.

'Good.' With a sniff, Danny turned back to Sergio. 'Now go and see if you can find any more padlocks.'

Sergio's jaw dropped. 'Huh?' he said.

'*Padlocks*,' Danny repeated testily. 'Don'tcha know what a padlock is?'

'Yeah, but—'

'I wanna lock both them gates. But I can't do it because I cut through the padlock on the gate next door.' As Sergio hesitated, Danny assured him, 'I've checked upstairs. The coast is clear. Now get up there and find me another padlock.'

To my surprise, Sergio did as he was told. He trudged from the room looking sullen but resigned, while Danny headed for the alternative exit.

They seemed to have forgotten my existence.

'Wait!' I cried. 'Hang on! Where are you going?'

'I'm gunna fetch poor Tyson,' Danny retorted. It took me a few seconds to work out that Tyson was the fourth dog – the one we'd left at the pool.

'But what about me?' I asked weakly. 'What should *I* do?'

'Stay right there,' he said. 'Just gimme the keys and I'll be back in a tick.'

Watching him march away down the tunnel, I had to swallow a sob. My head was in a whirl. I wanted to run after Danny and keep on running until I'd left the tanks and the house and everyone in them far behind. I couldn't believe what was happening to me. I couldn't believe that I was standing guard over a shackled prisoner, like some kind of Nazi.

In the silence, Psycho's throaty growl was clearly audible. So was the gurgle of Gary's ragged breathing. I knew that I should be watching him like a hawk, but I cringed at the prospect of catching his eye – just in case he made me feel even worse about being an armed guard. So I kept my own eyes fixed firmly on the darkness at the end of the tunnel, praying that Danny would return soon.

I was worried about what Lincoln might be doing in the tank next door. I was worried about what Sergio might be doing upstairs. What if he found another gun while he was searching for a padlock? What if he came charging down here with a crossbow or a cattle prod or some other exotic weapon? How would I deal with *that*?

Then suddenly, from the top of the staircase, his high-pitched voice reached my ears. And he didn't sound angry at all.

He sounded terrified.

'Toby! Quick! Come here!' he shouted. 'It's a car! I can hear it! *Someone's coming!*'

Chapter Twenty

There was a kitchen at the top of the stairs. I don't know why I found that surprising, but I did. Even more surprising, however, was the pale morning light creeping through the windows, which were hung with the ugliest curtains I'd ever seen.

According to the clock on the wall, it was nearly half past six.

'Listen!' Sergio was clutching the boltcutters. 'Can you hear that?'

I listened. Through the ticking of the clock and the hum of the refrigerator, I could just make out the low-pitched drone of an engine.

'Where's it coming from?' I said.

'How the hell should I know?'

When I crossed the floor, my feet peeled off the sticky lino – which was old and cracked and covered in grime (to match the cupboards). Spiderwebs fluttered from the ceiling. Dead flies littered every surface. The wallpaper was in shreds.

But *someone* had been using the kitchen; that much was obvious. Dirty dishes were strewn across the table and piled up around the sink. A plastic tidy bin was overflowing with beer cans. An electric fan whirred away in a corner.

Twitching aside one pineapple-print curtain, I peered out

at the desolate scene beyond. It was worse than I'd expected. Red dirt and blue-grey scrub stretched out to the horizon, relieved here and there by small, spindly trees that cast very long shadows. There was a lot of rubbish scattered close to the house, including rolls of chicken wire, rusty petrol drums, and weathered bones. (*God*, I thought, swallowing hard. *Let's hope those bones aren't human.*) On the other side of a dilapidated fence stood Lincoln's empty grey sedan, which was covered in dust and squashed insects. It didn't look so sleek anymore.

'They're closing in!' Sergio squeaked. He was right; the purring noise was growing louder. But I still couldn't see the car that was approaching us.

'Can you spot it?' I asked, because Sergio was at the other window. He shook his head.

'No.'

'It's out the front,' I decided, rushing through the nearest exit into a long, dingy passage. This passage led straight to the front door, past several rooms furnished with old mattresses and soiled sheets. I caught a glimpse of pill bottles, underpants, and a discarded shoulder holster, but no phones. There were no phones anywhere. There weren't even any phone jacks.

There was no glass in the front door, either. It was a solid slab of wood. To get a view of the driveway, I had to peer between the slats of a dusty, broken blind that hung in the living room.

I could feel Sergio's hot breath on my cheek.

'There!' he exclaimed, pointing over my shoulder. 'There it is!'

'Back off.' I could see the dust cloud hanging behind a distant vehicle. Both the vehicle and the cloud were moving along an unsealed road that passed the house. 'Is that a van?' I said. 'It looks like a van.'

'It is a van,' Sergio agreed. As the van slowed, he caught his breath. 'It's coming here!'

'Of course.'

'Oh my God!'

'Stop *shouting in my ear*, will you?'

The blue van had turned off the road. Passing between two whitewashed gateposts, it clunked over a cattle grid and crawled up the long driveway towards us.

'Shoot him when he gets out,' Sergio pleaded. I knew just how he felt. But I wasn't at all confident about discharging the rifle. I couldn't even be sure if the safety catch was off.

So I said, 'Calm down.'

'He might have a gun, Toby!'

'*Shut up!*'

To my surprise, the van stopped in front of the house instead of parking round the side, next to Lincoln's sedan. I couldn't have been more than fifteen metres away from the driver as he cut his engine. But he was just a murky shadow behind tinted glass.

'You can do it from here!' Sergio whispered, nudging me. Just then the driver's door popped open.

Sergio grabbed my gun.

'Stop it!' I hissed.

'Do it now! Through the window!'

'Are you crazy?'

'He's right there, look!'

I looked. And I gasped.

'That's Reuben,' I said.

'What?'

'I know that guy.' My shoulders slumped. My knees sagged. It felt as if something inside my chest had unravelled. 'He's a werewolf. He's the one that phoned Danny.'

'*Hey, Danny!*' Reuben called, surveying the house through wraparound sunglasses. He stood with his hands on his hips, chewing gum and frowning. Instead of his usual overalls, he was dressed in jeans and a grey singlet.

He didn't seem to be armed.

'How does he know it's safe?' I muttered. 'Who told him?'

Sergio didn't reply. He was too busy watching Reuben.

'*Danny?*' Reuben shouted. '*Are you there?*' When no one answered, he reached back into the truck and pulled out a big, heavy crowbar, before slamming the driver's door shut.

Then he crunched across the gravel in our direction.

'Wha-what's he doing?' Sergio stammered.

'He's coming inside.' It was time to make our presence known. There was no point skulking behind the venetian blind any longer.

As Reuben climbed the steps, I flung open the front door.

'Oh. Hi.' He stopped in his tracks.

'How did you know?' I asked.

'What?'

'How did you know the coast was clear? Who told you it was safe to come in?'

'Danny called. About ten minutes ago,' he said, his gaze sliding past me. 'This must be Sergio,' he added, removing his sunglasses. 'Hi, Sergio. I'm Reuben.'

I cut in before Sergio had the chance to respond.

'Whaddaya mean, Danny called you? How did Danny call you, when he doesn't even have a mobile phone?'

Reuben raised his eyebrows. 'Danny's got a satellite phone.

Ordinary mobiles don't work out here,' he explained, before turning to gesture at his van. 'I've got one too.'

Speechless with shock, I stared at him. I couldn't believe my ears. Reuben, however, was more interested in Sergio than he was in me. Fixing Sergio with a sombre look, he said, 'How long were you down in the tanks?'

'I dunno,' Sergio mumbled. 'A long time.'

'Danny's got a *phone*?' I interjected. 'Are you *kidding*?'

'It's the twentieth now. The twentieth of January,' Reuben told Sergio, ignoring me. Sergio's eyes immediately glazed over as he began to run some calculations.

'The *bastard!*' Boy, was I mad! If Danny had been there, I would have decked him. 'He wouldn't call my mother! He *lied* to me!'

'I've been down there ten months,' Sergio finally revealed. He was talking to Reuben. 'Ten months and seven days.'

'Yeah?' Reuben nodded slowly. 'I was down there for five years,' he went on, 'so I know how you feel.'

He grabbed my arm when I tried to brush past him. 'Where are *you* going?'

'To get your phone.' I couldn't shake him off, no matter how fiercely I tugged and twisted. He was a very strong guy. 'I need to call my mum.'

'Wait,' he said.

'But—'

'In a minute. When we've worked things out.' Before I could protest, he jerked the rifle away from me. 'Where's Danny?'

'He went to get his dog,' Sergio replied.

'Is that *his* truck, over there?' asked Reuben, squinting off to his left. Turning, I saw that Danny's motionless truck was now clearly visible in the distance.

So was the figure striding towards it.

'That's Danny,' I said. He was carrying the shotgun, and a black dog was bounding along behind him. 'Is he leaving?'

'Hell, no. He must be bringing the ute back here,' Reuben deduced, then scowled. 'So who's on guard duty?'

'The dogs,' Sergio and I both chorused.

'The *dogs*?'

'And we chained those guys to the floor,' I added. 'Both of 'em.'

'There are two?'

'Yeah,' I said.

'But there might be another one,' Sergio piped up. 'I saw another one a few days ago, only he's not here now.'

'Right.' Reuben shouldered the rifle. When he took a deep breath, bracing himself, I realised that he didn't want to enter the house. Perhaps it held too many bad memories. 'So they're down in the tanks?' he asked.

'Uh-huh.' I nodded. As he marched through the front door and down the hallway, I suddenly remembered the question that had been bugging me since I'd first woken up. 'Hang on. Wait,' I said, scampering after him. 'How did you find out I was here? Who told you?'

'No one told *me*,' he rejoined. 'But I know the guys who own this place. The McKinnons. And someone told *them*.' Hesitating on the kitchen threshold, Reuben pocketed his sunglasses. Then he proceeded towards the stairs. 'The McKinnons used to get tips about werewolf activity from a dogger. I told you about him, back at Sanford's place. Well, last night this dogger called up outta the blue. Said he'd been talking to some other dogger in Broken Hill, who musta been talking to your third guy. The Third Man. The one who's not here.'

'But—'

'Apparently, the Third Man was babysitting Sergio while his mates were in Sydney, tracking *you* down. And the babysitter boasted about it in a pub somewhere. Told his dogger friend that there was gunna be some kinda fight pretty soon. Dumb jerk.' Reuben stared down into the basement. Then he discarded his crowbar and unslung his rifle. 'So Dogger Number One heard about all this from Dogger Number Two,' he went on in a distracted tone, 'and called the McKinnons just to make sure they knew what was happening on their property. Which they didn't, of course. Christ, I can't stand the smell around here. Makes me sick.'

'So the owners told you? About the men in this house?' I demanded.

'Yeah.'

'Why?'

'Because we're all on the same side now – us and the McKinnons.' Before I could interrogate him further, Reuben went on to say, 'When I found out there was someone in the tanks, I figured it had to be you. I knew you were missing, see, because your mother decided to sic the cops on Father Ramon.'

'She *did*?'

'Bloody right she did. And she gave them my name, too. It was lucky we all had alibis.'

'But . . .' I was amazed. 'You mean she thought *you'd* kidnapped me?'

'Sure,' Reuben confirmed. 'It makes sense. Me and Father Ramon had been sniffing around, so she told the police all about us. I had to pretend I was a total flake – weird but harmless. I had to talk about crystals and poltergeists, so they'd figure

I was the kinda nut who always goes around telling people they're shapeshifters or water diviners, or whatever.' With a sigh, Reuben wrenched his gaze from the yawning hole in front of him so he could look at me. 'Thank God you've been in trouble lately. I reckon those cops think you ran away, because of that dingo-pen business.'

'And Mum? What does she think?'

Reuben shrugged. 'Don't ask me. I haven't talked to her. I've been too busy organising a rescue squad – it's a good job Danny lives so close to Cobar.' Suddenly he addressed Sergio. 'Danny says one of 'em's a Yank, is that right?'

'Lincoln,' Sergio agreed. 'The older one.'

'Figures.' Reuben gave a nod. Then he clattered downstairs, tucking the rifle under his arm. 'Let's see what Lincoln's got to say about Forrest bloody Darwell...'

I didn't try to follow him. I didn't even wait to see what Sergio would do. Instead I charged straight back into the hallway and out the front door, knowing that Reuben had left his phone somewhere in the cabin of his van.

I had decided that, come hell or high water, I was going to call my mum.

When I reached the van, I discovered that it was locked. But the driver's-side window was open about ten centimetres – and I figured that I was skinny enough to wriggle my arm through the hole, once I'd found something to stand on. So I searched the junk-strewn yard until I uncovered a rusty petrol drum, which I placed beside the door that I was trying to open.

Meanwhile, Danny's truck was bouncing towards me over the tussocks and salt-pans. It was a kind of race, I guess. By the time I'd groped my way down to the inside lock, Danny had parked nearby. And I'd only just gained entry to the van when a black dog sprang from the open door of his truck, barking and snapping, its lips curled back in a ferocious snarl.

'What the...?' I froze. The dog kept barking, but didn't bite. It just sat at my feet, *threatening* to bite.

I hardly dared move my lips. 'What's going on?' I croaked.

Danny jumped down from his truck.

'I dunno,' he retorted, pulling the shotgun out after him. There was a sardonic glint in his eye. 'You tell me.'

'I'm getting something for Reuben,' was all I could think of to say.

Danny didn't buy this story, though. 'Whyn't he give you the keys?'

'He forgot.'

'Oh yeah?'

'He did!' I insisted. When I saw Danny sneer, however, I lost it. 'You *lied* to me!' I bleated. 'You *do* have a mobile phone!'

'The hell I do.' He was grinning. 'I've got a satellite phone. It's a whole different gadget.'

'Arsehole!'

'Brat.'

'I've gotta call my *mother*!'

'Aww. Boo-hoo.' Danny's toddler imitation was like a slap in the face. 'Izza poor liddle boy missing his mummy?'

I was suddenly so mad, I stopped caring about the dog. I think I might have *wanted* it to attack me, so I could kick its leathery butt clear across the International Date Line. But when I reached for Reuben's phone, which was sitting beside the gearstick, it was Danny who pounced. He lunged forward and caught my wrist.

'Nuh,' he said. 'No way. You wanna use someone's phone, you ask 'em. Nicely.'

'Screw you!'

'See, that's not the magic word. That won't get yiz anywhere.' Yanking me out of the van, he nearly dislocated my elbow. 'You're supposed to say, "Please, Mr Ruiz, sir, can I use your phone?"'

'Ow! Ow! Let go!'

'"*Please*, Mr Ruiz, will you let go?"' He was putting on a high-pitched whine that I probably would have found insulting, if I hadn't been in so much pain.

'Ow! Ouch! Okay! Please!'

Whoomp! He kicked the door shut.

'We'll have a talk, we'll decide what to do, and *then* we'll start making phone calls,' he announced. 'We're not calling no one till we figure out what we're gunna say to 'em. All right?'

'All right! Jeez!'

'Where's me rifle?'

I explained that Reuben had it.

'Good.' He began to pull me towards the house. 'And the other kid? Where's he?'

'Sergio? I'm not sure.'

'That kid's about to blow. I know the signs. You better watch that kid; he's a mad dog.' Danny seemed to find this amusing; he snickered to himself as he shoved me ahead of him, through the front door and down the central passage. I didn't put up any sort of fight. Conscious of the fact that he was armed with a deadly weapon, I let him hustle me back into the kitchen – where Sergio was yanking open drawers and cupboards.

'I can't find a single one,' he told Danny.

'Huh?'

'I can't find any padlocks! You wanted padlocks!'

'Oh. Right.' Danny shrugged. 'It's no big deal. I might have something in the ute. Or Reuben might be able to help. Where is he, anyway?'

'Down there,' Sergio replied, pointing.

Danny raised his eyebrows. Then he dragged me over to the top of the stairs. '*Reuben! Oi!*' he yelled. '*You okay?*'

During the pause that followed, I could feel Danny's grip tightening on my T-shirt. At last, however, Reuben responded with a 'Yeah! I'm good!'

Danny's grip relaxed. 'Need help?' he queried, adjusting his volume a little.

'Nah. I'm fine,' came Reuben's muffled answer. 'This gate down here isn't locked, y'know.'

'I know. You got a padlock?'

This time the silence was so long that even *I* started to worry. Had Reuben been ambushed? Was he being held at gunpoint?

At last he said, 'Yeah,' very reluctantly.

'You wanna get it, then?' Hearing no reply, Danny continued – with a distinct edge to his voice. 'Once those bloody cells are secured, we can siddown and work out what we're gunna do next, eh? Before this kid calls his mum.'

'Yeah, yeah. Okay.' All at once Reuben appeared at the foot of the stairs. He was looking ruffled and tense. 'That American in there works for Forrest Darwell,' he revealed, jerking his chin at one of the cell doors.

But Danny wasn't enlightened. With a frown, he said, 'Who's Forrest Darwell?'

'Jesus, Danny, I told you about him!' Reuben snapped. 'He runs werewolf fights in the US! He tried to buy me from the McKinnons! Don't you remember?' Appeased by a grunt from

Danny, Reuben added, 'I'm gunna kill Forrest Darwell. I'm gunna get 'im down in a pit and rip his goddamn throat out.'

This didn't impress me at all. In my opinion, Reuben's priorities were skewed. Why the hell should we be worrying about someone living in America, when we had so many more immediate concerns?

'First we should warn the police!' I exclaimed.

'No.' Danny's tone was flat and hard. 'First we get the padlock,' he said. 'Then we secure the gate. Then we siddown with a cuppa tea and work out our next move.' He narrowed his eyes at Reuben. 'You good with that?'

'Yeah,' Reuben replied. 'I'm good with that.'

'Okay.' Danny released me at last, before slapping me on the back. 'Let's get this show on the road, then.'

Chapter Twenty-one

Reuben's padlock was attached to the rear door of his van, which he wouldn't let anyone touch. 'That van is borrowed,' he said. 'If you guys lay a finger on it, I'll tear you apart.'

He then went off to retrieve the padlock, taking his crowbar with him. He also parked the van in a shed that stood near the house. 'I don't want it getting too hot,' was the explanation he gave, when asked why he'd even bothered. Danny muttered something about mollycoddling perfectly healthy vehicles, before wondering aloud why Reuben had brought a van in the first place. 'Why not a four-wheel drive?' Danny wanted to know.

Reuben had a ready answer for that, too.

'I thought it would be a good way of transporting things secretly,' he declared. 'Just in case.'

Though he didn't elaborate, I figured he was talking about Gary and Lincoln. Danny must have thought the same thing, because he immediately stopped arguing. Instead he trudged downstairs with the padlock, while Reuben and I pieced together a scrappy meal consisting of milkless coffee, corn chips, pickles, diet cola, and fifteen slices of heavily buttered toast.

There was beer in the fridge as well, but only Danny had the stomach to drink *that* for breakfast. Upon finally sitting down at the kitchen table, he consumed three full cans of the stuff, one straight after the other. Then he produced a small bag of kangaroo jerky.

'It's homemade,' he revealed, offering it around.

Since there were no takers, he ate about half the bag. The rest went to his dogs, which had followed him into the kitchen. According to Danny, they were no longer needed downstairs. With Gary and Lincoln now safely locked up, the dogs were well overdue for a break.

'I guess so,' said Reuben, who had taken charge of the shotgun. It lay on the table in front of him, along with Lincoln's keys. Danny sat opposite, nursing the rifle; to *his* left was Sergio, facing me across a sticky expanse of red-checked plastic. Sergio couldn't take his eyes off Gary's pistol. It had been placed within easy reach, between the salt and the corn chips, like a tasty appetiser.

There was certainly no shortage of firearms. But I couldn't see a phone anywhere – and I wondered what had happened to *my* phone. Was it still in Lincoln's sedan? Or had he thrown it out the window during our trip to Cobar?

'As long as those dogs aren't allowed to wander,' Reuben warned Danny. 'They've gotta stay put, all right?'

'Yeah, yeah.'

'I mean it.'

'Lay off,' Danny growled. 'They'll be fine.' As he knocked back another beer, I said to Reuben, 'When can I call my mum?'

'Not yet.' Reuben looked around the table. 'First there's something I've gotta tell you. It's important. It'll affect the way we handle things from now on.' He paused for a moment to regard Danny, who belched as he stared right back. 'Danny? Are you listening?'

251

'Do I have a choice?' said Danny. Reuben sighed. He wasn't eating much, I noticed. And he kept squirming around in his seat, though this mightn't have been because he was anxious. It might have been because he was sitting on a pile of upturned kitchen drawers.

There weren't enough chairs, so we'd been forced to improvise.

'Before I left,' he began, 'I talked to Sanford and Nina and Estelle—'

'Who?' Sergio interrupted.

'They're friends. Good friends. They know about us.' Reuben turned to me. 'Toby's met 'em. Haven't you, Toby?'

'Yeah.' I couldn't deny it.

'Sanford's a doctor,' Reuben went on. 'That's why I decided to bring him along.'

'You *what*?' Danny yelped. Even *I* was gobsmacked. But Reuben just held up his hand.

'Wait,' he said. 'Hear me out.'

'Are you *joking*?' Danny snarled, ignoring Reuben's request. 'I thought you said we had to keep this quiet?'

'We do. We will. That's why I brought Nina with me, too.'

'How?' I broke in. 'Where is she? Did you leave her in the back of the van or something?'

'Hell, no!' Reuben's eyebrows snapped together. 'She's at a motel in Cobar. That's the nearest town. I was worried that things might go pear-shaped out here, and I didn't want her getting caught up in a gunfight.'

'This doesn't make sense, though.' I still couldn't get my brain around it. 'Why bring Nina? I understand the doctor, but why her?'

'That's what I'm trying to *tell* you!' Reuben barked. 'If you'd just let me get a word in edgeways!'

'So Nina's a doctor? Is that it?' Sergio queried, sounding lost. I decided to set him straight before his brain exploded.

'Nina's fifteen and looks anorexic,' I informed him. 'Which is why it's so weird that Reuben brought her all this way.'

'I *brought* her because of what you told your mum!' Reuben hissed. 'Doesn't your mum think that Nina's your girlfriend? Isn't that what you told her?'

Danny laughed. I flushed.

'Yeah, but—'

'So if your mum finds out that you've run off with Nina, she's gunna believe it. Right?' said Reuben.

I nearly fell off my chair.

'Are you *crazy*?' I squeaked.

'No. I'm not crazy. I'm *using my bloody grey matter*.' Reuben tapped his head as he thrust it towards me. 'Nina's grandma is gunna tell your mum that you and Nina eloped, yesterday.'

'But—'

'Estelle will say she had a call from Nina's uncle Barry, who lives right here at Wolgaroo. The story'll be that Nina dragged *you* out here, and Barry's worried, and Estelle wants to drive over with your mum and talk some sense into you both.'

'Hang on,' Sergio interjected. 'Who's Estelle?'

'Estelle is Nina's grandmother,' said Reuben, then resumed his conversation with me. 'Estelle will tell your mum that she doesn't want the police involved,' he explained. 'That way, we'll be able to talk to your mum, and show her this place, and convince her that you're a werewolf. Before she can freak out and spill everything to the cops. Understand?'

'Yeah.' I did, too. Not only that; I could see how it would

work. Mum didn't know that Estelle had any dealings with Reuben. In fact Mum might actually believe Estelle, because Estelle was a little old lady. I could just imagine them on a road trip together, fretting about the out-of-control kids in their care.

There was only one problem.

'I wouldn't run off just because Nina told me to. It's not like me. Why would I do that?'

Reuben spread his hands. 'I dunno, Toby. Why would you wake up in a dingo pen one morning? That's not like you either, is it?'

'Oh.' He had a point. 'No, I guess not.'

'You've run away once already. Why wouldn't you do it again?' Instead of waiting for me to answer, he ploughed on. 'This is our best chance of turning your mum around. Before she screws things up. And once we've done that, we can start thinking about Sergio's parents.' His gaze swung towards Sergio, who was slowly munching on a pickle sandwich. 'Whaddaya think, mate? Do your mum and dad know you're a werewolf? What would they do if you turned up outta the blue, after ten months – would they call the police?'

Sergio didn't answer at once. He chewed, swallowed, licked his lips and cleared his throat.

Then he said, 'I think they'd shoot me.'

Reuben blinked. 'Ah,' he murmured. Danny grimaced.

'I don't wanna go back home,' Sergio continued in a hoarse voice. 'I don't wanna go back there ever again.'

'Right.' Reuben nodded awkwardly. 'Gotcha.'

'Weren't you in foster care, though?' I couldn't help butting in, because I'd just remembered something that Sergio had told me about his recent past. 'I thought they put you in foster care. Because of the pizza oven.'

'The *pizza oven*?' Reuben echoed, before Sergio's expression made him back-pedal. 'No. It's okay. Don't tell me. I'd rather you didn't.'

'I don't wanna go into foster care, either,' Sergio said.

Reuben reached over and patted his arm in a clumsy, unpractised sort of way. 'We'll work things out,' Reuben promised. 'If there's no one you've gotta contact, then that just makes it easier for us.'

But Sergio hadn't finished. He turned his mournful gaze on Danny.

'Maybe I can live with *him*,' was Sergio's suggestion.

Danny gave a snort.

'Like fun you will,' he said. Even Reuben seemed alarmed at the prospect. The look on his face made me wonder what kind of rat-hole Danny occupied. Was it a windowless shack? A caravan smelling of dog piss? Or did he live in the back of his truck?

'Uh – I don't think that would be a good idea,' Reuben mumbled. 'Maybe we need some more input. Maybe we should ask Sanford. Or Toby's mother, when she arrives. *They* might know what to do. Or I could call Father Ramon – he knows lots of social workers...'

'Yeah, but hang on a minute.' Danny had been slumped in his chair, chomping on strips of sun-dried kangaroo as he listened to the rest of us. Now he straightened up and addressed Reuben. 'Are you saying we've gotta wait around till all these people get here? How long's that gunna take?'

'It took me just under eight hours,' Reuben rejoined. 'If we

255

call Estelle now, and she calls Toby's mum, they should be here early this evening.'

'Not the others, though,' I reminded him. 'They're staying in Cobar. You just said so. We could drive over there after breakfast and—'

'No!' Reuben stamped on this option as if it were a bedbug. He was so abrupt, I think he almost startled himself. 'No,' he said quickly. 'Sanford and Nina – they're asleep, by now. They need their sleep. They were up all night.'

'So was I. So were you,' I pointed out.

'Yeah – and look at us.' Reuben flapped his hand, encompassing the whole table in a single gesture. Glancing around, I could see what he was getting at. Everyone had bloodshot eyes, hunched shoulders and creased, puffy faces. 'I don't know about you,' he went on, 'but I'm trashed. I can hardly think straight. We need to be on the ball before we make any major decisions. That's why I've gotta rest up.'

'And in the meantime?' Danny rumbled. 'What are we supposed to do with those bastards downstairs while you're sleeping?'

Reuben shrugged. Then he rose to his feet, taking care not to topple the unsteady stack of kitchen drawers.

'They can wait an extra day,' he replied. 'I was down there five *years*.'

'Yeah, but suppose their mate comes along?' Danny was sounding more and more irritable. *Snap* went the ring-pull of yet another beer can. 'What's the plan for him? Do we blow his head off?'

Reuben frowned. 'Don't be stupid.'

'How's that stupid?'

'D'you *want* the police involved?' Reuben folded his arms.

'Because that's one sure way of bringing 'em down on top of us!'

When Danny opened his mouth to argue, I jumped in ahead of him – though not because I disagreed. On the contrary.

'Danny's right,' I said. Like Danny, I wanted to discuss the third partner. 'If that other guy does show up, he'll know someone's here. He'll see all the cars.'

'Not if we hide 'em,' Reuben assured me. Danny, however, was unimpressed.

'Screw you!' he spat. 'I'm not gunna skulk in here, hoping he'll go away! I wanna *get* that guy!'

'Me, too.' Sergio raised his hand, like someone casting a vote.

'Hell, I reckon we should hunt the bastard down,' Danny continued. 'Lure him out here and get stuck into 'im.'

The way Danny was talking, you could tell that he'd mapped out a really horrible fate for all three of the kidnappers. It was there in the depths of his chilly gaze and harsh, gravelly voice. Even his dogs picked up on it; they raised their hackles as he took a swig of beer.

But Reuben wasn't intimidated. Though smaller than Danny, he could match the bigger man scar for scar. And his baleful green glare was just as menacing as Danny's jagged brown teeth.

Even without the dogs to back him up, Reuben had a lot of muscle.

'Well...fine,' he said, grinding out the words. 'Sure, we need to deal with the third guy. But not right now. Right now, we've got the *other* two guys to deal with. Not to mention Toby's mother, and her missing person's report.' Seeing Danny lift his torn lip in a sneer, Reuben sharpened his attack. '*You* might have a police record, mate, but these kids are clean! And I want 'em to *stay* clean! I don't want you messing things up for 'em! Maybe when the kids are gone, we can tackle Forrest Darwell's crew. Until then, though...' He took a deep breath. 'Let's just say we keep it low key, all right?'

Danny shrugged. He seemed resigned, though peevish; Reuben had obviously struck a chord, though I wasn't sure how. Danny hadn't impressed me as someone who'd be concerned about protecting teenagers.

'You're right about the third man,' Reuben conceded, still addressing Danny. 'We should keep an eye out for him. That's why I need you on guard duty while I phone Estelle. As for you kids...' he nodded at Sergio, then at me, '... you should have a nap before things hot up again. I'll do the same myself, when I'm done making calls.'

'Can *I* make some calls?' It seemed worth asking, though I could sense that Reuben wouldn't approve. 'Can I talk to my mother?'

Reuben heaved a longsuffering sigh. 'Toby, what did I just tell you?' he said. '*Estelle* will be talking to your mother. You're not supposed to know they're on their way.'

'What about Nina, then? Why can't I call her?'

'Because she's asleep.' Seeing me glower at him, Reuben raised his eyebrows. 'You won't be popular if you wake her up. Especially if you're too damn tired to make any sense.'

This struck me as a gross exaggeration. 'I'm not *that* tired.'

'Well, you look tired. And you smell worse. In fact you might wanna freshen up before Nina arrives.'

Sergio tried to smother a laugh, which came out through his nose instead of his mouth. Danny leered at me.

Though I tried not to blush, it was a failed attempt.

'She's not *really* my girlfriend!' I protested. 'I hardly know her!'

'Yeah, yeah,' said Danny.

'It's true!'

Danny didn't reply. He just smirked as he staggered to his feet, crumpling an empty beer can before he tossed it onto the floor. Then he picked up his shotgun and headed for the stash in the fridge.

Reuben watched him, sour-faced.

'Think you can handle guard duty?' Reuben inquired. 'Or do you wanna get completely stonkered instead?'

'On five beers?' Danny scoffed. 'You must be mixing me up with some little fella.'

'Just take it slow, all right? I'm serious.'

'Y'reckon?' Danny's tone was scathing. 'If you were really serious, mate, we'd be scraping a couple of scumbags off the walls by now. Kids or no kids,' he insisted. 'Don't worry, though. I'll play it your way. And if I nod off, then the dogs'll wake me up. They don't miss a thing.'

And that was that. Once Danny had raided the beer supply yet again, Reuben decided that any further discussion would be useless. So the meeting broke up. Reuben went to phone Estelle. Sergio made a sudden dash for the bathroom. He told me later that he was keen to get there before I did, since he hadn't had a proper shower in ten months. 'I didn't want you to use up all the hot water,' he confessed. 'And anyway, you didn't smell nearly as bad as me.'

He may have been right, but I was still feeling self-conscious. So I took off one of my T-shirts – the sweatiest, raggiest, innermost one – which I bundled into a ball and tossed into a kitchen cupboard. Then I waited for Sergio to finish in the bathroom.

I didn't wait in the kitchen, though. Not while Danny Ruiz was there. I'd had my fill of Danny; when I saw him spitting beer into Psycho's mouth, I decided that I needed a bit of peace. The living room was also out, because Reuben had taken his phone into it and collapsed onto the only remaining piece of furniture – which happened to be a busted futon. That's why I retreated to one of the bedrooms. That's why I ended up using a mattress on the floor. There weren't any beds, see.

But I shouldn't have gone near that mattress. Not because it was smelly, or because it made my skin crawl. Not because I felt uncomfortable, parked on the floor with my knees around my ears. The fact is, I shouldn't have gone near *any* mattress, because I was far more tired than I realised. As soon as I sat down, I wanted to lie down.

I tried telling myself that the sheets stank of Gary – that I'd feel much better after taking a shower – that I had a whole lot to think about before I could spare the time for a nap. I tried to concentrate on Reuben's plan; was it the best plan for me? Was Reuben trustworthy, or would it be better if I just grabbed a phone and called my mum?

For at least five minutes I managed to stay upright. Gradually, however, my thoughts became muddled. Reuben's distant chatter began to sound blurred. I looked at the mattress and saw that it was blotched with stains. The sheets were all twisted. There was a scattering of crumbs on the pillow.

But I lay down anyway, reminding myself that I often did

my best thinking in bed. How many hours had I spent staring at my bedroom ceiling, reviewing the events of the day and dreaming about the future? *I just have to rest my body, not my brain,* I decided – and that's all I can remember.

I guess I must have fallen asleep.

Chapter Twenty-two

When I woke up, I was hungry. I was also stiff, parched, hot, and desperate for a piss. The sun was blazing through the window, so I figured that it had to be early afternoon, at least. I couldn't be sure, though, because I still didn't have a watch.

Someone had dumped my shoes by the bed while I was sleeping. Obviously Lincoln hadn't had time to throw them away. After pulling them on, I headed straight for the bathroom – which by now was unoccupied. Sergio had gone. He'd left a puddle of water on the floor and a damp towel hanging on the rail, but he didn't answer when I called his name. That's why I didn't immediately duck into the shower myself, once I'd emptied my bladder. The all-pervading silence was already beginning to unnerve me.

Where *was* everyone?

Back in the hallway, I spotted a closed door. It was one of the bedroom doors, and it squeaked as I pushed it open. Behind it, Reuben didn't even stir in his sleep. He was draped across a mattress like the one I'd used – a worn, grubby mattress that lay on the floor. His hair was wet and he smelled of soap. The shotgun had been placed beside him, within easy reach.

I wasn't even tempted to pick up that shotgun. Sergio would have done it; in fact I was surprised that he hadn't already. To me, however, it would have been like picking up a chunk of radioactive waste.

I slowly backed out of the room, then went to look for the others. There was no one in the kitchen. '*Danny?*' I called. '*Hey, Sergio?*' Still nothing. The table hadn't been cleared. The dirty dishes hadn't been washed. The rifle and the handgun were missing.

But Danny's truck was still there, as was Lincoln's sedan. I could see them when I peered out the window. I couldn't see Reuben's van, though, because he'd parked it in the shed. Unless someone had driven away in the van while I was asleep? That was possible. Unlikely, but possible.

I decided to go and check just in case. I wanted to make sure that Danny hadn't gone off without me and Reuben – and I also didn't want to look downstairs. I had a very bad feeling about those underground cells. I guess I just had a picture in my head: a picture of Danny and his dogs in the cells, tormenting our prisoners. The picture was so clear that it had set up a kind of force field, driving me away from the kitchen, out the back door.

'Danny?' I yelled. There was no reply. I moved towards the shed in a thick haze of heat. Stepping out of that house was like stepping into a blast furnace. Inside, the dim light and high ceilings had fooled me. It had been hot, but not unbearable. Outside, it was the middle of summer. The sun beat down on my head like a baseball bat. It poured into my eyes like molten lead.

Nevertheless, as I picked a path between the stacks of shredded tyres and rusty springs, I noticed movement on the horizon. Someone was walking around out there.

Squinting, I shaded my eyes. A small, dark figure was visible through shimmering waves of heat; I recognised Sergio because of his fuzzy hair and squat build. He was hovering at the edge of the pool, encircled by its lofty wire fence. The long, skinny shape in his hand was probably Danny's rifle.

'*Hey! Sergio!*' I yelled.

Maybe he didn't hear me – or maybe he didn't want to hear me. For whatever reason, he didn't react. I had to close the distance between us, trudging up the long, low, scrubby incline at the back of the house, towards the pool. It never crossed my mind that Sergio might actually be *with* someone. I assumed that he'd run off by himself, with Danny's rifle, so he could practise shooting at things.

'*Hey!*' I shouted, beckoning to Sergio – who heard me, this time, and glanced over his shoulder. But he shook his head, then turned his attention back to the bottom of the pool. I saw him train his rifle on something down there, though not as if he felt very confident. The gun barrel wavered in his hands.

I wondered if he was aiming at the petrol drum.

'*Hey!*' I warned, '*don't do that! What if the bullets ricochet or something?*'

That's when I heard raised voices. The sound was very faint, carried on a fitful breeze; even so, I identified the exchange as an ugly one. Somebody was threatening somebody else. And it was happening in the pool.

'Oh no,' I breathed, before pumping up the volume. '*Sergio! What are you doing? What's going on?*'

'Shhh!' he hissed.

'Where's Danny?' It was a rhetorical question, because I already knew where Danny was. Sure enough, when I reached the fence, I looked down and saw him. He was dragging Lincoln through the hatch, using an armlock and a pistol to hurry things

264

along. There was a growling dog stationed in each corner of the pool. As for Gary, he had been left kneeling by the drain, with a pillowcase over his head.

Sergio wasn't aiming at the petrol drum at all. He was aiming at Gary.

'Oh no,' I muttered again. It was the pillowcase that really freaked me out. 'No way. No *way*. This...this isn't gunna happen. Sergio? You can't do this.'

'Shut up,' he growled. Then Danny spoke.

'Right!' he said to Lincoln. 'D'yiz reckanise this little spot? Eh?'

He was drunk. I could tell. I wouldn't have described him as *falling-down* drunk, because there was nothing unsteady about the way he walked around. But his speech was slurred and his face was flushed.

'See, this time the shoe's on the other foot,' he continued, still addressing Lincoln. 'This time, *we're* gunna watch *you* fight to the death. And whoever wins gets to keep on breathing...'

'Okay, wait. I get it,' Lincoln interrupted. He sounded remarkably calm, even though he was damp with sweat, and his clothes were filthy, and there was a smear of blood on his walrus moustache, as if someone had punched him in the nose. 'You've made your point, so what's the deal?' he said, in a voice that was only slightly hoarse. 'Tell me what you want, and it's done. We'll do it.'

'I just told ya,' Danny replied, still holding his gun to Lincoln's head. 'I wanna see yiz put the boot in. Hard.'

'You've no idea how much money I can access,' Lincoln went on, in his rumbling drawl. 'There's half a million us dollars in my operational account, but you'd need the password to – oof!' He grunted as Danny pushed him to his knees.

'Don't move. Not yet,' Danny warned, edging away. 'Or I'll set me dogs on ya.'

'Hey, Danny!' I rattled the wire fence, causing him to squint up into the sun. 'I'll tell Reuben! Reuben won't like this!'

His only response was a snort. It was Lincoln who answered me.

'Kid, this guy's psycho. Once he's through with us, he'll go after – ouch!'

Danny had kicked him.

'Shuddup,' said Danny. 'One more word and I'll blow your brains out.' He whipped the pillowcase off Gary's head, exposing a black eye and a split lip. 'The rules are very simple: you wait till I'm outta the ring, then you rip each other apart. And if you don't, me dogs'll do it for ya.'

Gary mumbled something. He looked bad.

'Danny!' I shrilled.

'Piss off.'

'I'll tell the police!'

'Yeah, yeah.' He was heading for the ladder, and displayed no interest in what I was saying. 'Now, remember,' he told his two captives, stumbling a little as he reached for the bottom rung, 'Sergio's up there with a ten-gauge, so if anyone starts making trouble...' He didn't bother to finish, wagging his automatic instead.

I bolted. Before he had even climbed out of the pool I was on my way to fetch Reuben, galloping back down the slope with my mouth agape and my eyes popping. I dodged a ditch. I tripped on a rock. I vaulted a fence and slammed into a screen door, which I nearly wrenched off its hinges.

'*Reuben!*' I bellowed, hurling myself over the kitchen threshold. For a second or two I couldn't see; my eyes had trouble adjusting to the dimness inside the house. *'Hey, Reuben!'* I called again.

He must have heard my voice – or the *thud* of my shoulder bouncing off a doorjamb – because he was standing up by the time I reached his bedroom. When I flung open the door, I was met by a pair of bleary green eyes blinking through a mop of tousled curls.

'What?' he croaked, staggering slightly. When someone's that unsteady on his feet, the last thing you want to see is a gun in his hands. Reuben, however, was clutching that shotgun as if he couldn't stay upright without it. 'Whassa matter?'

'It's Danny!' I cried. I was gasping for breath. 'You've gotta come!'

'Why?'

'He's drunk...' I had to gulp down some air before continuing. 'He's at the pool with the dogs! He's making Gary fight Lincoln!'

'Oh Christ.' Reuben dashed past me before I could finish. Suddenly he was gone. Footsteps thumped down the hallway.

I followed him, still panting.

'Sergio's out there with the rifle!' I added. 'You'd better watch out!'

That's when I heard the gunshot.

I knew what it was, even though I'd never heard one before. The echo made me think of certain movies I'd seen. Though faint, it was a sound that stopped me in my tracks like a bullet. I reeled and choked. My knees almost buckled.

I had to steady myself against a wall.

'Oh no,' I said aloud. There was no response from Reuben – just the *crash* of a screen door slamming. When I reached the kitchen, he was already outside.

I have to admit that I didn't rush after him. One part of me wanted to crawl under the table, while the other part was desperate to know what had happened. But the longer I hesitated, the more antsy I felt. In that silent room, with only the *tick-tick-tick* of a clock to keep me company, I began to imagine all kinds of horrible things – until at last the pictures in my head became scarier than any real-life scenario.

That's what drove me outside. It wasn't courage; it was sheer cowardice.

Meanwhile, certain events were unfolding back at the pool. Surrounded by slavering dogs, with two guns pointed straight at him, Lincoln must have realised that he wouldn't be able to *talk* himself out of the arena. So he'd thrown a few punches at Gary – who had fought back with a couple of wild swings, one of which had made contact with Lincoln's jaw.

If it hadn't been a punishing blow, I don't think that Danny would have been fooled. Put it this way: I'm pretty sure that Lincoln must have gone down for real. But knocked out? I don't think so. I find it hard to believe that someone lying unconscious on the ground would suddenly wake up at the exact moment his sworn enemy was leaning over him. And even if that did happen, it's pretty near *impossible* to believe that the person on the ground would be alert enough, after sustaining a serious head injury, to make a lightning-fast grab for the nearest handgun.

To me, it seems obvious that Lincoln must have faked the whole blackout just to lure Danny back into the pool. And I suppose you could say that the plan worked, up to a point. While Lincoln and Danny were wrestling, Sergio wasn't able to fire his shotgun; if he had, he might have hit Danny. (That's what Sergio told me afterwards, anyway.) As for the dogs –

well, *they* had been told to keep Gary pinned down, in case he tried to launch an attack while Danny was busy examining Lincoln. But during the struggle between Danny and Lincoln, Danny's pistol discharged into the air. And that noise must have confused the dogs just long enough to make them relax their guard a little. I guess they were torn between their desire to obey Danny and their desire to protect him.

With the dogs' attention diverted, Gary seized his chance. Even as Reuben and I were charging towards the pool, Gary was flying towards its open hatch – which could be bolted shut from inside the tunnel. Though Mutt did manage to bite his calf, Gary gave the dog such a kick that it immediately fell back. That's when Sergio fired his shotgun. I heard it roar and ducked automatically, despite the fact that I wasn't in any danger. Maybe Gary ducked, too – or maybe Sergio was a lousy shot. Either way, Sergio missed. And Gary reached the hatch just in time to slam it in Psycho's face.

'*Quick! Go get 'im!*' Danny yelled. He had custody of the pistol by then, because at least two of his dogs were hanging off Lincoln's shirtsleeves. Sergio, however, faltered at the edge of the pool, as though wondering what Danny had meant.

'*Don't just stand there!*' Danny screamed at him, pressing Lincoln's skull into the tiled floor. '*He'll take his car, ya drongo!*'

'Oh!' Sergio suddenly realised that Gary was making for the house. So he began to run, though he hadn't gone far before he bumped into Reuben. They stood together for a moment, breathlessly talking and waving their arms. Then they both raced towards me.

'What is it?' I cried. 'What happened?'

Reuben skidded to a halt, loose gravel sliding and tumbling

269

from beneath his boots. 'One of 'em's in the tunnel!' he barked. 'We gotta head 'im off at the house!'

'Oh, man...'

'That bloody fool didn't lock up the cells!' Reuben added, before shooting off again. He didn't explain who the 'bloody fool' was. I assumed it was Danny.

As for Sergio, he didn't even bother to stop. He pelted straight past, legs pumping, eyes staring. I followed him. We were moving downhill at a pretty good clip, despite the fact that Sergio was wearing Lincoln's shoes. But we weren't fast enough. Before we'd even hurdled the fence, Gary had popped out of the kitchen door. We saw him racing towards the sedan.

'Jesus!' Reuben yelped. His pace eased off as he began to fidget with his shotgun. I couldn't help overtaking him; my momentum almost hurled me into the back of the shed, which I dodged at the very last moment. Sergio was lagging behind because his legs were so short – and because his rifle was weighing him down. But he caught up at the fence.

BANG!

Another shot. It nearly deafened me. I looked back and saw Reuben aiming his gun. A wisp of smoke dissolved into the super-heated air.

Then the sedan's ignition fired. *Chugga-chugga-chugga-vrrrOMM!* My head snapped around. The sedan was moving – slowly, at first. Its driver's door was still standing open. But Gary pulled the door shut while I was swinging my legs, one by one, over a rusty strand of fence wire.

'Dammit!' I exclaimed. Beside me, Sergio was fumbling with his weapon. I can only assume that he wanted to take a few pot-shots at the car before it was too late, though I'm not sure what his target would have been. Reuben was almost

270

certainly aiming at a rear tyre. His second shot hit the sedan just above its bumper bar.

Nothing happened, though. The sedan kept bowling along, picking up speed as it retreated.

'The van!' I cried. 'Quick!'

'No.' Reuben shook his head. Then he raised the shotgun to his cheek one last time, squinting along its barrel.

By now his target was almost invisible behind a cloud of dust.

'Don't you have the keys to the van?' I asked Reuben, who ignored me. He squeezed the trigger.

BANG!

Unfortunately, it was a hopeless attempt. The sedan was much too far away.

I don't know why Sergio couldn't see that. After scrambling over the fence, he began to give chase like a dog. Reuben lowered his gun, scowling.

'Don't you have the keys?' I repeated. 'Where are they? We should get them, quick!'

'We're not taking my van,' Reuben replied, then raised his voice. '*Sergio! Come back!*' he bawled. '*You're wasting your time!*'

'Why can't we take the van?' I couldn't understand his reasoning. 'What's wrong with it?'

'We'd never catch up in a heap like that,' he said. 'Anyway, it's borrowed. I don't want it getting trashed.' He turned to peer back up the slope towards the pool. 'What we need is Danny's truck,' he insisted, before cupping one hand to his mouth. '*Oi! Danny! Coo-ee!*'

'He'll never hear you.'

'I hope he's okay.' Reuben wedged the butt of the shotgun

271

into his armpit, so that its barrel was pointing at the blood-red dirt on which we stood. 'I shoulda checked the whole house for spare car keys,' he went on. '*God* I'm a fool. They musta hidden an emergency set somewhere, the sneaky bastards.'

'Where are you going?' I demanded, because he was beginning to retrace his steps.

'I'm getting the keys to Danny's ute,' he told me, with the air of someone stating the obvious.

I couldn't believe my ears.

'But that'll take *ages!*' I protested. 'We'll *never* catch up!'

'It'll take even longer if we stand around flapping our gums,' Reuben snapped – just as Sergio hailed us from the side of the house.

'Hey!' Sergio called. He was squatting right where the sedan had been parked. 'Guys! Look at this!'

'For Chrissake, kid,' Reuben warned, 'don't hold the bloody gun like that!'

But Sergio wasn't listening. 'It's petrol!' he exclaimed. 'Right here! On the ground!' Straightening his knees slightly, he shuffled backwards a few steps. 'It's a trail!' he added, pointing. 'Along here... and all down the track...'

That's when I smelled it. There's no mistaking the stink of petrol. It wafted past my nose, borne on a puff of hot wind.

Reuben's whole face suddenly brightened, though not in a pleasant kind of way. His eyes flashed and he bared his teeth.

'You little beauty!' he snarled. 'I musta hit the tank!'

'You musta hit the tank!' echoed Sergio. He was very excited. 'Can you believe that? You hit it and it didn't explode!'

Clearly, he had never watched *Mythbusters*. 'Bullets don't make petrol tanks explode,' I remarked. 'They've proved it.'

No one, however, was the least bit interested in what I

had to say. Sergio was already hastening towards us, clumsily heaving his rifle around like a bundle of curtain rods. Reuben was squinting at a cloud of white dust as it moved off into the distance. He looked like an eagle watching a rabbit, or a wolf gloating over a wounded fawn.

'That's right, scumbag,' he murmured. 'We'll get you now, my friend.'

Then he spun around and headed for the pool.

Chapter Twenty-three

Danny didn't hesitate. As soon as he heard what was going on, he dropped everything – including Lincoln. I was vaguely startled to see that Lincoln was still awake and breathing. I suppose that, somewhere at the back of my mind, I'd been expecting to find him smeared all over the pool on my return. But Danny had managed to restrain himself.

Or perhaps he'd just run out of time.

'The dogs'll stand guard,' Danny insisted, as he sprang up the ladder. Looking down at Lincoln, who was sitting with his hand pressed against his blood-smeared cheek, I realised that he wouldn't be able to escape even if he *did* kill every dog in the pool. Because once Danny had raised the ladder, there was no way out. Not for a man on his own. Not with the hatch bolted shut from inside the tunnel.

'He'll be fine,' Danny promised. I wasn't so sure. On the one hand, Lincoln certainly wasn't going anywhere. On the other hand, he was at the bottom of a tiled pit, with nowhere to shelter from the blazing sun. How long could he possibly last without water?

Then I realised that the dogs were down there, too – and that Danny wouldn't *dream* of leaving his dogs to die of heatstroke. So I didn't feel that I had to ask any awkward questions on my way back to the house. Instead I concentrated on keeping up with Danny, who was amazingly fast on his feet for such an old guy. Especially when you consider that he was wearing his heavy raincoat, which billowed out behind him as he ran.

Of course, he wasn't wearing much *underneath* his raincoat, except his boots and his boxers. But still...

I was out of breath by the time we reached Danny's truck. So was Reuben, who volunteered to ride out back with the shotgun. Sergio didn't agree with this; he wanted to carry the shotgun himself. So there was a short, sharp, vicious exchange as seats were assigned and weapons redistributed. For some reason, Sergio was forced to give the rifle to me, even though I hadn't asked for it. I mean, I couldn't even find the safety catch! But Reuben insisted, telling me to 'keep an eye out'. He didn't say for what.

When we finally set off, Danny was driving, Reuben was standing in the back of the truck, and Sergio was squashed into the cabin between Danny and me. I don't think that Danny should have been allowed to drive. Not after drinking all that beer. But he'd refused to hand over his ignition key, so Reuben had decided not to waste time arguing. 'Fine,' Reuben had said. 'Since there's nothing you can possibly hit out here, I guess it won't matter much.'

I can't say I entirely agreed with him. For one thing, Danny was nursing the pistol in his lap. Every time we hit a bump (and believe me, we hit a lot of bumps), I had a horrible vision of that stupid gun sliding off his knees and discharging a bullet into somebody's foot. It wouldn't have been Reuben's foot, either: oh no. Reuben was safe in the back of the truck, armed with a ten-gauge shotgun. *I* was the person who had to sit near

275

someone who was driving under the influence with a loaded automatic bouncing around in his lap.

If Sergio hadn't been Sergio, I might have suggested that *he* take the gun, just to be on the safe side. Sergio, however, wasn't the type of kid that you could really entrust with a firearm. Instead of shooting someone in the foot, he probably would have trashed a lung or a kidney.

'Can't we put that gun on the floor?' I finally asked, my voice wobbling as we juddered over the corrugated surface of the road.

'Nope,' Danny replied.

'Then can you point it in some other direction, please?'

Danny grinned. But he did move the pistol, without even sparing me a glance.

He was too busy scanning the road ahead.

'Is this the only way out?' was my next question.

'Yep.'

'What are we gunna do if we can't find him?'

'We will,' said Danny, with absolute confidence.

'And then what?' When he didn't answer, I drew my own conclusions. 'If you do something crazy, I'll call the police. I mean it. I won't even wait for my mum.'

Danny snorted. 'Give it a rest.'

'I mean it, Danny!'

'Yeah, yeah.'

'Is there any water?' Sergio suddenly inquired. I don't know if he was genuinely thirsty or if was trying to head off an argument; all I know is that I gave up, at that point. I was too hot and tired to make a big fuss. And even though I had the rifle, I didn't feel entirely safe.

So I decided to shut my mouth and have a drink of water.

Sergio and I shared a metal flask between us, our teeth clanking on its mouth whenever the truck swerved or jolted. The road was like a dry creek bed, all rocks and dips and meandering channels. As for the truck, it sure could have done with some new shock absorbers, though even they wouldn't have helped much – not while Danny was driving. That guy just planted his Blundstone boot on the accelerator and kept it there. Our heads would hit the ceiling and he *still* wouldn't slow down.

I don't know what it was like for Reuben out the back. He must have felt as if he were in a tumble dryer.

'Is that him?' Sergio suddenly piped up. He pointed through the windscreen at the white strip of road that was unfolding before us. There was a dark speck at the end of it.

'That's him,' Danny said. Then he cursed as the truck bumped over another ditch. *Bom-CRASH!* It was a miracle that we weren't shedding a trail of loose auto parts.

'Are you sure?' I wasn't convinced. 'It could be someone else.'

Danny sneered. 'Like who?' he growled. Then Reuben banged on the cabin roof.

'Vehicle ahead!' he shouted. We managed to hear him, despite all the clanging and chugging, because every window was wide open. Danny's truck wasn't air-conditioned, so the flies and the dust had free access.

'Don't do anything stupid!' I begged, when I saw Danny fondling the gun on his lap. 'It might not even be him!'

'It is,' Sergio assured me. 'That's Gary, all right. I recognise the car.'

'It's the wrong colour,' I objected. 'That's not his car, it's too pale.'

But Danny dismissed my doubts. 'It looks pale because it's

covered in dust,' he declared – and he was right. As soon as we were close enough to read its numberplate, I had to concede that the car was Gary's.

It was parked in the middle of the road, stranded by the leak in its petrol tank. Around it lay an endless stretch of outback, devoid of cover. Grey stones were strewn across red earth, none of them big enough to hide a baby, let alone a full-grown man. The saltbush was all knee-high. The scattered mulga trees were skinny and stunted.

When Danny turned off his engine, the silence was as vast as the landscape. It was a silence so smothering that every little noise seemed impossibly loud: the creak of springs, the slamming of doors, the crunch of footsteps. I wanted to speak, but I couldn't. I'm not sure if I was intimidated by the silence or by the car, which sat there looking ominous, as if it was about to explode. There was no one in the driver's seat.

We all stood for a moment in a semicircle, about six metres from the sedan's rear bumper. The stink of petrol was overwhelming; I could see drops of it on the road.

Danny plucked his rifle from my hand.

'Gimme that,' he said. I was glad to. And I was even more delighted when he didn't try to press his pistol on me. Instead, he shoved it into his waistband.

'Danny?' said Reuben. He was holding the shotgun, his finger resting lightly on its trigger guard. 'Has that car been searched?'

There was a pregnant pause. Then Danny hissed through his teeth.

'No,' he finally admitted. 'Unless you checked it out?'

'No.'

'Crap.' Danny was disgusted with himself. 'What a bonehead!'

'If there was a gun inside, he woulda used it already,' was Reuben's reasoning. 'He woulda fired at us back at the house.'

'Maybe.' But Danny wasn't taking any chances. 'You kids stay right here. Okay? Don't move.'

He didn't have to tell *me*. I wasn't going anywhere. Sergio, however, looked very disappointed. He scowled as Danny and Reuben advanced towards the car, guns raised.

I have to admit, my heart was pounding away like mad. I felt certain that Gary must be hiding in the car, because there was nowhere else for him to hide. Even if he'd tried to run, we still would have spotted him. It was probably no more than ten minutes since his car had died, and in that brief period he couldn't possibly have run far enough to become invisible. Not in that country. It was so flat and featureless, you could see for about fifty kilometres in every direction.

And there was no jogging figure on the horizon, whichever way I looked.

'Nup,' said Danny. He yanked open one of the car doors, which wasn't locked. 'Nothing in here.'

'What about the boot?' Reuben asked.

Danny sauntered towards the back of the car as Reuben examined the rear footwells. 'Okay!' Danny warned in a loud voice. 'I'm gunna shoot this lock out! Anyone in the boot better say so now, before they get a bullet in 'em!'

'For God's sake, Danny!' Reuben sounded cross. 'The key's still in the bloody ignition! You don't have to start blasting away at the goddamn thing!'

'Oh,' said Danny. 'Right.' He backed off so that Reuben could open the boot.

But it was empty.

'I don't get it,' Danny muttered. He straightened up and gazed around. 'Where the hell did he go?'

'Maybe he's gone too far,' Sergio offered. 'Maybe if we drive a bit further we'll see him.'

'Nuh.' Danny was adamant. 'He can't be that quick. I don't believe it.'

'He's out there somewhere,' said Reuben, shading his eyes as he scanned the surrounding wasteland. 'In a ditch. Or behind an anthill. Flat on his belly, like a lizard.'

'We gotta find 'im before somebody else comes along,' Danny announced. Then he jabbed a finger at us, one after the other, as if he was counting heads. 'North, south, east,' he said. 'Split up and fan out. I'll go west.'

'But—'

'I won't need this,' he continued, tossing me his rifle. 'All I need is a tyre jack.'

He then gave Sergio his automatic, while Reuben looked on with a frown, not entirely won over. 'Maybe we should do this in pairs,' Reuben objected. But Danny waved a dismissive hand.

'They'll be fine,' he said. 'They're bloody werewolves, they can look after themselves.' Having squelched Reuben, Danny addressed me. 'You'll smell 'im before you see 'im. Once you're clear of this petrol stink, you can use your noses. It'll be like an early-warning signal.'

'But what if he has a gun?' I quavered.

'If he did, we'd all be dead by now. He'da picked us off like bottles on a wall.'

'You should still be careful, though,' Reuben interrupted. 'He could have a knife or something, so watch where you're putting your feet.'

'He's like a landmine,' Danny finished, 'because he could blow up in your face any second.'

And that was all the advice he gave me. Next thing I knew, I was trudging out into the desert with no supplies except for a loaded rifle. I didn't even have any sunglasses, let alone a hat. The sun beat down, the flies descended, and the ants kept running up the legs of my jeans. They had big jaws, those ants, and they bit like tigers. I remember thinking, *What the hell? This is crazy. I don't belong here. How did this happen?* It occurred to me that I might be going mad – that I might actually be home in bed, hallucinating. But the sudden jab of an ant bite reassured me. It was far too painful to be a figment of my imagination.

I couldn't see Gary. I couldn't smell him, either. The scene ahead of me was devoid of human life; the further I went, the more isolated I felt. The stink of petrol faded away. The silence pressed down, as dense as the heat. The air filling my lungs had a hot, wild, dusty, peppery scent to it.

When I glanced back, I saw how far I was from Danny's truck. Though the others were still visible, I couldn't make out their features. They were just stick figures in a landscape, and they didn't interest me. I preferred to stare out at the limitless horizon, pretending that I was all on my own.

Maybe I should just walk off out of here, I reflected. But of course I couldn't have done that. A walk into the wilderness would have killed me. I *had* to go back, even though I didn't want to. Even though Sergio had flipped, and Danny was dangerous, and Reuben was paranoid. I could see that quite clearly now; the sudden taste of freedom had cleared my head. I knew I had to call someone: Mum, the police, it didn't matter who. I realised that the first thing on my agenda, once I returned to the house, should be a thorough search of the every bed, drawer and cupboard. Because Lincoln *had* to have a satellite phone. And it had to be somewhere in that house.

Unless it was in his car?

I looked over my shoulder again, towards the sedan – and that was when I saw Gary. At least, I assumed it was Gary. Though I was too far away to see his face, he wasn't hard to identify. Who else would have been scrambling out from beneath the rear axle?

I couldn't believe my eyes. I had to rub them vigorously, worried that I'd been fooled by a mirage.

But, no; there he was. Running for the truck.

'*Hey!*' I yelled. '*Hey! Hey! Stop!*'

My shout alerted the others. They heard my voice, even if they couldn't figure out exactly what I was saying. And when the truck door slammed shut, they drew their own conclusions.

'Goddammit!' I cried, as I raced back towards the road. I had a horrible feeling that Danny must have left his key in the ignition, though how on earth Gary could have worked that out, I had no idea. And how the hell had we missed *Gary*, for God's sake? Why hadn't we seen him skulking under the car?

It turned out, in fact, that he had been quite clever. As his car ran out of puff, he'd parked on a bit of road with a large pothole in it. Then, after rolling around in the dust for a while, he'd wriggled and slithered into this pothole – which was twice as long as it was wide. From a distance he'd been impossible to see, because the back of his head had been level with the surface of the road. That was why we hadn't bothered to hunker down and examine the car's underside. We just hadn't thought it necessary.

Of course, we didn't learn any of this until much later.

BANG! Sergio fired his pistol. When I heard Danny scream, '*Don't shoot at me truck, ya turkey!*', I realised how much ground I'd covered. Everyone else seemed a lot closer. We were all converging on the ute at top speed.

So why didn't it move? Why didn't the engine start? *There are no keys,* I concluded, with a sudden leap of the heart. We had him! He was ours! He couldn't get away!

Chugga-chugga-chugga . . .

The sound of that engine put wings on my feet. I surged forward, desperate to catch our quarry. It was a savage, animal feeling that surged up from somewhere deep inside, triggered by the shouts and the headlong pursuit. *Chugga-chugga-chugga.* Danny's truck was so old that it was easy to hotwire, though getting the ignition to fire was a challenge. Gary must have been frantic. *Chugga-chugga-chugga.* By this time I was so close that I could see him through the window, hunched over the steering column.

You might be wondering why Reuben didn't just shoot out the tyres. I wondered that myself, later. I even asked him. He waffled on about Danny being a lunatic about his truck, but if you ask me, that was just an excuse.

The truth is, we all had to catch that truck. All of us. The whole pack. We were in pursuit.

Vrrr-OOMM! As the ute lurched forward, I was about two metres from its rear wheel. So I hurled myself at the tailgate. It was a crazy thing to do – especially with a rifle in my hand. I could have killed myself. I nearly *did* kill myself. I was stuck there with my top half hanging over the tailgate and my legs waving in the air, like one of those tin cans tied to a newlywed's bumper. God knows where I would have landed if the battered old tailgate had fallen open.

To pull myself up I had to drop the rifle, which landed in the back of the truck and began to slide around, banging against all the toolboxes and other junk that Danny had put there. (Some of it didn't look too well secured.) The gun could easily have gone off and hit Sergio, who was clinging to one side of the truck-bed, trying to claw his way on board. But I wasn't worried about Sergio. I was too busy keeping a firm grip. That truck was fishtailing wildly, bucking like a horse as it hit the worst bumps at top speed.

Gary was trying to shake us off.

'*HAAAAH!*' someone bawled; I'm not sure who. Danny, probably. He'd thrown himself at the front grille and climbed across the bonnet, using the bullbar as a foothold. I could see the top of his head bouncing above the cabin roof – or were my eyeballs doing the bouncing? They were certainly hard to focus. My teeth were chattering and my bones were vibrating and my neck felt as if it was about to snap. I could barely breathe because there was so much dust in the air.

Still, I managed to throw a leg over the tailgate. That was when I heard Sergio laugh. He was laughing like a maniac. And when the truck's right wheels lifted off the ground in a heart-stopping swerve, he howled his appreciation.

Danny let loose an answering howl. He was braced against the bonnet, pitching back and forth, one hand wrapped around the radio antenna. His tyre jack was in his other hand, but he didn't smash it through the windscreen. I don't know why not. Maybe he didn't want to damage his truck.

'*Shoot! Shoot!*' he screamed at Reuben, who was hanging

off the passenger door. Despite Gary's desperate attempts to dislodge him, Reuben had managed to yank it open – and would have wriggled inside if the shotgun hadn't been slung over his shoulder. Its barrel had become wedged against the top of the doorway; every time he reached back to adjust the strap, we'd hit a bump and he'd have to grab the nearest handle just to keep from being thrown clear.

'*Ow-ow-owooo!*' Danny bellowed, as the truck zigzagged.

I was on my feet by then, groping for the rifle with one hand. The other was firmly clamped to the side of the truck. But before I could stagger close enough to help, a big jolt gave Reuben all the help he needed. The shotgun shifted, he let it slide down his arm, and all at once there was nothing standing between him and Gary.

I think it was the shotgun that freaked Gary out. To see Reuben climbing into the seat next to you would have been bad enough, but to see Reuben with a ten-gauge shotgun...?

No wonder Gary spun the wheel.

It was a dumb thing to do, at that speed. The truck almost did a backflip. Everyone in it was flung sideways.

As we tipped over, I took a flying leap into a billowing cloud of dust.

Chapter Twenty-four

So here I am, sitting here today, and I'm not dead. Go figure. I jumped off that truck while it was toppling onto its side at about a million miles an hour, but I hit the dirt without killing myself. How did I do it? Don't ask me. It all happened so fast that I'm not sure.

Maybe I should thank my quick reflexes. Or maybe I'm just lucky I hit bulldust instead of rock. That bulldust was like talcum powder; I was coughing it up for hours afterwards. Still, it was a lot softer than asphalt.

I know that I landed way too hard on one ankle. And even though I instantly sprang off it into a kind of lopsided forward roll, the pain was dire. What's more, I knocked the air out of my lungs. I was winded. For what seemed like forever, I lay there gasping for breath in a cloud of dust as fine as smoke.

'Ow...ow...ow...'

You know when you just have to writhe around for a little while, until the agony eases off? Well, that's what I did at first, rocking back and forth, clutching my injured leg. Then I spotted Danny's silhouette, looming out of the dust. He looked unsteady on his feet.

I saw why when he drew near. There was blood all over his face. His nose and mouth were bleeding, and so was the cut on his head. 'Lotht a tooth,' he mumbled, into his cupped palm. Blood dripped between his fingers. Flies were buzzing around his head.

'Toby?' said Reuben. 'Are you okay?'

He was over near the truck, which was lying on its roof. From the careful way he was moving, I could tell that he'd hurt himself. But since he wasn't limping or bleeding or nursing any particular part of his body, it was hard to work out exactly what he'd injured. His back, perhaps? His ribs? His shoulder?

His shotgun was nowhere in sight.

'Where's Sergio?' I asked, grunting the question through clenched teeth.

'I dunno...' Reuben coughed as he glanced around. But Danny was the one who pointed.

'There,' he said.

Sergio was curled up in a patch of saltbush, some distance away. He was covered in scratches and whimpering like a puppy. There was something wrong with his arm. Even I could see that.

'He'th all right. He'th breathing,' Danny announced, in a thick, dull, gluggy kind of voice. I guess he must have been lisping because of his lost tooth. Or maybe it was because of his fat lip. 'Where'th me rifle? Toby? Where'd you drop it?'

'I – I dunno...' I couldn't see the rifle, though all kinds of other objects littered the surrounding landscape. There was an upended toolbox, a tangle of nylon rope, a tyre jack, a shovel, a tarp and a bag of kangaroo jerky, among other things. 'It must be somewhere.'

'What about that arsehole scumbag?' Reuben wanted to know. He sounded immensely tired. 'Is he still inside your truck?'

'Mutht be,' said Danny, scanning the area. Without another word, Reuben shuffled off to see whether Gary was still alive. Danny followed him, while I tried to stand. But I couldn't put any weight on my injured foot.

I had to crawl over to where Sergio was lying.

'What's wrong?' I asked, certain that I already knew the answer. 'Did you break something?'

'I – I dunno.' He was gingerly holding his right forearm just above the wrist. 'Maybe. My arm hurts.'

'Can you wriggle your fingers?'

'Kinda...'

'Can you bend your hand forward?'

'*E-e-e-ow!* God!'

'Sorry,' I said quickly. 'Don't bend your hand forward.'

He shut his eyes and groaned. I averted my own eyes, fixing them instead on Danny and Reuben – who were crouched beside the upended truck. They were trying to peer through the driver's window, which had cracked into dozens of little white shards. As I watched, Reuben gave the doorhandle above his head a firm tug.

But the door wouldn't open. The roof was too badly buckled.

'Is Gary dead?' I asked, too dazed to care much either way.

'Dunno,' Danny replied. Then he said to Reuben, 'I'll knock that glath out.'

'Don't be an idiot.' Reuben's breathing was shallow. He winced as he straightened up. 'We can't drag him out over broken glass.'

'Why not?'

'Just find a bloody crowbar. Or a hammer or something.'

288

While they were scouring the scene for a crowbar, I wondered dully what the hell we were going to do. The truck was totalled. The car was a write-off. We were stuck out in the middle of nowhere without any kind of transportation.

'Did you bring your satellite phone?' I asked Reuben, who shook his head.

'It's under the mattress,' he croaked. 'Back at the house.'

'Under the *mattress*?'

'Look.' He stooped, very slowly and deliberately, to reach behind a bush. 'Here's the shotgun.'

It was the shotgun, all right, but part of its stock was missing. Reuben clicked his tongue over this damage; he said that the weapon was probably unsafe to use. Then Danny cried, 'Goddit!', and pounced on something. When he waved it at us, I saw that it was a crowbar.

'How are we gunna get back?' I demanded, still addressing Reuben.

'We'll work it out,' he promised. He was moving away, so I raised my voice.

'We don't have a car, Reuben!' I bleated.

'Just hang on a minute. One step at a time.'

Reuben clearly had his heart set on pulling Gary out of the truck, so I turned my attention to Sergio, who needed just as much help as Gary did. Unfortunately, the only bit of pain relief that I could offer was a sling constructed from my T-shirt – which had to be ripped down the middle before it was long enough. 'Don't worry,' I told Sergio, when he feebly protested. 'I've got another one back at the house.'

Meanwhile, Danny was busy with his crowbar. When he finally popped the driver's door, it shed sprays of broken glass as it swung open. The effort involved must have left him dizzy, to judge from the way he staggered backwards. It was Reuben who crawled into the overturned cabin, until only his feet were visible.

'He's alive,' Reuben announced, after thirty seconds or so. 'But he's unconscious.'

'Can you get 'im out?' asked Danny.

'I think so. Yeah. He's not stuck under anything.' A pause. 'Ah, jeez. This is gunna be hard.'

There followed a lot of grunting and cursing. I guess it was quite a struggle, extracting a dead weight from that cramped little box – especially for someone with sore ribs, or whatever. When Reuben finally emerged, he was pouring sweat and gasping for air. He had his elbows hooked under Gary's armpits.

As for Gary, he looked better than I'd expected. Though the knees of his pants were torn and bloody, his lolling head was still in one piece. It hadn't been caved in or ripped off.

'Whaddaya reckon?' said Danny, flapping the flies away. 'Ith he gunna wake up?'

'I dunno.' Reuben waddled backwards until his burden was well clear of the truck, then dumped Gary beside Sergio. 'You two guys can look after this one for a minute. Me and Danny have to fix the car.'

Fix the car? I couldn't believe my ears. 'But—'

'You got any spare petrol, mate?' Reuben interrupted. He was talking to Danny. 'Was that a jerry can I saw behind the seat?'

'Yep. I'll get it for ya.'

'We'll need soap and water, too. And maybe a bit of tubing, if the fuel line's taken a hit...'

It turned out that Reuben was a motor mechanic. When he started to ramble on about plugging holes in tanks, I suddenly remembered his oily overalls. *Thank God*, I thought, as he described how it was possible to patch up a petrol tank using a cake of soap mixed with water and bulldust. Luckily, there was soap in Danny's glove box – along with a razor, a toothbrush and a small first-aid kit. What's more, the water bottle was still half full. But the car was miles down the road, and I didn't much fancy being left behind with only a first-aid kit to sustain me. What would happen if Gary woke up? What was I supposed to do if he tried to escape?

'He won't wake up,' Reuben said flatly. 'And even if he does, he won't be doing anything. I mean, just look at the guy. He's comatose.'

'And if you're *that* worried, you can find the bloody rifle,' Danny growled. He was throwing soap and spanners and plastic tubing into a toolbox. 'I want that rifle. That rifle belongth to me.'

'I didn't lose it on purpose.' From the way he spoke, I could tell that he was wondering if I had. 'It wasn't *my* fault.'

'Yeah, yeah,' said Danny. He was such a fearsome sight, with his swollen nose and blood-caked mouth, that I decided to change the subject. There was no point getting him all worked up.

Instead I asked, 'Did you bring your phone?'

'Nuh.'

I didn't know whether to believe him or not. 'If there's a phone in the car,' I continued, 'you could call an ambulance.'

'An *ambulance*?' Reuben echoed. 'Out *here*?'

Danny simply snorted. So I tried again.

'What about the Royal Flying Doctor Service? Couldn't we call them?' When no one answered, I became more strident. 'Sergio's got a broken arm! He needs a doctor!'

'And he'll get one,' Reuben replied. 'Once we're back at the house, I'll call Sanford. Sanford's a doctor. He'll know what to do.'

By now I was feeling sick (from the shock, I reckon), so I gave up and watched in silence as Reuben and Danny trudged off down the road. Danny was lugging the toolbox and Reuben had the jerry can; they were no more than ten metres away when Danny suddenly scooped up the pistol, which had been lying at the bottom of a shallow ditch. Though he didn't turn around, he did hoist it above his head to give me a clear view of the thing. Then he tucked it into the pocket of his raincoat. 'Rifle!' he reminded me, in a loud voice.

I pulled a face at his retreating back.

'What's the time?' Sergio croaked.

'Good question.' I raised Gary's arm to study his watch. 'Twenty to four.'

'What happens if they don't come back for us?'

With a shrug, I said, 'If they don't come back for us, I guess we'll be eating Gary.'

Sergio didn't even crack a smile. 'They shouldna taken the water bottle,' he complained. 'It's really hot. We could die of thirst.'

I pointed out that there was shade behind the truck. But when Sergio scrambled to his feet, I wouldn't let him run for cover – not until he'd retrieved Danny's tarpaulin. My idea was that we should spread out the tarp, roll Gary onto it, and drag him into the shade. Dragging him would be easier than carrying him, I said.

Sergio, however, didn't see why we should bother about Gary. 'Let him sizzle,' was how Sergio put it. 'I don't care if he fries like an egg.'

'You will if some judge says it's manslaughter,' I snapped. And we were still locked in a waspish argument about criminal negligence when all at once Gary moaned.

I nearly had a heart attack.

'Oh my God,' I breathed. His lips were moving and his hands were twitching. He was definitely coming to.

Sergio quickly stumbled off to search for the rifle, hissing with pain at every footfall. I reached for the discarded crowbar as Gary opened his eyes.

'Gnaah,' he muttered.

His blank gaze was unfocused. Though it drifted about, it wouldn't settle on anything. I wondered if he had brain damage. It was the second time he'd been knocked insensible in less than a day; surely that couldn't be healthy?

'I found it!' Sergio cried, from the middle of a roadside salt pan. 'It's over here!'

'Is it busted?'

'I dunno. It *looks* okay.' Sergio held up the rifle with his good hand. It certainly seemed to be in one piece.

Then Gary mumbled, 'What happened?'

I studied him warily, my fingers closing around the crowbar. He still seemed out of it.

'You crashed the truck,' I replied.

'Huh?'

'You shouldn't move,' I added, with a sudden flash of brilliance. 'You've got a head injury. If you move, you might damage your spinal cord or something.'

I was trying to stop him from running away. And I must have succeeded, because he just lay there for a while, blinking in the glare.

With his beard growing out, and his pants all bloody, and

293

his shirt-tails flapping, he didn't look like a police detective anymore.

'So what do we do now?' asked Sergio, hovering at a safe distance with the rifle tucked under his good arm. The other was still wrapped in my homemade sling. 'Are we moving him or what?'

'Nup.' I winked. 'We might hurt him if we move him.'

Sergio frowned. 'Who cares?' he said roughly. When I scowled, it only puzzled him further; his face crumpled into a confused, fretful, impatient expression. 'What's up?' he demanded. 'I don't get it. You just said we had to move him.'

'Yeah, but we'd better not.' Wink, wink. 'It could be dangerous.'

'Why?'

'Sergio, he's got to *stay where he is*. He can't move a muscle. He *can't leave*.'

'Oh!' At last realisation dawned. 'Right. Yeah. Gotcha.' Sergio regarded me with more respect than usual. Before he could say anything, however, Gary spoke up.

'Who are you?' he whispered.

He was squinting at Sergio, who sneered.

'Yeah, sure. Like you don't know,' Sergio spat. 'Nice try, dickhead.'

'Is it Chris?' Gary sounded groggy. 'Did I crash your bike?'

'What?'

'I had a few too many...' As Gary trailed off, Sergio and I stared at each other. Sergio's eyes slowly widened. I sucked air through my teeth.

Then I gently prodded Gary's arm.

'Hey,' I said, 'd'you remember who I am?'

'Huh?'

'*Do you remember who I am?*'

'Uh . . . you're not Chris.' He didn't sound too sure. 'Is *that* Chris?'

Unless he was faking it, Gary seemed to be suffering from short-term memory loss. It was weird. It was creepy. But it was also kind of useful; I saw that at once.

'I'm Toby. That's Sergio. We're friends,' I declared. 'You crashed our truck.'

'I did?'

'Yeah. But we're waiting for some other friends, and when they get here, they'll take us to see a doctor. You need to see a doctor, Gary.'

'Yeah . . .' He lifted a hand to cover his eyes. 'Yeah, I feel pretty crook.'

'That's because you hit your head,' I informed him. Then I gestured at Sergio, indicating that he should put the rifle down. He wouldn't, though. He just stuck out a mutinous bottom lip.

'I don't remember this,' Gary continued. He was slurring his words. 'Where is this place?'

'The outback.' I didn't want to give an exact location, in case it jogged his memory. But he wasn't satisfied.

'The outback?' he repeated, grimacing. 'How come?'

'I dunno. Your car broke down and we gave you a lift.'

'You did?'

'Yep.'

'You were driving?'

'Oh no. Not me. Danny was driving.' As he opened his mouth to ask more questions, I cut him off. 'You should stay quiet. You shouldn't talk too much. Not with a head injury.'

'I feel sick.'

295

'Yeah. Well, that's what happens when you talk too much.'

'I'm gunna throw up,' said Gary, before abruptly rolling onto his side. Then he began to vomit.

I probably should have stayed with him. But in that heat, with so many flies around, I just didn't have the stamina. Instead I beat a hasty retreat, leaning on Sergio as I limped over to the little patch of shade cast by Danny's truck.

Here I sat to wait for the sound of an approaching engine.

'What if they can't fix the car?' Sergio queried, after a long pause. He was huddled beside me, poking through the first-aid box. 'If they can't fix it, they'll have to walk back to Reuben's van. It could take hours.'

'Yeah.'

'Maybe your mum will be here before then. Reuben said she'd turn up in the early evening.'

'Maybe.'

'There's no aspirin.' Frowning, Sergio slammed down the lid of the first-aid box. 'Can you believe that? He's got bandages and alcohol and antiseptic cream, but no painkillers. Why the hell not?'

'I dunno. Because painkillers are for wimps?'

'Brandy's a painkiller. I'll have some brandy,' Sergio decided.

I didn't even try to stop him. To tell the truth, I was trashed. Wasted. I didn't have the strength to worry. I was thirsty and tired and my ankle was throbbing and my head was aching. The glare was making my eyes burn. So after a while I closed them – and soon after that, I fell asleep.

I was still asleep two hours later, when Gary's car appeared on the horizon.

Chapter Twenty-five

By sunset, Danny's truck was upright again. Upon inspecting its undercarriage, Reuben had declared that it was 'in pretty good nick, all things considered'. So he'd roped the two vehicles together, hopped behind the wheel of the sedan, and pulled the truck over until its four tyres were planted firmly on the ground.

Danny had helped, of course. He'd used rocks, spare tyres and toolboxes to ensure a smooth and easy roll, propping the truck up here and holding it down there. But it was Reuben who had known where to tie the rope and apply the pressure. Without Reuben, I'd probably still be out there, my bones bleaching in the sun. Danny's truck would *certainly* still be out there. Because when he finally turned his key in the ignition, his engine wouldn't start.

Luckily, Reuben came to the rescue.

'It sounds like you've got loose battery terminals,' he said, before checking under the bonnet. 'Yep,' was his conclusion. 'Loose *and* corroded. You oughta clean your terminals, mate.' Then he fiddled around with spanners and damp rags for five minutes, after which the truck was just fine – except that its roof had caved in. When Danny was at the steering wheel, he had to hunch his shoulders until his chin was almost level with the dashboard.

That was one reason why no one wanted to accompany him back to the house. Another reason was the fact that he didn't look fit to drive, what with his beat-up face and trembling hands. The rifle propped up next to him wasn't much of an attraction, either. What's more, the sedan had air-conditioning. Danny's truck only had hot air blasting through the shattered driver's window.

Faced with a choice like this, the rest of us piled into Gary's car. Reuben made Sergio sit beside him, in the front. I was told to sit behind Reuben, with Gary next to me. I guess Reuben didn't want Gary anywhere within reach of Sergio – even though Gary no longer knew who Sergio was. Personally, I found it hard to stay mad at a guy who had to be shown how to fasten his seatbelt. Talking to Gary was like talking to a little kid, because I had to keep repeating myself. He'd forgotten everything I'd just finished telling him: my name, my cover story, the fact that I'd warned him not to move . . . I just couldn't see the point of hating a guy who wasn't even there anymore.

Besides, brain damage is scary. It's so scary that I soon forgot about the bad things Gary had done. I was far more worried about the things he might never do again – like feed himself, for instance. What would we do if he never recovered?

'Use him as a plant stand,' growled Sergio, without bothering to lower his voice. Not that it mattered much. Gary was slumped against a window, staring out at the passing scenery in a dazed kind of way. His eyes were half shut and his head bobbed around loosely, like a rag doll's, every time we hit a bump.

'He'll have to go to hospital,' I said. 'Reuben? Sanford's just an ordinary doctor. He can't fix something like this.'

'We'll see,' Reuben replied shortly.

'I dunno why you even care,' Sergio interrupted. 'That guy *deserves* to be brain-dead.' He craned around to peer at Gary, who said in a plaintive tone, 'My knees hurt.'

'Good,' Sergio snapped. When I opened my mouth, Reuben glanced up into the rear-view mirror.

'Sanford's the expert,' he assured me, before I could say anything. 'He'll know what to do. Once I drop you off, I'll go get Sanford and Nina.'

'You should go get Lincoln first,' I advised, having noticed how long the shadows were. The sun was very low and the light was tinged with red. 'He's been in that pit for hours. So have the dogs. They must be desperate by now.'

'Unless the dogs have eaten him.' Sergio spoke with obvious relish. But since he was probably just trying to annoy me, I pretended that I hadn't heard. Instead, I looked away, studying the reflection of Danny's truck in the driver's wing mirror. We were churning up so much dust that it was hard to see more than a blurred silhouette. The outline of Danny's dented roof, however, was clearly visible.

'Are you gunna use this car to pick up Sanford?' I asked, my mind on the punctured tank beneath us. I could still smell petrol.

Reuben shook his head.

'Nuh,' he rejoined. 'I'll use the van.'

That made sense. I could understand why Reuben wanted to get the hell out of Gary's car. In fact the sight of Wolgaroo's distant gate came as quite a relief to me; I'd been worried that we wouldn't make it.

'Can I go to Cobar with you?' was my next question.

There was a brief pause. Then Reuben said, 'There won't be room. Not in the van.'

He was right, of course. The van could only fit three people, squeezed onto a bench seat.

'You'll be okay,' he continued. 'I won't be gone long.'

'Yeah, but what if Danny . . .' I began, before I suddenly remembered who was sitting beside me. Even though Gary didn't appear to be listening, I found that I couldn't finish the sentence.

It didn't matter, though. Reuben knew what I meant.

'Danny won't be staying,' he announced – much to Sergio's surprise.

'Huh?'

'We don't need Danny anymore. He's been a godsend, but I think we'll be better off without him from now on.' Reuben was driving very carefully, because of all the potholes. Maybe that's why he kept his eyes fixed on the road ahead of him. Or maybe he was trying to avoid Sergio's gaze. 'Once we've got everything secured, I'll ask Danny to leave. It's not like he's a friend or a relative. And we don't want him freaking out your mum, Toby.'

'No. We don't.' I agreed with that one hundred and fifty per cent. But Sergio didn't.

'What if Danny doesn't wanna leave?' Sergio protested. 'What if he *won't* leave?'

Reuben sniffed. His fingers tightened on the steering wheel.

'Oh, he'll leave,' Reuben said flatly. 'I'll make it worth his while.'

Before he could explain how, we reached our destination. Reuben pulled up next to the house. Behind us, Danny's truck rolled to a standstill. As the dust settled and the engines fell silent, I was suddenly struck by a nasty thought. Suppose someone was inside the house, watching us? Suppose the Third Man had arrived during our absence, and had hidden his vehicle?

'You don't think anyone's in there, do you?' I muttered, nervously scanning the nearest windows.

'Nah. We woulda seen him.' Reuben was already halfway out of the car. 'There's only one road in, and we were on it.'

'Oh. Yeah.'

'Don't worry, mate. I've got the Glock. Danny gave it to me.'

Reuben patted the bulge beneath his singlet. Then he slammed his door shut – *bang!* But the noise didn't rouse Gary, who had drifted off. His eyes were closed and his mouth was open.

I prodded his arm, very gently.

'Hey,' I said. When he didn't stir, I poked him again. '*Hey!* Wake up!'

Still he didn't react. And I suddenly realised that he wasn't asleep at all.

'Oh no.' I recoiled in horror. From the front seat, Sergio declared, 'He's passed out.'

'*Reuben!*' I cried.

'Probably just as well,' Sergio went on.

'*Reuben!*' I pushed open the door beside me and swung my feet to the ground. Since I'd forgotten all about my injured ankle, the jolt of pain that shot up my leg served as a sharp reminder. 'Ouch! Argh!'

'What is it?' Reuben had been heading straight for Danny's truck. At the sound of my yelp, he stopped abruptly. 'Are you all right?'

'Gary's unconscious! He looks really bad!' I exclaimed.

Reuben frowned. Behind him, Danny was climbing down

301

from the truck's cabin. His spine crunched as he straightened out the kinks in it.

'Aahh,' he sighed. Then he slung the rifle over his shoulder.

'Danny.' Reuben signalled to him. 'You'd better come and help me with this.'

'Huh?'

'This bugger here needs to be carried in. I can't do it alone.'

Danny pulled a face. He pointed out that Gary could be dragged by the feet and not notice, but Reuben stood firm. Together, he and Danny wrestled Gary's limp form out of the car, while I hopped ahead of them into the kitchen, leaning heavily on Sergio. It was a difficult trip for everyone. By the time Reuben had shuffled backwards over the kitchen threshold, Sergio and I were draped across the table, puffing and groaning.

Sergio had bumped his broken arm on a doorjamb. I had badly jarred my foot.

'Come on,' said Reuben, pausing to address us both. 'Up you get, I need you.'

'Wha...?' I couldn't see why, since Danny had a firm grip on Gary's legs. 'My foot hurts,' I complained.

'Yeah, well, my chest hurts!' Reuben snapped. Then he adjusted his position, freeing up one hand so he could jerk the pistol out of his waistband. 'Here,' he said, offering the gun to me. 'You've gotta watch Gary, in case he's faking it.'

I didn't understand, at first. I just stared dumbly at the pistol. Danny remarked that there was one sure way of figuring out if someone was really unconscious or not ('just stick a bloody knife in his leg'), but Reuben ignored him.

'Take the damn gun,' said Reuben, fixing me with a hard green glare. So I took the damn gun.

'Why can't I have it?' Sergio whined. 'How come Toby always gets the guns?'

'Because he doesn't wanna fire 'em,' said Reuben. Sergio immediately began to sulk. He stuck out his bottom lip and wouldn't move.

I had to make my own way out of the kitchen, using walls and cupboards for support. Reuben and Danny couldn't help. They were having a hard enough time with Gary, who had to be carefully manoeuvred through narrow openings and around tight corners. At last, however, they reached the first bedroom, where they dropped Gary onto the mattress that I'd been using earlier that day.

When I finally caught up with them, Danny was flexing his shoulders, Reuben was bent double with his hands on his knees, and Gary was lying on a tangle of dirty bedclothes, dead to the world.

'His breathing sounds bad,' I muttered.

Danny sniffed. I could somehow tell that, in Danny's opinion, Gary was lucky to be breathing at all.

As for Reuben, I don't think he even heard me.

'Right,' he said, straightening up. One hand was pressed against his ribcage. 'You stay here, Toby. Keep an eye on this one while we go get that other one outta the pool. It won't take long. We'll use the tunnel.'

'And then you'll drive to Cobar?' I asked.

'And then I'll drive to Cobar.' Reuben shot a quick glance at Gary, whose eyes had sunk deep into bruised-looking hollows. 'This one will be okay in the meantime.'

'You think?' I couldn't agree. But since I wasn't feeling strong enough to argue, I just slid down the wall and parked myself opposite Gary. No one tossed me a pillow for my bad foot, or offered to bring me something that I could wear on my top half. Reuben just followed Danny out of the room, leaving me empty-handed – except, of course, for the pistol.

The pistol that I wasn't going to need.

Reuben, I thought, was being paranoid again. No *way* was Gary putting on an act. His face was the colour of putty. His breathing sounded like something heavy being dragged over wet gravel. As the minutes slowly passed, he didn't stir – not even when a fly crawled across his bottom lip.

It was awful, having to sit with him in the gathering dusk. The longer I waited, the worse I felt. What if he wet the bed? What if he choked and I had to give him mouth-to-mouth?

What if he died right there in front of me?

If this bloke dies, we're in big trouble, I decided. And then, all at once, I remembered Reuben's phone.

It was under the mattress, he'd said. Under the mattress in the opposite room. Surely it must still be there? Reuben and Danny had marched straight down the hall into the kitchen; they hadn't paused along the way. I'd listened to their footsteps recede, hoping that someone might double back with a drink of water. But no one had.

Cautiously I pushed myself upright, using the wall as a crutch. As long as you have something to lean against, it's easy enough to move along on one foot; you just have to keep swivelling from heel to toe. My other foot dangled in the air as I edged towards the doorway – heel, toe, heel, toe. When I reached the empty corridor, however, I had to cross it. And I couldn't do that without letting go of the wall.

Hopping was out of the question, since it would have

made too much noise. I had to crawl. Once I was in the other bedroom, it didn't take me long to reach the mattress, or to find Reuben's phone. But I had to spend about a minute trying to figure out how the phone actually worked. And then I was really stupid, because the first person I called was Mum. On our home number.

I guess I was just distracted. It's hard to concentrate when your ears are pricked for the sound of approaching footsteps.

As soon as our voicemail answered, I realised what a fool I'd been. Of course! She was on her way here! So I hung up and tried her mobile, which proved to be out of range. 'The number you have dialled...' said the recorded message, before I cut it off. Though my heart sank, I decided that not being able to reach her was probably good news. It probably meant that she was quite close, since I was in an area with no mobile-phone reception.

Suddenly a voice cried, 'I *knew* it!'

Looking up, I saw that Sergio had appeared in the doorway. He'd taken off his shoes, for some reason – maybe because they weren't his. I guess that's why I hadn't heard him coming.

'You *slimy bastard*!' he exclaimed, lunging at me. I squirmed away, desperately trying to key in an emergency number. But it was no good. When he kicked my arm, I dropped the phone.

'Ow! Jesus!'

I didn't stand a chance. He pounced on the phone while I was still rubbing my wrist. By this time the whole house was shaking from the impact of a heavy, urgent footfall. Someone was thundering down the hallway.

'Who did you call?' Sergio demanded shrilly. 'Who was it?'

And then Danny burst into the room.

His face and bare chest were still smeared with dry blood. His raincoat flapped out behind him like a bat's wings. He was big and filthy and covered in scars, and the whites of his eyes were tomato-red. Around his ankles swarmed a pack of barking, baying dogs.

But he wasn't carrying his gun, for some reason.

'WHO DID YOU CALL?' he bellowed. 'Huh? HUH?'

'N-no one,' I stammered. It was the wrong thing to say. Next thing I knew, he'd grabbed me by the hair.

'Ouch! Yeow!'

'Who did you call?' His broken nose and bushy brows swam in front of me; I could hardly see them through the tears that had sprung to my eyes. 'Didja call the copth? Didja?'

'No!'

WHUMP! He drove my head into the floor. It happened so fast that I only realised what he'd done a second or two after he'd done it. The pain wasn't as bad as the shock, at first. I felt a weird sensation, as if my eyeballs were bouncing off the inside of my skull (which they were, I suppose). But then the pain hit while Danny was hauling me up again. I think he may have wanted to hammer my head against the floor. And all the time he was shouting questions, which I couldn't possibly have answered. Not with my brain sloshing around like a heap of wet clothes in a tumble dryer.

I was lucky that Reuben appeared. If he hadn't, I probably would have ended up like that poor sod across the hall.

'Stop it!' Reuben shrieked. He must have jumped on Danny, though I didn't see it. I had my eyes shut. There was a tug at my hair and then Danny let go. I heard thuds and shouts as the floorboards quaked beneath me. I was close enough to smell the sweat and feel the vibrations. Someone hit a wall: *cr-r-runch*. The dogs were barking hysterically. Then one of them gave a startled yip, followed by a whimper.

I curled into a ball, shielding myself from the swaying, staggering bodies.

'*You want me to? Huh?*' Reuben yelled. '*I'll do it! I will!*'

Something went *click* – and suddenly the fighting stopped. There were no more creaks or grunts. All I could hear was the sound of panting. Even the dogs were silent.

I opened my eyes and saw Reuben. He was clinging to Danny's back, looking like a shell on a tortoise. Danny was bent almost double, clawing at the arm that was wrapped around his neck from behind. In his right hand Reuben held the pistol, which was rammed against Danny's skull, just above the ear. They were both gasping for breath.

'He wath calling the cops,' Danny croaked. But Reuben just tightened his grip, so that Danny grimaced.

'*You wanna make me do it?*' Reuben screeched. '*Do ya? Is that it?*'

'No . . .'

'*Because I bloody will! Because you're a mad bastard!*'

'Okay, okay!'

'*Because you're outta control, and I'm sick of it!*' As Reuben slid to the ground, he kept his arm clamped firmly around Danny's throat. This meant that the bigger man was pulled sideways, almost losing his balance. But the dogs didn't leap to his defence. Though they were pacing like wolves – hackles raised, ears back, fangs bared – they were also keeping their distance.

I couldn't understand why until one of them growled. That was enough to galvanise Reuben. His head whipped round, his teeth snapped, and he hissed like a crocodile.

307

The dogs all flinched. They slunk even further away, looking thoroughly squashed.

I couldn't believe it.

'Now. You gunna toe the line, or what?' Reuben asked, in a slightly calmer tone. He was talking to Danny, who had bent his knees and twisted his spine to accommodate Reuben's hold on his neck. 'Because I'm *fed up*, Danny. I've *had it* with you!'

'It was Toby's fault,' Sergio cut in. 'Toby was calling somebody—'

'Shuddup.' Reuben flashed him a look that made Sergio cringe like the dogs. Then Danny said hoarsely, 'Okay. All right. I thcrewed up.'

'Damn right, you screwed up!'

'I know. I lotht it. Just leggo, will ya?'

To my surprise, Reuben did let go. But he kept the gun trained on Danny.

'This isn't gunna work,' Reuben declared. 'You can't stay here. It's messing with your head.'

Danny stiffened. 'Nah,' he rumbled, hunching his shoulders in a shifty kind of way as he massaged his neck muscles. 'I had one too many beerth...'

'And let someone escape. And bashed a kid.'

'I made a mithtake. I'm thorry.' Danny pointed to where I was cowering. 'But if that little bugger called the copth—'

'Then *I'll* deal with 'em.' Reuben interrupted. Lowering his gun, he gestured at the door. 'If the cops are coming, you've gotta get out. You know what you're like with the police.' Seeing Danny hesitate, he took a deep breath and continued in a more measured, persuasive manner. 'Mate, you did a good job. But it's over now. You can't stay here.'

Danny was looking disgruntled.

'I like to finish what I thtart,' he said.

Reuben scowled impatiently. 'What's to finish, for Chrissake? The kids are out. The villains are trashed. One's brain-dead and the other has first-degree sunburn—'

'Yeah, but what about number three?' Danny objected. 'We haven't found *him*, yet.'

'So why don't you track 'im down, then?' Reuben asked. It was a good question. It certainly had an impact on Danny, who blinked and raised his eyebrows.

'Me?' he said.

'Go home, get cleaned up, and head for Broken Hill. Because that's where the bugger is.' Reuben must have realised that he'd struck a chord with this argument, because he kept plugging away at it. 'Sergio can tell me what he looks like, and we'll take it from there. In fact I'll call you. I might even join you, if I can get the time off.'

'Really?' Danny seemed to have been won over. His voice, though gruff, was also resigned. 'Well...okay.'

'You've gotta go, Danny. When this kid's mother shows up and sees what you've done to him—'

'Yeah, yeah. I know.' Danny waved a weary hand. 'Anyway,' he remarked, 'I need to get me truck fixed. I can do that in Broken Hill.'

'And I'll pay for the panel beating,' Reuben offered, clinching the deal. All at once Danny folded. He came to a decision and acted on it.

'I'll go,' he confirmed, clicking his tongue at the dogs. 'I can tell when I'm not welcome.'

'Thanks, mate.'

'If I hang around, I'll end up hitting people.' Danny glared at me as he moved towards the door. 'You wanna watch your back with thith one, though. *I* would.'

Reuben didn't comment. He just said, 'Your truck should be fine. But if it's not, gimme a yell. I can always take a look at it.'

Danny nodded. Then he vanished – and his dogs vanished too. I heard him stomping down the hallway, heading for the kitchen.

'*You can take the rest of the beer, if you want!*' Reuben called after him.

There was no reply. After a minute or so, however, the fridge door slammed.

I looked up at Reuben, who was listening intently.

'Where's his rifle?' I quavered.

Reuben didn't answer until Danny had left the house. When the back door creaked, it was like a signal. Reuben sighed. His muscles relaxed. His gaze dropped.

He fixed me with a hard, fierce, icy stare and said, 'If he was gunna shoot you, he'da done it already.'

'Yeah, but—'

'You dunno how lucky you are, mate. You have *no idea* how lucky you are.'

He reached for the phone just as an engine sputtered outside. It was a second or two before that ominous *ugga-ugga-ugga* was swallowed up by a throaty roar – and I don't think I was the only one who heaved a sigh of relief when it happened.

Reuben shoved the phone into his pocket. 'Didja call the police?' he asked me.

'No.'

'Are you *sure*?'

'I'm sure. I tried. But Sergio took the phone.'

310

Reuben grunted. After eyeing me for a second or two, he decided to take my word for it.

'All right,' he grudgingly allowed. 'So I guess you learned your lesson, eh? No harm done, except to your head. You should put some ice on it.' He paused briefly, distracted by the noise that Danny's truck was making as it drove away. 'Needs a new spark plug,' he mumbled, before giving himself a kind of mental shake. 'Right,' he announced, in a brisk voice. 'I'm off to pick up Sanford. You two can wait here till I get back. And don't go anywhere near the guy downstairs – he's fine as he is.'

With that, he beat a hasty retreat. But just as he crossed the threshold, he threw a sourly amused glance over his shoulder and drawled, 'Why don'tcha talk amongst yourselves, in the meantime?'

Then he snorted and left.

Chapter Twenty-six

Needless to say, Sergio and I *did not* spend the next two hours chatting. In fact we didn't exchange a single word until we heard Reuben's van approaching the house again, at about eight thirty. By that time we were sitting at the kitchen table, studiously ignoring each other. Sergio had swallowed a couple of aspirins that he'd found in Lincoln's gym bag, while I had taken a bath and put on the dirty T-shirt that I'd stuffed into a kitchen cupboard earlier that afternoon. (I figured that a dirty T-shirt was better than no T-shirt at all.) Sergio was combing his hair. I was holding a makeshift icepack to the lump on my head. We were also eating leftovers: pickles dipped in tomato ketchup.

I think we were both trying to pretend that Lincoln and Gary didn't exist. We certainly hadn't made the slightest effort to check on them. I mean, we couldn't do anything to help them, could we? And I didn't want to just sit and watch them suffer.

'Listen.' Sergio looked up. 'Is that what I think it is?'

I listened. 'Someone's coming,' I deduced.

'Quick! Turn the lights off!'

'*You* turn the lights off. My foot hurts, remember?' When he rose, I added, 'It's probably Reuben.'

'Yeah, but suppose it isn't?' Sergio flicked the switch by the door, plunging us both into darkness. 'I wish Reuben hadn't taken the gun,' he snivelled. 'What'll we do if it's that guy from Broken Hill? We'll have to hit him with a frypan when he walks in.'

Luckily, however, it wasn't the guy from Broken Hill. When Reuben pulled up outside, I was already peering through the back window. And my pulse slowed right down when I spotted his van.

'Don't worry. It's Reuben,' I told Sergio, who had started to scour the cupboards for a heavy pot. He immediately rushed over to join me.

'Has he brought any food?' asked Sergio.

'I dunno.'

'There must be *somewhere* in Cobar that sells food. Even if it's just salted peanuts...'

We both pressed our noses to the dusty glass, keen to catch sight of a pizza box or a bag of groceries. But we were doomed to disappointment. Though the cabin of the van was stuffed with people, not one of them seemed to be carrying so much as a bottle of water.

'Aw, crap,' Sergio complained. 'Would it have killed him to buy a couple of hamburgers?'

'They might have brought some chocolate bars,' I hazarded, watching the van disgorge its load. First came Reuben, jingling his keys. Then came Dr Plackett, in a truly ridiculous outfit. (Why the hell was he wearing a safari suit?) Then came Nina, looking very small and pinched in a droopy dress with flowers all over it. And then came... 'Who's that guy?'

Sergio frowned. 'Which guy?' he said.

'That guy.' I pointed at a short, balding, middle-aged man

313

with a broken nose and very little neck. He seemed to be grey all over; his face was grey, his clothes were grey, his hair was grey. 'I've never seen him before. No one ever mentioned *him*.'

'Isn't he the doctor?'

'No. *That's* the doctor. The one with the medical bag.'

'Oh. Right.'

'How did everyone fit in?' I couldn't understand it. They might have been skinny, but even so... *four*? All the way from Sydney? 'And what's with the sunglasses? It's night-time, for God's sake. Do they think they're movie stars or something?'

Much to my relief, the sunglasses didn't stay on. Nina took hers off as soon as she entered the house, and her two friends did the same. For a moment they stood blinking, their eyes screwed up against the light. Then Nina spotted me.

'Hello, Toby,' she remarked. 'You look a bit rough.'

I could have said the same thing about her. In fact I nearly did. Though I'd been feeling pretty sorry for myself, up until that moment, I was shocked when I first saw Nina in the harsh light of an unshaded hundred-watt bulb. She was gaunt and pasty-faced. Her eyes were ringed by dark shadows, like a raccoon's. She had hollow cheeks and cracked lips and bluish fingernails.

So did Dr Plackett, but you always expect older people to have health problems. When an older person is sallow and sickly, it doesn't seem so strange. As for the grey guy, he was actually tottering. Nina had to lead him to a chair.

'This is Barry,' she explained. 'He's a bit carsick.'

Carsick my arse, I thought. But all I said was, 'Why did you bring him, then? What's he here for?'

Reuben and the doctor exchanged glances. Before either of them could speak, however, Nina jumped in. 'He's supposed to be my uncle. The one who let us stay when we eloped.' There was a twinkle in her eye. 'Like that priest from Romeo and Juliet.'

I couldn't help blushing. To hide it, I limped over to a chair and sat down. Sergio, meanwhile, was bombarding Nina with questions.

'But wasn't that uncle story just a ruse? To get Toby's mum out here?' he asked. 'Aren't we gunna tell her the truth when she arrives? Why do we need a fake uncle – have I missed something?'

'Um . . .' Nina hesitated. She turned to Dr Plackett, who immediately took over.

'You must be Sergio,' he said, stepping forward. 'I'm Dr Plackett. Dr Sanford Plackett.'

Sergio didn't know what to make of this. Though he grudgingly let Dr Plackett shake his good hand, he also withdrew it very quickly, with a baleful and suspicious look.

'This is Nina Harrison,' the doctor continued, 'and this is Barry McKinnon. He's the owner of Wolgaroo.'

'*McKinnon?*' I echoed. But Dr Plackett hadn't finished.

'We felt that we couldn't prevent Barry from coming along to inspect the place,' he said.

Nina rolled her eyes at the ceiling. I sensed from her long-suffering expression that Barry hadn't been wanted.

'It's my house,' Barry croaked, as if he knew what I was thinking. 'I built it. I paid for it. It's supposed to be empty.'

His voice sounded rough and dry, like sandpaper. He had thin lips and a pale, lifeless gaze. His scars reminded me of Danny's.

'*You!*' Reuben spat. '*You* didn't pay for this house, *I* did! And

315

so did Danny Ruiz and Orlando Esteban and Lupe Calleja—'

'Yes, yes, we're all aware of that,' the doctor interrupted. 'Please, Reuben, this isn't the time to discuss culpability issues. You should save it for our next meeting.' He lifted a hand, as if to quell any further protests. 'This is obviously going to be difficult for everyone, in light of where we are, but there are far more important matters to address than the apportioning of guilt.'

'Like what?' Reuben growled.

'Like that arm, for instance.' Dr Plackett nodded at Sergio. 'And Toby's head.'

'You should look at Gary first,' I cut in. When the doctor raised his eyebrows at me, I added, 'He's really bad, you know. He acts like he's dying.'

Nina sucked air through her teeth. Dr Plackett rounded on Reuben, who yelped, 'Don't blame me! I didn't crash the truck, Gary did!'

'And it was Danny who made Gary fall downstairs,' I observed.

'That's right. It was Danny's fault. We'd all be fine, if it wasn't for Danny,' Reuben assured the doctor, who shook his head gravely before asking where Gary was.

'In there.' I pointed. 'He's still breathing, but only just.'

'You'd better show me,' the doctor said to Reuben. Together they vanished into the hallway, Dr Plackett carrying his medical bag and Reuben armed with his gun.

After they'd left, there was a brief, awkward silence – which I finally broke when I turned to Barry.

'So,' I said, 'aren't you the one who set up those tanks downstairs?'

Of course I knew the answer to this question. I just wanted

to see him squirm. And he did, too. His eyes skittered away as he hunched his shoulders.

In the end, it was Nina who replied.

'Barry's really sorry for what he did,' she insisted. 'Aren't you, Barry?'

He mumbled something.

'Hang on.' Sergio was frowning. 'Are you telling me this is the same guy? The guy who used to run fights here?'

'Jeez, Sergio, did you only just work that out?' I scoffed. But I don't think he heard me. A red flush was slowly creeping across his face.

'The one who kidnapped Reuben? And Danny?' he choked.

'Yeah, but he's paid for it,' said Nina. 'Swear to God, he'd be better off dead.'

It was the weirdest thing to say. What the hell did she mean? I shot her an incredulous look, which seemed to make her uncomfortable.

'In a manner of speaking,' she lamely amended. I think Sergio might have asked for more details then, if the sound of raised voices hadn't distracted us. An argument had erupted in the bedroom. I recognised Reuben's raised voice, though I couldn't hear his exact words. Dr Plackett's sharp retort was pitched a little lower.

'Oh, man,' Nina murmured. She sighed as she collapsed onto the last empty chair. Everything about her seemed to droop; her hair, her mouth, her spine... everything. Her arms were blue-white, and so skinny that I couldn't help myself. I just had to ask.

'Are you sick?' I blurted out. 'I mean, are you *really* sick?'

Thump-thump-thump. Angry footsteps were pounding down the corridor. Nina gave a nod.

'Yep,' she replied, 'I'm really sick.'

'You mean like cancer?' Sergio came right out with it, before I could say something a little less goddamn *blunt*. I scowled at him, just as Dr Plackett entered the room.

'Now – where's this staircase?' he snapped. Seeing that no one else was going to tell him, I gestured at the hatch in the floor.

'Under there,' I mumbled. Then Reuben appeared in the doorway.

'Lincoln's fine! I told you! We gave him some water!' cried Reuben. 'These other guys are *much* worse off than he is! Sergio's got a broken arm, for God's sake!'

'I doubt that,' the doctor rejoined. He was moving towards the hatch, but paused long enough to eye Sergio's makeshift sling. 'A broken arm is usually a lot more debilitating,' was his off-the-cuff diagnosis. 'This is probably a sprain. But I'll check it in a minute. Along with your head, Toby.'

'And my foot. My foot hurts too.' I didn't bother getting up to help him with the hatch. Though he was so feeble that he couldn't have managed it all on his own, he didn't have to; Reuben was with him. And Reuben had no trouble lifting the lid on that shadowy, brick-lined basement. 'I'll go first,' said Reuben, waving his gun. Then he plunged downstairs, closely followed by Dr Plackett. The noise of their bickering was soon overlaid by a jangle of keys.

'Is that American bloke down there?' Nina asked, much to my surprise.

'Yeah,' I answered. 'So Reuben told you about him?'

Nina shrugged. 'He gave us an update on our way over.'

'Oh. Right.'

This made perfect sense to me, but not to Sergio. 'Why?' he demanded. And when Nina and I both stared at him, he said brusquely, 'Who *are* you people? Why are you even here? What the hell has this got to do with you, anyway? Are you werewolves, or what?'

If Nina was taken aback, she didn't show it. Instead she just smiled a sad little smile. 'I wish,' she murmured. Again, it was an odd thing to say. I was about to tell her so, but I didn't get a chance – because all at once Barry lurched to his feet.

'I'm gunna be sick,' he groaned. Then he clamped a shaking hand across his mouth.

Nina stiffened.

'Where's the bathroom?' she shot at me.

'Uh – through there.' I motioned at the connecting door. 'Second on your left.'

As Barry stumbled out of the kitchen, he kept bouncing off corners and bumping into furniture. He moved like a drunk man, and I wondered if he might need help. From what I could see, Nina wasn't about to give him any; she just sat there, watching him stagger out of the room. And Sergio's only reaction was to pounce on Barry's vacated chair.

It didn't seem right that *I* should have to get up. I mean, I had a sore foot, for God's sake.

'Is he gunna be all right?' I asked, jerking my chin at the door.

'He'll live,' Nina said wearily.

'Can't the doctor do anything?'

She shook her head, even more wearily. 'No.'

'But if it's something he ate . . .'

'It isn't.' Nina hesitated, as if she didn't know whether to go on or not. Her dark eyes searched my face. She opened her mouth and took a deep breath.

Unfortunately, Sergio bumbled in ahead of her.

'Speaking of things to eat, did you bring any food?' he piped up. 'Like a chocolate bar, maybe?'

Nina blinked. She turned to peer at him, her expression dazed. 'A chocolate bar?' she repeated. You'd have sworn that he was speaking in a foreign language.

'We're living on pickles! That's all we've got!' he exclaimed. 'We're *starving* to death!'

'Oh.' She put a hand to her cheek. 'Yes. Of course. Food,' she muttered. 'I never thought...'

And then, suddenly, the back door burst open.

It was Danny Ruiz.

Surprised? You bet I was. I can't pretend that I didn't start, or gasp, or squeak like a mouse. For one thing, Danny was a fearsome sight, what with his scars and his rifle. On top of that, I was still nursing the bump he'd given me. It wasn't as if we'd parted on good terms.

But at least he wasn't the mysterious Third Man. That's what I told myself, anyway. *Better the devil you know*, I thought.

'It's okay,' I said to Nina, who had uttered a little cry of fear. 'It's just Danny. He's come back.' I cocked my head at him. 'Did the truck break down?' I queried.

Danny didn't respond. He stepped across the threshold, his coat-tails flapping, his dogs at his heels. The screen door banged shut behind him.

As he scanned the room, I realised that he'd pulled on a pair of jeans, though his chest was still bare.

'Where'th Reuben?' he snapped.

'Downstairs,' I replied – and this time I made an impression. He rounded on me.

'Where'th the gun?'

'The pistol, you mean?' I felt a twinge of unease. 'Reuben's got it.'

Nina tried to introduce herself. 'I'm Nina,' she said, rising from her chair. But Danny brushed straight past her, ignoring her outstretched hand. I figured that he must be heading for the basement.

Instead, he slammed the hatch down. *Crash!* I couldn't believe my eyes when he started to drag the heavy table across it.

'What are you doing?' I yelled. Without a second thought, I sprang out of my seat to stop him. And the pain, of course, knocked me straight back down again. '*Yeowch!* Argh! Ooh!'

The dogs were growling at Nina, their hackles raised. Danny was doing much the same thing; his gun was now trained on her. 'So what'th your angle? Huh?' he rasped. 'What are you up to?'

She lifted her hands, shaking from head to toe. She was much too scared to say anything.

Meanwhile, someone was pounding on the underside of the hatch. But it wouldn't budge. There was too much weight pushing it down, now that Danny had parked himself on the tabletop.

'Danny,' I spluttered, 'what the hell . . . ?'

'They were in the back of the van.'

'What?' I gaped at him.

'*They were in the back of the van.* I thaw 'em. I wath out there, watching. Down the road.' He was squinting along the barrel of his gun; his hands were rock-steady, though the table beneath him kept shaking. (*Bang-bang-bang* went Reuben's fists – or was it Dr Plackett hammering on the hatch?) 'I thought I'd wait till Reuben had gone,' Danny explained. 'And then I'd come back and help. I didn't think he shoulda left ya. Not without a gun.'

'Hear, hear,' Sergio squawked. He obviously believed that Danny had been concerned about our welfare.

I didn't. I figured that Danny had wanted to return when the coast was clear, so he could blast a hole through each of our prisoners.

'Reuben didn't drive to Cobar,' Danny went on. 'He parked down the road and opened the back of the van. Then he let *them* out. Her and the other two. And they waited for a while.'

I didn't understand. 'You mean—'

'They were in there all day. In the back of the van.'

'Don't be stupid.' I didn't believe a word of it. 'That's impossible.'

'Athk her,' said Danny. 'Go on.'

I turned to Nina, whose dry lips were moving slightly. When she looked back at me, there was something in her dark-ringed eyes that made me wonder.

No, I thought. *No, that's crazy. Danny's got it wrong.*

'You couldn't have stayed in the back of that van,' I argued. 'Not all day. You would have died in there. It was too hot.'

'Maybe it's a refrigerated van,' Sergio interjected. He might have been joking; I'm not sure. But Nina didn't tell him to butt out. She seemed lost for words.

So I said, 'If it was refrigerated, there wouldn't be enough air. Would there?' Sergio shrugged. Nina remained speechless. In the silence that followed, Reuben's muffled voice was faintly audible. '. . . *out* . . . *open* . . .'

More violent thudding ensued. Danny ignored it.

'And gueth what?' he snarled. 'D'you know who wath in that van with Morticia here? I'll tell you who.' He paused for effect. 'It wath Barry McKinnon. *Barry bloody McKinnon!*'

I'm not sure what kind of reaction he was expecting. Shock, maybe. If so, he didn't get it.

'Oh yeah.' Sergio nodded. 'We knew that.'

He cringed as Danny's rifle swung towards him.

'You *what*?' Danny barked.

Sergio raised his hands. When he spoke again, his voice was a tiny thread of sound. 'He – he told us. I mean, Reuben did . . .'

'Barry McKinnon built the tankth!' Danny roared. 'Didja know *that*?'

Sergio licked his lips.

'D'you know what he did to *me*?' Danny raved, his eyes nearly popping out of his head. That's when Nina spoke up, at long last. Don't ask me why. Maybe she was trying to protect Sergio.

'He's very sorry,' she bleated. 'Barry's very sorry for what he did.'

Once again, Danny whirled around. He shoved his rifle at Nina.

'Oh, he'll be thorry all right,' Danny promised. 'Now where ith he?'

Nina swallowed. Her hands were still in the air.

'You – you don't understand,' she stammered. 'He's already been punished.'

'Not the way I'm gunna do it.' Danny was grinding the words out between his teeth. 'Now *tell me where he ith.*'

'He's in the bathroom,' I volunteered.

You may be wondering why I said that. You may be thinking,

323

'What a weasel!' But the fact is, you weren't there. You didn't see the way Danny was looking at Nina. I did, and I was dead sure of one thing: he wasn't bluffing. Two more seconds, and he would have beaten the answer out of her – or worse.

There was something else, too. I happened to be sitting between Danny and the door, so I knew that, when he ran towards it, I'd have a good chance of stopping him.

I just wanted to get his gun out of Nina's face.

Yeah, yeah, I know. What a moron. Danny had a loaded rifle and four vicious dogs, and what did I have? An injured foot. Good one, Toby.

Mind you, I did manage to take him by surprise. He probably didn't think that I could get up at all, let alone grab his gun as he went past. Not that I had a hope of actually getting the gun *off* him. I just thought that if I could keep him occupied for a few seconds, Nina would have enough time to open the hatch and let Reuben out.

I didn't factor in the dogs, though. They went straight for me.

'*No! Stop! Get them off!*' Nina screamed, as I staggered backwards. My ankle gave way because the dogs were dragging me down; mostly they were pulling at my jeans, but Psycho had leapt right up and bitten my arm. *Snap!* It wasn't really a bad bite. He let go of me the instant I let go of Danny. Still, I was bleeding – and hurting, too. *Man,* did it hurt! (Dog bites hurt like you wouldn't believe.)

'*Stop it!*' Nina had picked up a chair. She was using it against the dogs, trying to drive them away. She looked like a lion tamer. '*Get off! No! Stop!*'

By that time, however, the pain had kicked in. And when that happened, I stopped being scared. I got angry instead. I got so angry that I hauled off and punched Psycho straight between the eyes. It was chaos, for a moment. Blood was dripping and dogs were barking and people were yelling and Nina was reeling back, looking sicker than ever. As for Danny, he'd freed himself and was heading for the hallway.

'Open the hatch!' I shouted at Nina. She'd dropped her chair, for some reason. Not only that; she'd retreated to the furthest corner of the room, where she was clinging to a benchtop as if she needed propping up.

It was Sergio who came to my rescue. I don't know why, unless he was afraid that he might be the dogs' next target. He weighed in and gave Tagger a huge kick, before treading on Mutt's tail. I had Psycho in a headlock by then, and he was hysterical, thrashing about like a shark on a hook.

'Nina, will you *open the hatch*?' I bawled.

She nearly passed out while she was moving from the sink to the table, but she did it. She got there. In the meantime, I was trying to keep Mutt away from my bad ankle. Sergio was waving a chair at Tagger. Somewhere down the hallway, Danny was bellowing at the top of his voice.

Scr-e-e-e-ech. A heavy piece of furniture scraped across the floor. Nina had leaned against the table and used her weight to slowly, noisily, push it a metre or so to the right. I didn't see Reuben lunging out of the basement. I was too busy fending off snapping teeth.

But I sure heard him fire his pistol.

BANG!

It was so damn *loud*. Even the dogs froze. For a split second I thought that Reuben had shot someone, until I saw that he'd aimed at the ceiling.

'GEDDOWN!' he roared. His eyes blazed and his veins throbbed

325

and he stamped his foot at the nearest dog – who happened to be Tagger. When Tagger growled, Reuben growled back.

Mutt was already slinking away. Psycho whimpered. They knew who was top dog in that kitchen.

Then Dr Plackett said faintly, 'Oh Christ. Is someone bleeding?'

I looked around to discover that he was halfway up the stairs. I had to think for a moment before answering. Was mine the only fresh blood in the room?

'It's just a dog bite,' I croaked. The words were hardly out of my mouth when a terrible scream rent the air. It was coming from down the hallway.

'Out.' Dr Plackett wasn't talking to the dogs. 'Get out. Quick. Everyone.'

'Not me,' said Reuben.

'Yes, you.'

'He's got a gun, Sanford!'

A huge THUD made the whole house tremble. There was a distant moan, followed by a series of uneven little thumps.

'For God's sake, get out!' cried Dr Plackett. Psycho was wriggling and whimpering. I had to let him go because Reuben grabbed my arm, hauling me upright.

It was Sergio who first spotted Danny. He yelled and pointed. I turned to look, vaguely aware that Nina was wringing her hands.

Danny stood on the threshold, swaying like a tree in the wind. His lips were blue. His expression was shell-shocked. His neck was streaming blood.

In a faint voice, he said, 'The rotten bugger bit me.'

Chapter Twenty-seven

Next thing I knew, I was outside. Reuben had hustled me through the back door.

'Get in the van,' he instructed.

'What?'

'*Get in the van!* Quick!' He darted into the house again, ignoring the fact that I was practically crippled. How was I supposed to get in the van when I couldn't move without some kind of support? As it was, I had to stand on one foot. And there was so much *junk* between me and the van, I could easily have impaled myself on a tangle of auto parts or a set of rusty bedsprings if I'd tried to hop through it all in the darkness, unaided.

Luckily, Reuben was back within seconds. He was dragging Sergio behind him.

'A vampire?' Sergio was saying. 'What d'you mean, he's a *vampire*?'

'They all are.' Reuben caught sight of me. 'Why aren't you ...?' he began. Then his gaze dropped to my foot, which was dangling off the ground. 'Oh. Right. Your ankle.'

'He reckons they're all vampires,' Sergio told me, in tones of dismay. 'Because Danny got bitten...'

'And you'll be next, if you don't get in the bloody van!'

Reuben snapped. Then he caught his breath, listening intently. At first I couldn't hear anything except the shouts and thumps and frantic pleas that were coming from the kitchen. Gradually, however, I picked up another sound: the faint hum of a distant car.

'Oh Christ,' said Reuben. He dashed around the side of the house, past his van, to get a good look at the road.

Sergio and I stared after him, completely gobsmacked.

'What's all this about vampires?' I finally asked.

Sergio shrugged. He couldn't seem to stop shaking his head.

'Who's supposed to be a vampire?' I pressed. 'Barry McKinnon?'

'And Danny, now.'

'Jesus.'

'Are they crazy?' Sergio demanded, his voice cracking. 'You know these people. What are they up to?'

'I – I dunno...'

'We gotta get outta here.' Sergio winced as something heavy hit the floor inside. The noise sent him scuttling towards Reuben's van.

'Wait!' I cried. 'Come back! What about me?'

But he didn't hear – or he didn't *want* to hear. I had to cast around for a crutch of some kind. It wasn't easy in the dark; eventually I came up with an old piece of fence-post, which I leaned on as I picked my way between all the clumps of garbage.

When I caught up with Sergio, he was tugging fruitlessly at one of the van doors.

'It's bloody locked,' he muttered, before whirling around and shrieking at Reuben, '*It's bloody locked! Where are the keys?*'

Reuben stood in a golden patch of light that was spilling through a kitchen window. Above him arched a glistening canopy of stars. Beyond him, in the middle distance, I could see a pair of headlights.

They were growing larger and larger.

Reuben hissed something under his breath. Then he whirled around, plunging a hand into his pocket. His other hand was still wrapped around the pistol.

'Is it – is it that third guy?' I quavered. 'The one from Broken Hill?'

'I dunno.' He pulled out his keys and hurried towards the van. I stepped aside so he could unlock it.

'Are we leaving?' Sergio exclaimed. When no one answered, he said, 'Who has Danny's rifle? Where is it now?'

'Here.' Reuben yanked open the driver's door. 'Get in.'

'Are we making a run for it? Are you gunna drive?' Sergio was becoming more and more shrill. 'I'm not getting in if you're not!'

'Just do it, will you?' Reuben ordered.

'No! I won't! We'll be sitting ducks in there!' Sergio shook him off, stumbling backwards. Meanwhile, I was watching the car as it bounced towards us. It was low to the ground. It had rectangular headlights. It seemed to be a dark reddish colour. And the softly illuminated numberplate read...

'Hey!' I squeaked. 'Hang on! That's our car!'

'What?' Reuben froze.

'That's Mum! In our car! It must be!'

It was. By that time I could see her face – a pale, narrow blur behind the windscreen – and I hobbled forward to greet her. You can imagine how happy I was. I forgot everything else: Danny, Gary, my foot, my empty stomach, Reuben's insane jabbering about vampires – everything. All I wanted to do was crawl into our car and drive straight home.

'Dammit,' Reuben muttered. 'I can't let her see me. Not yet.'

He must have slunk away, behind the house. I'm not sure, because I wasn't looking. My attention was fixed on Mum's car, which had braked near the front veranda. The engine stopped but the headlights stayed on. The driver's door popped open.

'Mum?' I said, picking up my pace a bit.

'*Toby?*' She emerged from behind the wheel, her eyes round with horror. 'Oh my God! What happened?'

'Huh?' For a second I didn't understand. Then I realised that she was staring at my foot. It was spotlit by the headlight beams. 'Oh. Right. This,' I mumbled, stopping to glance down.

'And your head!' she squealed. 'And your wrist! What happened to your wrist?'

I didn't know where to begin. With the overturned truck, perhaps? With Danny's assault? With the dog bite? All kinds of thoughts and images rushed into my brain as she threw her arms around me; I still hadn't settled on a good starting point when Nina's grandmother climbed out of the front passenger seat.

'Where's Nina?' she croaked, then erupted into a fit of coughing: *hack-hack-hack*. If it hadn't been for the cough, I might not have recognised her at first – not without her cigarette. Even her steel-wool hair was engulfed in one of those old-lady scarves that you see on the Queen sometimes. She also looked older than she had before, all creased and stiff and colourless.

Mum looked pretty bad too. She was wearing trackies, for one thing. And she didn't have any makeup on.

'Nina's inside,' I confessed. 'But—'

'She's here? Nina's here?' Mum broke in.

'Yeah.' I took a deep breath. 'There's a whole bunch of people here. That's what I have to tell you. It's a long story...'

Estelle, however, wouldn't let me finish. 'Who's this?' she squawked, nodding at Sergio. 'I don't think I've met *him*, have I?'

'That's Sergio. He's – we're —' I didn't know how to put it. Did Mum know the truth or not? Had Estelle filled her in, yet?

'Let's go,' Sergio said abruptly. '*Now*. Come on.' He was dancing from foot to foot, as if he needed to empty his bladder. I understood how he felt, but I also realised that Mum wouldn't be going *anywhere* unless I provided her with an explanation.

So I opened my mouth to give her one – just as somebody roared like a wounded buffalo inside the house.

Mum gasped. 'What on earth ... ?' she said, pulling away to listen. A muffled *crash* made her cover her mouth in alarm.

That's when I decided not to waste time explaining things. Not yet, at least. Not until we were well on our way. 'We should go. Right now,' I urged.

'Not without Nina,' Estelle insisted. She slammed the car door behind her, then trudged towards the house in what looked like a pair of orthopaedic sandals. She was wearing something that could have been a nurse's uniform.

'I wouldn't go in there if I were you,' Sergio warned. It sounded so much like a threat that I quickly tried to clarify the situation.

'It's not safe,' I said. 'There's a guy in there – Danny – who's had a bit of a meltdown.'

'You mean Danny Ruiz?' Estelle didn't seem especially

concerned. As she waved a dismissive hand, I suddenly remembered that she knew all about Danny. 'So what's new?' she said. 'He's always having meltdowns.'

'Yeah, but he's *really* mad this time.' I couldn't stress this enough. 'It's because Barry McKinnon's in there, and Danny doesn't like him.'

'Because Barry bit his neck,' Sergio added.

Estelle stopped in her tracks.

'He *what*?' she cried, in a strangled voice. 'Oh *Christ*, no!'

'What on earth are you talking about?' Mum sounded frantic. She flinched as another distant, animal roar split the night air. 'Isn't Barry Nina's uncle?'

Bang! The front door flew open. Danny Ruiz stood there, silhouetted against the light in the hallway. '*A-A-A-U-U-GH!*' he bellowed.

Then he lurched onto the veranda, still clutching his neck.

'Get in the car,' Estelle snapped. She beat a hasty retreat, waddling back towards the seat she'd just vacated. But the rest of us were rooted to the spot.

'Who – who—' Mum stammered.

'That's him,' I said. 'That's Danny Ruiz.'

'*O-o-o-a-a-a-gh!*' More bellowing. Danny kept losing his balance; he swayed and stumbled on his way down the veranda steps.

That's when I realised that he was twitching like someone with epilepsy.

'Let's – let's get in the car,' I croaked. Mum didn't argue. She grabbed my elbow, supporting me as I hopped along.

Sergio was ahead of us; he reached the car before we did, plunging into the back seat like a rat into a drainpipe. I was crawling in beside him when Reuben charged out of the house, waving Danny's rifle.

'Oh my God!' Mum shrieked. 'He's got a gun!' Then she dropped her keys.

I don't think she recognised Reuben at first. She was too busy scrabbling around in the driver's footwell. As for Reuben, I doubt he even noticed her. His attention was fixed on Danny, who was struggling to his feet again.

'For God's sake, Rowena, will you *close the door*?' Estelle said fiercely.

Mum did as she was told, groping around for her keys with one hand while she pulled her door shut with the other. *Whomp!* 'Oh my God,' she kept whimpering. 'Oh my God, oh my God, oh my God...'

'What's wrong with Danny?' Sergio's voice was high and frantic, like a police siren. 'Is he bleeding to death?'

'No,' Estelle replied. By this time Danny's dogs had surged onto the front veranda. But they were strangely subdued. Instead of running to join him, they hung back, looking disoriented.

Reuben ignored them. He advanced towards Danny, adjusting his grip on the rifle.

'For Chrissake,' Estelle hissed, before lowering her window a few centimetres. '*Reuben!*' she squawked. '*Get back inside!*'

Danny heard her. He must have, because he turned his head. He even took a step in our direction.

Something was wrong, though. His leg buckled. He fell to one knee.

Estelle quickly wound up her window again, coughing like a machine gun.

'I don't get it,' Sergio whined. 'Where's the doctor? Why doesn't he do something?' At that very instant, Dr Plackett emerged from the house. He was wearing his sunglasses, and he seemed to be arguing with Reuben.

'Where the hell is Nina?' growled Estelle.

Suddenly the engine roared. Mum had found her keys, at long last. She released the handbrake, craning around to check that nothing was behind her. Then she reached out to change gears.

'No!' Estelle yanked at the handbrake. 'Not yet.'

'*What are you doing?*' Mum screamed.

'Wait. Just wait.'

'*Let go!*'

Next thing I knew, Mum and Estelle were wrestling for control of the handbrake. I couldn't believe it. Outside, Danny was flat on his stomach, groaning and shuddering. Reuben was edging towards him, rifle raised. Dr Plackett was trying to grab Reuben's arm, without success; Reuben repeatedly shook him off.

'Nina's in there!' Estelle snapped. 'We can't go without Nina!'

'He's got a *gun*, can't you *see*?' Mum shouted back.

'Yeah, but he won't use it,' Estelle insisted. 'Not on us.'

'How do *you* know?'

'He won't, Mum.' I could be sure of that, at least. 'It's okay. Swear to God.'

'It's not Reuben we should be worrying about,' Estelle confirmed, before she dissolved into another fit of coughing.

Mum caught her breath. Her head swivelled. She stared through the windscreen.

'Reuben?' she echoed. 'Is that – is that *Reuben Schneider?*'

'Mum—'

'Oh my God! It *is* him! It's that lunatic!'

'Mum, listen—'

'It's all a plot! We've been kidnapped!' Mum rounded on Estelle. 'You *bitch!*'

She launched herself at Nina's grandmother, who raised her arms in self-defence. If I hadn't intervened, God knows what would have happened.

'Mum, don't!' I thrust myself between the front seats, before Mum could do any serious damage. 'Stop it!'

'*Get out! Get out of this car!*' she screamed at Estelle, past my left ear.

'Mum, listen! Someone *else* tried to kidnap me! Reuben was the one who stopped them!' I appealed to Sergio. 'Isn't that right? Isn't that what happened?'

'Yeah,' Sergio agreed, in a distracted sort of way. He was watching events unfold outside the car, where Reuben and the doctor were yelling at each other.

'And the rest of them too. They came here to help,' I went on, desperately trying to explain. 'Reuben and Nina and Dr Plackett—'

'Toby, this is all a conspiracy!' Mum cut me off. Her voice cracked on a sob as she fumbled for the handbrake. Her eyes were glazed with panic and she was trembling all over. 'We've got to get out of here, now!' she ranted. 'We've got to get away from these people!'

'Mum, you're *not listening*! Will you *listen* to me?' I gave her a shake, which surprised her so much that she seemed to snap out of her mad fit. She blinked, gasped, and shut up. 'What Reuben told us is true. Okay? He wasn't lying. I'm a werewolf, Mum.'

'Oh, *Toby!*' she wailed.

'Just let me finish—'

'You've been brainwashed!'

'I have *not!*' She was making me mad. 'Do you think I'm stupid? Is that what you think?' Before she could answer, I ploughed on. 'We're werewolves, Mum. Me and Sergio. And Reuben. And Danny. I swear to God, we're all werewolves.'

'Not Danny,' Estelle interrupted. 'Not anymore.'

I was so intent on convincing Mum that I didn't really absorb this comment. Not for a second or two, anyway. Sergio was the one who reacted first.

'Whaddaya mean?' he asked Estelle. 'Whaddaya mean, Danny's not a werewolf anymore? Of course he is! How could he not be?'

'Because Barry bit him,' Estelle rejoined. She spoke in a kind of hoarse, flat, weary drawl, rubbing her wrist where Mum had scratched it. 'Once you get bitten by a vampire, you're a vampire. Full stop.'

In the brief pause that followed this announcement, I heard the distant creak of rusty hinges over the noise of our idling engine. A quick glance informed me that Nina had finally pushed open the screen door at the front of the house. She was wearing sunglasses and carrying the pistol.

'Oh my God.' Mum dropped her face into her hands. 'You're insane,' she muttered brokenly. 'You're all lunatics, and you've kidnapped my son . . .'

It's funny; when I heard what she said, all my doubts fell away. Mum didn't believe in werewolves, but she was dead wrong. So why couldn't she be wrong about vampires, too?

'Are you serious?' I turned to Estelle. 'About vampires, I mean? They really exist? Really and truly?'

'Yeah,' she rasped.

336

'Oh, Toby,' Mum groaned. She raised her head. 'Can't you see what they're doing? They're trying to make you—'

'Shut *up*!' Sergio snapped at her like a dog. Then he addressed Nina's grandmother. 'So Barry's an honest-to-God vampire? Like in the movies?'

'No, love,' said Estelle. '*Not* like in the movies. Believe me, it's nothing like the movies.' She was peering out the window at Nina, who had shuffled over to join Reuben and Dr Plackett. 'It's a disease, that's all. It's just a bloody awful disease.'

'And that's why Barry bit someone?' Sergio pressed. 'Because he's got the vampire disease?'

'Yeah, but he must have been blooded.' Estelle frowned as Dr Plackett knelt beside Danny's motionless form. 'Barry must have smelled fresh blood,' she mused, 'or he wouldn't have gone for this bloke. Someone must have been bleeding.'

'That was me,' I admitted. 'One of the dogs bit my arm when I was holding Danny...'

'Well, there you are, then. That's what happened. Barry smelled your blood on Danny.' Estelle spoke so matter-of-factly that it wasn't hard to accept what she was saying. I didn't get the feeling that she was trying to coax or persuade anyone; in fact she sounded a little absent-minded, because she was watching Dr Plackett check Danny's pulse. 'See, the first time any vampire smells fresh human blood, you've got a problem,' she said. 'Either he bites someone or he doesn't. And if he does, he's always going to be trouble. But if he doesn't, then he'll pretty much behave himself till the end of time. Like Sanford, for instance. Or Nina.'

'*Nina?*' I nearly choked.

'Nina's been a vampire since 1973.'

'But—'

'She's my daughter, not my granddaughter,' Estelle confessed sadly. 'She's fifty-two years old.'

I was floored. Speechless. So was Sergio, whose mouth had dropped open. We exchanged a flabbergasted look.

Then Mum said, 'How dare you?' She was talking to Estelle in a trembling voice. 'How dare you tell such abominable lies to these children? How *dare* you involve them in your sick, pathetic fantasy?'

'*My* sick, pathetic fantasy?' Estelle gave a derisive snort. She didn't seem the least bit bothered. 'You're the one living in a fantasy world, darl, not me. You don't know what's really going on.' She pointed through the windscreen. 'Danny's turning into a vampire right now. In front of our eyes. And you want me to get out of the car?' She shook her head. 'Not on your nelly.'

'So are *you* a vampire?' asked Sergio.

'Of course not!' The old woman's tone was caustic. 'I just *told* you I didn't want to get bitten! It wouldn't matter if I was already a vampire, would it?'

'Yeah, but . . . I mean, if Nina . . .' Sergio trailed off suddenly. He seemed confused – and I understood why. How could you live with a vampire and not become a vampire yourself? Wouldn't you end up on the vampire's menu?

Unless, of course, the vampire was 'behaving' itself. Maybe that was what Estelle actually meant, when she'd referred to vampires who 'behaved'.

'It doesn't run in families, love. It's not like being a werewolf,' she told Sergio. Once again, her attention was fixed on the huddled group near Danny. Nina was wringing her hands, her brows knotted and her neck taut. Reuben was shaking his head in disbelief. Dr Plackett had rolled Danny over.

My stomach did a backflip when I saw that Danny needed mouth-to-mouth resuscitation.

'*What the hell is going on?*' Estelle shouted, after lowering her window again.

Two faces turned towards us. They wore shell-shocked expressions; the glare of the headlights had leached them of colour. Nina glanced at Reuben, who took a deep breath. But when he opened his mouth, nothing came out. He appeared to be lost for words.

Dr Plackett was still pushing on Danny's chest. He didn't pause to reply.

'Could you switch the bloody engine off?' Estelle asked my mother. 'I can't hear a bloody thing.'

Mum bridled. I could tell that she was about to refuse. So I leaned forward and said, 'Please, Mum? We have to know what's going on.' When she hesitated, I tried something else. 'It's the middle of the night. Where else am I going to find a doctor, all the way out here?'

'Yes, but—'

'That guy's a *doctor*, Mum! And I've got a *sore foot!*'

'Yeah, but he's a vampire too, isn't he?' Sergio objected. 'Can a vampire be a doctor? Or is he just a doctor for vampires?'

I could have strangled Sergio. There I was, trying to calm my mother down, and he'd started talking about vampires – a sure-fire way of making her mad. To my surprise, however, her only response was to turn her key in the ignition.

Silence fell, thick and heavy. The only sound was the rush of the wind.

Then Nina began walking towards the car: *crunch, crunch, crunch*. She wasn't holding the pistol anymore. It was stuffed into Reuben's waistband.

'So what's wrong with Danny?' Estelle asked her gruffly. 'Has he passed out? Is that it?'

'He – he...' Nina stalled for an instant. She had to swallow and clear her throat before continuing. 'He's dead,' she quavered, glancing over at the body in the dust. 'He just...he just...died.'

Chapter Twenty-eight

What do you mean, *dead*?' Estelle spoke indignantly. 'He can't be dead.'

'He is.' Nina's voice was thick with unshed tears. She jumped aside as Estelle pushed open the front passenger door.

Mum said, 'You've killed someone? *You've actually killed someone?*'

'It's impossible,' growled Estelle, struggling to her feet. 'He's passed out, that's all.'

'Oh my God, no.' Mum was beginning to lose it. She sounded hysterical. 'Oh no. Oh no . . .'

I didn't blame her. Do you know what I actually told myself? *This is just a dream.* Seriously. *This is just a dream. I'll wake up in a minute.*

'He must be asleep,' Estelle declared. Having extracted herself from the car, she stumped towards Dr Plackett, still arguing with her daughter. 'You always look like a corpse when you go to sleep. Your heart stops. Your breathing stops—'

'Yeah, but Danny's only just been infected.' Over by the veranda, Reuben had found his voice at long last. 'Remember how long it took with Barry? *Much* longer than this.'

'At least twenty-four hours,' Dr Plackett agreed. Then he sucked in a lungful of air before bending over Danny again.

'That's right. So he isn't a proper vampire yet,' said Reuben. 'Is he?'

There was no reply from Dr Plackett, who was blowing into Danny's mouth. It was Nina who observed, 'I've never known *any* of us to keel over at night. Isn't it only meant to happen during the day?'

By this time Sergio had scurried after Estelle, so I decided to follow his example. It wasn't easy. For one thing, I had my sore foot to contend with. And then there was Mum, who made a grab for me as she jabbered something about the police.

'Are you kidding?' I cried, shaking her off. 'The police will lock us *all* up!'

Ignoring her protests, I swung myself out of the back seat and leaned against the car so that I could hop a little closer to Danny. He looked bad. I mean, he looked *really* bad. Even in the harsh blaze of the headlights, I could see that he was turning blue.

'M-maybe it's his heart,' Nina stammered. 'Could it be his heart, Sanford?'

'His heart's stopped working,' the doctor said drily, 'if that's what you mean.' All at once he turned to Reuben. 'Go and get my bag,' he ordered. 'It's in the kitchen.'

Reuben sped off. Estelle was chewing her thumbnail. 'That bite's not going black,' she pointed out.

'I know.' Dr Plackett applied pressure to Danny's ribcage with both hands, pushing hard as he gulped down more air. Estelle wondered aloud if someone else should be doing the mouth-to-mouth – someone with a bit more stamina, like Reuben.

The doctor shook his head, then planted his lips over Danny's.

Nina said, 'It wouldn't be safe, Mum. The guy's just been fanged.'

'Yeah, but look at him.' Estelle nodded at Danny. 'It's not like he's much of a threat.'

'We don't know that.'

Estelle snorted. 'One minute you're saying he's dead, the next minute you're saying he might fang me,' she complained. 'Will you make up your bloody mind?'

'What's happening?' Sergio bleated. 'Is he dead or not?'

'No,' Estelle snapped.

'Maybe,' Nina had to admit.

'I hope not,' said Dr Plackett, straightening up. He wiped his brow, though he didn't appear to be sweating. I noticed a tremor in his hands.

'But you're a doctor!' Sergio wailed. 'Can't you tell?'

'It's not that simple.'

'Perhaps it's different for werewolves,' Nina said hoarsely. 'Perhaps...perhaps you can't fang a werewolf without killing him.'

Oh, man, I thought. *Is this a hoax?* I almost expected to look up and spot a camera crew, because nothing seemed real. Werewolves? Vampires? Dead people? Get outta here.

Suddenly Reuben banged through the front door and hurled himself down the steps, tossing Dr Plackett his medical bag. At the very same moment, Nina turned on her heel and stumbled away.

'Ah...Nina?' I said, as the shadows engulfed her.

'It's all right, love. She's feeling a bit off-colour,' Estelle explained. Sure enough, the sound of retching soon wafted back to us. 'Just let her alone and she'll be fine,' Estelle assured me. 'Vampires are always vomiting, poor things.'

'Do they – I mean – can they—'

'No.' She wouldn't let me finish. 'They can't fly, or turn into bats, or anything else. It's a dog's life.'

'Except that it goes on forever,' Reuben reminded her. He was watching Dr Plackett, who had produced a very long syringe from his bag. 'Dogs aren't immortal and vampires are.'

'But not invincible.'

'No,' Reuben conceded. 'You can say that again.'

'Did you check on our other patient?' Dr Plackett suddenly asked, drawing some kind of medicine into the syringe. When no one answered, he said, 'Reuben?'

'Huh?'

'Our suspected skull fracture.' The doctor's gaze was fixed on his syringe, which he tapped with one finger to dislodge the air bubbles. 'Did you check his condition while you were in the house?'

'No.'

The doctor sighed. Then, without warning, he plunged his needle into Danny's chest.

'Eeww!' Sergio protested. We all cringed like Danny's dogs, which were still skulking on the veranda. Personally, I didn't want to look anymore. I'd had about as much as I could take.

So I stared off into the darkness, wondering how Nina was doing.

'What the hell is that?' Estelle demanded. I guess she must have been talking about Dr Plackett's needle, because he said in response, 'It's a last resort.'

His tone was so grave, I couldn't help glancing at him. But Estelle refused to accept this grim diagnosis.

'Danny's not dead,' she insisted. 'He'll wake up soon.'

'I wouldn't bet on it.' Dr Plackett was feeling for a pulse. 'This isn't what normally occurs.'

'Yeah, but he's a werewolf, isn't he? It's like Nina says. Werewolves are probably different.' After a quick bout of coughing, she added, 'We should take him inside and give him a few hours. He'll come good – you'll see.'

Once again, the doctor shook his head. He sat back on his haunches and stared dully at nothing in particular. It was obvious that he'd given up.

'You could be right,' Reuben said. 'Sanford? She could be right.'

Dr Plackett's grunt wasn't very encouraging.

'We shouldn't put him in a bedroom, though,' Reuben went on. 'I mean, it wouldn't be safe. We could put him in one of the tanks, don't you think?'

'No,' Dr Plackett slowly, painfully climbed to his feet. 'Both of those tanks are occupied, remember?'

'Oh. Yeah.' Reuben cursed under his breath, but I was all at sea. And so, apparently, was Sergio.

'Who's down there besides Lincoln?' he asked, frowning.

'Barry,' said Dr Plackett. He had joined the rest of us in a kind of anxious huddle. 'We were able to lock him up, though it was a bit of a challenge. He'll be very hard to handle for at least another hour or two.'

I must have looked surprised, because Reuben kindly offered me an explanation. 'Barry's not so sick anymore. Vampires always perk up when they get a bit of fresh blood into 'em. Isn't that right, Sanford?'

'Unfortunately, yes. It has an immediate effect on the nervous system.'

Beep! Beep! The blare of a horn made us all jump; we whirled around to gape at my mother, whose white face and pounding fist were visible above the steering wheel of her car. She was yelling something as she sounded the horn, but I couldn't hear what she was saying.

'*What?*' Reuben shouted back at her. Mum started jabbing a finger at the windscreen.

'Mum, calm down!' I begged. Estelle cupped a hand to her ear.

'Huh?' she said.

Then a short, sharp scream cut through all the commotion. It was Nina. She had drifted back towards us, completely unregarded, and had positioned herself behind Reuben. As we rounded on her, she pointed past him.

'Oh my God!' she whimpered. 'Look! Look!'

We looked. Every head turned; every gaze dropped to the ground.

Danny was moving again.

'There!' Estelle said triumphantly. She didn't have to raise her voice, because the horn had stopped. (I guess we'd all seen what Mum had wanted us to see.) 'He *isn't* dead. I was right after all.'

Danny's eyes were open. His legs were churning up dust. His arms twitched feebly. 'Groa-a-ah . . .' he croaked.

The doctor gasped. 'I don't believe it.'

'That injection must have worked,' Reuben offered.

'I told you.' Estelle sounded smug. 'Didn't I tell you?'

Sergio and I were dumbfounded. We exchanged a bewildered glance.

'You blokes should go inside,' Reuben advised us, as Danny sat up. 'Or get in the car or something. You too, Estelle.'

'And you,' Estelle retorted.

Danny groaned again. He was slack-jawed and drooling as he stared blankly into the middle distance.

Dr Plackett ducked down beside him. 'Danny? Can you hear me?'

No response.

'Danny?' The doctor touched his arm. 'Can you get up?'

Slowly and ponderously, Danny's head swivelled in the doctor's direction. But he wasn't looking at anyone. His eyes were still unfocused.

Drool kept leaking out of his open mouth.

'See if you can get up,' said Dr Plackett, applying pressure to Danny's elbow. It seemed to work. While the rest of us backed away, Danny staggered to his feet.

'What's wrong with him?' Nina whispered.

'I don't know.' Dr Plackett had to swallow before continuing. 'This isn't symptomatic. I've never seen this before.'

'Maybe he's like Gary,' Sergio suggested. 'Maybe he hit his head.'

The dogs were whining. Danny didn't seem to hear, though – he was swaying slightly, his arms hanging loose, his head cocked, his gaze blank. An experimental prod from Dr Plackett seemed to have some effect; Danny took one step forward, then stopped.

'Oh, man,' Sergio muttered.

'*Danny?*' Reuben spoke in a sharp, loud, hectoring voice. But Danny just stared and drooled.

'Okay,' said Dr Plackett. 'This is extremely peculiar. I don't like this at *all*. We need to get him downstairs and locked up before he moves on to the next stage.'

'What next stage?' Estelle inquired.

'I don't know, but there's bound to be one.' Dr Plackett

started gesturing at people. He looked grim and pale and exhausted. 'Nina, you come with me. The rest of you stay well back. *Well* back.'

'Sorry, Sanford. No can do.' Reuben wouldn't cooperate. 'Where d'you think you're gunna stick this guy? In the Yank's tank? Then the Yank'll have to come out, won't he?'

'Yes, but—'

'You're not gunna leave 'em in there together, are you?'

'No, of course not!'

'In that case, you'll be needing my help.' Reuben adjusted his grip on the rifle. 'You won't be able to handle Lincoln. Not without me you won't.'

Suddenly I had an idea. 'Will you be bringing Lincoln upstairs?' I asked Reuben, who narrowed his eyes at me.

'I'll have to, won't I?' he said. 'Don't worry. We'll make sure he doesn't try anything.'

That was all I needed to hear. As Dr Plackett prodded Danny into the house, and Nina fluttered around them like a little white moth, and Reuben shooed Estelle and Sergio away from Danny, I hopped back to where my mother was sitting, hunched behind the steering wheel of her car.

'Hey, Mum? Mum!' I clutched at the windowsill. 'There's someone you have to meet, okay?'

She peered through her glasses at me, her expression dull and drained. 'He looks as if he's had a stroke,' she murmured.

'Huh?'

'Him.' She nodded towards Danny, who was lurching from foot to foot like Frankenstein's monster. 'He's lost control over his motor neurons. I've had stroke patients like that, only their weakness tends to be all on one side.'

'Oh.'

348

'He needs to go to hospital. Isn't *anyone* going to take him to hospital?'

'Maybe. I mean – it depends.' When she sighed in a despairing kind of way, I gripped the windowsill even more tightly. 'Things are really complicated!' I exclaimed. 'You can't help unless you understand what's happening! That's why you have to come and meet this guy!'

She was shaking her head. 'It's not complicated, Toby. It's very simple.'

'It's not!'

'These people are all *deeply* disturbed. They're using this paranormal cover story of theirs to involve you in some kind of human trafficking—'

'Okay – you know what? You're wrong. You don't know what you're talking about.'

'Toby, there's no such thing as werewolves or vampires. *They don't exist.*'

'Then where did the whole idea come from?' Before she could think of a snappy comeback, I tried another approach. 'I'm not talking about the stuff you see in movies, I'm talking about a *condition*. That you *inherit*. I know it's pretty weird, but what about the Elephant Man? Or those kids who can't go out in the sunlight?'

'Yes, but—'

'You've gotta keep an open mind! You're always saying that!' I pleaded. 'Mum, if I wasn't a werewolf, this place wouldn't even be here. You should *see* what's downstairs. They've got it all set up for werewolf fights, and it must have cost a fortune. You don't spend money like that for nothing.'

'You do if you're deluded,' she mumbled, staring in front of her. By now I was getting really impatient.

'How could they *all* be deluded?' I asked. 'You reckon they've been hypnotised or something?' When she wouldn't answer – or even look at me – I leaned down further and pushed my head through the window. 'They're not deluded, Mum, and I haven't been brainwashed. I haven't been here long enough to get brainwashed.'

At last she fixed her bloodshot eyes on my face. She was holding onto the steering wheel as if it were keeping her afloat in a stormy sea; her hair was a mess and her lips were dry and cracked.

'We have to go...' she said hoarsely.

'We will. After you've come inside.'

'Only if you tell me one thing.' She took a deep breath. 'Are there drugs inside that house? Illegal drugs?'

Oh, man, I thought. And aloud I said, 'You think we're all *stoned*? Is that it? You think Nina's mum is having hallucinations?' Even though I was famished, and frightened, and suffering from half a dozen aches and pains, I couldn't help smiling. Estelle on hard drugs? *Puh-lease*. 'Honest to God, there's *nothing* inside that house. No food. No medicine. Nothing. That's why I wanna leave as much as you do.'

'So get in the car and we'll go!'

'I *can't*. Not yet. I'm part of this now. I have to make you understand.' And then all at once a spark plug fired in my head. Being different wasn't an illness. She knew that. She *believed* in that. 'Mum, what do you think I was doing in that dingo pen? I was there because I'm a werewolf. It's who I am. Can't you accept who I am?'

Maybe I'd hit a nerve – or maybe she was just too tired to argue. Whatever the reason, she suddenly gave in, switching off the headlights and stepping out of the car. There was no one else around. While Mum and I had been talking, Dr Plackett must have coaxed Danny through the front door. Nina and Reuben must have followed them inside, while Estelle and Sergio had also disappeared – around the back of the house, perhaps? Everything seemed very dark, though a golden glow was still spilling through the kitchen window.

With Mum's help, I made my way up the front steps. If we'd had a torch it would have been a lot easier, but I managed somehow. On the veranda we ran into Danny's dogs; they were pacing around, whining and yapping, as if they didn't know whether to wag their tails or sink their teeth into the nearest human body part.

'They ought to be locked up,' Mum said, peering nervously at their restless, shadowy shapes. 'You can tell they're unstable. And they're in a pack, too – packs are always hard to control.'

'Yeah, well...' I shrugged. 'We can't lock 'em up, because the tanks are full.'

'Who do they belong to?'

'Danny.'

'Oh.'

'They're pretty well trained. They won't do anything unless he tells 'em to.'

'Well, that's a problem in itself,' Mum observed, 'since I don't think Danny will be saying much in the near future. Not if he's had a stroke.'

Luckily, the dogs didn't attack us as we moved inside. The first thing I did, once I'd crossed the threshold, was to turn the hall light on. Then I headed for the kitchen, refusing to lean on Mum while there was a perfectly good wall to support my weight.

'Who's that?' she suddenly demanded. She had reached the

door to Gary's bedroom; even though I was a few steps behind her, I could hear the gasp and rattle of his breathing.

'Oh – well – that's Gary. He's one of the guys who kidnapped me,' I explained. 'He was in a road accident.'

'He's cheyne-stoking.'

'Huh?'

'He's dying,' she said flatly. 'That's cheyne-stoking respiration. It means that he's dying.' Her fierce gaze flashed around the empty corridor. 'Where's the phone?'

'There isn't one,' I confessed. 'I mean, there isn't a landline. Not here. Reuben has a satellite phone—'

Mum didn't wait for me to finish. She marched ahead until she reached the kitchen, while I hobbled along in her wake. By the time I'd caught up with her, she was haranguing Estelle, who was sitting at the table puffing on a cigarette.

The only other person in sight was Sergio. I couldn't believe my eyes when I saw that he was chewing ravenously on a muesli bar. Had Estelle given it to him?

'—dying in there!' Mum was shouting. 'He needs to be in hospital!'

Estelle squinted through a cloud of smoke. 'Are you sure?'

'Of course I'm sure! He's cheyne-stoking! You probably don't know what that means—'

'I know what that means,' Estelle interrupted. 'I'm a hospital volunteer, remember?' As she lumbered to her feet, I suddenly realised. Of course! Estelle must have been the one who'd put Father Ramon's letter in my hospital room!

But I was more interested in the contents of Estelle's pockets than I was in her volunteer work.

'Can I have a muesli bar too?' I asked.

'Nope. All I've got left are some mints.' She reached the top of the stairs and yelled down them. *'Oi! Sanford! This bloke up here is cheyne-stoking!'*

There was a moment's pause. Then a 'What?' came drifting up.

'That fractured skull!' she bellowed. *'He's cheyne-stoking!'*

'So can I have the mints, then?' You must think I'm a bastard, the way I was obsessing about food at a time like that. But my stomach was growling, and Gary wasn't exactly a friend of mine, and there was a weird, dreamlike quality about the whole scene, anyway; somehow I couldn't believe that Gary was *really* dying. 'Please?' I begged. 'I've hardly had anything to eat all day...'

Estelle reached into the pocket of her cardigan and pulled out a packet of mints, which she passed to me without a word. Meanwhile, Dr Plackett was slowly emerging from the hole in the floor, his feet thudding rhythmically on the stairs. He'd taken his sunglasses off, exposing a sunken pair of eyes. With his cadaverous face and bad colour, he looked almost as sick as Gary did.

Mum didn't let that stop her, though. She got stuck into him anyway.

'Gary needs to go to *intensive care!*' she ranted, waving her arms around. 'He's in a *critical condition!*'

'I'll have a look at him,' said Dr Plackett.

'He doesn't need you, he needs a hospital!' Mum cried, as the doctor trudged past her, carrying his bag. 'We have to call for help! This is an emergency! If you don't bring me a phone, I'm going to report you!' When he disappeared into the hallway, she screamed after him, 'You can't possibly handle this on your own!'

'It's all right, darl, I'm here to back him up,' said Estelle, who had offered her chair to me. But Mum wasn't impressed.

'*You!*' she spat. 'Hah! You call yourself a health worker, and you're *smoking*! In front of these *children*!'

Estelle blinked. I wasn't expecting her to apologise, but she did more than that. She blushed, cleared her throat and stubbed out her cigarette.

'Sorry,' she muttered. 'I keep forgetting. You can't kill vampires with second-hand smoke. And I seem to spend most of my bloody time with vampires these days.'

Mum scowled. She was so disgusted with all this talk about vampires that she probably would have thrown something at Estelle, given the chance. But there were no cups or knives or pieces of furniture within easy reach – and before she could even consider hurling her shoes or her car keys, Reuben's arrival distracted her.

He had come up from the basement, red-eyed and reeling with fatigue. The rifle was tucked under his arm.

'What is it?' he asked no one in particular. 'What's happening?'

'We need your phone,' Mum snapped, before Estelle could speak. 'Toby says you have a working phone – is that right?'

'Yeah, but—'

'Gary is dying. He needs emergency intervention.' When no one did anything but stare at her numbly, Mum stamped her foot. 'Did you hear me? He's *cheyne-stoking*. He won't last another hour!'

Reuben scratched his shaggy head. 'Have you told Sanford?' was all he could think of to say.

Mum gave up, then. For some reason the question broke her. Tears sprang to her eyes; her shoulders sagged and her voice cracked. 'Don't you understand?' she said. 'Aren't you listening to me? There's nothing a doctor can do – that man needs a hospital!'

Everyone else exchanged sheepish glances. Even Estelle grimaced like someone with bad indigestion. But nobody knew what to do next. Certainly not without the doctor's input.

I couldn't say a word because my mouth was full of mints.

'If you don't act now, you'll be guilty of manslaughter,' Mum warned, much to Sergio's annoyance. He scowled ferociously.

'It wasn't *our* fault,' he protested. 'Gary's the one who crashed the truck. We wouldn't even *be* here if it wasn't for Gary!'

Mum ignored him. 'The longer you wait, the worse it will be. For *everyone*,' she told the entire group. Then she focused on Reuben. 'Where's your phone?' she asked.

He hesitated. For the first time in ages, I remembered that he was actually quite young. Though he hadn't been fazed by vicious attack dogs, armed lunatics or out-of-control utility trucks, righteous mothers really seemed to throw him off balance.

As he opened his mouth, we heard footsteps in the corridor.

'Ah,' said Estelle. 'Here we go. This is the man we should be talking to.' She didn't even wait for Dr Plackett to appear in the doorway. Instead she just shouted her next question. '*So what's the score, Sanford? How's he doing?*'

A split-second later, Dr Plackett stepped into the room. He was so green around the gills that he had to prop himself against a wall – but I don't think Gary's condition was making him sick. Neither Reuben nor Estelle even asked the poor bloke if he was feeling all right; judging from their general lack of interest in his health, I could only assume that he spent most of his time looking absolutely wasted.

When his sombre gaze fell on us, we knew that something bad had happened.

'Well?' said Mum, breaking the extended silence. 'Is he dead?'

I stopped chewing.

'No,' Dr Plackett replied hoarsely. 'No, he's not dead. Not yet. But there's only one thing we can do for him, at this point.' He turned to Reuben, licked his lips and braced himself. Then he took a deep breath before finally coming out with it. 'We don't have a choice,' he stammered. 'We're going to have to...um...to let Barry deal with him.'

Chapter Twenty-nine

You've gotta be kidding,' said Reuben.

Estelle erupted into a coughing fit that left her purple and bug-eyed.

'It's the only course open to us,' Dr Plackett continued gravely. 'And there isn't much time to make a decision.'

'Jeez, Sanford.' Reuben looked shell-shocked. 'I dunno...'

'There must be something else we can do,' Estelle wheezed.

'No.' The doctor shook his head. 'There's no alternative. Not at this point. Either we let the man perish, or...' He shrugged.

'Or what?' Mum asked. She was utterly mystified. But no one took any notice.

'Maybe he'd be better off dead,' Estelle proposed – and that was when I suddenly figured out what was going on. If Gary turned into a vampire, he wouldn't be *able* to die. So Dr Plackett was suggesting that Barry be allowed to bite one more person.

Oh, man, I thought. *Tell me this isn't happening.*

'I mean, can you really call it a life?' Estelle went on. 'Nina doesn't seem to think so. This bloke – what's-his-name – might not thank us when he wakes up.'

'Who cares?' Reuben snapped. 'He bloody *deserves* to be miserable forever. He's a scumbag. It's not him I'm worried about; it's us. We'd get stuck with 'im, wouldn't we? He'd end up at our group meetings.'

Estelle winced. Dr Plackett sighed. 'I'm afraid so,' he conceded. 'On the other hand, getting stuck with a corpse would be worse. Dead bodies are terribly hard to dispose of.'

Reuben made a scornful noise.

'Are you kidding?' he exclaimed. 'We've got a whole desert out there to dump a corpse in!'

'Yes, but I'm not a killer. And neither are you.' Dr Plackett was talking directly to Reuben, as if the rest of us didn't exist. 'I vote in favour. I think we should do this.'

'Do what?' said Mum. She was still in the dark. 'Are you saying there's something you can do for this man?'

'Uh – Mum—'

'And you're actually wondering if you *should*?' She was scandalised. 'Are you insane? Of course you should!'

'Mum—'

'Nina's not going to like it,' Estelle grumbled, ignoring my mother. 'Where is she, anyway? In the bathroom? Is she sick?'

'She's downstairs,' Reuben admitted. He explained that he had left Nina to guard Danny, who was no trouble at all. 'It was only for a minute,' Reuben assured Estelle. 'And she's got the other gun. We were trying to work out what cell to put him in, but then you wanted Sanford to come up, and the whole thing kinda got hijacked...'

'We should put him in Barry's cell,' Dr Plackett interrupted, moving across the kitchen. He called to Nina, who came to the bottom of the staircase. While she and Reuben and the doctor were engaged in a brief yet heated argument about Barry, Sergio leaned towards me and said in a low voice, 'They want the other vampire to bite Gary, right?'

'Right,' I agreed.

'Like Danny got bitten?' When I shrugged, Sergio added, 'That didn't work too well.'

What could I say? 'Gary's not a werewolf,' I pointed out.

'Oh my God.' Mum had twigged, at long last. 'Is *that* what this is all about? Turning people into vampires? *That's* the solution they're proposing?' When I nodded, she began to wring her hands. 'What are we going to do?' she whimpered. 'We'll end up in gaol, I just know it!'

By that time, I didn't care. My dog bite was sore and so was my foot. My head was throbbing. The mints hadn't filled me up much. I felt weirdly detached from the whole scene. 'Didn't Lincoln have some aspirin in his bag?' I asked Sergio.

'Yeah.'

'Are there any left?'

'I think so . . .'

'Let me fetch them,' Mum offered. But she didn't get the chance to try, because all at once Dr Plackett made an important announcement.

A decision had been reached, he said. Since these were highly unusual circumstances, the Reformed Vampire Support Group's ban on fanging people would be lifted for one night only. Barry McKinnon would be allowed to infect a dying man as part of an emergency treatment regime. All non-vampires would have to lock themselves in the bathroom while Barry was at large. There could be no exceptions to this rule. Nina and the doctor would escort Barry upstairs while Reuben stood guard in the bathroom with his rifle.

Reuben objected. He didn't want to stay in the bathroom. According to him, Barry would be hard for two sickly vampires to control, handgun or no handgun. 'You'll need a bit of muscle,' he said. 'You'll need someone who doesn't throw up at the drop of a hat.' But Reuben was outvoted.

Even Estelle wanted him in the bathroom.

'When I was a barmaid, I once held off six drunken bikers with a cricket bat and a bottle of Guinness,' she revealed, 'but right now I don't have a cricket bat *or* a bottle of Guinness. And this lot won't be much help if Barry breaks down the door – not with all their sprains and whatnot.' She cocked her thumb in my direction, then fired off another salvo before Reuben could open his mouth. 'Besides,' she said to him, 'you saw what happened to your mate Danny. I reckon you'd be worse off than most people if Barry got his teeth into you. At least Nina and Sanford can still get dressed without help.'

In the end, she won. Reuben's protests fell on deaf ears. Everybody who wasn't a vampire – and who hadn't been confined to an underground cell – trooped into the bathroom, which was the only room in the house that could be locked from the inside. Sergio brought a couple of chairs with him, Mum brought Lincoln's bag, and Reuben brought the rifle. What with all this extra stuff, plus five bodies, it was a bit of a tight squeeze; the room wasn't very big to begin with, and since it hadn't been renovated (or even cleaned) since about 1958, most of the available space was filled with massive, weighty fittings in shades of snot-green or pus-yellow.

But we managed to cram ourselves in somehow, once Sergio had climbed into the bath and I had parked myself on the toilet seat. 'Don't come out till we've given you the all-clear,' Dr

Plackett instructed, slamming the door in our faces. Then he hurried back downstairs.

It was Reuben who turned the dinky little lock on the flimsy aluminium doorknob.

'Like *that's* gunna stop a blood-crazed vampire,' he groused.

No one responded. As Dr Plackett's footsteps faded away, the only sounds to be heard were the *drip-drip-drip* of a leaky tap and the distant rattle of Gary's breathing. It was the breathing that got to me. At first I was able to distract myself by rooting around in Lincoln's bag for an aspirin, which I swallowed with a scoop of tap water. After a while, though, I had to do something else.

'What's the time?' I asked.

'Nine fifteen,' said Mum.

'Mmmph.' No wonder I was starving. 'So what's the deal with these vampires?' was my next query. 'How did you find them, anyway?'

I was addressing Reuben, who had his ear pressed to the door.

'I didn't find them,' he replied. 'They found me. Remember how I told you I was rescued from the tank downstairs? Well, they're the ones who did it: Nina and Dave and Father Ramon. And Sanford sent them, so I guess he was involved too . . .'

'Hang on.' I did a mental double take. 'Who's Dave?'

With a shrug, Reuben said, 'He's another vampire.'

My jaw dropped. Sergio gave a little yip of surprise. Mum covered her face with her hands, shaking her head in despair.

'You mean there are *more*?' I demanded.

'Love, there's no end to them,' Estelle informed me. She was sitting on a chair, looking like someone who desperately needed a smoke. 'You've already met Bridget, but there's also Dave and Gladys and Dermid and George—'

I cut her off. *'Bridget's* a *vampire?'* I couldn't have been more astonished. 'You're *kidding!'*

'Who's Bridget?' Sergio wanted to know.

'She's a little old lady.' I stuck out my hand. 'She's about yay high, she has bad hips, and she makes scones.'

'She was eighty-three when she turned,' Estelle explained. 'Bridget's as good as gold. You don't have to worry about Bridget – she wouldn't hurt a fly. And Dave's a lovely bloke. He's the nicest fellow you could ever meet, even though he doesn't say much.'

'And George is all right,' Reuben grudgingly allowed. 'Not that you'd wanna go anywhere near 'im, but at least he's not a pain in the arse.'

'The rest of them have bitten people.' Estelle made a sour face at the thought of it. 'They're not to blame, God love 'em, but it makes them a bit...'

'Unstable,' Reuben supplied.

'That's it. If you fail your first blooding, then you're always going to have problems. Not like Nina or Dave.'

'Or Sanford or Bridget,' said Reuben.

'There are some vampires you can trust, and some you can't,' Estelle finished. 'Just like everyone else on earth.'

In the silence that followed, a faint commotion reached our ears. It was the distant sound of an argument, which gradually grew louder until we could just make out what was being said over the scuffle of approaching feet and the creak of floorboards.

'... wasn't my fault!' somebody insisted. 'I told you, I was defending myself! You would have done the same, I bet!'

I couldn't put a name to the voice, which wasn't resonant like Danny's or American like Lincoln's. It didn't sound like Barry's voice, either; it was too strong and brisk and fierce.

'Any mitigating circumstances will be taken into account.' That was definitely Dr Plackett. I recognised his clipped, reedy vowels, which were drained of all energy and enthusiasm. 'It wasn't a premeditated act, so the penalty won't be too extreme. But there are other ways of defending yourself, Barry.'

Barry! I couldn't believe it. He was talking like a totally different person – like a normal, healthy person.

'Not against a gun, there aren't,' he snapped. 'What was I supposed to do, let 'im shoot me?'

'You were lucky he *didn't* shoot you,' Dr Plackett rejoined. By this time he was right in front of our door – and I probably wasn't the only one holding my breath inside the bathroom. 'Bullets do just as much damage to vampires as they do to other people; don't fool yourself.'

'So you shouldn't try anything stupid,' Nina interposed.

'That's right,' said the doctor. 'Because I won't hesitate to use this. Not if I have to.'

'Yeah, yeah, I know.' Barry's tone was deeply resentful. 'You'll blow me away if I fang the wrong guy.'

'This is a medical emergency. It's not open slather. Is that clear?' A pause. Dr Plackett seemed to be waiting for some kind of assurance. 'Barry?' he said at last. 'Are you listening?'

At first there no response. Then came an awestruck, 'Bloody hell.' In the blink of an eye, Barry's entire attitude had changed. His accusing growl had become a hushed murmur. 'Is that him?'

'That's him,' Dr Plackett confirmed.

'He looks bad.'

'He is bad.'

Another pause. 'Is he gunna taste funny?'

Even Reuben grimaced when he heard *that*. Estelle gave a hiss. I felt a twinge of nausea. As for Mum, she nearly burst a blood vessel. 'Oh, this is monstrous,' she spluttered, turning bright red. '*Monstrous*. How can you people just stand there and . . . ? Aaugh! You're all *sick*.'

I guess she must have been talking just a bit too loudly, because silence fell out in the hall. Then, after about ten seconds, there was a lot of shuffling and rustling and whispering as Barry was dragged into the opposite bedroom. I only realised what had happened when a door clicked shut nearby – and then I was filled with an overwhelming sense of relief.

The last thing I wanted to do was eavesdrop on Barry's slurping noises.

Estelle must have been thinking the same thing, because all at once she said loudly, 'So we'll have to call Dave some time soon. Eh, Reuben?'

'I guess,' Reuben muttered.

'He'll be worried about Nina,' Estelle went on, before peering at Sergio. 'Where do *your* parents live, darl? We'll have to call them too, I suppose.'

Sergio shook his head. 'Nuh' was all he could manage.

'Are you sure?' Estelle looked surprised. 'Won't they be worried?'

Sergio just stared down at his makeshift sling, leaving me the job of explaining.

'They were glad to see the back of him,' I volunteered. 'They shut him up in a pizza oven.'

Estelle blinked. But it was Mum who echoed, 'A *pizza oven*?'

'Because he's a werewolf. They were scared of him, see. That's why he was put in foster care.' Suddenly I remembered what I'd been meaning to tell Reuben for quite some time. 'By the way,' I added, turning towards him, 'I figured out how Lincoln must have tracked us both down. He must have heard about us from this doctor we've been seeing. Dr Passlow. He was Sergio's doctor, too.'

'Really?' said Reuben. He was so interested, he actually pulled his ear away from the door. 'You think?'

'Yeah. I think Dr Passlow told another doctor in America, and the other doctor told that bloke who hired Lincoln – what's his name?'

'Forrest Darwell.'

'Him. Right.'

'Wait – wait just a minute,' Mum broke in, urgently flapping her hands to slow us down. She was being bombarded by too many unwelcome chunks of information. 'Toby, listen to yourself. Do you realise what you're saying? You're saying that your paediatrician is involved in some kind of *international conspiracy*. Doesn't that seem a little farfetched to you?'

'Nope,' Reuben said bluntly, before I could speak. 'Illegal werewolf fighting is a global industry worth millions of dollars. As long as it exists, your son is in danger.' He narrowed his eyes as Mum pursed her lips. 'Whaddaya think we're doing here, for God's sake?' he exploded. 'We're trying to stop all the abuse and the exploitation!'

'All right, all right...' Mum wasn't about to start throwing punches. She tried to calm things down a bit. 'Let's say that's true—'

'It *is* true!' Reuben spat.

'Fine,' she said. 'Then why don't you just go to the police?'

There was a momentary pause. Everyone else exchanged longsuffering glances. Then we all began talking at once.

'We can't go to the police,' I told her.

'People *hate* werewolves,' Sergio insisted.

'You want Toby on some official werewolf register? How safe would he be then?' asked Reuben. 'D'you think your neighbours would want a werewolf living down the street?'

'He'd never be able to get any kind of insurance, love,' was Estelle's contribution. 'And he'd spend the rest of his life on rental blacklists.'

'People would try to kill him.' (That was Reuben, again.) 'Or do medical research on him.'

'And if the police find out about Toby, then they'll find out about Nina,' Estelle concluded. 'Which would be a nightmare, believe me. When it comes to bad press, vampires are even worse off than werewolves.'

Poor old Mum. This furious barrage left her reeling; she just sat there for a moment with a stunned expression on her face. Perhaps she would have recovered, eventually. Perhaps she would have thought of something clever to say, if we hadn't suddenly heard Gary's bedroom door creak open.

Listening hard, I could make out a cough, a sniff, a grunt, and the scrape of dragging footsteps. But Gary's strangled gasps were no longer audible.

'Sanford?' Reuben said sharply. 'Are you there?'

'Don't come out,' Dr Plackett warned, in a weak little voice. 'Just stay where you are.'

'Why? What's wrong?'

'Nothing.' Dr Plackett heaved a sigh. 'It's done.'

Reuben caught his breath. Everyone else in the bathroom stiffened.

'Did it work?' Reuben asked. 'Is he any better?'

'I don't know. It's too early to tell.' After a moment, the doctor admitted, 'His breathing has improved.'

'Okay. Well… good.' Reuben seemed more amazed than pleased. 'So what happens now?'

'Now we'll take Barry back downstairs,' said Dr Plackett. At which point Barry himself spoke up, loudly and aggressively.

'I don't wanna go downstairs! I'm fine! I promise!'

'No, you aren't,' Dr Plackett replied.

'I won't *do* anything!'

'Sorry. We can't take the risk.' After another short silence, the doctor said, 'Go on. Move.'

'No,' snarled Barry.

Reuben grimaced. He adjusted his grip on the rifle; I think he wanted to rush out and stick it in Barry's face. Before he could even reach for the doorknob, however, Dr Plackett wearily remarked, 'If you don't move right now, Barry, I'll stick you so full of drugs that you won't be *able* to move. Not for a week at least.' And this threat must have done the trick, because Dr Plackett aimed his next set of instructions straight at the bathroom door. 'I'll be back directly, all right? Reuben? Don't come out till I secure Gary. He's been infected, so he's not safe. You'd be risking an attack.'

'Yeah, yeah.' Reuben's tone was bored and impatient. 'Like he'll really leap out of bed and fang someone.' When the doctor said nothing, Reuben squashed himself against the door. 'Hello? Are you there? Sanford?'

'Nina?' Estelle butted in, raising her voice. '*Are you all right, Nina?*'

'I'm fine,' Nina affirmed, from somewhere out in the hallway. She didn't sound fine, though. She sounded as if she were going to be sick. 'We're both fine. Don't worry.'

'Nina—'

'I'll be back in a second, Mum.'

And that was that. Inside the bathroom, everyone listened to three sets of feet slowly moving out of earshot. At last Estelle said glumly, 'Another bloody vampire.'

'Another bloody *dickhead* vampire,' Reuben amended. 'Like we don't have enough in the group already.' He squinted at me through a curtain of tangled hair and said, 'Do you actually know anything about this guy? Like where he lives, or if he's got family . . . ?'

'Gary, you mean?' When Reuben nodded, I shrugged. 'He's a bastard.'

'Yeah, but apart from that.'

'He hates his ex-wife,' Sergio piped up. 'He wants to kill her.'

Estelle gave a snort. 'That figures,' she rasped.

'He knows people in Melbourne,' Sergio continued. 'And he used to sell drugs. I heard him telling Lincoln about it.'

'A real thug, in other words.' Estelle shook her head. 'God knows, the McKinnons are bad enough. Nina's always complaining about the way they carry on at group meetings. But now she'll have to put up with *this* nasty piece of work . . .'

Estelle trailed off, still shaking her head. I couldn't help it; I had to ask.

'There are meetings?' I said. 'What kind of meetings?'

'Oh, you know. Group therapy sessions. That kind of thing.'

'For *vampires*?'

My tone made her cross. 'It's not easy being a vampire,' she snapped. '*You* try living with a chronic illness forever and ever.'

'Vampires have a harder time than we do,' Reuben was forced to concede. 'But now that we've got the numbers, we could probably start our own group. For werewolves only. That's if Father Ramon wants to pitch in and help—'

'*I* think he should start a second Reformed Vampire Support Group,' Estelle interrupted. 'Just for the hardcore villains. So decent types like Nina and Dave don't have to put up with people who ought to be in gaol.'

Reuben sniffed. Mum said softly, '*You're* the ones who ought to be in gaol.' I flashed her a disapproving look while Sergio shifted uncomfortably in the bath.

'When's that doctor gunna come back and fix me up?' he whined. 'Me and Toby, we've been waiting for *hours*. It won't be much longer, will it?'

If he was trying to make everyone feel guilty, he certainly succeeded. Mum bit her lip. Estelle hunched her shoulders. Reuben took a deep breath and pushed his hair out of his eyes, like someone about to make an apology.

But he never got to speak. Because at that very instant, we heard the muffled sound of gunshots.

BANG! BANG!

There was a short break, then another three shots: BANG! BANG! BANG!

By the time the sixth (and last) shot was fired, Reuben had already yanked open the bathroom door.

Chapter Thirty

My injured ankle slowed me down. By the time I reached the kitchen door, everyone else was way ahead of me. Reuben and Sergio had already plunged into the basement. Even Estelle had arrived at the top of the stairs.

'*Nina!*' she squawked. '*What happened? Nina?*'

She was barely audible above all the shouts and screams and thumps. Someone was bellowing like an animal below us. Nina was squealing. Reuben was firing off orders; I couldn't quite hear what they were. A hoarse voice was begging, 'Get him off! Get him off!'

Estelle began to clump downstairs. Mum hovered behind her, ducking and weaving in an effort to see was going on. '*Stay back!*' cried Dr Plackett. He must have been yelling at Estelle, because she stopped suddenly, her chin level with the kitchen floor.

'What happened to you?' she exclaimed. 'Where's Nina?'

No one replied. But in the clamour that followed I could just make out Nina's frantic pleading, which was muffled and indistinct.

Mum clapped her hands over her mouth, her eyes widening.

'What is it?' I demanded, limping towards her. Estelle wouldn't budge. Reuben's voice cut through all the commotion, strong and loud and urgent despite the fact that he was somewhere underground. 'I've got 'im! Quick! Hurry! Move!' The sound of moaning sent a chill down my spine.

'Did – did somebody get shot?' I asked. 'Mum? What's going on?'

'He's hurt,' she whispered.

'Who is?'

'That doctor. He was holding his eye.'

'Where?' I couldn't see. Estelle was blocking my view. All at once, however, she began to retreat, backing up the stairs as a small knot of people advanced towards us both.

I flinched when I realised that one of these people was Lincoln.

'Oh my God,' Mum quavered.

I'll never forget what Lincoln looked like. He was hanging between Nina and Sergio, his legs dragging as he pressed a crumpled sheet to his bleeding neck. His white shirt was drenched in blood; his trousers were stained and dusty; his grey hair was like a dirty old mop above his drawn, yellowish face.

I've seen less mangled things peeled off the side of the road.

'Who – how—?' Mum stammered.

Sergio ignored her. 'It was Danny,' he told me, goggle-eyed.

'Huh?' I said.

'Danny *bit* him! He tried to rip his throat out!'

'Oh my God,' Mum repeated. I didn't say anything. My mouth was too dry.

Nina started to move again, lurching along under the weight

of Lincoln's right arm. She was ashen, dishevelled, and shaking like a leaf.

'Are you all right?' her mother wanted to know. 'Nina? Are you hurt?'

Nina shook her head. As Sergio hauled Lincoln over to the nearest chair, she struggled to keep up. Lincoln was moaning again. The instant his butt hit the seat, Nina disentangled herself. She withdrew to the farthest corner of the kitchen.

'Psychopath,' Lincoln muttered thickly. 'Oh Christ...'

I was still trying to absorb Sergio's announcement. It didn't make sense to me.

'*Danny* bit him?' I'd been assuming that Barry was responsible. 'But I thought Danny was out to lunch. Why would he suddenly go for Lincoln?'

When Nina answered, she spoke in the tight, rapid, creaky voice of someone who was trying not to breathe.

'Because Lincoln shot Danny,' she said.

Everyone froze. 'He *what?*' That was Estelle. Mum nearly fainted. I thought, *This can't be happening.*

Down in the basement, silence had fallen.

'Is he – is he—?' I couldn't finish. Sergio gaped at Nina.

'Danny was *shot?*' he yelped. 'But how could ... ? I mean, he wasn't even...'

'He didn't seem to mind,' Nina admitted brokenly. She was still holding her breath.

'He was gnawing on Lincoln like a beaver,' Sergio informed the rest of us, in amazement. 'Reuben had to jump him from behind.' Turning back to Nina, he said, 'Are you *sure* Danny got shot? It didn't look like he was even hurt. Maybe Lincoln missed him.'

'I saw it,' Nina replied, her face crumpling. Then she slapped a hand across her mouth. 'I can't stay in here,' she bleated. 'The blood – it's too much for me...'

'But what happened?' Estelle asked the question before I could. 'Where's Barry?'

'He's locked up. We put him in Danny's cell.' Nina was edging towards the doorway as she mumbled into her hand. 'We thought it would be safer, and it was. They didn't go for each other. I don't think Danny even knew what was happening.'

Estelle frowned. 'Then—'

'Then we took Danny and put him in Lincoln's cell. I left Danny standing near the door. I was pointing the gun at Lincoln while he was being marched into the stairwell.' Nina's voice began to wobble. 'He was passing me – Lincoln was – and he made a grab for the gun. I don't know if he meant to pull the trigger, but he did. And when Sanford tried to stop him, he punched him in the eye...'

Lincoln groaned.

'...and Sanford collapsed, and Lincoln tried to run, but Danny was in the way, and he – I mean Lincoln – he just – he just—'

Nina broke down.

'Shot Danny?' Sergio finished.

'In the chest!' Nina wailed. Then she bolted from the room.

Estelle sat down heavily. I could hear someone climbing the basement steps: *thump, thump, thump*. Lincoln looked as if he was going to pass out.

I reached for one of the empty chairs, just in case. Since there was no telling who might be trudging towards us, I needed *some* kind of weapon.

'In the chest?' Mum croaked. 'God help us...'

'Yeah, but that's impossible,' Sergio countered. 'You don't get shot in the chest and then power on like a steamroller.'

'*Who's that?*' Estelle was loudly addressing the person on the stairs. '*Is that you, Sanford?*'

'It's me,' said Reuben. His head suddenly appeared, closely followed by the rest of him. 'Don't worry. It's only me.'

'Where's Sanford?'

'He's coming.' Poor Reuben was so tired he could hardly put one foot in front of the other. Nevertheless, when his gaze fell on Lincoln, he took a deep breath and squared his shoulders. 'We've gotta get *this* guy under lock and key right now,' he declared. 'God knows what'll happen otherwise.'

'Did he really shoot Danny?' Sergio asked.

Reuben swallowed. Then he nodded. Then he moved towards Lincoln.

'But I *saw* Danny!' Sergio protested. 'He was on this guy like a dog on a bone! He was like a wild animal!'

'Right. And now he's standing there like he never got hurt.' Reuben grasped Lincoln's arm, still talking to Sergio. 'Danny was fanged, okay? He's a vampire now. You can't kill a vampire with a bullet.'

'Can't you?' This was news to me. After everything I'd been told by Estelle, I found it hard to believe that vampires had any kind of stamina at all. 'You mean they really *are* invincible?'

'Immortal. Not invincible,' Estelle corrected. 'If Nina got shot, she'd be on her back till the end of time. A bullet wouldn't kill her, but it would do a lot of damage.'

'Yeah,' said Reuben, as he dragged Lincoln to his feet. 'Christ, remember what happened when Barry tried to brush his teeth with toothpaste? How many teeth did he lose? Not to mention all those blisters . . .'

'Auugh.' Lincoln staggered. He dropped the sheet that he'd been using to staunch his own blood.

I stooped to pick it up again, grudgingly. No one, I felt sure, wanted to look at Lincoln's ragged neck wound. I certainly didn't.

'So what's the deal with Danny, then?' Sergio wanted to know. 'How come *he's* so different?'

'Beats me.' Reuben shrugged. 'Ask Sanford. He's on his way up now.'

It was true. I could hear someone else slowly mounting the stairs. And I thought, *What about Danny?*

'I need to lock this one in the bathroom, quick smart,' Reuben continued, steering Lincoln towards the corridor. It wasn't easy, though. Lincoln was a dead weight; he could hardly walk. And Reuben had only one free hand, because the other was occupied with his rifle.

'Nina's in the bathroom,' Estelle warned him. 'She's being sick.'

'Then she'll have to be sick somewhere else. This guy could get his second wind any minute, and I don't want anyone else getting fanged.'

Estelle screwed up her nose.

'You think *he's* been infected?' she queried, cocking her head at Lincoln.

Once again, Reuben shrugged. But he didn't say a word.

'Vampires *bite* people,' Estelle pointed out. 'They don't tear chunks off 'em. This doesn't seem right to me...'

'It's not,' said Dr Plackett. He had finally emerged from the stairwell, tottering a little. His left eye socket was already a strange, greenish-grey colour. 'Something else is going on here. Something I haven't encountered before.'

'Like what?' Reuben asked. Dr Plackett didn't answer immediately. Instead he collapsed onto the nearest vacant chair, which I'd just put down. Then he closed his eyes and took a few deep breaths.

'Sanford? Are you going to vomit?' Estelle inquired.

The doctor shook his head.

'Are you sure? Because if you are, you should do it in the sink.'

'I'm all right.' He opened his eyes. 'Just give me a minute. I'll be fine in a minute.'

'What about Danny?' I couldn't keep silent any longer. 'Is *he* going to be all right?'

Dr Plackett's gaze flicked towards me. After a brief pause, he muttered, 'That's a good question. I honestly don't know. All I can do is monitor his condition.'

'But he's been *shot!*' Mum exclaimed. 'He needs surgery!'

Dr Plackett sighed. He began to massage the bridge of his nose. 'Mrs Vandevelde,' he said, with barely suppressed impatience, 'surgery would be useless. You don't perform surgery on a dead man.' Before the rest of us could do more than gasp in horror, he added, 'The fact that Danny's still upright suggests that something is seriously amiss. Even a vampire wouldn't be standing up after a shot through the heart, and I'm not even sure if Danny *is* a vampire.'

'But he was fanged!' Estelle cut in. 'He's got to be a vampire if he was fanged!'

'Not necessarily.' Seeing her open her mouth again, Dr Plackett lifted his hand. 'So far, Danny hasn't exhibited any of the normal transformation behaviours.'

'Because he's a werewolf?' Sergio proposed.

'It's possible.'

Reuben frowned. 'You think werewolves react differently when they're infected?' he asked, just as Nina appeared on the threshold. She was so weak that she had to lean against a doorjamb. Nevertheless, Dr Plackett said to her, 'Ah. Good. You're back.' He nodded at Lincoln. 'This fellow here has to be stitched up. In the bathroom. I'll need your help.'

'That's okay,' Reuben offered, when he saw Nina's expression. 'I'll stand guard. Nina's not well enough.'

'No.' The doctor was adamant. He stood up and shuffled over to his medical bag, which was sitting on the table. 'I don't want any uninfected people nearby. It's too risky. After seeing what Danny did, I'm not about to stick a suture into this fellow here without taking precautions.'

'But you just told us that Danny's not a vampire,' Estelle objected. 'How could this bloke be infected if Danny's not a vampire?'

'Yeah,' Reuben agreed, prodding Lincoln's shoulder. 'And he hasn't been *acting* like someone who's just been infected. He hasn't puked. He hasn't passed out...'

'And he hasn't been acting like Danny did, either,' Sergio interposed. 'I mean, he can still talk and everything.'

'Look, I *don't know* what's going on!' the doctor snapped. 'And I won't know until I've got more data! I'll have to monitor Danny. I'll have to monitor the other two. In the meantime, there are more urgent matters to address – like that neck wound, for instance.' He gestured at Lincoln. 'There's also Sergio's arm, and Toby's foot... I might even give you a shot for that dog bite, Toby. Just in case.'

To be honest, I'd almost forgotten about the dog bite. It had merged into my general sense of misery. 'Oh! Sure. Whatever,' I said.

'And when I've done all that,' he went on, turning to my mum, 'I'm going to ask if you'd take these two boys back to Cobar, Mrs Vandevelde. So you'll be out of harm's way.' Glancing at his watch, he concluded, 'It's not even ten yet – with any luck some of the pubs will still be open, and you'll be able to get a couple of rooms for the night.'

Mum stared at him. It was Reuben who said, 'And then what?'

'Then we'll play it by ear. We might have to stay here another forty-eight hours or so, until our three casualties have stabilised.'

'Not without guinea pigs,' Estelle warned. 'There are no more guinea pigs, remember?'

Dr Plackett gave a grunt. I thought I must have missed something. Or had I fallen asleep? Was this all a fragmented nightmare? Were the chairs about to grow wings and fly off?

'*Guinea pigs?*' I echoed.

'These vampires live on guinea pigs. One a day,' Estelle advised me. I don't know what kind of weird face I must have pulled, because she quickly added, 'It's better than sucking the blood out of *people*.'

'We'll organise something.' Dr Plackett was trying to reassure her, I think. 'If the worst comes to the worst, there are always alternative sources of nourishment. Feral pigs and so forth.' At the sound of Nina's wordless protest, he suddenly lost his cool, shoving the leather bag under his arm as he marched over to grab Lincoln. 'Look, all I'm saying is that we have *options*!' he barked. 'But at the moment I'm applying triage procedures, and taking things one step at a time! So if you'd kindly let me handle this like a professional—'

'Wait!' I could tell that he was about to push Lincoln out of

378

the room, and I didn't want that to happen. Not until I'd made one more attempt to convince my mother. She was standing there with her eyes shut, gnawing her fist and shaking her head as if she'd given up on the lot of us; I wanted her to listen and understand. I wanted her to *stop being so close-minded*. 'Wait,' I said to Dr Plackett. 'Before you go, can I just...I mean, it would be good if...'

'If what?' he snarled. 'Hurry up!'

'If he could tell Mum what he did to me.' I finally managed to spit it out, aiming an accusatory finger at Lincoln as I did so. 'Mum, this is the guy who kidnapped both of us. Me and Sergio. Okay? This is the guy who locked us both downstairs in the underground tanks.' When Lincoln didn't react, I was suddenly filled with rage. 'Didn't you? Huh? *Didn't you?*' I yelled, making everyone jump.

Even Lincoln responded. His bleary eyes rolled in my direction. 'Uh...yeah...' he mumbled.

'Tell her why you did it!' I leaned towards him in a threatening kind of way, but no one tried to pull me back. Not even Nina. 'Go on! Tell her why!'

Lincoln licked his cracked lips. 'For – for the money?'

'No! I don't mean that.' Before Sergio could jump in, I rephrased my question. 'Why did you choose us in the first place? Huh? Why did you go to all this trouble?'

'Be-because you're werewolves,' Lincoln croaked. It was the reply I'd been angling for. Triumphantly, I turned to my mother.

'See?' I said. 'What did I tell you? Why would *he* lie?'

Mum's eyes filled with tears. 'Oh, Toby,' she murmured, her voice breaking, 'can't you see the state he's in? He's been terrorised. He'd say anything. He's hurt. He's *scared*.'

379

I couldn't believe my ears. Neither could Estelle, to judge from the way she snorted. Reuben heaved an impatient sigh. Sergio scowled. Dr Plackett cast his gaze towards the ceiling.

Then all at once, out on the front veranda, there was an explosion of furious noise.

Danny's dogs were whipping themselves into a frenzy.

I don't think anyone stopped to consider what this actually might mean. We simply stampeded towards the kitchen door out of the room, desperate to see what was going on. Reuben reached the hallway first, with Sergio close at his heels. Estelle and Dr Plackett were next in line; they tried to muscle their way past the other two, without much success. Even Mum rushed to have a look. Nina lagged behind because she got stuck with Lincoln, who had to be herded along. And I, of course, had my dud foot to contend with.

When at last I caught up with the others, they were all peering down the corridor. At the very end of it, in a pool of yellow light, Gary Santos had thrown himself against the front door – *whump* – which slammed shut as he sagged against it. He was gulping down air, his knees shaking. Over a volley of hysterical barks, I could just hear the scratching of claws and the thump of low, heavy bodies.

Clearly, he had tried to sneak outside, not realising that four traumatised dogs were lying in wait on the welcome mat.

'Ugh...ugh...ahh,' he panted, pushing at the bolt with trembling fingers. Then, slowly and haltingly, he turned to confront us.

'I'm gunna be sick,' he moaned.

Chapter Thirty-one

Once my mother had laid eyes on Gary, she became an instant convert. I didn't have to worry anymore. To see him up and about was all it took to change her mind about everything.

Not that she was much use after that. For the next half-hour she hardly said a word, sitting chalk-faced in one corner as Dr Plackett treated Lincoln's neck, and my foot, and Sergio's arm. Nina had to look after Gary, who spent a good twenty minutes with his head in the toilet bowl. As for Estelle, she retired to bed. 'I need my beauty sleep,' she drawled, 'since I'll be the day nurse tomorrow.' Then she took a chair into one of the bedrooms, wedging it under the doorknob so that nothing could pounce on her while she was catching her forty winks.

By the time I was ready to go, Mum had recovered slightly. When Reuben gave her his contact number, she was able to enter it into her own electronic phone book. When he asked her to call him in the morning, she promised – feebly – that she would. And despite the stunned look in her eye, she managed to pull herself together when she slipped behind the wheel of our car. The drive to Cobar might have been slow and silent, but it passed without a single mishap. She didn't run us off the road or anything.

As Dr Plackett had promised, one of the hotels in town was

still open. So while Mum and I scored a twin-bedded room with squashed flies on the wall, Sergio spent the night in a kind of enclosed veranda, lying on a trundle bed with squeaky springs. The next morning, we didn't rush off to Sydney. I'd been expecting that we would, because I figured that Mum would want to. We hadn't had time to talk; I didn't understand how she felt. But instead of calling the police when she woke up, she called Reuben – who then drove all the way from Wolgaroo in his van, so that he could join us for breakfast in the dingy hotel dining room.

I'll always remember that meal, because it was the start of a new era for me. There we were, the four of us, all stiff and sore and puffy-eyed, hunched over four greasy stacks of egg and bacon. We weren't especially scared, or excited, or angry. We were too tired to be anything much. But in that nicotine-stained dining room, surrounded by dusty lampshades and sticky tabletops and old sauce bottles, being a werewolf suddenly became part of my everyday life. Without even knowing it, I'd moved on. My panic and disbelief had been replaced by a kind of weary acceptance.

Not that we actually mentioned werewolves – not while Bill the hotelier kept waddling in and out with coffee and toast. Reuben used the word 'condition' a lot, and Mum referred to my 'problem' until he corrected her. My genetic heritage wasn't a problem, he insisted. In many ways it was a bonus, as long as everyone concerned had the right attitude and took the right precautions. We didn't, however, discuss those precautions in any detail over breakfast. There wasn't enough time. Reuben had to get back to Wolgaroo, and he wanted Mum to go home, where she could await further instructions on her own turf. He told her not to worry about Danny or Gary or Lincoln.

Her job would be to take care of Sergio for a day or two, until Reuben and Dr Plackett had worked out some kind of strategy. 'Sergio needs as much help as Toby does,' Reuben explained. 'We can't just sling him into foster care, or something bad might happen.'

Mum didn't argue. Without a word of protest she took Sergio back to Sydney, where she fed him, clothed him (in some of my old stuff) and let him sleep on our couch. It was really nice of her, because he wasn't a perfect house guest. As well as being moody and messy, he had very loud nightmares – and whenever there was washing-up to be done, he would claim that his wrist was too sore. Luckily, he didn't stay with us for long. After three days, Reuben turned up with Father Ramon to offer Sergio a room in St Agatha's presbytery.

It was only a temporary measure, of course. Officially, Sergio became my foster brother. Officially, he's now living at our house. And sometimes he really *is* at our house, because the Department of Community Services likes to check up on these things. But for the most part he just lives with Reuben, even though it means a very long hike to school every morning.

Estelle would have been a better choice of foster mother. Her house is closer to Reuben's and has a lot more space than ours does. With a vampire on the premises, however, she can't afford to have social workers constantly tramping through her front door. That's what she told us, anyway. That's what she decided at the meeting we held just a few days after everyone had come back from Cobar.

It was an emergency meeting, which took place at St Agatha's church hall. Father Ramon was there, along with Reuben, Sergio, Estelle, Nina, and Dr Plackett. Mum and I showed up, of course, as did Bridget and one person I didn't yet know – Dave, who turned out to be a big, hairy vampire in blue denim. I was kind of surprised that Barry didn't attend, until Nina told me that he was being 'punished'. (She didn't tell me how.) Lincoln and Danny were too sick to come. Gary Santos wasn't there either; according to Dr Plackett, he wasn't safe enough to invite.

'It's too early,' the doctor explained. 'Once he's been blooded we might be able to risk it, but I couldn't be sure even then...'

He went on to confirm that Gary, who had mutated into a fully fledged vampire, was now living under his direct supervision – though not for much longer. The aim of the Reformed Vampire Support Group was to help its members live useful and self-sufficient lives. One day, Gary would move into his own residence. He would learn how to manage his own symptoms and hold down some kind of vampire-friendly job. Until then, however, he would need a whole lot of help; as well as adapting to an endless series of physical changes, he would have to separate himself from everyone in his past.

'But that's not your concern,' Dr Plackett assured all the werewolves at the meeting. 'You have other things to worry about.' He then gave us a complete rundown of what Gary had told him about Forrest Darwell's werewolf-fighting operation.

Apparently, Darwell had been keeping an eye on Wolgaroo through his agents in Australia. At first his only concern had been tracking down the McKinnons; there was bad blood between the two parties (I'm still not sure why), and Darwell had been hoping that Barry or his son might eventually return to Wolgaroo. Gradually, however, it had become obvious that the McKinnons' deserted property would serve as a fine outpost for Darwell's organisation. 'Our friend Mr Darwell must have decided to kill two birds with one stone,' the doctor related. 'On the one hand, he wanted to catch the McKinnons. On the other hand, he was keen to fill the vacuum that Barry had left behind.' So Lincoln had been sent to Australia, with orders to establish a new 'fight pit' like the ones in the States.

According to Gary Santos, I had been right about Dr Passlow. Although the paediatrician wasn't an associate of Forrest Darwell, his colleague in Chicago was – and Dr Passlow was always sending notes on interesting cases to Chicago. Upon hearing of Sergio's existence from the American doctor, Darwell had entrusted Lincoln with Sergio's name and address.

It had been Lincoln's job to organise Sergio's capture – and mine, as well.

'The trouble is, Forrest Darwell might send another agent,' Dr Plackett remarked. 'If he doesn't hear from Lincoln or Gary, he might try to find out what's been going on. And since Forrest Darwell was the one who gave Lincoln all of Toby's details . . .' Trailing off, the doctor looked anxiously at my mum. 'Maybe you should think about moving,' he suggested. 'I know it's a lot to ask, but we don't want this chap turning up on your doorstep.'

'Are you *kidding*?' Reuben exclaimed. 'That's exactly what we *do* want!' He turned to my mother, who had blanched. 'Don't worry, okay?' he said. 'If Forrest Darwell ever *does* show up, I'll teach him a lesson he'll never forget. And if he doesn't, then I'll take the fight to his front door. I can do that, now. Because I've got inside information.' Gazing around the cramped little room in which we'd gathered, he tried to drum up some excitement. 'This is the best chance we've ever had to get even with that bastard! We might even be able to lure him over here! Into a trap!'

'Oh no.' Mum raised her hand like someone directing traffic. 'No, we're not getting involved in any kind of elaborate revenge scenario.'

'But—'

'*No*, Reuben. This isn't a game. Your job is to *protect* us from Forrest Darwell.'

'But I can't do that unless I get rid of him!' Reuben protested. It was a stupid thing to say. I couldn't believe my ears; surely he wasn't serious?

'That's not true,' I piped up. 'If you pretend that Lincoln's killed off all his werewolves and can't find any more to replace them, there won't be any reason for Forrest Darwell to come sniffing around.' As everyone absorbed this suggestion, with many grunts and nods and frowns, I added, 'All we have to do is get Gary and Lincoln to lie. Which shouldn't be a problem. I mean, it's not like they're giving us any trouble, eh?'

I looked at Father Ramon when I asked this, because he was the one taking care of Lincoln.

The priest shifted uneasily.

'No...well, no...' he muttered. I felt sorry for the poor guy. Lincoln had turned into a kind of human slug; he lay in bed all day like someone with chronic fatigue syndrome. Though he was able to eat when prompted, he barely had enough energy to speak, let alone go to the bathroom.

Having someone like that in your house isn't much fun. Especially when he has to be kept away from other people.

'So how *is* Lincoln?' Estelle inquired. 'Has there been any change so far?'

'No,' said Dr Plackett.

386

'He hasn't perked up at all?'

The doctor shook his head.

'Oh well.' Estelle shrugged. 'It could be worse. Even if he *is* infectious, at least he won't be attacking anyone.'

'I don't think he's infected,' Nina weighed in. 'How could he be? He's eating real food. Vampires can't eat real food.'

'Even so, he can't stay in the presbytery forever. I have too many other guests – homeless families and so forth,' Father Ramon reminded us. There followed a long, involved discussion about spare rooms. At that point, Gary was living with the doctor. Danny had been parked at Dave's house. Sergio was dividing his time between Mum's place and Reuben's, while Danny's dogs had been distributed among Reuben, Father Ramon, and a couple of Reuben's friends. So finding enough space for Lincoln wasn't easy. I don't think Reuben would even have tried, if left to himself. And he wasn't the only werewolf present who would have tossed Lincoln onto the street without a twinge of guilt.

But the vampires outnumbered the werewolves, so we had to thrash out a more humane solution. In the end, it was decided that Lincoln should move in with George. I'd heard about George, though we hadn't met; he lived in a big old house with a brick wine cellar, which Reuben had identified as a perfect full-moon retreat. So there was a bit of an argument about whether Lincoln should be transferred to George's house before Reuben had finished werewolf-proofing its cellar for me. Then there was an argument about the cost of the conversion. And after that, there was an argument about the old refrigerated meat locker at Bridget's place, which had once been a butcher's shop. Wouldn't it be an ideal space to stash Sergio during the next full moon?

At last we sorted things out, and the meeting broke up. There was another meeting a week later, but I didn't attend that one. Neither did Sergio. To be honest, we haven't had much to do with the vampires since then, even though they've been a big help. It's partly because they're only awake at night, and partly because they're kind of annoying. (They complain a lot, for one thing, and they seem to spend most of their time sitting on their butts, yakking away.) The main problem, though, is that werewolves and vampires don't mix. And it's not just because of our different energy levels, or because they're sick and we aren't. It's because when you mix a werewolf with a vampire, you get a zombie.

That's Dr Plackett's diagnosis, anyhow. After weeks of monitoring Danny Ruiz, he reckons that we have a zombie on our hands. 'After all,' he's said, more than once, 'Barry can't be the first vampire who's fanged a werewolf. And the whole idea of zombies must have come from *somewhere*.'

It's hard to disagree. Right now Danny isn't acting like a vampire *or* a werewolf; all he does is sit and drool. He's still got a hole in his chest, which doesn't seem to be healing very quickly (though it doesn't seem to bother him much, either). If you stick something in his mouth, he'll swallow it – and if you give him a push, he'll start moving. Sometimes he'll wet himself. Sometimes he'll groan. If he goes anywhere near sunlight, he'll shrink away. If you shoot him, he'll try to chew your head off.

But that's pretty much it. After running a lot of tests, Dr Plackett has decided that Danny's a walking vegetable. Not that anyone's given up on him; as the doctor always says, it's early days yet. There's no telling what might happen. Various treatments have already been tried, including a special diet and a carefully monitored exercise program. Danny will happily spend hours doing push-ups or jogging on a treadmill. He doesn't seem to mind being massaged. And Mum claims that he's responding well to speech therapy, though I can't see it myself. A groan is a groan, as far as I'm concerned. Maybe you have to be an expert to spot the difference. Maybe she's right, and he really *is* making connections in his head. Even if it's true, though, he's got a long, hard road ahead of him – and when you consider where that road actually leads, you have to wonder if it's worth the effort.

I know, I know. What a bastard, eh? I shouldn't be saying something like that. But the guy used to be a menace, and now he's not. He doesn't wave guns around anymore. He doesn't bash heads in, or sic dogs on people. These days he isn't even a problem when the moon is full, because lunar cycles have stopped having any effect on him (thank God). Once you wouldn't have wanted Danny occupying your spare bedroom. What with his gun and his dogs and his temper, it would have been like sharing the house with a stick of dynamite. These days, however, he's the world's easiest guest. He doesn't raid the fridge. He doesn't leave the lights on. He doesn't make snide remarks about your favourite TV show. Apart from the odd spot of drool, you wouldn't even know he was there half the time – or so Dave says.

You're probably thinking, *Yeah, it might be good for other people, but what about poor Danny? He's not having any fun.* And you're right. He isn't. But the thing is, he never did. He was always a very unhappy guy. According to Reuben, Danny was one of those paranoid, hard-drinking, traumatised loners who wouldn't accept any kind of help. Danny's only friends were his dogs; he'd fought with everyone else he knew. His only hobby

389

was shooting feral pigs. He hated just about everything – and distrusted what he didn't hate. 'He nearly cracked my head open half a dozen times,' Reuben revealed to me in private one day. 'I've seen him knock out his pit-bull with a single punch.'

Reuben seems to think that Danny's a lot happier than he used to be. Maybe I'd tell myself the same thing, if I'd persuaded Danny to get involved in a rescue attempt that had turned him into a zombie. It's better than feeling guilty, right? But I have to admit, I agree with Reuben. Danny really does seem to be a lot happier.

It's hard to say the same thing about Lincoln, though. For one thing, he keeps *telling* everyone how miserable he is; it's practically his only topic of conversation. Not that he talks much. He's too tired. All the same, whenever he *does* open his mouth, it's usually to complain about the fact that he can't get out of bed and kill us for what we've done to him.

Even Bridget can't dredge up a lot of sympathy for Lincoln.

I guess he's a kind of half-zombie now, with a very mild case of whatever Danny's got. It looks as if zombies are only slightly infectious. As for half-zombies, no one knows how infectious they are. That's why Dr Plackett has put Lincoln in quarantine, though the chances of anybody getting bitten by a guy who can't brush his own teeth are pretty remote. Mind you, there *is* an outside chance that his 'condition' might wear off. Dr Plackett says so. But if that happens – if Lincoln finally regains enough stamina to wreak his revenge – will he still be infectious? I doubt it.

Dr Plackett is very interested in the whole zombie phenomenon. He's thrilled that Danny transmitted the vampire disease in a form which, though grossly mutated, was also much less virulent than normal. According to the doctor, this is a medical breakthrough. It opens the door to a possible cure for vampirism. He says that he's changed the direction of his research, thanks to Danny Ruiz, who won't have become a zombie in vain. However, since this 'change of direction' seems to involve taking a lot of werewolf blood samples, I'm not all that thrilled about it myself.

In case you're wondering, I should probably make it clear that Dr Plackett doesn't draw his own blood samples. He wouldn't dare risk it. Instead he packs us all off to a pathologist, because he's still got some kind of medical ID (don't ask me how), and can do a lot of stuff that ordinary doctors do: write prescriptions, refer to specialists, order tests. So I really don't see much of him, despite all the medical research. I don't see the other vampires, either. I try to avoid them, in fact, because there is always a bit of a risk that someone might smell blood, and (as I mentioned before) werewolves and vampires don't mix.

That's what I said to Nina, after the emergency meeting had broken up. She was standing at the door of the church, with Estelle at her side, when Mum offered them both a lift home. But Dave stepped forward to put his arm around Nina's shoulders. 'It's okay,' he announced. 'I'm the designated driver at these things.' And I suddenly realised that Dave was Nina's boyfriend.

Not that I cared. I mean, she's fifty-two, right? *Way* too old for me. Besides which, she's a vampire. 'Car-pooling's probably not a good idea,' I said, 'because vampires and werewolves don't mix.' Nobody argued, so I guess they all agreed.

I haven't laid eyes on Nina since then, although Mum and Estelle have met a few times over lunch. According to Mum, it's nice to talk to another person who's in the same boat.

'We've got a kind of support group,' she once explained. 'For mothers of the paranormally afflicted.'

Ha-ha. Pardon me while I piss myself laughing.

Speaking of support groups, I belong to one myself, these days. It's called the Abused Werewolf Rescue Group. Reuben's the chairman, I'm the secretary, and Sergio is the treasurer. We meet at St Agatha's Church Hall every Thursday at 6.00 PM to discuss important issues: how we should trick Forrest Darwell, for instance, or what we should tell Dr Passlow, or how we're going to find Lincoln's mystery partner, the Third Man, who's apparently left Broken Hill for an unknown destination. There are always lots of things to talk about. At our last meeting, we talked about the previous full moon – which we'd each spent in our own private little gaol. Father Ramon had locked me in George's wine cellar, Reuben had let himself into Dr Plackett's bank vault, and Estelle had shut Sergio up in Bridget's meat locker. Meanwhile, as an extra safety measure, all the vampires (except Dave) had moved to Estelle's basement for the night, leaving the coast clear for us werewolves.

Even a vampire wouldn't want to be around if a werewolf escaped from his cage on the night of a full moon.

In the end, everything worked like a charm. I woke up with a few bumps and scratches the next morning, but you have to expect the odd scratch after a transformation. It's part of being a werewolf. That's what Reuben told me, anyway, and he should know. He's the expert. Even Mum pays attention to him now, though she doesn't always agree with what he says. For example, she argued long and hard against his suggestion that we invite Fergus and Amin to our group meetings. She's always there herself, of course, and so is Father Ramon (who acts as a kind of information conduit between the werewolves and the vampires). When Reuben proposed that we take on two extra members, however, she nearly hit the roof.

'Are you insane?' she protested. 'Why on earth would we want to do that?'

'Because Toby's friends already know that he's a werewolf,' Reuben replied, 'and a little knowledge is a dangerous thing. It might be better if they realise how important and serious this whole situation really is. Plus we'll get to keep an eye on them, and make sure they don't go hatching any dumb plots. Don't you think, Toby?'

I shook my head. 'Uh-uh.'

'You don't?' Reuben looked surprised. 'Why not?'

'Because if we let those boys come here, they'll find out about the vampires!' Mum interjected. 'Do we really want that?'

'No,' the priest said firmly. 'We don't.'

'But if we're very careful . . .' Reuben began.

Mum wouldn't let him finish. 'Something's bound to slip out. It always does,' she insisted. 'The same goes for anything those silly boys are told about werewolves. If they hear about it, they'll talk about it, so the less they know the better.' She turned to me for support. 'Toby agrees. Don't you, Toby?'

'Yeah,' I confirmed. And then I told Reuben why we *shouldn't* let my friends know how important and serious the situation really was. Instead, we had to do the opposite. We had to give them the impression that being a werewolf was as dull, annoying and restrictive as having an allergy to sugar.

If we did that, I explained, then Fergus would quickly lose interest. He would move onto other, more absorbing projects – and Amin would almost certainly follow his example. I had already begun to lie to them, with some success; every time I said that I couldn't do something because I was a werewolf, or because I had to go to the pathologist, or because I had to hunt down a few wild-dog population figures on the Internet, Fergus would become more and more disillusioned. 'For Chrissake,' he'd said to me, 'why can't werewolves have any fun? Sometimes I wish you *did* have epilepsy. At least it wouldn't be so boring.'

My ultimate goal, I said, was to discourage both Fergus and Amin from coming over to my house at all. 'Just in case Sergio's there,' I explained. 'They've already met him once, and I don't want it to happen again.'

'Why not?' Sergio scowled. 'Don't they like me, or something?'

'It's not that...' Fergus, in fact, had been all over Sergio at their one and only meeting. Even though Sergio had been sulking in front of the TV with his wrist in a sling, Fergus had refused to leave him alone, prying and pestering and generally making a nuisance of himself until Sergio had hurled a TV remote clear across the room. What with Sergio being so traumatised and Fergus being so tactless, I didn't think they ought to spend a lot of time in each other's company.

'Fergus can be a real pain in the arse,' I informed Sergio. 'He's just gunna bug you, is all. And if you knock him out, his older brothers might get cheesed off.'

Sergio grunted. He seemed to understand. It was Reuben who said, 'But won't that be kinda tough? I mean, won't you miss your friends if they don't come over?'

With a shrug, I replied, 'It's no big deal. I'll see 'em when I see 'em.'

'Are you sure?' Reuben didn't seem convinced. 'You don't have to change your whole lifestyle just because you're a werewolf. That's not what this group is all about.'

'Reuben's right,' Father Ramon agreed. 'In the past, a lot of werewolves have suffered because of their condition, which has been portrayed in a very negative light. Our job here is to emphasise the positives. Any changes you make have to be for the better, or you shouldn't be making them.'

'It's okay,' I said. 'It's not a problem. I know what I'm doing.'

Though I had to repeat myself about half a dozen times, I finally persuaded them that I really *did* know what I was doing. And I do. Because I'm not the same as I used to be. I'm different, but not for the reason you think. Sure, I have to spend every full moon in an underground wine cellar. Sure, that sets me apart. There have been other changes as well, though, and the big one is this: I don't want to run with the pack anymore.

Ever since that day at Wolgaroo, I've gone off the whole idea of crazy schemes that end up in high-speed pursuits. Like that business with the bomb and the fire extinguisher, for example. You start on a basic level, looking for kicks, because you don't realise how badly out of control things can get. It's all just a game, right? A bit of a laugh? Then all of a sudden you're hanging off a runaway truck, surrounded by guns and blood and howling maniacs, and it's no fun at all. I mean, it's *scary*. You soon realise that, even though you've had the adventure of a lifetime – full of werewolves, vampires, zombies, guns, and underground passages – you didn't enjoy it one little bit.

I've had it with bombs. I've also had it with spy technology, homemade rockets, booby traps, Halloween, lock-picking, fake blood, and practical jokes. Now that I've seen the real thing, this stuff no longer excites me. And since Fergus isn't interested in much else, it's no wonder that we don't seem to get along as well as we used to.

I might have a change of heart, I guess. The shock of my experience might wear off, and I might forget how good it was to get back home after the long drive from Cobar. Until then, however, I'll be spending more time doing normal things, like walking dogs and going to dance class (which I'm paying for with my dog-walking money).

Of course, the Abused Werewolf Rescue Group isn't exactly normal; I realise that. Sometimes I wish I could just forget about it. Sometimes I'm tempted to go out and experiment with Amin's nail gun, as a way of distracting myself from all my worries. But according to Dr Plackett, that's only to be expected. It's a normal response. He says that he'd recommend a bit of professional counselling, if it wasn't entirely out of the question.

There wouldn't be any point going to a counsellor if I couldn't talk about my life as a werewolf.

So I've been doing the next best thing. I *have* been talking about my life as a werewolf, only I've been speaking into a recorder. That's what I'm doing right now, as a matter of fact. And when I'm finished, Nina's going to transcribe the recording so she can send it to her publisher. (She's an author, see; she writes vampire detective fiction.) Naturally, I'll be changing all the names and dates and places before she submits the manuscript, so don't bother looking me up in the phone book. I'm not even called Toby Vandevelde. That's simply a name that Nina invented.

Still, the essential story is true. And we've decided to publicise it because there must be a whole lot of young werewolves out there who need information and reassurance. If you're one of them – and you've read this book – you'll know that it's not a fantasy novel. You'll know that it's a thinly disguised piece of non-fiction. And by now, with any luck, you'll also know that you're not mad, or evil, or all alone in the world. You're just another werewolf who needs to take precautions.

I can't tell you how to get in touch with us at the Abused Werewolf Rescue Group. The risk of exposure would be too great. But rest assured that we're keeping an eye out, and that we understand what to look for. If necessary, we'll even come and rescue *you*.

Until then, just try to hang in there. And always remember: there's an 'I can' in 'lycanthropy'.

Just because you're a werewolf doesn't mean that you can't live your life exactly the way you want to.

Have you read . . . ?

Turn the page to read an extract . . .

Chapter One

Nina was stuck. She didn't know what to write next.

So far, her teenaged captive had been dragged into a refrigerated meat locker by two thugs armed with a gun and a boning knife. But Zadia Bloodstone was already waiting for them. Hanging upside-down from a meat hook, wrapped in a long, black cape and covered by a thin layer of frost, Zadia had cleverly disguised herself as a harmless side of beef. Only when she'd spread her arms wide had the crackle of breaking ice announced her presence.

Bang-bang! Two bullets had promptly smashed into her ribcage. But Zadia wasn't troubled by bullets, because her vital organs could regenerate themselves at lightning speed. Somersaulting to the floor, she'd walked straight up to the bigger thug and kicked the gun from his hand. Then she'd whirled around to fight off his friend. Within seconds, the two baddies had been knocked out – leaving a very important question unanswered.

What would the rescued boy do?

Obviously, he would be grateful. He might even be dazzled by Zadia's flawless face and perfect figure. But if he saw her sink her fangs into anyone's neck, he would also be frightened.

He would realise instantly that she was a vampire, and run for the door.

He would be unaware, at this point, that Zadia was a heroic crime-fighter who only preyed on lowlife scum.

Nina chewed away at a lock of her hair, thinking hard. She was in the middle of chapter eight. The room in which she sat was illumined solely by the glow of her computer screen; barely visible in the dimness were her brass bedstead, her Indian cushions and her lava lamp. A poster of David Bowie hung on the wall, curling at the corners. A small bookshelf contained multiple copies of *Youngblood* (*Book Two of the Bloodstone Chronicles*), by someone called N. E. Harris.

Splashed across the cover of *Youngblood* was a glamorous, slinky young girl with white skin, black hair and ruby-red lips. She wore high-heeled boots and lots of black leather, as well as an ammunition belt. Her canine teeth were long and pointed, but she was stunningly beautiful nonetheless.

She appeared to be leaping from rooftop to rooftop, her black cape streaming out behind her.

'Nina!' somebody shouted, from beyond the closed bedroom door. Nina didn't respond. She stared unblinkingly at the computer screen, still gnawing at her hair – which was thick and dark, and cut in a heavy, clumsy, old-fashioned style that didn't suit her bony little face.

It was about time, she decided, that Zadia made friends with the boy she'd rescued.

Zadia hesitated, Nina wrote, *torn between her desire to punish the wicked and her need to reassure the tall, pale, handsome teenager with the big brown eyes.*

'Nina!' a distant voice called again. Ignoring it, Nina deleted the word 'pale'. Her hands on the keyboard were like chicken's feet, all scaly and dry. Her skin was the colour of a maggot's, and her legs were so thin that her tights were wrinkled around the knees.

Her boots had flat heels on them.

'Nina!' The door burst open to admit a withered old woman in a quilted nylon dressing-gown. 'For God's sake, are you deaf? Father Ramon's outside – you want to keep him waiting?'

Nina sighed. She shut her laptop, moving sluggishly.

'All right,' she murmured. 'I'm on my way.'

'Aren't you feeling well?' the old woman wanted to know. She had the hoarse rasp and yellowed fingertips of a chronic smoker; her hair looked like a frayed clump of steel wool, and her scarlet lipstick was bleeding into the cracks around her mouth. 'Because if you're sick,' she said, 'you shouldn't be going.'

'I'm not sick, Mum. I'm fine.'

'That's what you always say, and you never are. Is your head giving you trouble?'

'No!'

'What about your stomach?'

Nina didn't reply. Instead she rose, reaching for her sunglasses – which shared the cluttered surface of her desk with a Pet Rock, a pile of vintage vampire comics, and a netball trophy awarded to the 'Junior Regional Inter-School Champions' of 1971. On a noticeboard hanging above the desk-lamp were pinned various faded photographs of laughing teenage girls.

If any of these girls was Nina, it wasn't immediately apparent. They were so sleek and glossy and bright-eyed that they could have belonged to an entirely different species.

'Are you nauseous?' her mother nagged. 'You are, aren't you?'

'There's *nothing wrong*,' said Nina, on her way out of the room. It was a lie, of course. There was always something wrong.

And her mother knew it.

'If you get sick, I want you to come straight home,' the old woman advised, as they descended a narrow wooden staircase together. 'Dave won't mind bringing you back early, if you can't stay to the end. And don't leave it till the last minute, the way you did before. Dave won't want you throwing up all over his sheepskin seat-covers again . . .'

Nina winced. It was true. She had ruined Dave's precious seat-covers. Was it any wonder that he didn't exactly beat a path to her door? Was it any wonder that she spent so much of her time in imaginary meat lockers with the stylish and vigorous Zadia Bloodstone? At least there were no uncontrollable bouts of vomiting in Zadia's world.

Nina pulled open the heavy front door of her mother's terrace house. Outside, the darkness was relieved only by the soft glow of a nearby streetlamp; stars were scattered like sequins across a coal-black sky. Yet Nina had already donned her sunglasses, which were big, heavy, wrap-around things that made her pinched face look smaller than ever . . .

You know what? This isn't going to work. I can't write about myself the way I write about Zadia. It's too weird. It's confusing. Next thing I'll get mixed up, and start making me do things that I can't actually do. Like turn into a bat, for instance. Zadia can do that, but I can't. No one can.

The plain fact is, I can't do anything much. That's part of

4

the problem. Vampires are meant to be so glamorous and powerful, but I'm here to inform you that being a vampire is *nothing* like that. Not one bit. On the contrary, it's like being stuck indoors with the flu watching daytime television, for ever and ever.

If being a vampire were easy, there wouldn't have to be a Reformed Vampire Support Group.

As a matter of fact, I was going to a group meeting that very night. Father Ramon had come to pick me up. It was a Tuesday, because all our meetings are held on Tuesdays, at 9.30 p.m., in St Agatha's church hall. And in case you're wondering why I couldn't have driven myself to St Agatha's . . . well, that's just one of my many problems. I still look fifteen, you see. I still *am* fifteen, when all's said and done, since I stopped ageing back in 1973, when I was infected. So I'd attract far too much attention behind a steering wheel. (Besides which, Mum doesn't have a car.)

As for the public transport option, Sanford Plackett has ruled that out. He's always ruling things out; you'd think he was our lord and master, the way he carries on. He's forbidden any of us to travel around Sydney on buses or trains, for instance, in case we stumble across something that Father Ramon would probably describe as 'an occasion of sin'. I suppose Sanford's worried that we might encounter a bleeding junkie rolling around on a station platform, and won't be able to stop ourselves from pouncing.

'You think you'll never succumb,' he once said to me, 'because you can't come to terms with your true nature. You refuse to concede that you're really a vampire, with a vampire's weakness. But you are, Nina. We all are. That's why we have to be careful.'

5

And being careful means not catching cabs. According to Sanford, it's too risky. Staring at the back of a cab-driver's exposed neck would be quite stressful for most of us – especially if someone's been bleeding onto the seats beforehand. Sanford also insists that no one in our group should go wandering the streets all alone. He says that we wouldn't stand a chance against the drunks and addicts and muggers on the loose out there. He says that everyone should follow his advice, because he's been around for so long and has so much experience, and because, although Father Ramon might be our group facilitator, even a priest with counselling experience can't be its *leader*. Not if he isn't a vampire himself.

That's Sanford's opinion, anyway. He's got a lot of opinions, let me tell you. And he's never shy about airing them, whether asked to or not.

He was already in the car when I reached it, because he can't drive either. People who grew up before the First World War rarely can. Back then, even doctors like Sanford didn't own motor vehicles – and he certainly couldn't risk learning to drive now. None of us could. We'd be exposing ourselves to the kind of official scrutiny that you need to avoid at all costs, when you're toting fake IDs. Most of the vampires I know have changed their identities at least once, and Sanford has done it twice, owing to the fact that he doesn't look his age (believe it or not). Despite his balding scalp and clipped moustache – despite his preference for three-piece suits and fob-watches – you'd never guess that he was a hundred and forty years old. The very fact that he's not six feet underground is a dead giveaway. And he's no different from the rest of our group, which is full of people living precarious lives, under assumed names, with forged papers.

It's a real drag, believe me.

'Hello, Nina,' he said, as I slid into the back seat of the waiting Nissan Pulsar.

'Hello, Sanford.'

'How are you, Nina?' Father Ramon inquired, pulling out from the kerb.

'Oh – you know. Nauseous. As usual.'

I didn't want to complain too much, because that's what vampires do. They complain too much. But I needn't have worried. Gladys did the complaining for me.

'I bet you're not as nauseous as I was last night,' she said, moving over to give me some space. 'I was trying to sell a timeshare, and I spewed all over the phone. At least a cupful of blood. It no sooner went down than it came back up again. I lost the sale and everything – didn't I, Bridget?'

'Oh, yes,' said Bridget, who was knitting. Bridget's always knitting. She was eighty-two when she was infected, so she can't do much else. Even climbing stairs can be a problem for Bridget, because of her hip joints.

There's only one thing worse than being a vampire, and that's being an elderly vampire with bad hips.

'Have you been taking your enzymes, Gladys?' asked Sanford, from the front seat. He craned around to peer at her. 'Every morning, before you go to bed?'

'Of course I have!'

'What about other treatments? Have you been drinking those herbal concoctions again?'

'No!' Gladys exclaimed, sounding defensive, though it was a perfectly reasonable question. Gladys goes about smelling weird, like a hippy, because she's always treating her manifold health problems with miraculous new oils or exercises or

7

meditation techniques. She even looks like a hippy, in her beads and her shawls and her long, flowing skirts. Having been infected back in 1908, she can't bear to expose her legs; ladies didn't do that sort of thing in the old days, and Gladys likes to think of herself as a lady – even though she was actually a common streetwalker. She also likes to think of herself as a *young* lady, despite her old-lady obsession with bowels and feet and joint-pain, because she was only twenty-four when she first got infected. But I'm here to tell you, she's about as young as a fossilised dinosaur egg.

'I haven't even been burning scented candles,' she whined, 'and I'm still getting that rash I told you about. The one on my stomach.'

'It might be a bad response to the supplements,' Sanford mused. 'I could adjust your levels a bit, I suppose. Have you had any dizzy spells?'

'Yes! This morning!'

'What about headaches?'

'Not since last week. But the other night one of my toenails fell off in the bath –'

At this point I could restrain myself no longer.

'Hey! Here's an idea!' I growled, my voice dripping with sarcasm. 'Let's all talk about our allergies, for a change! That'll be fun.'

There was a long pause. Father Ramon glanced into the rear-view mirror, shooting me one of those reproachful-yet-sympathetic looks in which he seems to specialise. Sanford sniffed. Gladys scowled.

'Well, what do *you* want to talk about, then?' she demanded. 'What have *you* been doing lately that's so wonderful? Watching re-runs of *Buffy the Vampire Slayer*?'

'I've been writing my book,' I said, knowing perfectly well what sort of reaction I'd get. And when Sanford removed his sunglasses briefly, to massage the bridge of his nose, I braced myself for the usual guff about how I was putting everyone at risk (even though I write under a pseudonym, and use a post office box for all my correspondence).

'Yeah, yeah, I know what you think of my books,' I added, before Sanford could butt in. 'Spare me the sermon – I've heard it all before.'

'They're not doing us any good, Nina,' he replied. 'People are scared enough already; you're only making things worse.'

'Zadia's not scary, Sanford. She gets fan mail. She's a *heroine*.'

'She's a symbol of your flight from reality.' This was one of Sanford's stock remarks. For at least twenty-five years he'd been telling me that I was stuck in the 'denial' phase of the Kubler-Ross Grief Cycle (rather than the 'anger', 'bargaining', 'depression' or 'acceptance' phases), because I had refused to embrace my true identity as a vampire. 'You feel compelled to invest vampires with a battery of super-human powers,' he said, making reference to Zadia Bloodstone, 'just so you can tell yourself that you're not really a vampire. You're living in a dream world, Nina.'

'No – *you're* living in a dream world.' I was trying to be patient. 'You talk to me like I'm still a kid, even though I'm *fifty-one-years-old*. Do you know how boring that can get?'

He did, of course. Everyone did, because I'd mentioned it often enough. It had been a good thirty years since our group's first meeting, so we knew each other pretty well by this time. We'd also covered every subject known to man, over and over and over again. It's something that tends to happen when you don't mix very much with other people.

Sometimes I look around St Agatha's vestry on a Tuesday night, and I think to myself: *If I never see any of you ever again, I'll be a happy vampire.*

'You might have lived for fifty-one years,' Sanford chided, without even bothering to glance in my direction, 'but you're still a kid at heart. You're stuck in a teenage time warp. You still think like a teen. You still behave like a teen.'

'What – you mean like this?' I said, and flipped him the finger. Gladys giggled. Father Ramon changed gears abruptly, though his voice remained calm.

'Come on, now,' he remonstrated. 'That's enough. If you want to argue . . . well, you should at least wait until the meeting.'

Then Sanford's mobile phone began to trill. While he fumbled inside his jacket, I turned my face to the window. Outside, streetlamps were gliding past, illuminating the kind of neighbourhood that I've always enjoyed looking at. House-fronts were shoved up hard against the pavement. Though the gaps between shrunken curtains and broken cedar slats I could see flickering television screens, curling drifts of cigarette smoke, and people rushing from room to room, slamming doors.

But I couldn't see enough. I never can. I always get a fleeting glimpse of normal life before it's whisked away – before I'm back in a crowded car with a bunch of vampires.